Other Works by Tracy Broemmer
Writing as **Therese Kinkaide**

Published by **Wings E Press**

Luther's Cross, 2008
Fairytale, 2011

Independently Published

Just Like Them, 2011
Small Hours, 2011

Writing as **Tracy Broemmer**

Independently Published

Picket Fences, 2013
Two Story Home, 2013

Lorelei Bluffs Series
Every Little Thing, Book 1, 2014
Two A.M., Book 2, 2014
Blind, Book 3, 2015
Leaving July, Book 4, 2015

The Williams Legacy
Truth Is, Book 1, 2015

Other People's Ugly
The Williams Legacy, Book 2

by

Tracy Broemmer

Women's Fiction

Published by Tracy Broemmer at CreateSpace

Cover Photo by Can Stock Photo

Cover Artist: Trisha FitzGerald-Jung

All Rights Reserved

Copyright © 2015
ISBN#: 978-1517130992

Names, characters, and incidents depicted in this book are products of the author's imagination or are used fictitiously. Any resemblance to actual events, locales, organizations, or person, living or dead, is entirely coincidental and beyond the intent of the author.

No part of this book may be reproduced or transmitted in any form or by any means, electronic or mechanical, including photocopying, recording, or by any information storage and retrieval system, without permission in writing from the author.

A note to my readers: The Williams Legacy is set in Quincy, Illinois. However, I took certain liberties and made changes to street names and numbers and local shops and restaurants. I think natives and those of you in the area will 'see' the setting the same way I do.

One

The sounds of a party greeted her as she climbed out of her Passport. Mind on the shoot she'd just finished, it took a moment for the laughter and the music to reach her, to penetrate the wall in her mind. With a shiver, she leaned back into the SUV and grabbed her black rain jacket, for all the good it would do her. As she shrugged into it, she thought she recognized her daughter's voice from somewhere behind Luke Ashley's house.

What the hell were they doing outside, anyway? Wishful thinking? It was March, for God's sake, and the nice, warm days were the exception rather than the rule, and Amber jammed her hands in her pockets as she walked up the drive to the house.

She passed Liv's Traverse and Ezra's truck and wondered if Wade was here and really what the hell was going on with Liv and Wade, anyway. *Well*, thanks to Ingrid she knew the basics, but she was curious. How the hell had her sister gone from happily married for, like, a hundred years, to restless and having an affair? Was she still having an affair? Had it even *been* an affair, or had it just been a fling? Liv had been Amber's ideal. Her hope. She'd been putting Nathan off for a while, okay for over a year....maybe two, sure, but in the back of her mind she'd considered his proposal. Her parents' marriage had always been what had slowed her down. Made her hesitate. And Liv and Wade had always been what made her think, but *what if?*

Finding out about Liv's infidelity had crushed her, and then finding out about it from Ingrid instead of Liv had sort of ripped her apart and left her completely wrecked. Amber had thought she and Liv had grown closer through the years, since she'd gotten a little older and settled down, and Ingrid had remained at large.

But apparently, old habits died hard, because as soon as Ingrid had come home in December, she and Liv had been thick as thieves, and Liv had gone back to treating Amber like a pain in the ass third wheel little sister.

Which, technically, she was.

By the time she reached the house, Amber was shaking with the cold, and her hands, still jammed in her pockets were ice cubes. The tantalizing aroma of meat on the grill assaulted her as she reached to open the screen door. Okay, so she was hungry, *okay starved*, but that still didn't mean she wanted to freeze her ass off outside at a mid-March cookout. Why couldn't they hang out inside? Where there was heat?

The house, well, it was more like a lodge-a big ass ski lodge in the mountains of Colorado, complete with fireplaces and whirlpool tubs and a hot tub out on the patio (Amber had almost cried with envy when she'd first come here with Ingrid a week ago) was cozy and warm when she stepped inside. The party sounds, Amber supposed they were more like family dinner sounds (Party sounds were more like earsplitting music and TVs blaring the game of the day and drunken people calling to each other from one room to another. At least those were her memories of party days.) were louder inside. Amber wiped her boots on the rug at the door, but after inspecting them, she glanced at the hardwood floor and then leaned over to tug them off. Really, they weren't too muddy. But the thought of crossing the gleaming hardwood with even a smidge of mud on the hiking boots made her feel guilty.

She followed the sounds of laughter and conversation to the kitchen. Rather than finding the scene comforting-she couldn't even be relieved that they did seem to be hanging out inside-she was irritated. And further irritated because she didn't know why she felt that way.

Ingrid stood at the counter, eyes on a cookbook, glasses perched on the tip of her nose. This woman was such a mystery to Amber, it sometimes hurt to look at her. Before she could look away, though, Ingrid looked up and caught her staring. Amber felt a little stroke of warmth spread through her belly when Ingrid flashed her a little grin.

"Hey."

Amber turned to Liv, sitting at the high top table in the corner. Fingers curled around a glass of wine, she raised her eyebrows at Amber. Amber frowned. What was the huge stack of papers in front her? More stuff from Mom and Dad's house? Probably. The thought made her head hurt even worse.

"Hey." She said it so quietly, probably none of them heard her. Luke, back to her at the counter with Ingrid, turned and hollered a greeting to her.

"Just in time," he told her. She nodded as he disappeared out the backdoor, she assumed to check the grill.

"Where's Hadley?" she asked as she stepped further into the room.

"Jeez, Amber, chill," Ingrid mumbled.

Amber took Ingrid's words like bullets. She glanced at Liv to see if she'd heard Ingrid. But Liv was now holding the wine glass halfway to her lips, and her eyes were on the stack of papers.

"I just asked where Hadley is." Amber sighed. James Taylor sang a plea not to let him be lonely tonight as she slipped out of her jacket and tossed it on the back of a chair. The party had sounded bigger from her SUV. Where were Ezra and Shay? Wade? The kids? She didn't ask. God only knew what Ingrid would say if she did.

"She's outside," Ingrid told her as she looked up again. She picked up a bottle of Sam Adams Winter Ale and took a long drink.

"She's not in the hot tub, is she?" Amber asked quickly. Her phone, tucked away in her back pocket, buzzed.

"No." Ingrid shook her head. "I mean, we wouldn't want her to have too much fun at her aunt's house, would we?"

Amber paused in the act of pulling her phone from her pocket. She lifted only her eyes to look at Ingrid.

"She's been complaining of a sore throat," Amber mumbled. "She doesn't need to be in the hot tub if she's getting sick."

"I don't think any of us need to be in that hot tub," Liv announced. "I think it's Ingrid's new favorite place to have sex."

"Eeww." Amber shivered.

"They're all down by the fire pit." Ingrid glanced back at the mixing bowl on the counter, as if she was afraid it had run off. Or maybe, Amber thought, she was hoping it had run off. "And actually, that table where you're sitting is a pretty good place to have sex, Liv."

Amber snorted when Liv looked up in alarm. She made a show of looking at the table and then at the floor.

"You'd have to climb a ladder to get up here." She rolled her eyes.

"Yeah?" Ingrid shrugged. "Luke's a handy man, remember? He's got ladders."

Amber licked her lips and shook her head when Ingrid winked at her.

"I just hope you clean the house now and then," Liv mumbled.

"That's just sick." Amber finally looked down at her phone.

"Want something to drink?"

Amber nodded as she looked at Nathan's text.

Having dinner. Call you later.

"Wine?" Ingrid asked her. "Or would you rather have a beer?"

"How about water?"

"Beer." Ingrid nodded. Amber frowned at her back as she crossed the small area behind the counter and then yanked the refrigerator door open. "Winter Ale or Miller Lite?"

"Are you kidding me? This is like taking a test or something." Amber reached up to rub the back of her neck.

"Winter Ale it is." Ingrid reached into the fridge to grab a bottle and then turned back to hand it to her. When Amber only stood there, bottle in hand and eyebrows arched in question, Ingrid pointed at the drawer behind her.

"Seriously?" Amber mumbled as she turned to pull the drawer open.

"What does that mean? I'm supposed to open it for you, too?"

Amber rooted through the drawer until she found a bottle opener. Settled it over the top of her beer and then pulled the top off. She glanced at Ingrid as she dropped the opener back into the drawer.

"You're settled in enough that you remember where things are? I don't even remember where half the stuff in my house is, and I've lived there for three years."

"Three years?" Ingrid repeated. "I didn't know you'd been there that long."

"Think about it, Amber." Liv, still at the table, eyes still on the stack of papers-Amber looked at her over her shoulder-sounded distracted. "What's the first thing Ingrid's going to familiarize herself with?"

"You mean besides the hot tub?"

Liv finally looked up and grinned. "Well, yeah-"

"Why are we picking on me tonight? I thought it was Amber that was into-"

"The kitchen?" Amber shook her head at Liv.

"Well, she had to know where Luke keeps his bottle opener, didn't she?"

Amber chuckled. "Very true." She took a drink of the beer and shivered a little. "And yes, Hadley and I've been in the house for three years."

"Are you?" Liv asked Ingrid. "Settled? I haven't noticed many boxes sitting around."

"Then you're not looking," Ingrid answered. "Not settled."

"Did you get everything from your apartment?" Amber asked her. "Or are you guys gonna have to make another trip?"

"Nope." Ingrid shrugged and turned back to the mixing bowl and the cookbook. "Got it all the first time around."

"I never saw the place," Amber said quietly. She moved to stand beside Ingrid, looked over her shoulder at the cookbook. "What are you trying to make?"

"Brownies."

"Easy. Preheat the oven. Open the box."

"From scratch." Ingrid turned her head to look at Amber. This close, Amber could see the fine lines around her sister's eyes. The lines reminded her of the scar Ingrid had only just told them about and the cancer scare and their mom.

"Why?" Amber stared at her boldly.

"Just thought maybe they'd taste better."

"Brownies, Ingrid," Amber told her. "You don't improve brownies."

"What'd Nathan say?"

"What?"

"Was that him? That text?"

Amber twisted around, as if she needed to see her butt to reassure herself her phone was still there and that Nathan had actually texted her.

"Yeah."

"What'd he say?"

"That he'd call later."

"Where's he at?" Ingrid turned her attention back to the bowl. Amber watched her long, slender fingers slide over the cookbook. Her nails were bare, but they were the perfect length and shape. Funny. Ingrid wore some heavy duty eye makeup, and Amber thought she was the only person she knew personally who had a dark purple streak in her short, spiky hair. But she rarely saw her with painted nails.

"Florida."

"Working?"

Amber raised her eyes when Ingrid nudged her with her elbow.

"What?"

"Is he working?"

"No." Amber cleared her throat. She watched Ingrid pick up a big wooden mixing spoon and dip it into the bowl.

"No?" Ingrid shot her a frown. "What's he doing in Florida?"

"Bachelor party."

"Nathan is in Florida for a bachelor party?"

"Yeah." Amber shrugged when Ingrid stopped stirring the brownie mix and looked at her. "What?"

"Do you trust him?"

Amber cocked her head and frowned at Ingrid. "Of course I trust him. What kind of question is that?"

Ingrid shrugged her lips innocently and looked back at the brownie batter. "Okay."

"No. Not okay. What do you mean by that? Do you trust Luke?"

"Yes, I do." Ingrid nodded.

"Then why shouldn't I trust Nathan?"

"Well, you should."

"Then why would you ask me that?" Amber nudged Ingrid with her elbow. "Do you know something I don't?"

"What?" Ingrid looked at her over her shoulder again. "No. Of course not."

"Then why would you ask me that?"

Ingrid sighed and took a step back from the counter. She turned to Amber, but Amber noticed the way she glanced at Liv before she looked at her.

"What?"

"Huh?" Ingrid shrugged. "I just-"

"Why'd you look at Liv? Before you started to answer me-"

"Jesus H., Amber, I don't know. I just asked about Nathan, because you made a comment about him cheating, so why get married?"

"I never said he cheated."

"I know you didn't," Ingrid agreed. "But you used that as one of your reasons not to marry him. Because he might cheat when he's out of town."

Unaware that she'd been holding her breath, Amber let it out now on a long, drawn-out sigh. "I did?"

"You did." Ingrid nodded. She turned back to the bowl and picked up the spoon again.

"Who's getting married?" Liv asked.

Amber leaned her back on the counter and glanced at Liv. "No one."

Liv rolled her eyes.

"Nathan is at a bachelor party?" she prompted Amber.

"Oh." Amber took a drink and then folded her arms over her chest. "A guy he went to college with."

"Why didn't you go with him?"

Amber licked her lips and studied Liv curiously. "Really? To a bachelor party? What would I be? The girl who jumped out of the cake?"

Ingrid snorted and nodded. "You could totally pull that off."

"Yeah." Amber sighed and stared at the top of Ingrid's head.

"You could've just gone to Florida. Soaked up some sun while he's out golfing. I'm sure he's been down there for longer than tonight for a bachelor party."

"Nathan golfs?" Ingrid, finally done mixing the brownies, looked up at Amber. She licked the spoon and raised her eyebrows.

"Mm-hmm." Amber nodded. "Why do you get to lick the spoon?"

"My house."

"No fair." Amber reached for it and tugged it out of Ingrid's hands.

"Do you love that? Saying that?" Liv asked.

"I do." Ingrid's face lit up with her smile. "I love it here."

"As long as I've known him, I would never have thought…this." Liv looked around the kitchen and put her hands out, palms up.

"I never thought this," Ingrid nodded her head back and forth, " was possible for me."

"The house?"

"Luke," she answered simply. "After Scott, living alone for so long, I just thought…I was gonna be a crazy cat lady or something."

"One with no cats," Liv mumbled.

"Well. Yeah."

"So anyway," Liv sighed and looked back at Amber. "Why do you get to lick the spoon? And ewww. That's gross."

"We're sisters."

"Yeah, but I can't get my mind around where Ingrid's tongue's been already today."

Amber closed her eyes and shivered. "That's just wrong."

"Quit," Ingrid told Liv. "You're making her jealous."

"Um. No."

"Not of Luke." Ingrid swatted Amber's arm. "How long's Nathan been gone?"

"Six days."

"A six day bachelor party?" Liv yelped.

"Two days in Florida. He flew out from Indiana."

"Job?" Ingrid clarified.

Amber nodded.

"I think it's only fair that I lick the bowl," Liv announced as Ingrid pulled a spatula from the drawer. Amber watched her spread the brownie batter into a square pan. "And seriously, chocolate would go much better with my red wine than beer."

"Pretty much everything goes with beer," Ingrid argued. She handed the nearly empty bowl to Amber and nodded toward Liv.

Amber grabbed a clean spoon from the drawer and then walked over to the table to hand Liv the bowl.

"So. Why didn't you? Go to Florida?"

"Because I had a few shoots scheduled."

"Coulda rescheduled."

"I can't just waltz in and out of town. Not with Hadley. What are you reading? Is that stuff from Mom and Dad's?"

"Hadley could stay with us," Liv offered.

"She could stay with us," Ingrid said from across the kitchen.

Amber shrugged. She pulled a chair out and hiked her leg up to climb up and sit down. "Whatever. Maybe next time."

"Whatever? Seriously?" Liv reached for her glass, only to stop when she realized it was empty. She dropped her hand on the pile of papers.

"I said maybe next time."

"Amber, what are you afraid of? He loves you."

"What is that?" Amber ignored Liv's question. "Did you find it in the attic? Like what? Tax papers or something?"

Liv sat back when Amber reached for the top paper on the pile.

It wasn't a tax paper. Wasn't anything legal. Not a contract. Not an instructional manual. Amber glanced over the sheet; her eyes skimming the words quickly. Something about a dark alley. Thunder. The stench of fire in someone's clothes.

"What is this?" She looked up at Liv with a frown. Turned to Ingrid when Liv didn't answer her immediately.

"Just-"

"You're letting Liv read your manuscripts now?" Amber glanced at the paper again. Definitely a page of a book.

"Well. No." Ingrid shrugged. "Not really."

Amber arched her eyebrows at Ingrid and then glanced at the paper in her hand.

"*The memory of the flame was stronger even than the smell of the smoke that Mark still carried in his clothes, his hair. His skin. The smell was embedded in his skin, and yet, it was the memory of that heat, that deadly heat that woke him most nights.*" Amber cleared her throat. "Seems pretty much like a page of someone's manuscript." She looked up at Ingrid and then flicked her eyes to Liv. "Are you writing books now, too? This your manuscript?"

Liv snorted. "You're kidding, right? I write lesson plans."

"So it's your manuscript," Amber said to Ingrid. "And Liv is reading it."

"Are you seriously gonna be upset about this?" Ingrid asked quietly.

Amber almost said yes. *Almost*. But she wasn't upset. Not like, angry, upset. But hurt. Jealous. Insanely jealous and hurt, but she swallowed it all down with another drink of her beer. Slipped off the chair and shook her head.

"No." She shrugged. "I'm not."

"Amber." Ingrid turned as she watched Amber walk through the kitchen to the backdoor where she'd seen Luke walk outside earlier. "It's just-it's old. I wrote it a long time ago-"

She pulled the door open and stepped out onto the deck, Ingrid's words cut off when she closed the door behind her.

Two

"Hey." Luke glanced at her as she stepped further out on the deck. Amber eyeballed the grill for a moment. Watched the chicken sizzle and the flames reach up through the grate and lick the meat. When she realized she was thinking about the smell of smoke rather than the chicken on the grill, she looked up at Luke and offered him a tired smile.

"Hey."

"Shoot today?" he asked her, but his attention was back on the grill. She watched him use tongs to turn each piece of chicken, one at a time. Even though he was intent on the job at hand, Amber felt like he was really listening as she told him she had done a shoot earlier in the day and that she'd spent a while in her dark room, too, and she almost told him about the kink in her neck that had crawled in and settled a week ago, but she caught herself.

"Do you ever use a digital camera?" he asked her.

When he looked at her over his shoulder, she found herself smiling again. Liv and Ingrid never asked her about her work. Okay, so asking her if she ever used a digital camera wasn't like asking her the meaning of life, but still. It was nice that someone was interested in something she did, and she loved to talk about photography and lighting and exposure settings.

"I do sometimes," she answered him. "But I like film. I like the process."

He nodded as if he completely understood what she was saying, that he agreed with her.

"What kind of equipment do you use?"

Amber raised her eyebrows as he set the tongs down, picked up his beer and turned to look at her.

"Mom?"

She looked toward the steps when she heard Hadley call to her. Within seconds, her daughter's long hair appeared and then her shoulders and finally all of Hadley crossed the deck and gave her a big hug.

"Hi." Amber kissed her cheek. "How ya feeling?"

"Good." Hadley nodded as she stepped back to look at her. Amber let her eyes travel over Hadley's face, noting the sparkle in her eyes and the pink in her cheeks.

"Yeah?" she asked skeptically. "No sore throat?"

"Little bit," Hadley admitted.

"And you think sitting outside in this cold, by a fire pit is a good idea?"

"Grace and Charlie are down there," Hadley whined. "With Uncle Wade."

Amber rolled her eyes. "Okay. I'm gonna call them when you end up really sick. They can take care of you."

"I got a B on my algebra quiz today," Hadley announced.

Amber, still concerned about Hadley's little bit of a sore throat, reached for her daughter's hand. She winced and wrapped her fingers around Hadley's icy fingers.

"Could you at least put your gloves on?"

"Don't have them with me," Hadley mumbled. "Besides, how would gloves help a sore throat?"

Amber heard Luke snicker. She glanced at him over her shoulder and grinned but wiped the grin away before she turned back to Hadley.

"You're just not dressed very warm for being outside."

"Did you even hear me?" Hadley's voice climbed an octave.

"Of course I did." Amber nodded. "You got a B on your algebra quiz."

"And?" Hadley raised her hands out, palms up.

"That's great. I'm proud of you."

It sort of pained Amber to say it. Always before, Hadley had been a straight A student. This year, the whole teenager thing, the *pissy, sullen teenager thing* had descended upon her daughter and turned her into the bad girl who snuck out at night to meet boys and go to parties and the kind of girl whose grades didn't matter. All of her grades had taken a hit, but algebra and English had gone down hard.

The door opened, and Ingrid, twisted around and talking to Liv, leaned out. Amber ignored her, even when she turned to the deck and hollered at her.

"You're not proud." Hadley pushed her lips out in a pout. "You're still mad at me."

"I'm not, Hadley," Amber insisted. "I'm glad you got your act together."

"But if I hadn't dropped the ball in the first place," Hadley mumbled with a perfect eye roll. Amber watched her slip up beside Luke and lean in to study the meat on the grill. "That looks good."

"Are you hungry?" he asked her.

Hadley giggled and touched her stomach. "I'm, like, starved," she told him.

"Amber."

Amber turned from Luke to Ingrid, who was still leaning out the door.

"Hmm?"

"Come inside for a minute?" Ingrid cocked her head. "I wanna show you something."

That quickly, her sister had forgotten that she'd hurt Amber's feelings. Again. Amber took a deep breath and followed Ingrid back inside the house.

"What's up?"

Determined to hide her frustration, her envy for her sisters' relationship from both of them, Amber drained her beer and rinsed the bottle out. She set it on the counter, next to the row of dead soldiers already there.

"I wanted to show you this picture I found," Ingrid told her.

Amber reached for the snapshot as Ingrid handed it to her. In the photo, a possibly sixteen-year-old Ingrid held a probably three-year-old Amber on her back. Ingrid and Amber were both mugging for the camera, but Liv, in the foreground, carrying Hodge, their dog, was looking away.

"Wow." Amber's smile was sincere, but sad. She stroked her fingers over the picture, as if she could pet Hodge. "I forgot all about Hodge."

When Ingrid didn't say anything, Amber looked up. Their eyes met. Ingrid watched her expectantly and finally looked away, but not before disappointment crept over her face and settled in the lines around her eyes and her mouth.

"Where'd you find it?"

Ingrid squatted in front of the oven and pulled the door open just enough to peek at the brownies.

"Um." She cleared her throat, looked at Amber, but quickly looked away and then stood up. "Kitchen drawer at Mom and Dad's house."

Amber answered with a nod. She let out a slow, deep breath and turned away from Ingrid. Something dark inside her yawned, stretched itself out to claim more of her. Maybe she could have forgotten the manuscript thing if Ingrid had said she'd had the picture at her apartment in Chicago.

Liv groaned softly, still at the table across the room. Still with the manuscript in front of her. Wine glass full again. Amber fought the urge to look at her. Lost. Of course.

"It's just an old manuscript," Ingrid said softly. "I wrote it a few years ago. Tucked it away."

Amber looked at her, but she said nothing.

"It was just on top of a pile of stuff. When she came in," Ingrid continued. "She saw it and asked what it was."

Amber shrugged one shoulder. "Yeah. Whatever." She nodded. "Where's Ezra? Didn't I see his truck?"

"Wade has it today." Liv barely spared Amber a glance. "Wade's is in the shop. He had some stuff he wanted to haul today so he borrowed Ez's truck."

"Mm." Amber nodded. "Ezra and Shay aren't coming?"

She'd talked to Shay earlier today. She'd said they would be here. Hadn't guaranteed they'd bring the baby, but she'd said she and Ezra were coming.

"Um." Ingrid frowned. "I don't know?"

"What does that mean?" Amber snapped.

Ingrid sighed. Amber watched her take a few steps backwards and then turn to pull the fridge door open again.

"Ezra said they wanted to come, but he wasn't sure." Ingrid grabbed another beer and handed it to Amber. Amber almost laughed, but she held it down and settled for a small grin. Maybe Ingrid saw it as a smartass smirk. Probably was more of a smartass smirk, really. Tame the bitch. Give her a beer. "Shay sounded up for it the first time I talked to her."

Amber turned her back to Ingrid to find the bottle opener again.

Ingrid cleared her throat.

"So. You don't remember Hodge?"

"I do now," Amber said quietly. "But I'd forgotten all about him before I saw that picture."

She dropped the bottle opener back into the drawer and pushed it closed. Leaned around Ingrid to toss the bottle cap in the garbage.

"Makes you wonder what else we might have forgotten, doesn't it?" Ingrid mumbled.

Amber blinked at her and then took a long drink.

"Do you remember Ulysses?"

"S. Grant?" Amber leaned on the counter at her back. "Eighteenth president of the United States?" She cocked her head at Ingrid. "Never met him."

"Our dog." Ingrid rolled her eyes and turned her back to Amber.

"We had a dog named Ulysses?"

"Mm-hmm." Ingrid busied herself with cleaning up the spot where she'd just mixed the brownies.

"When?"

"Um. Well. Dad had him put down...I guess Ez was a baby...so."

"Before me." Amber nodded. "Well, maybe I'm glad there was a Ulysses. Since Mom was into vowels, I might have been Ursula if there hadn't been a Ulysses."

Ingrid snorted.

"Good point."

"What kind of dog was he?"

"Just a mutt." Ingrid shrugged. "Kinda dumb, really. For a dog."

"Are you kidding me?" Liv took her glasses off and set them on the pile of papers in front of her. She pushed the stack away and picked up her wine glass. "He used to get Dad's paper for him."

"That's all he could do."

"But that's cool."

"But he couldn't even roll over."

"Seriously?" Amber felt her phone vibrating in her back pocket again. "He couldn't roll over?"

"Well, he could," Ingrid admitted, "but not, like, if you told him to."

Amber pulled her phone from her pocket and glanced at the screen.

"Hey."

"What're you guys doing?"

Amber grinned as the rush of words exploded on the other end of the call. Gretchen Calloway didn't have a medium speed or volume. As long as Amber had known her, she'd been full-blast in everything she did. Only one reason Amber loved her.

"Nathan's in Florida."

"Because I'm thinking we should go to-wait. What?"

Amber laughed softly. Feeling two sets of eyes on her, she wandered around the kitchen counter and into the hall. Stepped into the living room and propped herself next to the front window.

"Bachelor party."

"Oh. Damn. You told me about that, didn't you?"

"I did, yes." Amber nodded.

"Okay. So you're free. Come with us."

Amber wasn't going anywhere. Not because she was at Ingrid and Luke's (that still sounded weird) for a family thing, but because she wasn't about to leave Hadley alone while she was out having fun. Just because Hadley had towed the line for a week or two didn't mean Amber was ready to trust her again.

"What're you doing?"

"Live music at The Boathouse."

"Who's playing?" Amber was curious, but she didn't care who it was. She wasn't leaving Hadley alone.

"Swimming Venus."

"Really?" Amber winced. She liked Swimming Venus.

"Wanna go? I'll swing by and get you. Steve's picking me up in an hour."

"I can't."

"Why not?"

"Hadley-"

"Oh. Yeah." Gretchen sighed on the other end of the line. "Shoot."

"I'm at my sister's anyway. We're doing a family thing."

"Mm-kay. Well. Tell Liv hi-"

"I'm at Ingrid's."

"What?" Gretchen asked quickly.

Amber laughed softly. "Ingrid moved back home. She's living with Luke Ashley."

"I.G. Arensen finally came home, huh?"

"She's got nice digs here." Amber surveyed the stretch of yard in front of the house. The gravel road in the distance. Their cars lined up in the driveway. Her eyes fell on Ezra's truck. She was disappointed Ezra and Shay weren't here. She'd feel more comfortable with them around.

"Okay."

Amber stood up straight, recognizing Gretchen's wrap up. She'd sincerely wanted Amber and Nathan to go out with them tonight, but knowing they couldn't, she was ready to move on and get ready for her night out.

"Call me tomorrow," Amber told her. "I wanna hear about it."

"Oh, I'll call you tonight, if they sing 'Plastered in Paris'. You'll feel like you're really there."

Amber ran her fingers up through the back of her hair. She grinned and then stretched.

"Have fun."

She heard Gretchen say thanks and then the line went dead. With a quiet sigh, she slipped her phone back in her pocket.

"She can stay here if you wanna go out."

Amber jumped and looked over her shoulder. Ingrid hesitated, on the far side of the room, as if Amber might attack her if she got too close.

"No, it's fine." Amber shook her head.

"Spare boyfriend?"

Amber chuckled. "Gretchen Calloway."

Ingrid shook her head as if to say she didn't know Gretchen.

"She lived in the same dorm when I was a freshman."

Ingrid nodded. "Okay. Well. I just. If you'd rather go out, Hadley can stay here."

"I don't, really," Amber answered. And she didn't. As much as she loved Swimming Venus, as much as she loved Gretchen, she didn't want to go anywhere. Except maybe home. This might have been okay if Ezra and Shay had come, but she didn't love being in close quarters with her sisters.

Amber looked around the living room and almost laughed.

Okay, so this wasn't close quarters. She could get lost here and maybe not see either one of them for days. But. Still.

"Do you guys double?"

"What?"

"Your friend. Do you just hang out together? Or does she have a guy?"

"Both." Amber shrugged. "She and Steve are going to The Boathouse. Swimming Venus is playing."

"Swimming who?"

"Local rock band," Amber explained.

"Never heard of them."

Amber raised her eyebrows, but she managed to keep her smartass comment to herself. Ingrid wandered further into the room. Stopped to stand just a few feet away from her.

"I was looking through a box earlier. Um." She shrugged and then rubbed her forehead with the tips of her fingers. "Trying to find some other pictures to show Liv. She found the manuscript."

Amber cleared her throat, prepared to argue again that she was fine, not upset about the manuscript.

"It's just...something old that I wrote. I didn't like it, so it got buried."

They stood almost toe to toe now, and the wall was at her back, so Amber had nowhere to go. She answered Ingrid with a slow nod, but Ingrid continued.

"Do you wanna read it?"

Of course she wanted to read it. But she wasn't about to jump on it. Not now. Not since it had become a big deal. And besides, was Ingrid only offering because she'd seen that it had upset her earlier? If she hadn't noticed Liv reading it, would either of them have even told her?

"Sure." She shrugged, unwilling to give Ingrid too much. To show too much enthusiasm.

"Um." Ingrid nodded to the back of the house. "I'm sure dinner's ready. If you're staying."

"I'll be right there," Amber said quietly. Ingrid watched her for a moment, as if she might turn and run out the front door, but finally, she offered Amber a small smile and then turned and left her alone by the window. Amber glanced outside again. She would read the manuscript. She would read anything Ingrid wrote, but she wouldn't admit that to her sister.

She heard a shriek of laughter outside and watched as Luke's dog-well, she guessed Bella was now Luke and Ingrid's if the house was Luke and Ingrid's-streaked across the front yard, Liv's son, Charlie, following, though not close, behind.

Hadley used to ask her at least once a week if they could get a dog. She'd always told her no. And then there'd been the time Hadley had asked in front of Nathan, and he'd said yes. When Amber asked him about it later that evening, after Hadley had gone to bed, he'd told Amber he didn't think it would hurt anything for the three of them to get a dog after they were married and he was living there on a permanent basis.

Trouble was, she'd never said yes, they'd never gotten married, he didn't live there on a permanent basis, and they still didn't have a dog.

Amber's breath fanned out on the window as she watched Charlie and Bella race through the yard. Funny how she'd forgotten Hodge. No, she'd never known they'd had a dog named Ulysses. But she remembered Hodge now.

She wasn't thinking about the dog, though. She was remembering the relationship she'd had with her sisters when she'd been a little girl. They'd been a hell of a lot closer when she was only three and didn't think for herself or make her own decisions.

Kind of telling, Amber.

Three

Time spent in her dark room always helped her unwind. At least a little. It wasn't just watching the picture come to life, seeing if her creative vision paid off that she loved. It was the whole process. Seeing the potential for raw beauty and visceral emotion, taking the shot, making the contact print of her negatives, choosing which photos to enlarge. Which photos to submit to photography publications, which to submit to other publications-such as the picture of a three-year-old Hadley to the parenting magazine that had actually sparked her true interest in photography. She even loved negotiating with the publishers, though nowadays her agent did the majority of the legwork.

Lately, though, the dark room wasn't therapy enough. Nothing was, really, and Amber's heart was beginning to hurt the same way her neck did. Started like a little pinch and then grew to a cramp and these days, it was pretty much just an all out ache.

It wasn't just Ingrid coming home. Sure, that had added to her anxiety level, in a way she still didn't quite understand. Add that prodigal sister to her daughter asking questions about her father, to losing Pop just after Christmas, to the tension in the air now every time she and Nathan were in the same room together. Amber felt like the familial pressure inside the house was growing, the way the barometric pressure outside gathered and rose just before a storm.

There was a storm coming. A personal storm for her. She just wasn't sure when, and she wasn't sure she was prepared for it. Prepared for the aftermath.

Leaning over the paper, hands wrapped around her coffee mug, she sighed and then groaned when she heard the light tap at her door. She glanced up, wondered who it was. Who showed up on someone's doorstep on a Saturday morning, anyway? She glanced at her wrist, but she wasn't wearing a watch, so she had no idea what time it was. Before she could move, her visitor knocked again.

With another wasted sigh, (wasted, because whoever was outside couldn't possibly hear her frustration) she flattened her hands on the old oak dining room table and pushed her chair back. She ran her fingers through her hair and then reached to open the door.

"Hey." Ingrid flashed a smile at her and held up a small waxy bag in offering. "Hungry?"

Amber raised her eyebrows and started to say she wasn't hungry, but she only shook her head and stepped back to let Ingrid come inside. She closed the door slowly and then turned to lean against it. Ingrid, dressed in jeans and a lavender sweater, set the bag on the table and then looked back at Amber.

"Coffee?" Amber cleared her throat and headed to the kitchen before Ingrid could answer her.

"I didn't get you up."

"Um. No." She glanced over her shoulder to look at Ingrid and then shot a meaningful glance at her coffee mug. "I was up."

"Hadley still sleeping?"

"Yeah." Amber nodded. She glanced at the microwave when she stepped into the tiny kitchen. Not quite ten. "We watched a movie when we got home last night. Didn't go to bed until after midnight."

"You guys did?" Ingrid followed Amber into the kitchen. Amber tried not to think about the fact that Ingrid had only dropped in at her house once or twice as her sister wandered through the small room and eyeballed her stuff.

"Mm-hmm." Amber nodded and grabbed a mug from the cabinet above the toaster.

"What'd you watch?"

"*Anger Management.*"

She noticed Ingrid's eyebrows jump when she turned to offer her the coffee. Barely held a laugh in when their eyes met.

"Maybe that's a good thing," Ingrid whispered.

"Shut up." Amber rolled her eyes. "What's in the bag?"

"Pumpkin bread."

"In March?" Amber had been hoping for donuts. She couldn't hide her disappointment.

"Um." Ingrid took a sip of her coffee and cocked her head at Amber. "Yes? What's wrong with pumpkin bread in March?"

"Pumpkin bread is for fall."

"What?"

"Like September through December."

"You're kidding me. You have rules on when you eat pumpkin bread?"

"Do you need cream?"

"You have cream?" Ingrid arched an eyebrow skeptically.

"Yes." Amber nodded slowly. "Why wouldn't I have creamer?"

"Hadley went off on me not long after I got back. About the horrible stuff in creamer. How bad it is for you."

"Hadley's fourteen," Amber mumbled. She ducked around Ingrid to pull the refrigerator door open. "What do you care what she thinks?"

Ingrid laughed. "I love to hear what she thinks, actually."

Amber leaned into the fridge and grabbed a bottle of hazelnut creamer. She set it on the counter.

"I thought you gave up coffee." Ingrid took the creamer, but pointed with the same hand toward the living room.

"What? No."

"Yes. I offered you coffee at Dad's house a few weeks ago, and you said no, because you were getting too much caffeine-"

"Mm." Amber remembered the conversation. "Yeah, well, that didn't work. Obviously."

"Hazelnut, huh?" Ingrid set her cup on the table and popped the top on the bottle. "Is this good?"

"I dunno." Amber stretched her arms up over her head. "It's Hadley's. I drink mine black."

"Hadley's." Ingrid nodded. "Of course it is."

Amber reached backwards and grabbed the little coffee spoon from the counter and handed it to Ingrid.

"Is this from Dad's house?" Ingrid made a big deal of studying it before she dipped it into her cup. When Amber didn't answer her right away, Ingrid looked up at her expectantly.

"Am I gonna get the third degree because the coffee spoon ended up here?"

Ingrid raised her eyebrows and took a deep breath.

"No. I was just asking."

"Then, yeah, it was at Dad's house."

Amber took the bottle when Ingrid was done with it and put it back in the fridge. When she pushed the door closed, Ingrid leaned in to study the pictures held to the freezer door with magnets shaped like the letters of the alphabet.

"And no, the magnets didn't come from Dad's house." Amber propped her hip on the counter and watched her sister drink in the pictures.

Ingrid laughed softly, but she didn't look at Amber.

"I have this picture," she said softly. Amber couldn't imagine what picture she was talking about, so she moved to the right to stand shoulder to shoulder with Ingrid. Ingrid tapped the letter P. Hadley's fifth grade school headshot. She'd worn a pink and purple plaid button up blouse. Had her hair in a French braid. She looked adorable, but there was only so much you could see in a school headshot. Frankly, Amber hated them.

"Why do you have that picture?"

"I think Ezra sent it to me."

"Ezra?" Amber couldn't hide her surprise. "What? Were you guys pen pals or something?"

Ingrid frowned and looked back at the picture. "I dunno. Maybe it was Liv. I just know I have that picture. It was a…three by five or something. It's the only picture I have of Hadley. Funny. Considering her mother's a photographer."

Ingrid glanced at Amber, but she only shook her head.

"So. What'd you do with it?"

"What?"

"The picture of Hadley. What'd you do with it?"

"It's probably still in a box at Luke's. Why? Do you want it back?"

"Do I want-what?" Amber sighed. "No. I just…was it on your fridge?"

"No. I had it framed. With Charlie and Gracie's pictures. Kept them in my office."

Amber swallowed hard when Ingrid turned her head again to look at her.

"I need my coffee-"

"Who's this?" Ingrid ignored her and tapped a snapshot in the upper right hand corner of the fridge. Under the letter F.

"Me and Gretchen."

"Gretchen," Ingrid repeated. "The girl you were talking to last night."

"Mm-hmm." Amber turned to walk out of the room. "Grab plates, would you?"

"Yes, because I know where you keep your plates."

"Kitchen's pretty small. It's not that hard to figure out."

Amber padded barefoot to the dining room and eased back into the chair at the head of the table. The table and the six chairs had come with the house when she'd bought it. All of it-the house included-had seen better days, but it was home, and it was comfortable, and Amber rarely allowed herself to think about the possibilities of a newer home and someone to share it with.

"She's pretty."

Amber looked up when Ingrid appeared with a small stack of napkins in one hand and her coffee mug in the other.

"I do have plates."

"We don't need plates. This way you don't have more dishes to wash."

"I know how to wash dishes." Amber hated the note of petulance in her voice, but she couldn't pull the words back now. Shockingly, Ingrid chose to ignore it. She set the napkins down and pulled a chair out.

"Hadley?" Amber asked. She picked up her own mug and took a drink.

"What?"

"Who's pretty?"

"Hadley's beautiful," Ingrid said simply. "She looks so much like you. I meant your friend."

"Mm." Amber sat back and drew her legs up against her chest. Curled her toes over the edge of the chair.

"I still feel bad that I kept you from going out last night."

"If we hadn't been at your house, we'd have been at home."

"Really?"

Amber watched Ingrid open the blue wax bag and pull a slice of pumpkin bread out. She picked up a napkin and handed both to Amber.

"Thank you."

"You're welcome." Ingrid reached for the other piece of bread.

"And, yes, really. I wouldn't have gone out...with Hadley here."

Ingrid met her gaze across the table. Hadley had been sneaking out for quite a while when she'd found herself in over her head at a party a couple of weeks ago. Rather than call Amber, she'd called Ingrid for help.

"Okay." Ingrid nodded. "But I meant it. She's welcome to stay at our house."

"I'm not sure staying at your place would align with her punishment."

"Oh, I don't know," Ingrid said with a sarcastic laugh. "Not sure either of you loves to hang out at my house."

Amber tried to hide her grin behind her mug, but she couldn't hold in the giggle that bubbled up inside her.

"Well, true, but damn. That's like a ski lodge. All you need is some snow."

"Oh God." Ingrid shivered. "Don't even say that out loud."

"Mm." Amber nodded. "True. Sorry, powers that be. Do not send snow. Please."

"Powers that be?"

"I'm just not that committed to what's out there. Up there."

"So. Yeah. Like I said. I'd be happy..."

"To what? Babysit my fourteen-year-old? She sneaks out, Ingrid. You really want that responsibility?"

"Where's she gonna go? Out there?"

"Hell if I know. Kesh could find your place if he wanted to."

"She's still talking to him?"

"I don't think she has in a...since...that night. I haven't forbid her to talk to him. Just grounded her from texting and talking on her phone."

"Got any pictures of this guy?"

"Why? So you can call the cops if you see him on the property?"

Ingrid laughed. "Yep. If she ever stays over, I'll sit up all night with binoculars."

Amber set her coffee down and reached for her phone.

"I don't have any pictures of him down here. Hadley probably does upstairs. But I'm not goin' up there. Not about to wake her up."

"How can you be a photographer and not have pictures?"

"I don't do portrait photography-"

"Not even of your own kid?"

"Well, yeah. But not Kesh."

"Why didn't you ever send me pictures of her?"

Amber winced and looked away from Ingrid's intense stare. She tapped the photo icon on her screen and looked through her pictures. Plenty of Gretch and Steve. Plenty of Hadley. Several of Hadley and a few of her girlfriends. Nathan. None of Kesh.

"I dunno, Ingrid. You never asked."

"I never had to ask Liv. Or Julie."

Amber glanced up at the mention of Ingrid's best friend.

"Talk to her lately?"

"Couple days ago."

"Yeah? And?"

"And." Ingrid shrugged. "Nothing. Things are good right now."

"Good." Amber looked back at her phone and tapped the Facebook icon. She typed in Hadley's name and then scrolled through her pictures. "I thought you saw him. At the party. When you picked her up that night."

"I did." Ingrid pinched off a piece of her bread and popped it in her mouth. "But it was dark, and it was quick, and I was upset."

Amber found a picture, tapped it to enlarge it and then handed Ingrid her phone.

"Hmm." Ingrid pursed her lips.

"Hmm, what?"

"Look at this picture, Amber." She passed the phone back to her. Amber studied the picture. Kesh, good-looking, older than Hadley, an arm around her shoulders. Amber had always seen the way he threw an arm around her or a hand on her back as protective.

"What?" Amber glanced up at Ingrid. "What am I looking at?"

"Look at his hand."

Amber cocked her head.

"It's right here."

She tapped the spot below her shoulder.

"I don't think so."

"Oh, come on." Amber rolled her eyes. "It's a neutral zone. He's like a big brother to her."

"A big brother that makes out with her sometimes? When he's between girls?"

"Didn't you have someone you made out with? Someone that probably didn't love you half as much as you thought you loved him?"

"Yeah, but not when I was fourteen."

Amber shook her head.

"Where's Liv?"

"What?"

"Where's Liv today?"

"I don't know." Ingrid shrugged. "Why am I supposed to know where Liv is?"

Amber shrugged. "I just thought…" She finally reached for the slice of pumpkin bread and ripped it in half. "Nevermind."

"No. Don't *nevermind* me. You just thought what?"

"I just figured if you were coming here with breakfast or coffee, you'd bring Liv."

"Because you'd rather hang out with Liv? Than me?"

Amber met Ingrid's gaze again. "No. I know you like having Liv around as a buffer."

Ingrid bit her lip, but she didn't say anything. When she finally did perk up, as if to say something, Amber felt her phone buzz in her hand. She expected it to be Nathan, or maybe even Gretchen, but she felt her stomach twist into a tight knot when she saw the name on her screen.

It wasn't a call from Nathan or Gretchen.
It was a text.
One she'd been dreading for days.

Four
"What's wrong?" Ingrid sounded concerned. Amber was tempted to cave. To open her mouth and let the words and the dread and the fear that had been coiled up in her stomach, pumping through her body for weeks- hell, months now-all gush out. When she was sick, whether it was a real flu or a brown-bottle flu, she always felt better after vomiting. Would it be the same now? If she could just vomit out the fear? What would it look like? Black and murky? Runny or thick and vile? Would it stain the table? The carpet?

"Amber."

Amber blinked and looked up at Ingrid. She wouldn't, though. She wouldn't tell Ingrid anything.

"Nothing." She shook her head once and set her phone down. Picked at the pumpkin bread again, although she wasn't sure she could swallow it now. Pretty sure it'd get stuck in the middle of her throat and then she'd be coughing and trying to talk to Ingrid, and her eyes would water, and Ingrid might think she was crying.

"Nothing." Ingrid licked her lips. "You just froze up there. Like, you were in the middle of slamming me, and then you froze."

Amber looked away. Stared at the piece of bread in her fingers and wondered how it got there. She couldn't eat this, could she? She reached for her mug, but sighed in defeat when she saw that it was empty.

"That's not like you," Ingrid told her. She stood up and reached for the mug. Amber reached for her phone in a panic, afraid that Ingrid was going to pick it up. "Chill. Just gonna get you more."

Amber nodded. She watched Ingrid walk out of the dining room and picked up her phone the second she was out of sight.

Hey Amber. What's up?

Amber hated him. On principal. It wasn't entirely fair of her to hate him. She knew that. Hated him anyway.

When Ingrid returned and set her full mug in front of her on the table, Amber turned her phone over so Ingrid wouldn't see the screen.

"I'm not trying to see your phone," Ingrid told her. "But I am asking you what's wrong."

Amber swallowed hard, but the knot of emotion stayed lodged in her throat. She stared at Ingrid silently. Wondered if it were Liv sitting there, if she would tell her what was going on.

Before she could decide, before she could say anything, they heard Hadley on the stairs. Both of them turned to watch her come out of the enclosed stairwell. Hands rubbing her face, she didn't see them at first. Amber watched Hadley closely, looking to see if there was something different about her this morning than there'd been last night. If she'd snuck out, if something had happened with Kesh, would Amber be able to tell? Just from looking? She could see a hangover, sure, but would she know if her daughter handed her virginity over to Kesh?

She looked away quickly when Hadley dropped her hands and noticed them at the table. Hoped Ingrid hadn't seen the way she'd been watching her. That Ingrid hadn't known exactly what she was doing.

Then again, who knew? Maybe this part of her fear was common to motherhood. To mothering a teenager. Not like Ingrid would get that.

"Hey."

"Hi." Hadley yawned. She stretched her arms up over her head, pulling her tank top up just an inch. Amber's eyes wandered down over her stomach and her long legs. Roamed back up to her messy ponytail. Hadley cleared her throat and then coughed a little. Amber winced when she lifted her hand and rubbed her neck.

"Sore throat?"

Hadley nodded. "Sort of."

"Think we should go to the walk-in clinic?"

"No." Hadley shook her head. "I'm fine." Hadley turned her big eyes to Ingrid. "Hi."

"Hi."

"Is there coffee?" Hadley turned her frown to Amber. Amber glanced at Ingrid, who shook her head.

"I'm sorry," Amber said sincerely. "I'll make more-"

"I got it." Hadley waved Amber back into her seat. "What're you doing here?"

"Just came by for a visit," Ingrid answered. "I would have brought you something, but I'm never sure where you are with what you eat."

Amber snorted.

"I'm gonna make coffee. And go back upstairs."

"Feel that bad?"

"I have a few chapters to finish that book."

"Mm." Amber nodded. "Okay."

"What're you reading?" Ingrid called as Hadley disappeared into the kitchen.

"*The Raven Boys.*" Hadley leaned around the doorway to look at Ingrid. "Excellent book."

"Yeah?" Ingrid raised her eyebrows. "Maybe I should read it."

"It's young adult."

Ingrid shrugged. "Does that mean I can't read it?"

"No." Hadley shook her head. "You can borrow mine."

"Great. Thank you."

Ingrid turned back to Amber in time to see her cup her hand around her phone.

"I watch her sleep sometimes," Amber whispered. "Used to be that I just wanted to watch her sleep. Now I just want to make sure she's at home. In her bed."

"That guy broke her heart the night of the party," Ingrid said quietly.

"She's fine now." Amber shrugged.

"I know. She's young," Ingrid agreed. "But you know how that feels. Rejection from a guy you really like, and-"

"Stop talking about me," Hadley called from the kitchen.

"Can you hear us?" Amber aimed a grin at Ingrid.

"No, but I hear you mumbling so I know you're talking about me."

"Maybe we're talking about Ingrid and Luke," Amber suggested. "Or me and Nathan."

"That's worse." Hadley leaned around the corner again. "Just put it on pause until I go back upstairs."

Amber shook her head at Ingrid, but Ingrid shrugged. They sat quietly, listening to the sounds of Amber making coffee. When she was done, she slipped back through the dining room and darted into the bathroom. Closed and locked the door.

"She told me once she hated to read."

Amber shrugged. "She can be a little difficult."

"Hmm." Ingrid laughed, but she nodded enthusiastically. "Wonder where she gets that."

"Probably you," Amber decided.

Ingrid tossed her hands in the air, but she laughed. "Yeah, probably so."

Hadley opened the door a few minutes later and crossed the dining room quickly. Amber twisted in her seat as Hadley perched on her lap.

"Do your ears hurt?" Amber rubbed her hand over her back.

"No." Hadley stared absently at the center of the table.

"What time did you go to sleep?"

"I dunno." Hadley shrugged. "I was reading. Woke up around four with my lamp still on. My face in the book."

"You didn't drool in it, did you?" Ingrid asked with a small grin. "If you did, I'll just buy a copy."

Hadley blinked and turned her head to look at Ingrid.

"That's so gross." She shivered and then turned to look at Amber over her shoulder. "Kesh asked if I could go to a movie with him tonight."

"You're grounded, Hadley," Amber reminded her.

"I've been grounded for, like, years. Can I go, please?"

"Nope."

"Mom."

"Besides, how are you talking to Kesh? If you're grounded?"

"He texted me."

"Do I need to take your phone?"

"Mo-om!" Hadley whined. "It's just a movie."

"A movie theater's a good place to make out, Hadley."

"That's just...gross." Hadley stood up. "I don't wanna make out with him."

"What movie?" Amber asked her. Not that it mattered. She wouldn't let her go no matter what it was.

"I dunno. Some horror movie he wants to see."

"Nope."

"God." Hadley climbed to her feet. "I'm gonna be fifteen."

"Yeah, in about six months, and even if you were fifteen, you might still be grounded."

"No kidding."

Again, Amber and Ingrid waited quietly for Hadley to grab a cup of coffee. They watched her march stiffly through the dining room and then step into the staircase and slam the door before they heard her feet pound the steps.

"How many times did you make out in a movie theater?" Ingrid asked her.

"I didn't."

"Really? You didn't?"

"Nope."

Ingrid raised her eyebrows.

"I take it you did."

"Yeah." Ingrid shrugged. "A few times."

"I was a backseat kinda girl." Amber leaned back in her chair again. "I don't know what to do with her."

"Hold the reins. Just like you're doing."

"Sometimes Nathan handles her better than I do."

"Maybe you're too much alike."

"Me and Hadley?"

Ingrid nodded.

"Maybe."

"Who texted you?"

Amber took a deep breath and slowly shook her head.

"Are you ever gonna trust me?"

"It's not about trusting you, Ingrid," Amber mumbled. "I just don't wanna talk about it."

"Will you tell Liv?"

Amber lifted her right shoulder in a lazy shrug.

"Was it Nathan?"

"No."

"Is it that you think Nathan might cheat?" Ingrid met her gaze and held it boldly. "Or do you not wanna commit to him?"

"What?"

Ingrid stared at her silently.

Amber glanced at her phone, hand still curled around it protectively.

"You think-?" She shook her head.

"Usually a reason why someone's so jumpy-"

"I'm not cheating on Nathan. I don't wanna cheat on Nathan."

"Then who texted you?"

"Are you always such a bully?"

"Why am I being a bully?"

"Why does it matter who texted me? Why are you pushing this? Can't you-"

"I don't know," Ingrid said softly. "I guess I just wish we could bridge the last twenty years. I wish we could talk like-"

"Twenty-five, actually."

"What?"

"You were gone for twenty-five years, Ingrid," Amber told her. "And no, we can't possibly bridge twenty-five years in one morning. I'm not going to-"

"I've been back since December."

"Okay, we can't possibly bridge twenty-five years in three months. This isn't like a *Doctor Phil* thing. I don't wanna talk about it-"

Ingrid sighed. She stared at Amber for a moment and nodded.

"'kay."

"I mean, I have friends, Ingrid. I have Gretchen. I have Liv. I have Nathan. I don't need…"

"Me," Ingrid finished for her. "You don't need me."

Amber rested her head on her chair and closed her eyes.

"Ezra sends you stuff?"

"What?" Ingrid snapped.

"You said earlier that it might have been Ezra that sent you the picture of Hadley."

"Yeah? And?" Ingrid stood up. "What? You want the picture back? Is that it?"

"I didn't know you and Ezra were that close."

"Ezra's…"

46

Amber opened her eyes to watch Ingrid gather the napkins and the breakfast bag.

"He's what?"

"He's a guy." Ingrid shrugged. "He doesn't play games."

"This?" Amber lifted the hand with her phone in it. "You think this is a game?"

"No." Ingrid shook her head. She stepped away from the table and pushed her chair in. "I think *we're* a game. To you. Or *I'm* a game to you. Or something. Ezra's not like that."

Amber didn't move when Ingrid carried the napkins and bag into the kitchen. She didn't look at Ingrid when she came back to the table and picked her coffee mug up. Carried it to the kitchen.

"I've got some work to do," she announced as she walked back into the dining room. "I'll see you later."

Amber stood up and followed her to the door. She expected Ingrid to say something else, but her sister walked out of her house without another word. Amber felt that awful dread and fear cocktail, now with a dash of guilt, roll around her stomach.

"Kyle," she said quietly. Ingrid didn't even glance at her when she climbed into her Subaru she'd parked in the alley by the front porch. "It was Kyle Carpenter."

Five
"What're we doing?"

Amber, on her knees beside the ancient upright freezer in her parent's basement, didn't bother to look when she heard Ingrid's voice. As far as she knew, Liv was still down here somewhere. She could deal with Ingrid.

"Ezra said there was an emergency," Ingrid tried again. "Something about water in the basement."

"Yeah, well..." Liv's voice answered from another corner. Amber couldn't quite make out where Liv was, but she didn't care to put much effort into figuring it out. She and Hadley had gone another round this afternoon, much more animated than it had been when Ingrid had been over earlier. Amber was a bizarre mix of restless energy and anger and exhaustion.

"Well?" Ingrid called. Amber could tell she'd wondered closer to her because her voice was louder now.

There wasn't water in the basement. Not now. But there had been. Near the east wall, at the back of the house. Wasn't particularly a good thing to have water in the basement, but on the other hand, Amber wasn't sure anything down here needed to be salvaged anyway. For instance, the old freezer at her side was dirty, and it smelled moldy, and she figured it hadn't worked since she'd been lucky enough to join the Williams family thirty years ago. But apparently, the water issue was yet another problem they had to fix before they listed Mom and Dad's house.

"Hmm." Ingrid cleared her throat. "Remember how Mom always used to get freaked out when we came downstairs to play?"

Amber, still on her knees, rested her hands on her legs and looked up at Ingrid over her shoulder.

"Um. No."

"Really? She'd always get so worried we'd play with that freezer."

"Oh yeah." Liv suddenly appeared behind Ingrid. "Because old freezers are the place to hide in hide and seek."

Liv looked as exhausted as Amber felt. *Interesting.* They'd only just come downstairs within the past hour. Amber wondered if Liv had something on her mind, too. Ingrid turned to look at Liv.

"You can get stuck in old freezers and refrigerators," Ingrid recited, apparently mimicking their mother. Amber had no recollection of ever playing in the basement, let alone being told not to play by the old freezer. "You could suffocate."

"No shit, Ingrid," Amber mumbled. "Why would you wanna play down here anyway? It's creepy as hell."

Amber swept her gaze up and over the stone walls and the ceiling beams. Cobwebs hung in every corner. Amber was pretty sure she'd walked through six or seven of them on the steps alone. The front wall, on the west end of the house, was fresh dirt. Well. She wondered how fresh it could be, if everything else in the basement was moldy and ancient and wrapped in cobwebs.

"What're you working on?" Ingrid asked with a smirk. She rubbed her thumb over a streak of dirt on Liv's cheek.

"I found a box of cookbooks in the corner."

"More cookbooks?" Amber asked.

"Some of them must have been Grandma's."

Amber felt a little pang of jealousy, sadness when Ingrid's face lit up. Mom's mom had passed away when Liv was ten and Ingrid was eight. Long before Amber was born.

"How do you know?" Ingrid asked.

"Well, because they're old," Liv answered with a shrug, "and Grandma wrote in some of them."

"Show me." Ingrid laid her hand on Liv's arm and pushed her around to lead her to the box of cookbooks. Amber stayed where she was, feeling distinctly apart from the conversation. She looked back at her hands and pulled on the rubber gloves she'd carried downstairs with her. Lifted her knees off the cellar floor and reached to pull the freezer door open.

She coughed, squeezed her eyes closed the way you might when watching a horror movie, and then slowly peered into the freezer. Nothing. Just some pent-up moldy air. She almost laughed. What had she been expecting? Decapitated human heads in jars? No, wait, that was the stuff in Ingrid's novels. Not real life. Actually, she'd been afraid to find mice or mice skeletons in the freezer. She stood up and peered around it to make sure the thing was unplugged. Satisfied that it was completely useless, she slapped a yellow sticky note on it- what they'd all decided they'd use as a disposal flag and glanced over her shoulder when she heard Ingrid's and Liv's quiet voices coming from the far corner of the basement.

"Are you sure?" Ingrid asked, but both of them stopped talking and looked at Amber when she approached them and lifted a foot to rest on the bottom step. In Amber's opinion, the steps needed a yellow sticky note, too. Pretty sure someone could break his or her neck coming or going. One step was completely broken. You had to skip it altogether, and it was the fifth down, so it was basically right in the middle of the flight, and if you weren't paying attention, you could step wrong there and go down ass over head and break a few bones.

"Yeah." Liv licked her lips and offered Amber a tired smile.

"What's going on?"

"Nothing." Ingrid shook her head.

"One of Wade's clients is dodging his calls. Sent him a bad check, and he's got like, ninety-eight more payments on his account."

"Mm." Amber arched her eyebrows. "Is he gonna turn him over?"

"I don't know." Liv shrugged. "Wade's so easy-going. He hates to do that to people."

"Liv, it's his livelihood. You don't get anywhere being easy on people that don't wanna pay their way."

"Yeah, I know." Liv nodded. "Believe me, I know. But tell that to Wade."

Amber noticed a pile of books in front of the huge, warped, water-damaged box her sisters stood beside. The top one was indeed a cookbook, but she couldn't make out the rest of them, though their spines were turned toward her. Not that she cared. She didn't cook much, and what she did throw together in the kitchen was usually an Amber/Hadley concoction. That Nathan pretty much vetoed when he'd come around and they'd make it again for him.

Maybe she should marry him, so she and her daughter would always have a good meal. Then again, she might get fat.

"Nathan home?" Liv asked.

"Um." She looked at her wrist, but she couldn't really see her watch in the gloomy corner, with her back to the bare yellow bulb that hung at the bottom of the steps. She stretched and leaned to get out of the light and saw that her watch said it was after three. "Should be getting home soon."

"Going out tonight?"

"God, no." Amber rolled her eyes.

"What's wrong?"

Amber noticed that Ingrid wasn't looking at her. She was picking at a hangnail on her right hand, and she seemed intent on not acknowledging Amber.

"Hadley and I went at it earlier." She shrugged. At this, Ingrid did look up.

"Didn't seem that bad to me."

"You missed the real fireworks," Amber told her. "She came back down after finishing her book. Demanded that I let her go with Kesh tonight."

"Go where?" Liv asked. She shifted and leaned against the steps. Amber winced as Liv's hair hit a cobweb. "Ew. Yuck."

"Yuck." Amber nodded. She stepped closer to her and reached to pick it out of Liv's hair.

"Some horror movie," Ingrid told Liv. "Right?"

"Yep."

"I thought she was grounded."

"She is. She got really pissed when I took her phone this afternoon."

"Ouch." Liv flinched. "Did you lock it up?"

"It's in my back pocket as we speak."

"Oh wow. Do you read her texts?"

"I'm not planning to read anything on her phone. I just don't want her using it right now. Especially not to be making plans with Kesh."

"Horror movies are good to make out to." Liv nudged the stack of books with her toe. "Ya know? You don't really wanna even watch them, but your guy does, so you just huddle in close and close your eyes. There's always nudity and sex, so that's gonna put him in the mood-"

"Since when do guys need something to put them in the mood?" Ingrid interrupted her.

"Well, Wade does."

"I don't think eighteen-year-olds do."

"True," Liv agreed.

"Did you make out at movies?" Amber asked Liv.

"Of course. Didn't you?"

"No. I actually watched the movies."

"Who'd have thought you'd be so square?"

Amber laughed and playfully punched Liv in the arm.

"Did you talk to Gretchen today?" Liv asked. "How was the band last night?"

Amber grinned. "Yeah. She called around noon. Said it was great. They had a bunch of new music they did."

"Really?"

"You shoulda gone out." Ingrid glanced Amber's way, but she didn't actually look at her. "Sure you would've had a better time with your friends."

Amber sort of wished she'd have gone out, but last night hadn't been terrible. She liked being around Liv and Ingrid. She just wished it didn't take so much effort, so much energy to be in the same room with Ingrid. Seemed like relationships shouldn't have to be that hard.

"Gretch say when they play again?"

"Yeah, but I don't remember now."

"We should go."

"We?" Amber blinked.

"Yeah. The three of us." Liv nodded. "Or we could take the guys, and the six of us could go."

"What kind of music do they play?" Ingrid directed her question to Liv.

"They remind me of The Wombats."

"Not helpful." Ingrid shook her head.

"The Kooks." Amber tried again.

"Really?" Ingrid almost sounded interested, but she still wouldn't look at Amber.

"You know who the Kooks are?"

"Yeah, I do." Ingrid sighed. "What do you think? I live in a box? What do you think I listen to?"

"I dunno. Maybe creepy serial killer music."

"So, I sense a little tension here." Liv moved to reach inside the box again. "Yuck. Some of these books are mildewy...but...I just need to interrupt the coming squabble to ask this."

"What?" Ingrid sounded annoyed. Amber arched her eyebrows when Liv looked at her.

"What's creepy serial killer music? I mean, like, what do creepy killer people listen to that's different from what we listen to?"

"Guess you'd have to ask Ingrid," Amber said with a shrug. "She specializes in creepy killers."

"You know what?" Ingrid stood up and turned to face Amber. "It doesn't matter to me what you think. About my moving back. It doesn't matter if you like it or not, because I came home for me. And for Luke-"

"Wait." Liv shook her head and reached for Ingrid's arm. She pulled Ingrid a few steps back. "How did we go from a little bit tense to you going off on Amber? I don't think she said a word about you being back-"

"Ingrid is pissed at me because I don't wanna share my secrets with her."

"What secrets?" Liv's tentative smile faded. "Why do you have secrets?"

"We all have secrets, Liv-"

"No, we pretty much don't. You both know my secret. We know what Ingrid was holding back when she first came home."

Amber sighed.

"Is it Nathan?" Liv pressed. "I mean…is there really a reason you don't wanna marry him?"

Amber sank to the steps and turned her head, but she couldn't hold back the little sob.

"Maybe I do wanna marry him, but I can't."

"Why can't you?" Liv asked softly.

Amber shook her head, careful not to look at Liv or Ingrid. But Liv moved to stand in front of her. Squatted down and took her hands in hers.

"Amber, what's wrong?"

"There's…" Amber raised her shoulders and turned her head to wipe her face on her shirt. "There's just too much going on."

"Like what? What's more important than you and Nathan?"

"Hadley, Liv. Isn't she more important than what I might want?"

Six

"Wait." Liv leaned forward, resting her knees on the bottom step. "Ouch. Now I know why I was never a catcher when I was younger."

"Well, either that or you're just old now," Ingrid told her. "Why are we having a conversation like this down here? I feel bugs crawling on me."

"We're not having a conversation," Amber announced. "I'm not talking about this. And besides, we're down here because the drill sergeant insisted we work down here to get things cleaned up."

"Thanks, Amber." Liv nodded. "That's great. Not only do you blow off my concern, you-"

"Oh for God's sake," Amber groaned. "I actually agree with Ingrid this one time. I feel imaginary bugs all over me. And I'm-"

Ingrid leaned over and smacked at Amber's arm. "Not so imaginary, actually."

"What do you mean?" Liv asked softly.

"I hate this basement. Unlike you guys, I never played down here. I don't have good memories of anything-"

Ingrid snorted and then laughed out loud. "Liv, do you remember when we were playing spy and base and Brian Moody got locked down here?"

"What the hell is spy and base?" Amber looked up at Ingrid with a frown.

"You never played spy and base?"

"What is it? I've never heard of it."

"One person's a spy. He hides. Everyone else has to find him. He has to sneak around and get back to base before anyone finds him."

"So it's a messed up version of hide and seek." Amber raised her eyebrows.

"Well. Yeah. Except it's like…the reverse-"

"A messed up version of hide and seek," Amber repeated.

"He hid under the pool table." Liv grinned.

"What pool table?" Amber asked Liv.

Ingrid laughed again. "And when Cory Preston looked for him under the table, he climbed up just enough that Cory couldn't see him. It's always so dark down here. We ended the game, went outside with those popsicles Mom gave us. And she locked the basement door. Brian was still down here."

Liv laughed now, too.

"Oh my God, I'd forgotten all about that."

"He was so pissed when we finally heard him."

"You heard him?"

"Yeah. He heard us out in the backyard. And he started pounding on the cellar doors. The ones back there." Ingrid gestured over her shoulder. "Liv heard him. Cory got the cellar doors unlocked and let him out."

"Yeah, that's just creepy." Amber shivered. "If I got locked down here as a kid, I'd probably turn into a psychotic killer." She looked up at Ingrid again and narrowed her eyes. "Are you sure that didn't happen to you and not some other kid you guys knew?"

"Amber." Liv half scolded her and half cajoled her. "What're you worried about Hadley for? What's-"

"Are you kidding me? Don't you think I have reason to worry?"

"Sure, but it's all typical teenage stuff," Liv answered. "Charlie's getting interested in girls now. You think I'm not more than a little worried?"

Amber took a deep breath and pushed Liv's hands away. "Yeah. Well. I don't wanna talk about this. So let's get back to work."

"It's Hadley's father. Isn't it?" Ingrid asked quietly. Amber made herself sit still, because any reaction would be telling. She wasn't sure she'd ever want to talk about this with anyone, pretty sure she'd never want to talk about it with Ingrid, and she sure as hell didn't want to talk about it down here in Creepsville.

"Hadley's father," Liv repeated. "Is that it? Did he just make a sudden reappearance in your life? Is he making demands?"

Amber bit her lip.

"Wait a minute." Ingrid nodded slowly. "That's who texted you this morning. Isn't it?"

"He texted her?" Liv asked quickly. "So you guys are…talking? Are you…does Nathan know? Is that why you can't marry Nathan? You have feelings for-"

"Oh my God." Amber took a deep breath. She stood up and turned away from them. Her knees felt a little weak, but she wasn't sure if that was the topic of conversation or if she needed to get out of the basement, out of the mold and mildew and God only knew what else grew down here.

"Where are you going?" Liv asked as she started up the steps. "Amber?"

She put her hands up at her sides as she climbed the stairs. Pressed them against the walls as they materialized around her. Stepped expertly over the broken step. Tottered for a moment at the top. She stood for a few seconds and blinked her eyes. The kitchen was lit with afternoon sun, and just that quickly, Amber's knees were solid and she breathed easier.

Her tennis shoes made no noise as she crossed the linoleum floor. She hadn't said so to her sisters or Ezra, but she thought the linoleum should be replaced. It was yellow to begin with, and yellow linoleum kind of said *barf* to her anyway, and then take into consideration that it was at least thirty years old, had to be older because Amber was thirty years old and her parents had lived here long before she'd come along-so now it was *aged and worn and curled in the corners* yellow linoleum.

Her mind wandered as she pulled the fridge door open. To Ingrid at her house earlier today. Looking at the snapshots on her fridge. The picture of Hadley that Ingrid thought maybe Ezra had sent her. That had blown Amber away. She could see Liv sending Ingrid things about her or Hadley, just trying to keep the peace or at least keep the lines of communication open. But not Ezra. He was as absent from this family as Amber. Maybe not as aggressively, but still. Far as Amber knew, Ezra wasn't invested in keeping the Williams family in one piece.

They'd never been in one piece, though, had they? Weren't they separate, by design?

Amber eyed the water bottles and then looked at the six-pack of bottled Rolling Rock she'd left here the other day. Two bottles gone. She reached for water but decided against it and snagged a beer. Pulled it from the fridge and turned to find Nathan walking down the hall.

"Hey." He grinned at her.

"Oh my God." She laughed and cried as she set the bottle down and hurried around the counter to throw herself at him. Nathan laughed out loud as he scooped her up and closed his arms around her back. "When did you get home?"

"Just came from the airport. Decided to swing by when you didn't answer your phone."

Amber slid her hands up over his arms and shoulders.

"I'm pretty tempted to start singing 'Cowboy Take Me Away.'" She ducked her face in the crook of his neck and breathed deeply.

"Happy to oblige you, ma'am, but I left my hat in the south."

She giggled. "Let's just go west."

Nathan loosened his grip on her and then reached to cup her chin in his right hand. Leaned in to kiss her. Amber sighed contentedly when he fanned his fingers over her jaw.

"Did you miss me?" His voice was gruff.

"More than you can know," she answered.

"Amber!"

She tensed in Nathan's arms when she heard Liv call up the steps.

"Basement duty today, huh?" Nathan asked her. She eased backwards reluctantly, nodded in response and turned to the steps as Liv and Ingrid stepped into the kitchen.

"Hey, Nathan." Liv greeted him with a smile. "When'd you get back?"

"Just now," he answered. "Straight from the airport."

Amber wiggled her phone from her back pocket and pressed the home button. He'd called her about forty minutes ago. She figured she'd been navigating the steps at that time. Or maybe standing at the bottom of the steps, surveying the disgusting basement and hoping she'd get out alive.

She'd hoped for a call from Hadley. True, she had her cell phone, but Hadley could have used their landline to check in with her. Her eyes roamed over the text from Kyle Carpenter. The one from this morning, that she hadn't answered. She felt a little flash of something in her gut-wasn't guilt, nothing to feel guilty about-and glanced at Liv and Ingrid.

"Where's Hadley?" Nathan asked her. She shoved her phone back in her pocket and reached for the beer she'd abandoned earlier in favor of Nathan.

"At home."

"Are you sure?" Ingrid cocked her head and arched her eyebrows at her.

Amber bit her lip and edged around the counter. She twisted the cap off the bottle as she moved around Ingrid. Took a long drink as she pulled the cabinet open to toss the cap in the garbage.

"She's not feeling well." Amber ignored Ingrid and directed her answer to Nathan. "Sore throat. She said her head hurts."

"Great." Nathan winced. "Did you take her to the walk-in?"

"No." Amber sighed and leaned on the counter. "This morning she insisted she'd be fine, but later this afternoon, she decided she was really getting sick."

"Maybe you should call and check on her," Ingrid suggested.

Amber cut her gaze to Ingrid's.

"Maybe I'll just go home and check on her."

"You can't do that." Ingrid shook her head. "We've got another eighty-six thousand boxes and piles to go through downstairs. No reason you should miss out on that much fun."

"Ingrid-"

"I'll go check on her," Nathan offered. He raised his eyebrows in question. Amber nodded slowly. Yes, she was a little worried that Amber might have been playing her, though she really hadn't looked good when she'd left the house. She'd still been curled up in the middle of her bed, pajamas on, blankets piled on top of her. But she'd begged and yelled about going out with Kesh, too, so who knew how she really felt.

Might be good for Nathan to check on her. Trouble was, Amber wanted to walk away from Ingrid and Liv and go with him.

"Okay." She nodded.

"I'll unpack and check on her. See if she needs anything."

"Thank you." Amber nodded again.

"C'mon." Nathan reached for her hand. "Walk me out."

Amber squeezed back around the counter, around her sisters, and slid her fingers through his. She set her beer down on the counter and then turned her back to Ingrid and Liv.

"See you guys later," Nathan called over his shoulder.

"Absolutely," Liv agreed.

"Rolling Rock." Amber heard Ingrid. She waited, shoulders tensed, for Ingrid to complain about it, but she didn't hear her say anything else.

"What's going on?" Nathan asked as he opened the front door. Amber shook her head as he followed her out to the front porch. "That was pretty tense."

"Same old thing," she mumbled.

"Is Hadley really sick?"

"I think so." She nodded. "But she and I did get into it twice today."

Nathan frowned. He settled his hands on Amber's shoulders and leaned over to drop a kiss on her forehead.

"What about?"

"Apparently Kesh asked her to go to a movie tonight."

"How did he ask her anything if she's grounded from talking or texting?"

Amber shrugged. She pulled Amber's phone from her pocket and held it out. "I asked her that. Which only made her angrier. And I told her no, she wasn't going anywhere with him. Or anyone else right now."

"So, do you think she's at home?"

Amber nodded. "She looked pathetic when I left. And besides. Who sneaks out in the middle of the day? It's more fun to sneak out at night and do bad stuff."

Nathan laughed softly. "Well, then, maybe you and I should sneak out tonight and do some bad stuff."

Amber offered him a small smile as she covered his hands with hers.

"I would very much like to do some bad stuff with you anywhere tonight, Nathan Marquardt."

"Good." He winked at her. "Okay. You go play nice with your sisters-"

"Only if you promise me some really, really bad stuff later."

He studied her face for a few moments, finally lifted his lips in a crooked grin and leaned over to drop a quick peck on her lips.

"I just came home from a bachelor party. I am full of wicked ideas, Amber."

She laughed as he dropped his hands and stepped away from her.

"Now I'm scared."

"You probably should be." He nodded and stepped off the porch. "I'll call you. After I see Hadley."

"Okay." She nodded.

"Amber?"

"Hmm?"

"I love you."

"I love you, too."

Seven

Ingrid was perched on a barstool when Amber wandered back into the kitchen. Liv, beer in hand, leaned against the counter. Again, Amber felt like she'd walked into the middle of something. Same as always. The little pain in the ass sister, interrupting the big girls. She snagged her beer from the counter and turned to the steps without a word.

"Going down there alone?" Ingrid asked her.

Amber didn't have the energy to argue with her. Not right now. Not when she was worried what Nathan was going to find when he got to the house. Instead she took a deep breath and turned to look at her sisters.

"Don't you just wanna get this done?" she asked quietly.

"The basement or the house?" Liv asked. She was chewing something. Amber noticed an open bag of tortilla chips on the counter.

"Isn't it just kind of the same thing right now?"

Liv shrugged. "Not really. Yes, I wanna get the basement done, because it is a little creepy down there. But..." She shook her head.

"But what?" Amber urged her to finish her thought.

"I don't wanna be done. With the house. I don't wanna just...let it go."

"We've talked about this," Ingrid reminded her. "We can't just hold onto the house and let it sit here empty-"

"I know." Liv rolled her eyes. "I know that, Ingrid. All I'm saying is I hate it. I hate that one of these days, we'll be done and we'll walk out of here, and we'll never come back."

"Where's Ezra today?" Ingrid ducked her head and rubbed vigorously at her face. She finally looked up again, mouth wide open in a huge yawn.

"He's got Samuel today." Amber told them. "Shay had a thing."

"A thing?"

Amber shrugged. "Some family thing. A shower or something."

"So." Liv cocked her head to study Amber. "How come you get to have secrets?"

"It's not so much that I have secrets. I just don't wanna talk about any of it."

"With us." Ingrid nodded. "Or more accurately, with me."

"It's just…" Amber shook her head. "It's a big deal. It's huge. And I can't just…talk about it. Once things are said, it's easier for them to be repeated. And repeated again. And then they're real. And they have the potential to really hurt people-"

"You think I don't know that?" Liv asked quietly. "Look at how quickly Ingrid told you about me cheating on Wade."

"Yeah." Amber licked her lips. "I still don't really get that, either. Why would you do that to Wade?"

"Do you think I don't worry every day about one of you two saying something in front of him?"

"So you think we're that trustworthy? That we'd run and tell him-"

"No." Liv looked at Ingrid. "Just that it's easy to let something slip and then the whole world knows-"

"Why did you cheat on Wade?" Amber repeated.

"I don't know, Amber. I'm bored. We're boring. It's the same thing with us. Over and over-"

"Do you mean sex?"

"I mean everything. The same dinners. The same conversations. The same TV shows. The same dates, if we do go out. And yes, the same sex."

"So do something different."

"Like what?"

"Take a weekend away somewhere."

Liv shook her head.

"Give a little more. Maybe he'll do the same."

"Julie and Rafe are going to Cancun next month," Ingrid told Liv.

"Okay, so what if Wade and I go to Cancun? For a weekend. And we have the little fruity drinks with umbrellas in them, and we take long romantic walks on the beach, and we make love in some cozy little beach cabin and it's all wonderful. What about when we come back home? And we're in our house? Living our lives again? When there's no more sand? No more moonlit beach? No coconut oil to rub over each other's skin-"

"Then you put in a little effort," Amber said simply. "Get his coffee for him in the morning. Touch his hand when you leave the room. Spend a few extra minutes in bed in the morning. Give him a backrub. Take the time to..." Amber tossed her hands up. "To do something for him."

"Give him a blowjob," Ingrid translated for Amber. "Or a hand job. Make it about him."

Liv blinked and looked from Ingrid to Amber.

"If he doesn't do the same for you, ask him. Tell him what you want."

"We've been together for over twenty years. He knows what I want."

"But ask, Liv." Amber shrugged. "Talk to him when you're together. Make him remember how it used to be."

"Luke mentioned going to Colorado. Later this summer."

Amber and Liv both stared at Ingrid expectantly.

"To see..." Liv nodded.

"Hannah." Ingrid finished Liv's thought.

"Do you want to go?"

"Sure, but I'm scared to death to meet his daughter."

Liv looked back at Amber and arched her eyebrows expectantly.

"It's just." Amber shrugged. "Hadley's been asking about her father."

"And?" Liv coaxed her gently.

"I don't know…" Amber sighed.

"You don't know who her father is?" Liv asked incredulously.

"Yes, I do," Amber snapped. "God, this is what I'm talking about. This isn't a joke. This is real. This is my life. Hadley's life. His life."

"If you and Nathan…" Ingrid hesitated. Amber bit her lip as she stared at Ingrid.

"What?" She finally shrugged her shoulders when Ingrid didn't continue.

"Nothing." Ingrid shook her head.

"What?" Amber repeated. She heaved a big sigh and stepped over to the counter. Sat down on the barstool next to Ingrid's.

"I just wondered…" Ingrid stared at her bottle rather than look at Amber. "If she would still be interested…in finding her father. If you and Nathan got married."

Amber swallowed hard.

"I mean." Ingrid lifted her eyes and turned to look at Amber for a second. "If you got married, would Nathan…adopt her? Give her his last name?"

"I don't know." Amber tucked her hair behind her ear and stared at Ingrid boldly. "He wants to. Nathan's great. He's so good with her."

"But?" Liv reached for the bag of chips and started to fold it over.

Ingrid smacked at her hands and reached into it when Liv put it back down.

"How can you guys eat those without cheese or salsa or something?"

Ingrid shrugged as she popped a broken chip into her mouth.

"We should call Ez and have him whip up some homemade salsa."

"He makes killer guacamole," Amber told Liv.

"So?" Ingrid nudged Amber with her elbow.

"I don't know what Hadley wants."

"She wants you to tell him yes," Ingrid said quickly. "She told me that."

"But I don't know what she wants as far as her relationship with Nathan."

"So ask her," Liv suggested.

Amber winced. She reached for a handful of chips. "I just...I'm not sure I'm ready to do that. I don't know if I'm ready to open that whole can of worms."

"You said she's been asking about her father," Ingrid reminded Amber.

"Yeah. But."

"When did she start asking?"

Amber looked at Liv and took a deep breath. "Um. Well. The first time she asked she was four. It was a daddy daughter day at preschool. And she wanted to know why I was there with her, instead of her daddy."

"You went with her?" Ingrid's face lit up with a smile.

"Yes." Amber nodded.

"What'd you tell her?"

"I just told her that our family was just the two of us. That I loved her as much and more than a mommy and daddy could."

"That worked?"

Amber glanced at Ingrid again.

"Yeah. She asked again when she was nine or ten. Gets harder to answer the older she gets."

"What'd you tell her then?"

"I just told her that her dad wasn't in the picture."

"So when did it come up this time?" Liv turned her back to them and opened the refrigerator door. "There's, like…nothing….here to eat."

"Are you that hungry?" Ingrid asked her.

"I am so damned hungry."

Liv turned back to catch Ingrid and Amber exchange a look.

"I'm not pregnant. I ate half a grapefruit for breakfast. Haven't eaten since."

"Order something."

Liv looked at Ingrid curiously.

"What about the guys?"

"If you're hungry, order something," Ingrid repeated.

Liv sighed and leaned on the counter again.

"So?" Liv turned to Amber.

"It was…" Amber cleared her throat. "A week or two before Thanksgiving. They were studying genetics in science class. She asked me one night if she got anything from her dad. I mean…she looks just like me. She-"

"She's got your attitude," Ingrid agreed before Amber could say it.

"Shut up." Amber laughed softly.

"Does she?" Liv asked. "Does she take after him at all?"

"I see things, but no one else would because no one else knows."

"Like what?"

"Um. Her laugh. Her eyes. Some of her mannerisms-"

"Hadley totally has your eyes," Liv argued.

"She does, but if you knew him, you'd see him, too."

"Did you tell her that?"

"Well, I was gonna lie and tell her no. She didn't get anything from him. But she looked so sad. Even before I opened my mouth to lie to her, she looked so sad.

So. I told her that the older she gets, the more of him I see in her."

"Oh." Ingrid winced.

"So, of course, she asked again." Amber ducked her head and rubbed the back of her neck. "We've argued about it. Round and round and round. And then Dad died." She lifted her eyes to look at Liv. "You know how close she was to Pop. It really hit her." She turned to look at Ingrid. "I know you think I'm a horrible mom, and that she's the antichrist, but she's been a good kid. Up until…all of this."

"I never said you were a horrible mom-"

"You don't have to say a word, Ingrid. I read it in your face anytime you're around me and Hadley."

"What does Nathan think?"

"About Hadley?"

"About her wanting to know who her dad is."

"We haven't talked about it much."

Liv sunk her teeth into her lower lip.

"Don't you think you should? If you're close enough that he's asked you to marry him, and he wants to adopt Hadley, don't you think this is all stuff you should be talking about?"

Amber shrugged.

"So this is why you're putting him off?"

Amber looked up at Liv and arched her eyebrows.

"Tell me why we need to be married, Liv." Amber shrugged. "Tell me why. What's so good about being married? How long have you and Wade been married? You've got a house together. You've got children together. You go out. You stay in. You share money and bills. Nathan and I do all of that. Why do we need to be married?"

"Amber."

"You're not happy. You're bored with being married. Ingrid's divorced. Mom and Dad weren't happy. Ezra and Shay aren't happy-"

"What?" Liv stood up straight and looked around. She patted her pockets and then reached to pick up the chip bag again.

"What're you doing?" Ingrid asked.

"Looking for my phone," Liv answered. "I'm ordering pizza."

"What do you mean Ezra and Shay aren't happy?" Ingrid looked at Amber.

"Nothing." Amber shook her head. "My point is I think Nathan and I are fine the way we are."

"But Nathan doesn't. Nathan wants more."

"It's over there," Ingrid told Liv as she pointed at the end of the counter by the table.

"How'd it get over there?" Liv trailed her fingers over the counter as she slid against it until she was close enough to pick her cell up.

"What's going on with Ezra and Shay?"

"Nothing." Amber sighed. "Nothing. Forget I said anything."

"Amber."

"So. Wait." Liv tapped her phone in the palm of her hand. "Is there more to this thing with Hadley's father?"

Amber chewed on her lip. She pulled her own phone from her pocket, willing it to ring. She was anxious to hear from Nathan, but she was also desperate for a way out of this conversation.

"I don't know."

"Do you...do you talk to him?"

"Ingrid, if Luke asked you to marry him, would you?"

"Yes. I told you that a long time ago."

"Even now. You've moved in with him. You guys are happy. You have everything. Why would you wanna marry him? What's wrong with the way it is now?"

"I don't know." Ingrid shrugged. "But I'm crazy about him, and I'd marry him in a heartbeat if he asked me. I want that bond with him. I want to promise the rest of my life to him. I want his last name. I want everything he wants to give me."

"Amber."

Amber looked at Liv.

"Do you talk to Hadley's father? Is he someone in your life right now?"

"Kind of."

"Kind of?" Liv repeated. "That's not an answer."

"It is, though," Amber mumbled. "It's an answer. It's *my* answer."

"What kind of pizza do you guys want?" Liv looked down at her phone.

"I'll eat anything," Ingrid answered.

"Doesn't matter," Amber agreed.

"And Amber?"

Amber looked up at Liv as she tapped the screen of her phone.

"Things aren't…perfect with me and Wade. But I'd marry him again tomorrow. If he asked."

Eight

They'd moved back down to the basement after Liv ordered the pizza. Amber hated the damp, dungeony feel to the basement, but it beat hanging around upstairs talking about stuff. Didn't it? Part of her wished, once they were back downstairs, that they were still gathered around the kitchen counter talking about Liv and Wade or even Hadley and her father and Nathan.

Sure, she'd told Gretchen when Nathan had first asked her to marry him. She'd had to tell someone, because her utter shock at his proposal and her being unable to give him an answer had led to a horrible fight and a few sleepless nights and a few more silent treatment days before she and Nathan had talked and she'd promised him she loved him, she just wasn't ready to talk about marriage. Gretchen hadn't judged. She hadn't agreed with Amber, but she hadn't pushed her toward the big commitment either. She'd only listened. Pointed out some good things and bad things about Nathan, about marriage.

Funny. When Gretchen pointed out the bad things about Nathan-traveled too much for work, left the toilet seat up ninety percent of the time, didn't put the lid on the mayo jar tight enough-Amber had jumped to his defense immediately. She loved him like crazy. She'd never doubted her feelings for him.

She just didn't believe in marriage. She'd reminded Gretchen of her family's track record when it came to marriage. Gretchen, whose parents had been married thirty-eight years, had flinched and then quietly reminded her that some people did commit and make it work and enjoy it.

Amber had asked Gretchen if she planned to get married one day. She'd said yes, though she'd readily admitted now wasn't the time. And most likely, Steve wasn't the guy.

She'd never talked to Gretchen about Hadley's father, though. No one on earth knew who he was, other than Amber. Maybe she should've talked to Gretchen about it. Probably she could've, probably Gretch would've listened and committed the secret to that best friend vault that most best friends have. But she'd never been able to do it. She'd never been one to confide those deep down to the bone secrets. Not to anyone.

Even as much as she loved Nathan, she still felt like there was a big part of herself she kept hidden from him.

Amber had to admit that a small part of her wished she could just sit down and talk to her sisters. Just tell them who Hadley's father was and why she hesitated to tell Hadley and why she was afraid to tell him. And why she kept pushing Nathan away.

She wanted to come clean about all of her fears. But she was afraid to trust either one of them.

Not that they would share her secrets. She didn't believe either of them would betray her. But she was afraid *of them*. Of the look she'd see pass between them. Of the things they might say to her. The things they might say about her to each other.

Because really, she was afraid they loved each other more than they'd ever loved her and knowing that for a fact would devastate her. Wasn't holding back because of fear better than going all in and facing that rejection?

"Hey."

She hunched her shoulders when she felt Liv's fingers in her hair.

"Bug?"

"Huh?" Liv leaned over and squeezed her shoulder. "No. How's it going?"

"I don't know. I don't even know what I'm looking at."

Liv squatted down beside her and reached for the box. She pulled out a handful of papers and books and clothing patterns. All of it looked ancient, most of it was damaged from mildew and mold.

"We need to just have the guys carry the boxes upstairs."

"Yeah, that'd be great. We could unleash a rodent infestation upstairs just before we put the house on the market."

"Have you seen-"

"No, but, God, Liv, I'd bet my left boob that there's mice down here."

"How would that work then? If you won the bet? Would you, like, gain a boob?"

"Only if we doubled or nothinged." Amber shook her head and glanced up at Liv.

"Who's gaining boobs?" Ingrid asked. Amber and Liv both looked up as Ingrid made her way in baby steps across the basement. She carried a book of some sort in her hands, eyes on the book, feet hesitantly moving across the floor.

"Amber is," Liv answered.

"Yeah? Like, what? Miracle-Gro or something?" Ingrid finally looked up. "Do you add it to your drinking water or rub it in?"

Amber snorted.

"What do you think about having the guys just help us drag these boxes upstairs? So we can go through them up there."

Amber looked from Ingrid to Liv, as Liv climbed to her feet.

"I'm all about getting out of this basement, but you really wanna put these boxes upstairs?"

"I'm saying!" Amber nodded. She looked back down at the box she'd been working on.

"Well." Liv sighed. "I know...but on the other hand, we have to get rid of all this stuff, anyway. Don't we? One way or another. We can't sell the house with a basement and garage full of junk."

"Garage," Ingrid groaned. Amber looked up and caught her gaze.

"What if we had the guys take it outside? We could go through it in the backyard?"

"What if it snows? Or rains."

"We'd just have to be fast."

Again, Amber met Ingrid's gaze and was rewarded with a grin and an eye roll.

"We could put it in the garage."

"Have you been in the garage lately?" Ingrid asked Liv. "There's not room enough to step in and turn around."

"So you wanna just stay down here?"

Amber finally stood, wincing when her knees popped along the way.

"I don't, no." She shook her head. She laughed and swatted Ingrid's hand away when she reached out and pulled her t-shirt down straight. "What are you doing?"

"Looking to see if you're really getting more boobs."

Amber pushed her away again.

"Let's go upstairs," Liv suggested. "We can call the guys and have them haul this stuff up. We'll figure it out from there. Probably not much worth keeping anyway."

"Ya think?" Ingrid raised her eyebrows. "I just found the instruction manual for the toaster they had when we were kids."

"What?" Liv frowned and reached for it.

"An instruction manual for a toaster?" Amber repeated. "Are you serious? Isn't it pretty obvious how to use a toaster?"

Ingrid shrugged. "I know, right?"

"I wonder, though," Amber said, as she followed Liv up the steps, both of them careful to step over the broken stair.

"Wonder what?"

"If any of that kind of stuff would be valuable."

"Moldy instructional manuals for toasters?" Ingrid laughed.

"Well." Amber shrugged. She stepped into the kitchen behind Liv at the top of the steps. Coughed and then rubbed her face. "Yuck. I feel like I need a shower."

"Did you hear from Nathan?" Liv asked.

"Yeah. He texted. Said Hadley was sleeping when he got home. PJs and stuffed animals, sleeping. No faking."

"She *must* be getting sick." Liv nodded.

"I know. I probably should've taken her to the walk-in today. Now she'll probably miss school on Monday."

"You could've just called me. Taken her."

Amber shrugged. She watched Liv wash her hands and then bumped her out of her way with her hip so she could do the same.

"She didn't want to go. Said she'd be fine."

"So at what age do you let the kid decide?"

Amber looked at Ingrid over her shoulder as she dried her hands. "What?"

"I'm just asking," Ingrid mumbled. "I mean...at some point, kids know enough to know if they need to go to the doctor. Right? We did." She glanced at Liv.

"I dunno." Liv shrugged. "Maybe ten or twelve?"

Ingrid turned her eyes to Amber.

"Probably." She shrugged. "How long is that pizza supposed to take?"

"Half hour to forty-five minutes." Liv pulled the fridge open again. Finding only the same bottled water and three Rolling Rocks, she closed it. "We need something to drink."

"There're three beers in there," Ingrid reminded her.

"No one can drink just one beer when eating pizza." Liv shook her head.

"Water," Amber suggested.

"You'd rather drink water? With pizza?"

"Nope." Amber shook her head. "Just saying there's water in there."

"Let's make a beer run." Ingrid looked at Amber hopefully.

"Who's gonna be here to get the pizza?"

"I'll stay," Liv offered. "I'm gonna call and check in with Wade."

When Amber looked back at Ingrid, she was watching her expectantly.

"Sure. Why not?"

"What do you want?" Ingrid asked Liv.

"Surprise me."

Ingrid grinned. Liv rolled her eyes. "Nothing weird."

"Define weird."

"If you're not back, I'll eat it all."

"We're going!" Ingrid grabbed her purse and keys from the counter and glanced at Amber again. "Ready?"

"Yep." Amber patted her back pocket to make sure she had her phone and followed Ingrid out the backdoor. "Hey. It's nice out today."

"It is," Ingrid said with a nod. "I'm so ready for warm, spring days. Cool nights."

"Yeah?" Amber looked at Ingrid over the top of her Subaru. Ingrid pulled her door open. "Do you guys sleep with the windows open?"

"We haven't yet." Ingrid climbed into the SUV and pulled the door closed. Amber slid into her seat. "Too cold right now."

"So when it warms up, will you?"

"I don't know." Ingrid shrugged. She stuck the key in the ignition and started the car. Reached to turn the radio down. "Why?"

Amber shrugged. "I dunno. I just...what if you want the windows open, and he doesn't?"

"Then we won't open them." Ingrid shook her head. "You're thinking about Nathan again?"

"Thinking about the disastrous marriages I've witnessed..."

"Okay, wait." Ingrid dropped the SUV into gear and backed slowly out of the driveway. "You totally can't count my marriage. It should never have happened."

"But it did."

"Yeah, but Amber," Ingrid slowed the SUV to a stop at Maine and watched the traffic for a moment, "I was a kid. And Scott was a kid. And we'd just traded in years of friendship for steamy sex, and we thought it was love."

"You must have felt something for him."

"I did. I was crazy about him. But I wasn't in love with Scott. I never was. He never felt that way for me. We had a few good months, and I dunno...maybe it was an opportunity to get out. At least, maybe it was for me."

"Were you that desperate to get away from home?"

"Weren't you? When you were eighteen?"

Amber shrugged and looked out her window.

"Scott and I parted as friends."

"Really?"

"Yes, really. No hard feelings. Neither of us cheated. We just both kind of...figured out...that it wasn't...right. Wasn't what we thought it was."

"Do you still talk to him?"

"No. But if I saw him at the liquor store right now, I'd be happy about it."

Amber nodded. "And what about Liv? And Wade?"

"They'll figure it out."

Amber pressed her lips together and stared straight ahead.

"She loves him, Amber. She's crazy about him. They're just...they'll figure it out."

"Do you think she should tell Wade?"

"That she-? No. I don't. I don't think she should hurt him like that."

Amber sighed and turned in her seat. "Okay, what about Mom and Dad?"

Ingrid bit her lip. She glanced at Amber and then looked back at the road.

"They reconciled, Amber. Remember? They reconciled, and they had you and Ezra, and they were happy."

"Do you really think so?"

"Yes, I do." Ingrid nodded. "You don't?"

Amber raised her eyebrows.

"What?" Ingrid signaled to turn left at Twenty-Fourth. She groaned quietly when the traffic light turned yellow. Slowed to a stop again. "You don't think they were happy?"

"I don't know," Amber whispered. "I was too busy being a pain in the ass to notice. But when I think about it now, when I think about Mom and Dad, I wonder how they ever had time for each other when they always had to deal with me."

She was afraid to look at Ingrid, so she stared out the windshield at the red light and when it changed to green, she dropped her gaze to her hands, folded in her lap.

"Amber," Ingrid said quietly. "You...that's..."

Amber took a deep breath and lifted her head to look at Ingrid. "Forget it."

"No-"

"No. Just forget I said it."

"But-"

Amber sighed in relief when her phone buzzed in her back pocket. She lifted her butt from the seat to wiggle her phone out. Glanced at the screen and saw that Liv was calling.

"Hey."

"Get some cookies, too."

"What?"

"What part of that did you not get?" Liv asked with a laugh. "Get some cookies, too."

"Cookies," Amber repeated. Ingrid glanced at her.

"Yes. And grab me a pack of Dentyne, would you?"

Amber raised her eyebrows and nodded. "Sure, Liv."

"Thanks."

She lowered the phone to her lap and looked at Ingrid with a frown.

"We need cookies. And Dentyne."

Nine

Amber hated sending Hadley off to school when she knew she wasn't feeling well. True, Hadley wasn't dying. She didn't even have a fever, hadn't had one all weekend. Just that damned sore throat. And it wasn't like Hadley was a little kid anymore. If she felt that bad at school, she knew she could call and come home. On the other hand, it was when Hadley was sick that she regressed to her younger, sweeter self (most of the time) and wanted to snuggle with Amber or at the very least, she'd gather her blankets and stuffed animals and make a nest on the couch to be somewhere near Amber.

Probably, she should have taken Amber to the doctor Saturday. Now she couldn't justify pulling her out of school to take her to the doctor, because if she really was getting sick, she would be missing school. On the other hand, if she'd gotten her to the doctor earlier, she might have been able to hang in there and not miss school at all.

Amber heaved a sigh and gave herself a mental shake. It was done. Hadley was at school. A glance at her watch told her Hadley was probably in third hour by now. She'd last the day and then they could start the evaluation process over again this evening and again in the morning.

She adjusted her lens to draw the old barn into focus. Took a deep breath and released it slowly. Pressed the shutter release. Wondered again about Hadley.

Wondered if it was easier for Liv. If having Wade there to back her decisions or to argue and point out the flaws in her thinking made parenting any easier. Amber wasn't naïve. No parent's job was ever one hundred percent smooth sailing. Life wouldn't be perfect if she and Nathan were married. But would it be better?

She honestly didn't know.

Maybe it would be easier to handle the guy stuff. The thing with Hadley wanting to be around Kesh all the time. Maybe that would be easier if Nathan were around all the time. But he wouldn't be. Even if they were married, Nathan wouldn't be around much more than he already was. Not with his damned job.

Amber, crouched in the gravel drive that led to the old barn on the old Schuler property just north of town, lowered her camera and stared at the barn with her naked eye. It was beautiful, really. The faded red. The chipped paint and the big white cross bar on the door. The weeds, the fescue that shot up around it like a moat. Just weeks ago, the weeds had been choked by snow and ice, and Amber had taken several shots then, too. They'd turned out perfectly, but today she wasn't feeling it. There was the barn, the clear blue sky, the hint of spring in the air, and she couldn't focus.

Wasn't the damned camera. It was her brain.

Too much on her brain.

The house. God, she agreed with Liv. They couldn't just sell Dad's house. Not after they'd invested their time and money into a major overhaul. It was a gorgeous old brick house, and even if it wasn't, even if they hadn't done a damned thing to it, how could they just sell it? How could they hand the key over to strangers and walk away and let another family walk the hallowed ground of their childhoods? Even if they'd grown up separately, they'd all grown up there, and the house belonged to them.

Then again, she didn't want it. She sure as hell couldn't afford to buy the place. She couldn't afford the heating bills. The upkeep. What the hell would she and Hadley do rattling around in that house anyway? She couldn't keep track of her daughter as it was. No way she wanted to give Hadley that much more room to roam and hide.

She didn't want her siblings to have it, either.

She stood up and looked over her shoulder. No one around. She was surrounded by rolling fields of weeds, caught in the seasonal mix of brown and green, and trees that were still bare and a blue sky that stretched as far as her eye could see.

She loved the barn. The bicycles she shot. The houses. The antique furniture. The profiles of laughing faces, sad faces, thoughtful faces. She loved the beauty in life that she could frame in her viewfinder.

But sometimes she thought what she loved most about her job was the solitude it offered her.

She wondered briefly if Ingrid felt the same way. Thought of all the heated words exchanged between herself and Ingrid lately, cringed at how petulant and immature she was in her memories, and shrugged the shame away. She'd been a little kid when Ingrid had left. She'd loved her sister with the abandon that only a child knows to love with, and Ingrid had crushed that innocence when she'd walked away and left Amber as if she had been a childhood toy, a doll, maybe, that Ingrid had outgrown.

Sadly, she didn't get along with Liv much better than she got along with Ingrid. She'd been an absolute pain in the ass for her parents, and she knew Liv, being so much older, had thought she was horribly spoiled and that she should have grown up and treated her parents better.

She didn't care.

Maybe she'd like to see Ezra get the house. Mostly, she was close to Ez. They talked a lot. Maybe not about everything. He'd known Nathan had asked her to marry him, and he'd known she'd said no. She'd confided that to Ezra. Hadley had run her mouth about it to Ingrid, and Ingrid had, of course, told Liv. She knew Ezra and Shay weren't as happily married as everyone else seemed to think they were. She even know a little bit about why; she loved Shay, but she knew she was a little bit crazy.

Ezra might never tell her everything. She was okay with that. Because she had no intention of telling him about Hadley's father. About the way Hadley begged her just for his name. That when she wouldn't tell Hadley, she'd turn on her and say all those hateful things teenagers say when they're angry and hurt. That she'd finally given in and contacted him.

That Kyle Carpenter had responded.

And that now she was so sick with regret, with dread that she'd ignored his text. Deleted his text. That she'd binged on cheap wine and hit the hard stuff the night she'd opened that Pandora's box. And that since Kyle had answered her, she'd been unable to sleep through a night.

That she hadn't mentioned any of this to Nathan.

She took a deep breath and walked slowly down the drive. Maybe a new perspective would do it.

Kyle had texted Saturday morning. It was Tuesday now. She hadn't answered him yet. Maybe he'd forget. Maybe nothing would come of it, and rather than walk through her days tense and scared that he would suddenly become a part of their lives again, that Hadley would meet him and like him and prefer him to her, maybe it would all just go away and she could go back to being the bitch mom who won't share her secrets.

As she slowed at the end of the gravel drive and turned back to look at the barn, she shoved down the next thought to pop into her head.

Hadley had a right to know, didn't she? To know who her father was? But was fourteen too young? Should she wait until she was sixteen?

Amber lifted the camera, framed the barn with the nearly dilapidated feeding trough beside it, and hit the shutter release.

What difference was two years going to make? Hadley wasn't just going to grow up and accept it in two years. Amber didn't really want her to grow up that fast anyway. But then, when *was* the right time? When Hadley was twenty-one? And then Hadley would have missed out on twenty-one years of knowing her father instead of fourteen.

Amber snapped a few more shots and then walked purposefully toward the barn again. Glad for her hiking boots, she wandered around the barn, looked at it from the sides, the back. Moved far away, into the trees, and then back again to stand close enough to touch the wood. The wind was sharp, and she was cold, but she wasn't ready to leave yet. She had some good shots; she knew that much. But she didn't have what she wanted yet.

New angle, she told herself again. She moved again to the back of the barn, a few feet to the west. Knelt in the weeds and cringed when she felt the damp seep into her jeans. Hoped like hell it was too cold for any snakes to be out today. Lifted the camera and caught only the front corner of the old building.

Slightly askew in her viewfinder, she saw a piece of the barn, the long gravel drive that led to the longer, lonelier two lane highway, and only a small spot of dull gray at the bottom, that she knew was the feeding trough.

She needed to talk to Nathan. About Hadley. About Kyle. They weren't married, no, but they talked about things. They talked about work, if they had particularly good days or bad. They talked about families. Nathan had an older sister with MS, and her husband had just left her last summer. Amber knew that Nathan had been consumed with anger at his brother-in-law, worry for his sister. Amber spoke candidly with Nathan about how she felt about Liv and Ingrid. They weren't married. But there were no secrets.

Not until now, anyway.

She pressed the shutter release over and over again, picturing the barn in the next coffee table book she'd recently signed a contract to do. No title yet, but Amber was looking for simplicity. Not necessarily country, though today's setting certainly fit the bill.

Satisfied that she had the shot, she stood slowly and wandered back through the knee high weeds and down the gravel drive. She'd parked her Passport at the end of the drive, just off the highway. Since she'd been here-over an hour-there'd been no other traffic on the asphalt ribbon that cut through the boundless brown and green.

Before she got in, she dismantled her camera and packed it away carefully. Stowed the bag behind her seat and then climbed into the SUV. She pulled her phone from her pocket and looked at it. No service out here in the boonies, though. She'd assumed that would be the case, so if Hadley had decided she was too sick to stay at school, Amber had told her to call Ezra and have him come and get her. Ezra would call Amber and Amber would swing by and get her on the way to her studio. Drop her off at home.

Or take her to the doctor.

She drove slowly back to town. Watching. She was always watching her surroundings, looking for a shot. Looking for something stark or eye catching. Something to record. She figured she probably missed out a lot on the actual living of life, because she was always trying to capture the beauty in life. The curse of following her dreams, maybe.

Maybe she and Ingrid were alike that way. No, Ingrid didn't tote a camera around and hide behind it and use other people's everyday to create something extraordinary to savor and share. But she used her eyes and her heart to observe other people, and she hid behind her Mac, and she created the extraordinary from her observations and her imagination.

Amber sighed and punched the power button on the radio. Immediately touched the button to change the radio to her iPod and without looking at the screen, pushed the play arrow on the Classic.

She raised her eyebrows appreciatively when she heard Vance Joy's voice. Wasn't even lunchtime, and she was exhausted already. They were all meeting again tonight at Dad's house. Liv had asked Wade and Charlie to bring all the boxes up from the basement Sunday afternoon. So Amber guessed those boxes were now either dumped in the kitchen or else tossed outside. Luckily, it hadn't rained, so anything outside should be okay.

Amber was more concerned about what Wade and Charlie might have unleashed in the kitchen when they left boxes there. She hoped they'd checked and double-checked to make sure no rodents were roaming the boxes.

She wasn't sure she had the energy to deal with it tonight. Knew she didn't have the *desire* to deal with it tonight. They'd give her a pass. If she told them Hadley was sick, they'd tell her to stay home. But Nathan would be at the house if Hadley needed anything, and there was a tiny little perverse slice of herself that looked forward to seeing her sisters. She'd lost count, but there was no doubt they'd go another round. About something. Amber loved them both; actually, Amber loved them with a fierceness that surprised her, but none of them seemed capable of expressing that feeling. Or even capable of getting along for fifteen minutes at a time.

Her phone beeped letting her know she was back inside the coverage area. She waited, though, to pick it up until she could pull over to look at it. Ordinarily, she'd let it go until she got where she was going, be it the house or the studio, but because she was worried about Hadley, she couldn't do it.

She slowed on Highway 24 as she neared the entrance to a factory and an old motel. Flipped her signal on and turned into the lot. Tapped the brakes and eased into an actual parking spot, just to make sure she didn't hinder any traffic and end up with another ticket-she hadn't told her sisters about her speeding ticket last month-and picked up her phone.

If Hadley was still at school, she'd just go there now and pick her up. If she was with Ezra, she'd run by his place and get her.

Mouth suddenly dry, she tried to swallow. Her stomach clenched, and she felt a shot of adrenaline kick her heart and make it beat harder, faster.

Not Hadley. Not Ezra.
Kyle Carpenter. Again.

Ten

Amber felt the tension thread through her shoulders and neck before she even pulled the keys from the ignition. She took a deep breath to steady herself, not surprised when it left her feeling breathless and a little bit sick to her stomach. Seemed a touch unfair that she'd spent the morning talking herself down, backing things up and looking at the bigger picture only to sit now in her SUV in the ruts in the yard that had passed for the driveway at her parents' house as far back as she could remember and worry about the same stuff all over again. Dread, slow and thick, wound itself around her heart and her stomach and her lungs and squeezed painfully tight.

She still hadn't talked to Nathan about it. She'd seen him at the house before she'd come over here, and she'd told him there was something she wanted to talk to him about. But she hadn't said what, and as she'd made her way across town, she decided she shouldn't have said anything to him, because now he would sit and wonder what she was thinking. And too much wondering and thinking didn't do anyone any good.

Finally, deciding if she didn't get moving, Liv might come barreling out of the house and open her door and drag her ass out of her SUV, Amber pulled her key from the ignition, grabbed her purse and opened the door. Slid down out of the SUV. Distracted by the house-Liv was right, it was going to kill her to see other people live here-she pushed her door shut and leaned on the SUV for a second. Stared up at the attic dormer. She'd told the truth the other day. She'd never played in the basement. Had no idea if Ezra had, but she hadn't. It was dark and dank and creepy as hell, and Amber had never even wandered close to the door if it happened to be open.

The attic was a different story.

She'd loved the attic when she was younger. She'd nearly lived up there when she was thirteen or fourteen. Those really dark, angsty teen years. Ezra had come up now and then, but Amber had logged a lot of time up there, reading, talking on the phone-until her parents realized she was on the phone again and yelled at her to get off-daydreaming about boys.

Probably the reason she'd fallen in love with the old house where she and Hadley lived. She'd been more excited about the upstairs bedroom suite for Hadley than Hadley herself, until the past year or two. Hadley was old enough now to appreciate her own space, and so much of it at that.

Did you need to speak with me about something?

Kyle Carpenter.

Almost formal this time. Not particularly friendly. Then again, they hadn't exactly ever been particularly friendly. Physically intimate, but not friendly.

She had to talk to Nathan. She glanced at her phone. He was at home right now with Hadley. Hadley, who had suffered through the day with the same sore throat. Who was probably now working that sore throat to her advantage. Nathan would bend over backward to make her happy. Make her pudding. Get her ice cream. Rent a movie for the two of them to watch together.

Maybe she should just go home. She should be with her daughter, shouldn't she? Isn't that what Ingrid had been-not so subtly-drilling into her head the past two months? That a good mom spent time with her child and knew exactly what he or she was up to? Well, news to you, Ingrid, no parent knows what his or her child is doing twenty-four/seven.

"You comin' in or what?"

Amber looked up when she heard Liv holler, saw her sister at the end of the drive, standing near the garage. She wore jeans and a black hoodie, and probably a frown because as of five minutes ago, Amber was probably late.

She didn't need to be here. Nothing in the boxes they'd pulled up from the dungeon pertained to her. She highly doubted anything in them would be of value.

Suddenly she realized she didn't see Ingrid's SUV. Just Liv's Traverse parked between her Passport and the garage. She stood up straight and headed toward Liv. Hands jammed in her pockets and her chin tucked to her chest. She'd spent her afternoon hours looking over the photos she'd taken last week. The fire pit and the old stone patio behind the house at the end of her block. They were okay. Only okay. Until she'd come to the last one in her hands. It hadn't jumped out at her Friday morning when she'd looked at the negative.

Today it had nearly brought her to tears.

Wasn't her photography, though, that had left her so emotional. It was her messy, screwed up life. The way she continued to spiral out of control and hurt everyone near her. Kinda like she was playing tag, and she was determined to take everyone out with her since she was It.

"Hey."

"Hey." She nodded but didn't look at Liv.

"How's Hadley?"

Amber shrugged as her eyes surveyed the space between the house and the garage. One box. From where she stood, it appeared to hold the guts of a greasy, dirty machine of some sort.

"She's going to school," Amber mumbled, "but still not feeling great."

"Why don't you go back home to her? I'm fine here."

Amber finally looked at Liv, met her gaze.

"Nathan's with her. Where's Ingrid?"

"Running late. Working on edits or something."

Amber wondered why Ingrid could get stuck working late and get out of the family fun. It'd be different if she was writing and running late. Amber supposed you didn't just turn the creativity on and off, and if you got lucky enough that the writing was going well, you didn't particularly want to be interrupted. But editing was a whole different ballgame.

She noticed Liv square her shoulders and take a deep breath. Getting ready for a fight, she decided. Amber wouldn't give her one. Not tonight.

"Okay." She nodded. "Stuff inside?"

"Oh yeah."

Amber didn't move, though. That little pinched line between Liv's eyebrows was prominent right now. Sort of a worry line, but Amber thought more like a heavy thought line. Something was bothering Liv. Something more than this stuff. The house. And the contents of the boxes.

"What's wrong?" she asked quietly. She didn't expect an answer. She and Liv had grown somewhat close all those years when Ingrid was gone. They'd come to respect each other, to *like* each other. But given the age difference, and now with Ingrid being back in town, Amber knew there were a million things Liv would never tell her.

Liv bit her lip and shrugged.

"Bad day."

Amber nodded silently, not surprised to be put off. Hands still in her pockets, she took a step toward the house, but paused when Liv spoke again.

"Ingrid and I got into it. Again."

Not terribly surprising. Amber waited to see if she would say anything else. When she didn't, she closed the distance to the house and let herself in. The wind carried a chill, but it was stuffy and uncomfortably warm in the house. Smelled musty, too, and Amber assumed it was the years of memories and mildew now on the kitchen floor.

With a tired sigh, she peeled her jacket off and dropped it on a barstool. Made her way to the window above the sink and pushed it open. She should get moving. Try to be a little bit productive so she could get out of here and get home to Nathan and Hadley. But her eyes caught the big Maple in the back, and she remembered days when she was a kid and climbed as high as she could go. Ezra tried, God love him. For being a boy, he'd never been much of a tree climber. He'd actually fallen out of that tree on more than one occasion. Banged his knees and shins up at least every other day. Never cried, though. Then again, he was the big brother. Wouldn't do for him to let his little sister see him cry, would it?

      Unfortunately, he seemed to hold to that self-imposed rule now, too. Amber knew him well enough to know he wasn't particularly happy these days, but Ezra rarely said much to her about his personal life.

      "Did you have a shoot this morning?"

      Amber had heard the door open and bang against the wall before Liv could catch it, so she wasn't surprised when Liv spoke.

      "Yeah. I was on the old Schuler farm. Some barn shots." Amber answered Liv without looking at her.

      "I used to think it would be lonely for you," Liv said quietly. "Being out like that. By yourself. The travel."

      Still with her back to Olivia, Amber's eyebrows arched in surprise. She'd never considered that Liv would think anything about her profession or how she felt about it. Reluctantly, she tore her eyes off the Maple, still thinking about Ezra, and turned to look at Liv.

      Was she lonely? Yeah. Sometimes. But mostly, she only felt lonely in a crowd. She didn't consider the solitude of her profession a bad thing. It was her breathing space. Her thinking time. Not to mention it was usually best for her concentration.

      "Now I'm a little bit jealous of you," Liv admitted.

      "Jealous of me?" Amber drew back, again surprised by Liv's words.

"I spend my workdays surrounded by teenagers. Other teachers. Parents." Liv shrugged. "I come home at night to my own teenagers and my husband."

Amber felt that word like a bruise on her heart. *Husband.* Liv hadn't meant for it to hurt her. How could she? Amber had repeatedly sworn she didn't need a husband, so why would Liv know that it would bother her now? Suddenly?

Amber gave herself a mental shake and looked back over her shoulder. The tree was still there. The picnic table where she and Ezra had eaten lunch some days, ice cream treats on others. She squeezed her hands together in fists, almost feeling the sticky popsicle juice that would inevitably end up dribbling down her chin and over her fingers.

"I'd love to walk away from everything and be alone somewhere for a while." Liv's words were a gruff whisper.

Amber nodded.

"It's..." She raised her eyebrows and then looked at her hands, saw that she still had them balled up and made herself relax them. *Therapeutic? Soothing?* Either answer might invite questions she wasn't sure she wanted to answer. Questions she didn't care to answer might invite an argument. She wasn't up for an argument. Instead, she simply nodded.

She cleared her throat and looked back again, out the window.

"How do you suppose Ezra was so bad at climbing trees if you and me and Ingrid lived in that one?"

Liv grinned. "Maybe he got his tree-climbing skills from his dad."

"Liv!" Amber laughed softly.

"So." Liv stepped further into the room and edged onto a barstool. "Ingrid is pissed because I haven't called any realtors yet. Haven't scheduled an appraisal."

"Kinda hard to do that when we still have all this stuff piled everywhere." Amber glanced, with a frown, at the boxes strewn over the kitchen floor. From where she was standing, she could see four, and she knew there were at least three more.

"Thank you." Liv nodded enthusiastically. She yawned and rubbed her forehead and then her cheekbones. "She's also pissed because the guy…" Liv sighed, propped her elbows on the counter and rested her chin in her hand. "I…"

Amber nodded when she shrugged.

"He keeps texting me."

"Booty calls?"

Liv bit her lip, but she answered with a tiny nod. "Yeah."

"And?"

"And what?"

"Are you answering him?"

"No."

"So why's she pissed?"

"I guess the whole idea in general pisses her off."

"Well." Amber arched her eyebrows. "I get that."

"I know." Liv nodded again. "I get it. I screwed up. I'm trying to untangle myself…get out of the situation."

"You get how…" Amber's gaze skated over Liv's face and then jumped to the wall behind her and around the kitchen to the door of the mudroom and then finally she gave in and looked back at Liv.
"How…your…situation…makes me weary of marriage. Don't you?"

"Sure, I do." Liv tucked a strand of hair behind her ear. "I get it. But…"

"But what?" Amber's voice was tight and low. Startled to realize she was shaking, she rested her hands on the counter at her sides to steady them. Was she asking

Liv to confirm her fears, her anti-marriage beliefs? Or was she asking her to change her mind?

"You can't live your life according to everyone else's successes and failures."

Amber licked her lips.

"I mean, you're brilliant with a camera, Amber. But that doesn't mean I could pick it up and walk outside and shoot the tree and have something beautiful like you do. I messed up, and I've done something that would really hurt Wade. But that doesn't mean you would."

"What about Mom and Dad?" Amber cleared her throat.

"What about Mom and Dad?" Liv shrugged. "It's the same thing. Just because they…" Liv sighed. "None of that has to do with you."

"But maybe it does," Amber argued. "I mean, maybe that's our legacy. Mom and Dad separated. Mom cheated. You and Wade-maybe that's our legacy. We lie. We cheat."

Liv shook her head. "Ingrid and Ezra haven't done that. It's not written in our genetic code. Every marriage, every relationship is different, Amber. You know that."

Amber avoided Liv's eyes. She swallowed hard and then stood up straight.

"Liv."

"Hmm?"

Amber circled around the counter and surveyed the mess at her feet. Two boxes full of old magazines and books. One with what appeared to be photographs.

"Pictures?" she mumbled. "That's awesome. I'm sure they're ruined."

"I don't even know what those are." Liv turned on the barstool and stared at the same box Amber was studying. "I looked through some of them, and I'm not sure I know anyone in them."

"Weird," Amber said softly. She squatted down and reached into the box. Irrationally, she felt like she pulled out a cobweb or two and maybe a mouse with the photos, and she shivered at the thought. "I don't know what to do."

"About Nathan?"

"No." Amber eased from a squat to her butt on the floor. She drew her legs together, Indian style, and eye balled the top photo. From honest curiosity or a need to not look at Liv, she wasn't sure.

"Then what?"

Liv's voice was soft, gentle. Amber thought of their mother. Wished for maybe the billionth time since she'd been gone that she could talk to her.

Wondered if maybe having sisters was God's way of giving her Mom back to her.

"Kyle Carpenter."

Eleven

"Who's Kyle Carpenter?" Liv asked.

Amber jumped when the screen door banged shut. She looked up to see a harried-looking Ingrid step into the kitchen. She tossed her keys on the counter, dragged her other hand through her spiky black and purple hair and turned cold eyes on Amber.

"Yeah, Amber." She nodded. "Who's Kyle Carpenter?"

Amber took a deep breath and ducked her chin to her chest. She rubbed the back of her neck, wishing she could just say it. Just dump it here. The kitchen was already a mess. What difference would a few words from Amber make?

"So." Ingrid toed the box in front of Amber, but Amber didn't take the bait. "Kyle Carpenter is Hadley's father."

She was wrong. Those words, whether she said them or Ingrid said them, added a whole hell of a lot to the mess in front of her.

When Amber didn't answer Ingrid, Liv nudged her with a gray and purple Nike.

"Is that true? Is Ingrid right?"

Throat so tight, she couldn't breathe, Amber gave Liv a quick nod in response.

"Why are you okay telling Olivia that? What the hell is your deal with me, Amber?"

Amber ignored Ingrid. She wiped at her eye and then heaved a big sigh.

"I mean, you were so pissed at me in December. In January. Hell, up through maybe last week, you blamed me for everything. Everything wrong in this family is because I left home when I was younger. What is it now? I moved back-"

"Ingrid."

Amber heard the warning in Liv's voice, but apparently Ingrid missed it.

"What is it, Amber? You put me off all weekend, and the second you're alone with Liv, you just spill your guts?"

"I hardly spilled my guts, Ingrid," Amber mumbled.

"Jesus, Ingrid, chill."

Amber turned her head enough to see Liv slide off the stool, but she hid behind the curtain of hair that protected her from Ingrid.

"I just wanna know why you feel like you can tell Liv but not me. What am I doing-"

Amber dropped her hands to the floor, noticed that it felt a little bit grimy and thought again about new linoleum, and gracefully pushed herself to a standing position.

"I'm-" She cleared her throat and tried again. "I can't do this." She glanced at Liv. "I'm gonna-"

Olivia simply nodded.

"What?" Ingrid shook her head. "What was that? You can't what? You can't talk to me? You can't be in the same room with me?"

"Get off her back!" Liv snapped. "What the hell is eating you?"

"You wanna know what's eating me?" Ingrid threw her hands up in anger. Amber took a step back. She remembered she'd tossed her jacket on a barstool and then stepped forward again. Found it scrunched up in the back of the same seat Liv had been sitting in. She grabbed it and then patted her pockets down for her keys and phone. "I was working. I was editing. I hate edits. I hate reading my own work and hearing my voice and wondering how I'm a bestseller when what I'm reading sucks. And I knew you would be pissed because I got over here late, and I knew I would walk in and find you two together."

"Ingrid." Liv shook her head. Ingrid looked over Liv's head, searching for Amber. She pinned Amber in place with a hard look.

"I can't help it. Sometimes I have to work. I have deadlines. I can't just walk way from something when it's five o'clock. I'd think you both could understand that-"

"We do-"

Ingrid looked back at Liv and shook her head.

"And it hurts that even though I'm here...even though I'm back, Amber Williams, you still choose to trust Liv and not me, and-"

"I didn't choose to trust anybody!" Amber exploded. "It just...it's been on my mind for several months, and I just keep thinking about this and trying to figure out what to do. If I screwed up. If I should have just kept my mouth shut about it. I'm not...trying to keep secrets from you to hurt you. Either one of you. This is me. This is the biggest thing in my life right now! Do you get that? I feel like I'm holding dynamite in my hands, and I'm so fucking scared about it, and you think I'm playing games. You think I'm choosing-"

"I was right there beside you Saturday morning when he texted you!" Ingrid lunged at Amber, but Liv stepped in front of her and cut her off. "What the hell do you think I'm gonna do? Go tell Hadley-"

Breathless, Amber felt her lungs and ribs ache with the need to cry. To breathe. To let go. She looked from Ingrid to Liv and opened her mouth to ask Ingrid to stop. To stop talking. Stop yelling. But her throat ached, and she couldn't form the words she wanted to say and only a sob fell from her lips. She turned away from them, then, and she wished she were at home with Nathan and Hadley, or even better, that her parents were still alive and well, and her family wasn't actually two different families her parents had tried to cleave together like two halves of a whole.

"Amber?"

Back to her sisters, Amber took a deep breath. Swiped at her face and shook her head. She took two steps and then two more, and then she was in the hallway and the kitchen was behind her, and she wondered what Nathan and Hadley were doing.

"Don't leave."

If Ingrid had still sounded pissed, put out, she might have. She might have strode down the hallway and walked out without another word. But Amber couldn't deny, even to herself, that she heard the plea in Ingrid's voice.

"Don't leave, Amber." Ingrid, again.

She swallowed again, trying to ease the pressure in her throat, her chest. As she turned to them again, she saw the front door and thought of an eleven-year-old Ezra jumping down the steps four at a time, losing his balance on the last step and barreling into the door, shoulders and head first. He'd sprained his shoulder, whacked the back of his head and gotten an ass-chewing from Mom and Dad.

Did Liv and Ingrid even know about that? Did they know she and Ez used to stay up late and sneak outside and talk about the stars and their futures and that Olivia and Ingrid never came up? That there had been moments in her and Ezra's lives where Liv and Ingrid never even existed?

"I've never..." She licked her lips as she met first Ingrid's gaze and then Liv's. "I've never said his name out loud. Until today."

Ingrid squirmed under her heavy stare when she looked back at her.

"I just..." Ingrid's words trailed off. She shrugged and looked away from Amber. "You've made it clear that you-"

"You know how you didn't tell us about..." Amber circled her hand in the air, unable to say the words. The thought of Ingrid finding a lump in her breast, after losing their mother to breast cancer, still scared the hell out of her.

Ingrid nodded.

"It's like that. I didn't choose not to tell you or Liv or Mom and Dad. I chose to bury that name inside myself for Hadley's sake." Amber looked to Liv, but she moved her eyes back to Ingrid quickly. "I still haven't told Hadley his name. Nathan doesn't know. No one knows, but you two."

"I moved back to be..." Ingrid deflated and leaned against the wall at her back. Amber, a moment ago so angry with Ingrid she wanted to smack her, took a deep breath. Saw the circles under her sister's eyes. Wondered what was going on in her head, in her life that she looked so washed out. Again. She'd looked that way when she'd first come home, when Dad had passed away and Liv had called her. But Amber had seen Ingrid transform as the days passed. She'd seen the way life had filled her again, as if she'd been a flat black and white cartoon and the longer she stayed here, the more colorful she became. She and Liv hadn't realized it, but Ingrid had been busy falling in love.

"What's going on with you?" Liv asked suddenly, and Amber looked at her, startled, wondering if Liv had read her mind.

"Involved," Ingrid ignored Liv's question and directed the word at Amber. "To be part of this. I wanted to know you and Liv. To know what's going on in your lives-"

"You moved back here to shack up with Luke." Amber felt her stomach sink as the words tumbled out of her mouth. Maybe Luke had some bearing on Ingrid being back, but she'd gone too far with that comment. Ingrid's eyes flashed with a volatile mix of hurt and anger.

Amber steeled herself for Ingrid's next shot. She deserved it. No matter what Ingrid fired back, Amber deserved it after what she'd just said. Ingrid was trying to get to know her, to be involved in her life, and Amber had mostly rebuffed her attempts to be friendly and even thrown it all back in her face on more than one occasion. Immature and petulant. Maybe one more reason she had no business getting married. She still had a hell of a lot of growing up to do.

Then again, she and Nathan never fought at this level. Apparently, Amber saved the childish behavior for her siblings.

Ingrid ignored the tear that escaped. Probably, it pissed her off that Amber and Liv would see it; it would certainly piss Amber off. She simply nodded, glanced at Liv and then looked back at Amber.

"Okay." She licked her lips. "If that's what you think…okay."

She shrugged and then ducked through the mudroom.

"Ingrid." Liv rushed to go after her. Amber almost did. But Ingrid had put her keys on the counter; she wasn't going anywhere. Unless she planned to hoof it all the way back out to her place.

"So this conversation started out about Kyle, and it didn't even involve you, and then you show up, and it's all about you-"

"What the hell is wrong with you?" Liv snapped. Amber had slipped around the island counter again to stand at the window. "Shut up, Amber! God-"

Amber laughed softly. She sighed and dragged her fingers back through her hair. Looked over her shoulder to see Liv with her back on the doorway to the mudroom. Amber squirmed under her hard, accusing eyes.

She hadn't heard the screen open, but she knew Ingrid was still in the house anyway. She sensed her there in the mudroom.

With a deep breath, she turned around, heaved herself up to sit on the counter. Her mom, she knew, would swat at her and give her hell if she could see her now. The counter was not a place to sit.

"Your books don't suck," she mumbled. "Why would you even think that?"

Liv, still lounging against the doorframe, turned her head to look at Ingrid. Amber heard Ingrid mumble something, but she couldn't make out her words. Liv snorted and shook her head.

"You and Luke okay?"

"Jesus."

Amber heard Ingrid that time.

"Luke and I are fine."

"'kay." Liv nodded. "Maybe..." She shook her head. "Maybe we just need to...be done. Throw this stuff away. And move on."

Amber curled her fingers around the edge of the countertop. Stared at the dried mud caked on her hiking boots and realized belatedly that she should have taken them off.

"I didn't come home to just throw stuff away and move on," Ingrid said quietly.

Liv moved her feet and slid down the frame until her butt hit the floor. She looked at Amber again.

"Why does it bug you so much that I'm living with Luke?"

Amber looked away from Liv when she heard Ingrid. She lifted her left shoulder in response and shook her head.

"Maybe..." She started, but stopped herself. Thought for a second. "Maybe what bothers me is how sure you are."

"What?"

Amber looked back toward Liv when she heard movement in the mudroom. She waited to see if Ingrid would come back to the kitchen. Was almost relieved when she only saw her shoes appear in the doorway. Apparently, Ingrid was crashed on the floor in there, and she'd only scooted close enough to put her feet in the doorway.

"I've been with Nathan for almost two years, and I'm still scared."

"Amber-"

"Especially now."

"Because of..."

Amber nodded and looked at Liv. "Yeah. Because of that."

"Who is he?" Ingrid asked.

"You don't know him?"

"Well, he'd have been, maybe in preschool, when I was a senior in high school."

"Actually, that's not true," Amber said softly.

Ingrid picked her feet up and scooched closer to the door so she could see Amber.

"What do you mean?"

"He's..." She shrugged. "He graduated a few years behind you."

"What?" Liv shook her head. "So...when you were sixteen, he was..."

"A teacher."

"What?"

"Yeah. He was...a teacher. Just a substitute then, but...I think he was...twenty-five or twenty-six...when it happened."

"Did he force you?" Liv asked incredulously. "Why didn't you tell Mom and Dad? He could've-"

"Didn't force me," Amber said quietly.

"Amber, that's statutory rape," Liv reminded her.

"I know that." She nodded. "But...it wasn't...it was...just sex."

Ingrid took a deep breath and bent her knees to draw her legs up. She rested her forehead on her knees.

"So he was...maybe a freshman when I was a senior? Is he from around here?"

Amber nodded.

"Wish I could find my yearbook."

"Please don't do that," Amber whispered. "You're talking about Hadley's father. He was my mistake, but he's her father. And I don't know what to do about it."

Twelve

"So." Liv rested her head on the wooden frame behind her and closed her eyes. "How...did that work?"

"Happened...after school one day."

"Where?"

"Um." Amber cleared her throat. He'd picked her up two blocks away from school, but she wasn't sure she wanted to tell her sisters that. "We'd flirted the whole week. He was subbing in my chemistry class."

"So you guys had chemistry."

Amber shot Ingrid a look of anger, but she had to laugh when their eyes met.

"Yeah, I guess we did."

"You came onto him? I mean, how does a sixteen-year-old girl know how to do that?"

"I didn't come on to him, Liv. I just...talked to him. Or I tried to. He made me nervous. Made me feel like a little girl with a crush."

"You were a little girl with a crush," Liv reminded her.

Amber shrugged and nodded. "That Friday I was walking home. He found me two blocks away. Pulled over. Offered me a ride."

Unable to bear their eyes on her any longer, Amber turned sideways on the counter and leaned against the refrigerator.

"If Dad could see you now, he'd come unglued."

"Don't I know it?" Amber agreed with Ingrid.

"Did you know?" Liv asked. "When you got in his car?"

"Well, I knew something was gonna happen, yeah. Did I know we were gonna fuck in the backseat and make Hadley? No."

"Did he at least have a big car?"

Amber snorted. She looked out the window and then turned to look over her shoulder at Ingrid.

"No. It wasn't a big car."

"Big-"
"Ingrid." Amber rolled her eyes.
"Was it your first time?"
"No."
"Are you kidding me?" Liv sounded surprised.
"I did it once before with a guy in my class."
"You were only with this guy once?"
"Yep. One time." Amber nodded. "I've seen him around through the years. And really, I feel nothing. I don't...regret it. Because I have Hadley. I don't hate him. I don't like him. I don't want anything to do with him."

"But you knew how to contact him?" Ingrid's voice jumped an octave. Amber looked back at her again to find her eyebrows drawn down in a curious frown.

"Facebook friends," Amber explained. "Damned Facebook. If you looked at someone in high school, he friends you years later."

"So. Did you friend him or did he friend you?"

Amber looked away from Liv. Turned back to the window. Thought about the afternoon when she was maybe twelve, and Ingrid was home visiting and they'd had a cookout in the backyard. How had her parents opened their arms to her when she'd left that way? They'd been so angry at first when Ingrid married Scott and ran off to Chicago. Amber had been just a little girl when Ingrid had left, but she remembered the way her parents had fought. The way they'd blamed each other. The way the house had become so gray, so dark that Amber had been scared her eyes were broken. That she wouldn't see light again.

"I friended him," she said softly.

"But you wanted nothing to do with him," Liv reminded her.

"I don't. For me." Amber tore her eyes away from the window and looked down at her hands. "I just...you know. For Hadley."

"Is he married?

"He's been married for a long time. And he has kids. And that's why I feel like I've made a huge mess of things."

"But he's her father?" Ingrid asked. "You're sure?"

"I'm sure." Amber nodded.

"So then, he should have helped you out. All these years. He should be helping you. He could help support-"

"I don't want his money." Amber's voice was cold and hard. "I don't want anything from him. My daughter wants to know who her father is. I can give her his name. I can show her a picture. But I'm scared to death that it won't be enough. That she'll want to push it further. That she'll want to meet him." Amber took a deep breath and swung back around to slip off the counter. "And I'm scared she's gonna get hurt."

"Maybe…if you could…" Liv hesitated. "Hold her off a little longer. Maybe tell her when she's sixteen or something."

"And what, Liv?" Amber shrugged. "She won't get hurt because she's sixteen?"

Liv shook her head and mumbled an apology.

"I think you need to talk to Nathan."

"I know."

"I mean…I still wonder…"

Amber looked at Ingrid expectantly.

"Well, I just wonder if she would still want to know so badly if she saw Nathan as more of a father…than what he is now."

"What if she does?"

Ingrid raised her eyebrows. "I don't know. But I still think you need to talk to Nathan. I mean…maybe she'd still want to meet her father. And maybe she would, and it might not work out as she wants, and she might be hurt. But she has you, and she has Nathan. You both love her. She'd be okay, Amber."

"You really think so, Ingrid? Aren't you the one constantly warning me about how much trouble she could get in? Haven't you been telling me I'm raising a slut just like I was?"

Ingrid opened her mouth to answer her, but instead she sunk her teeth into her lip and groaned softly.

"Amber."

Amber flicked her eyes to Liv, but she looked quickly back at Ingrid.

"I'm sorry," Ingrid said softly. "I know-"

"You know it sounded that way, but that's not how you meant it-"

"No." Ingrid shook her head. "I think I did mean it that way when I first...said it...but, I'm sorry. It was a horrible thing to say."

Stunned by her apology, Amber caught her breath. She ambled down the counter only to find yet another box at the end, between the counter and the table. Squatted down and reached for the pile of material on top.

"Yuck." She shivered in disgust. An apron or tool belt, she supposed, hung, pinched between her thumb and her finger. Holes had been eaten away through the material, and Amber assumed it was mice or rats that had done the handiwork.

"Maybe..." she mumbled to Ingrid, though she wasn't sure either of her sisters was even listening now. "Maybe you're right."

She shivered again, fought the urge to gag, and dropped the tool belt to her side on the floor. Reached back into the box.

"Right about what?" Ingrid's voice carried over the counter.

"Well, we know what kind of person I am." Amber leaned against the cabinet and closed her eyes. "And maybe I am raising my little girl to be just like me. I had no idea she'd ever messed around with-"

"She'd be lucky," Liv interrupted her.

"What?" Amber licked her lips. She opened her eyes and stared at her hands, which she'd drawn back away from the box.

"If Hadley grows up to be like you, she'll be lucky."

Amber raised her eyebrows. "Yeah. Sure, Liv." She nodded. "Look. Can we get busy? I either need to do something here, or I need to get home. Talk to Nathan."

"Go ahead," Liv told her. "Ingrid and I can deal with this tonight."

"No." Amber scooted forward away from the cabinet. She sighed and reached for the box again. "No. If you're gonna work, I'll stay and work."

Truth be told, she didn't want to walk out now and leave them alone. To talk about her. Because they would. Amber wouldn't be able to talk to Nathan. Not wondering what her sisters were saying about her.

No. Not true. Under the cover of the cabinet, she swiped at her eyes and took a quick breath. Her throat felt painfully tight, so she splayed her fingers around it and rubbed gently, trying to knead the emotion back down. To her heart, maybe, or her stomach. Probably her stomach, because she could feel it churning now.

As much as she wished she were at home with Nathan, she had to admit at least a small part of her wanted to be here. With her sisters.

How pathetic was she that she wanted to be with her sisters so badly that she'd choose arguing with them over going home to her daughter and boyfriend?

"Wait."

Amber blinked and looked up when she heard Liv's voice right above her.

"Hey." Liv squatted down in front of her and reached out, as if to touch her. Amber cleared her throat and looked away when Liv let her hand drop to her own lap, rather than touch Amber. "You okay?"

"Yeah." Amber nodded.

"How about if you stay you go through that other box?"

"What other box?" Amber cleared her throat. She blinked again and looked around, positive there were at least five boxes scattered around the kitchen floor.

"The photographs."

"Well, if you don't know anybody in those pictures, I'm sure as hell not gonna know anyone in them."

"Yeah, but you're the photography guru." Ingrid's voice was closer now, too. Amber wished they'd given her another couple of minutes to get herself together. She hated losing control; she hated crying. She especially hated to break down in front of her sisters. If she couldn't be close to them, if they couldn't treat her as an equal, she didn't want to bare herself to them. She wouldn't let them in. Not that her refusal to give either of them a piece of herself was a punishment to them.

She was only hurting herself.

"Maybe you could just go through the pictures and see if there's anything interesting."

Amber nodded.

"Sure." She cleared her throat and climbed gracefully to her feet, hoping to hell she didn't look as wrecked as she felt at the moment. Avoiding their eyes, she tried to step around Liv, to get back to the box with the photographs.

"Hey." Liv reached out again, and this time, she did touch Amber. Laid her hand gently on her shoulder and gave her a little squeeze.

Amber glanced at her, but she looked away before they could make eye contact. She flashed a breezy smile and tried again to move around her. This time, Ingrid grabbed at her from behind. She snatched a handful of Amber's shirt and pulled gently.

"What?" Amber's throat still hurt, and that knot of emotion was still rolling around in her stomach and fighting to come back up. She wanted to lash out at both of them, ask them to please leave her alone. Why was it always hardest to control your emotions when people were smothering you with attention, asking if you were okay? Unless it was just someone acknowledging that she was...sad? Well, that didn't begin to cover it, did it?

And it wasn't just that someone was acknowledging anything. It was that her *sisters* were asking, and Amber knew the attention was fleeting and that within the next two minutes, one of them-most likely Ingrid-could and probably would say something hateful and hurtful, and so Amber wanted to grab onto this. To smash the clocks and the phones and let this moment linger. To make it stick.

"I'm sorry." Ingrid's voice was small and tight as Amber turned to look at her. "I'm sorry. Hadley's a beautiful girl, and I'm sorry for what I said."

Amber nodded, uncomfortable with the attention, with the intimacy in Ingrid's stare.

"I just...worry about her."

Amber caught herself before she could speak. Before she asked Ingrid where the hell she'd been the first fourteen years of her daughter's life.

"I mean...she's so young," Ingrid whispered. "I just want her to be a kid...a while longer..."

Amber felt raw under Ingrid's intense stare.

"I love her, Amber," Ingrid said simply. "I don't want anything to happen to her. I'm more concerned about her getting hurt with Kesh than her father-"

"Yeah, I know-" Amber started to argue, to lash out at Ingrid, but again she caught herself. Because she didn't want to argue anymore, and because honestly, Hadley could get hurt hanging out with Kesh, and maybe nothing would ever come of Kyle Carpenter, and she was exhausted, and it was ridiculous, but her hands felt dirty and grimy from touching the tool belt she'd found, and she wanted Ingrid to stop looking at her.

Ingrid stepped closer and drew Amber into a hug.

"I just...it hurts, Amber," she whispered, "that you have a life that you don't want me to be a part of."

Ingrid kissed the top of her head, smoothed a hand over Amber's back and then let go. She moved away swiftly, as if she'd swallowed the sudden rush of emotion, locked it away with a key, and she was ready to get back down to business.

Amber stood for a moment, a little stunned by the past five minutes, and then took a deep breath and glanced over her shoulder in time to see Ingrid squat down at the other end of the counter. When she looked back the other way, she found Liv on the floor by the box that had held the tool belt.

She turned on her tiptoes and stepped over the box. Placed her foot on the other side with precision, so as not to kick the box at Liv, and then stepped with her other foot. Ran her fingers through her hair, regretted it instantly because she felt dirty and now her hair was going to feel dirty, and made her way to the box of photographs.

"I saw Gretchen last night." Liv's voice drifted through the kitchen after several moments of silence.

Amber studied a small black and white photograph, the perfectly square kind from an ancient one twenty six camera, the kind you had to stick the perfect little flash cube on top of when you used it.

"Where at?" she asked Liv, eyes taking in the details of the photo. Not that you could discern much detail in a small black and white photo like this. There was a woman in the photograph. Standing beside an old car. Amber had no idea who the woman was, what kind of car she stood beside. Wondered if Wade would know.

"The grocery store."

Amber raised her eyebrows, not sure seeing Gretchen at the grocery store was newsworthy.

"Know what we did last night?" Ingrid asked a moment later.

"Yeah, we probably do," Liv answered. Amber snorted softly and shook her head.

"Get your mind outta the gutter," Ingrid told Liv. "We played board games."

"You and Luke played board games?" Liv sounded shocked.

"Yeah. It was kind of fun."

"Like what?" Amber still wasn't sure she wanted to have a nice conversation with either of them, but the words shot out of her mouth before she could stop them.

"Well, we started with Aggravation."

"The marble game?" Liv asked. "Ouch. Dammit." Her words were punctuated with a hissing sound.

"What'd you do?" Amber looked over her shoulder, but she could only see Liv's back. She was still wearing the black hoodie.

"Bent my fingernail back." Liv sounded like she had a mouthful. Amber assumed she'd stuck the injured finger in her mouth.

"Yes, the marble game." Ingrid sounded annoyed. "And then we played Battleship."

"Battleship." Amber nodded. She had to admit that sounded kind of fun.

"You always cried when I beat you," Liv told Ingrid.

"Because you cheated."

"I didn't cheat-"

"You cheated," Ingrid argued. "Amber, whenever we played, as soon as I would sink one of her ships, she'd have to go to the bathroom. Or she'd need a drink or a snack. She would look at my board when she came back."

"Bullshit-"

"She did, Amber!" Ingrid called to her.

Amber tucked the picture of the woman by the car at the back of the pile. Smiled in case either of them happened to be looking at her, but their bickering about Battleship only made her feel sad.

The next picture was of a storefront. She studied the glass windowpanes, but she couldn't find a sign to tell her what store it was. She twisted a bit to stretch and pop her back. She wasn't sure what her sisters thought she might find in these pictures, but it was going to be a long, boring project.

"Ez and I used to play Battleship," she mumbled after several minutes of quiet had passed. "And I cheated," she admitted. "But he let me."

Ezra had let her get by with pretty much anything when she was younger. She lifted her eyes from the pictures in her hands and yawned.

"Ezra needs to fix us all dinner again," Liv announced.

"God, no kidding." Sounded like Ingrid groaned with approval or longing or something. "Who the hell knew he could cook like that?"

"He watched Mom a lot," Amber mumbled.
"What?"
"Ez. He used to watch Mom a lot."
"Mom never cooked like that."
"Mom was a good cook-" Liv argued.
"Yeah, but she didn't do fancy stuff. She made comfort food."

"So he went from watching Mom to Gordon Ramsey." Amber shrugged. "I just know he used to hang out in the kitchen a lot with Mom."

"Let's take a break tomorrow," Liv suggested.
"What?"
"I think we could all use a break."
"From work?" Ingrid asked.
"Maybe we need some time with our families."
Ingrid laughed. "Amber, she's saying she needs a break from us."

"No," Liv said quietly. "It's just…that Wade's…been acting kind of weird."

"What do you mean?" Amber shivered. Wasn't so much what Liv said, but how she said it that filled her with fear.

"I dunno. I think maybe he knows."

Thirteen

"You're sure?" Amber asked Hadley. Hadley groaned and pulled her blanket up over her head. Even under the blanket, Amber saw Hadley burrow deeper into the couch.

"Mom. Yes, I'm sure."

"I just don't-"

"A walk." Hadley's voice floated out from under the blanket. "You're going for a walk. You'll be back soon. I'm fine."

"Want me to get you some more juice-"

"Nathan's probably already to Eighteenth by now," Hadley told her.

Amber laughed. Hadley pushed the blanket down and eyeballed her with irritation.

"I'm fine. If I need juice, I'll get it."

"I can-" Amber had started back across the living room, but Hadley threw off the blanket and reached for the juice glass.

"I have strep throat, not a broken leg." She frowned at Amber. "Go spend some time with him. He's been rattling around in the house like a ghost dragging chains since he's been back."

"What does that mean?" Amber watched Hadley take a sip of the juice. She felt a flash of empathy for her daughter when she winced. Why Hadley drank orange juice on strep throat, she'd never know. Not that anything went down easy with strep.

"Nothing, Mom. Just go."

Amber nodded slowly.

"Okay, if you're sure-"

"I am so sure!" Hadley laughed. "Get out!"

Amber chuckled and ducked out of the living room before she could change her mind again. Nathan, stretching on the front porch, looked up and flashed her a smile when she stepped outside.

"She all set?" He stood up straight.

"Well, she told me to get out." She shrugged and grinned. Nathan reached for her hand. Amber slid her fingers through his as they set off walking. "You're not gonna take off at a run and drag me along behind you, are you?"

"No." He leaned over to kiss her head as they walked. "Thought I might run after we come back home."

Amber nodded. "Hadley said you've been dragging around the house like a ghost with chains since you've been home."

Nathan glanced at her.

"Just miss you when you're not here," he said quietly.

She arched her eyebrows as if to say, *really?*

"Yeah, I know the feeling."

They hadn't talked last night. Nathan had clearly been ready to sit down with her and listen or talk or whatever she might have needed from him. But she'd been exhausted, physically but even more so emotionally, after the evening with Liv and Ingrid, and she couldn't imagine getting into a discussion about Hadley's father. Not at that hour-it had been after ten-and not after being put through the ringer at her dad's house.

"So." Nathan bumped her shoulder with his. "What's on your mind?"

Instead of talking last night, they'd gone to bed. Amber had closed her eyes, ready to dive into sleep. A sleep so deep that the thoughts that had been nagging at her for months now couldn't slip into her dreams to haunt her. Nathan had slid his leg over hers and then slid his hand up her thigh and before she could say no, that she was too tired, he'd told her it was okay. Just to relax.

He'd made love to her. He'd done all the work, including a tender massage, and soft, lingering kisses all over her body, and she'd come hard and fallen apart in their bed, only to be gathered up in his arms and then she'd slept hard and there'd been no nightmares.

"Oh, Nathan." She shook her head.

"Something bad?"

She looked up and shook her head quickly when she saw his frown.

"Well. Not about us, no."

"What?"

"Hadley."

"Hmm." He nodded slowly and tore his eyes away from her. She waited for him to say something, to add something to that *hmm* so she might get a glimpse into his brain. Into his thoughts. When he didn't say anything, when he didn't even look at her again, she tugged on his hand.

It had been a pretty day, but as the hours ticked by and evening settled in, it had gotten colder. Amber shivered in her fleece jacket.

"What *hmm*?" she asked finally.

"What?"

"What does that mean?"

He finally looked at her. His eyes were distant, his jaw firm. She thought about touching him. Fanning her fingers out over his jaw. The scratchy feeling of his beard stubble on the palm of her hand. On her thighs and her stomach last night.

"Nothing." He shook his head.

"It meant something," she pushed.

"I just…"

"What?" She squeezed his hand when his words trailed off. "You what?"

"When you said you wanted to talk to me…" He shrugged and let his words trail off again.

"Nathan."

"I thought maybe you'd…made up your mind."

Amber frowned and shook her head.

"Watch your step." He reached with his other hand to point out the uneven sidewalk so she wouldn't trip. The same uneven spot they stepped over every time they took a walk together.

"Made up my mind?"

"About us. Marrying me."

"Oh." She nodded once and looked away from his warm golden brown eyes.

"*Oh?*" He repeated. "What's that? I mean, you sound put out-"

"It's not about making up my mind, babe," she said softly. "I love you. Only you. But I don't want…to get married."

She snuck a quick peek at him. Saw that he wasn't looking at her. His eyes were on the path ahead of them. She felt his anger, though. His disappointment.

"So. What is it then?" He cleared his throat. "About Hadley."

"Um." She swallowed hard. Wondered if talking to him about this was a good idea. "She's…been asking a lot of questions lately."

Nathan glanced at her and then looked up to watch an old Ford pickup truck trundle down the street. He coughed and blinked his eyes when they were left in a cloud of exhaust.

"About?" He shrugged. "What? Sex?"

Amber barked a laugh and shook her head.

"No. I think I could almost handle that, if she would just ask me."

Nathan gave her a small smile and arched his eyebrows. "About us?"

"About her father."

Nathan stared at her blankly and then slowly, as if the words were just hitting him, just rattling around in his brain, he nodded once and then twice and looked away from her again.

"You know what?" He refused to meet her eyes. "I forget sometimes. That she's not mine. You kinda threw me there."

"Nathan." Amber leaned into him and rested her cheek on his shoulder. He didn't slow down, though, and it was hard to stay snuggled with him when their steps jostled her around.

"Sorry. I guess that's presumptuous-"

"Nathan." This time she stopped walking. Nathan walked until their arms were stretched to the limit while still holding hands. Finally he stopped walking, but he didn't look back at her.

"So what've you told her?" he ignored the whine in her voice.

"Nothing. She's been asking me...seriously asking me...since the holidays."

"The holidays?" He shot her a dark look and then dragged his eyes away. Shook his head. "And you're just now telling me about it?"

"I'm just...I've been trying to figure out what to do-"

"Amber." He let go of her fingers and pulled his hand back to his side. She watched him shove it into the pocket of his jacket.

"What?" she whispered.

"It's just..." He took a deep breath. "Why-I don't get why you wouldn't have said something sooner. To me."

She swallowed hard and let her gaze fall to the sidewalk between them. Worked at a crack in the sidewalk with the toe of her Nike. Thought of Liv's purple and grey Nikes last night, when she'd toed her in the shoulder to get her attention. All the things she and her sisters had said last night.

"I wanted it to just go away, and I knew that if we talked about it, I had to really deal with it."

"Who is he?"

They started walking again, separate this time. She waited to see if he'd reach for her hand again. Slipped it into her pocket when he didn't.

"Kyle Carpenter," she said quietly. Nathan shook his head.

"I don't know him."

Amber cleared her throat. Watched the cars zip by. Swiped at her eyes when the cars were suddenly blurry out there on the street.

"He was a substitute teacher," she whispered.

"A teacher?" Nathan repeated.

Amber shrugged when he glanced at her.

"He was young. Too old for me, but young," she explained. "He was…" She cleared her throat, a little uncomfortable telling him this story. She'd thought it was hard to tell Liv and Ingrid. "He was subbing in my science class. For a week…I guess there was something…"

She lifted her eyes to meet his gaze. Saw him nod for her to continue.

"I was walking home that Friday. He happened to drive by where I was…picked me up."

"So…did it…was it a thing? Or just that one time?"

"One time."

"You know if anyone…touched Hadley that way, I'd kill him."

"I know." Amber nodded. "I would, too."

"Okay."

Amber watched him swallow hard, watched his Adam's apple bob up and down. Wished he'd take her hand again. Balled it into a fist in her pocket. Wondered about Hadley right now. She'd given in earlier today. Called Amber at her studio and told her she felt horrible. Amber had picked her up just before lunch and taken her straight to the walk-in clinic. She didn't particularly like anything about the walk-in. Certainly wasn't convenient, as she and Hadley had wasted the better part of two hours waiting to be seen. She didn't love the three doctors there currently, either. But she'd needed to get Hadley seen today, and by three o'clock, she'd had Hadley and her probable strep throat diagnosis at home on the couch, with her first dose of antibiotic down.

"So. Do you..." Nathan blew out a rush of air and shrugged. "Do you know this guy now?"

"Facebook friends," she mumbled apologetically. It bothered her to feel that way. She had no contact with Kyle Carpenter, other than friending him on the social media site a couple of years ago. As she'd told Liv and Ingrid, she'd only reached out for Hadley. For a *just in case* sort of thing that was now beginning to materialize.

"Yeah?" Nathan looked at her and arched an eyebrow in question.

"I don't talk to him. I just...I saw that he had a page, and I thought maybe something like this would come up one day." She licked her lips and dragged her eyes away from his. She shouldn't have to feel guilty about this. She had hundreds of friends on Facebook, probably ninety percent of whom she never talked to. Of course she was friends with other men, on Facebook and in her real life. Nathan had female friends on his page. In his real life.

Wasn't the Facebook page that was shooting pangs of guilt through her right now, though. She hated to admit it, but it was the whole marriage thing. Why couldn't Nathan just be happy with the way things were? Why did he have to keep bringing up the whole marriage thing? She hated this sick feeling that crawled inside her and camped out for days on end whenever he brought it up.

"Know anything about him?"

Why was he acting like this? So normal. Why was Nathan talking to her about Hadley's father when she was swimming in guilt and maybe even a little dread about the marriage stuff? What if one day he asked, and she put him off, and he walked away? What if she said yes, and they got married, and they ended up hating each other and divorced in two years?

"Um." She took a deep breath and forced herself to focus on this conversation. Nathan had clearly moved on for now. He wasn't hung up on the thoughts, wasn't stewing about everything that could go wrong. Not like she was. Contrary to what Ingrid believed about her, Amber worried about every goddamned thing there was in the world to worry about.

Needing his touch, Amber took her hand from her pocket and hurried a few steps to catch up with him. She slipped her hand inside his pocket and linked her fingers through his. Funny how she felt a little better just from him curling his fingers around hers, gently squeezing her hand.

"He's married. Been married for…ten years, I think."

"Do you know his wife?"

"No."

"Kids?"

Amber nodded. "Yeah. He has kids."

"Is he still a teacher?"

"Yeah. He's a…college algebra teacher now. His wife…is a dentist. His kids…are pretty active in sports."

Nathan nodded.

Amber followed his lead when he turned the corner at Sixteenth Street and headed south. They walked the whole block in silence. She was anxious for Nathan's thoughts, but she tried to be patient. To give him some space. Her eyes flew over the old houses on the block. Some in the state of disrepair. Some all sparkly and shiny from recent remodels. Hers was somewhere in between, moving rapidly to disrepair, and sure, Amber wished for more for herself and Hadley. And Nathan.

She'd asked him more than once to just move in with them. Couldn't they find a nice house, maybe something in a subdivision just outside of the bustling city streets, and live together? Did they have to say *I do* for things to be real?

The houses spoke to her as they walked. Good thing because Nathan had yet to answer. She wondered if he was thinking about how it would feel to be married with children and then have a young girl like Hadley show up at his door claiming to be his daughter. Or if he was thinking about Amber riding Kyle Carpenter in the back seat of his car, setting the rest of this story into motion. Or if he was thinking about something entirely different. Work, maybe.

She squeezed her left hand so tight in her pocket that her fingernails dug into her palm. She wished she had her camera. Now and then she carried one with her when they walked. Mostly, Nathan didn't seem to mind. But there were times when Amber became so caught up in the picture in her viewfinder that Nathan ended up slipping away and jogging home without her.

"So?" she finally asked.

"What?"

"What do you think?"

Nathan pursed his lips and sort of shrugged his eyebrows.

"I guess you need to tell her."

"You really think so?" She was surprised by his words.

"You don't?"

"I just…" She bit her lip and shook her head. "I don't know. It scares me, Nathan."

"Everything scares you, Amber. You gotta live a little. Before you die and realize you were too afraid to try anything."

"But this is Hadley-"

Nathan shook his head and met her eyes. "I think that guy has the right to know he has another child out there in the world."

Amber blinked. Shocked by the direction Nathan's thoughts had gone, she didn't know what to say.

"What if he hurts her?" She finally found her voice.

"What if he doesn't?" Nathan countered.

Amber nodded and looked away. Tears brimmed in her eyes, so she kept them trained on the street to her left.

"So...if someone out there had your baby..." She didn't know if he could hear her, but she couldn't possibly speak louder. He'd stolen her wind, her courage. "You'd wanna know about it?"

Nathan hesitated for just a moment, but when she glanced at him, he nodded.

"Yes. I would."

"Even if it caused problems between you and me? You'd wanna know?"

"Why would it have to be a problem?" he asked quietly. "How would it be different from you having Hadley with another man?"

Amber opened her mouth to answer him, but it took her a moment to remember they weren't really talking about her and Nathan.

"It wouldn't," she answered. "I just...I'm thinking of his wife."

They turned the corner again and headed west. Amber's legs ached, and she shivered in the cold. Wished she were back home on the couch with Hadley.

"Maybe," Nathan conceded. "But sometimes, Amber, I think you only think of yourself."

Fourteen

Amber picked up her phone and glanced at it as she pulled into a parking space across the street from Java Infusion. Wondered briefly what Kyle Carpenter was like. Saw that it was Gretchen calling. She wanted to talk to her. But she didn't have time right now. She let it go to voicemail. Figured she'd call Gretch back after this meeting. Then again, at the rate she was going, maybe she should give herself a little time and give Gretchen some distance. She hadn't talked to either of her sisters since the other night at the house. And things really hadn't gone that well with Nathan. Maybe at first he'd been okay with the whole idea of making contact with Hadley's father, but somehow (as always seemed to be the case these days) they'd ended up talking about their own relationship, (at least Amber assumed Nathan's parting shot had been in regards to their personal relationship) and they'd walked the rest of the way to the house in silence. Amber had curled up on the couch with Hadley, and Nathan had thrown his stuff in his duffel, told Amber he was going to go home to get some laundry done and get packed because he had to leave town the next day. Most of the time, Nathan spent as much of his time in town as possible with her and Amber. Most of the time, Amber did his laundry for him. Most of the time, he left her house just to pack his bag and leave.

With a deep breath, Amber pulled her keys from the ignition and climbed out of the Passport. Swung the door closed, beeped the lock and then looked up and down Maine to check for traffic. None coming, of course. Nothing to delay her walking into JI. From seeing him. As she crossed the street, she studied the cars parked around her. She had no idea what Kyle Carpenter drove these days. Didn't particularly care, except she wondered if he was already here. If she'd kept him waiting.

She noticed a Volvo parked a few spots down from her Passport and wondered if it belonged to him.

He'd been jock cool back in the day, and Amber wondered if he'd grown into hipster. Or maybe the Silverado pickup truck she skirted to step onto the sidewalk was his.

Because her hands were shaking, she curled the left around the strap of her bag. Shoved her right hand, keys and all, into her pocket. Skipped up the steps to the big, heavy wooden doors with a confidence that belied that fire of nerves in her belly. When she stepped inside and the door dragged to a close behind her, she let her eyes jump over the photographs and drawings on the walls. Normally, she would take her time moving to the counter or the tables, and she'd admire the work on display. Today, she felt raw and exposed, like everyone in the place was looking *at her*. Even if he wasn't here yet, she felt like everyone in the café knew why she was here, whom she was meeting. As if they could see right through her.

She pulled in another deep breath through her nose and stepped around the waist high wall into the café itself. Allowed herself to look up and see just who was here. Four tables were occupied. One appeared to be moms hanging out with their babies, talking animatedly about breastfeeding and making baby food, and Amber fought the urge to vomit on the dark green marble flooring. She'd never been that kind of woman. Not the kind that breastfed or made her own food for Hadley. But the kind that gushed to other moms and crooned about how great it was to be friends and share stuff and spoke in that god-awful nasally voice and ended every sentence like a question.

Another table was occupied by two businessmen, judging from their dark suits and ties. Bankers, maybe? Investors? Amber didn't care. The next table was a lone woman, dressed in a dark suit, also. Fingers of her left hand curled around a mug, and her right hand holding a book open. The last table was a man reading a paper, but he had silver hair and wore glasses and looked nothing like

Kyle, and Amber heaved a huge sigh of relief. She'd beat him here. Just that much gave her the slightest edge.

Technically, she didn't need an edge. She had the big gun. But the potential for fallout was huge, and she knew she had to be careful.

She turned away from the tables and stepped up to the counter. Ordered regular coffee, remembered not long ago telling Ingrid she'd given up coffee and wished she could've stayed with that longer than two days. Her stomach growled, reminding her she hadn't eaten this morning. Wasn't sure she could now, but maybe having something to hold in her hands-a fork-would be a good thing. She added a blueberry muffin to her order, unzipped her bag and dug around for her billfold.

Found it and pulled a ten dollar bill from it and handed it across the counter. She looked up and scanned the room again. Still not here. She was irritated for a moment that he was late. Not that her time was that important that she couldn't wait a few moments to talk to the father of her daughter. More that she would have to sit and worry. Practice this damned conversation in her head yet again. Even after going over it fifteen times, anytime her body slowed, her brain brought it up again.

She put her billfold away, took the plated muffin from the woman behind the counter, and then the empty cup the woman handed her.

What if he didn't show up? She'd finally returned his text last night. After Nathan was long gone. Amber had simply told Kyle there was something she'd like to talk to him about. Asked him if he could meet her for coffee.

He'd suggested Java Infusion. She'd suggested today. Nine o'clock. He'd agreed, but that didn't particularly mean anything, did it? After all, he'd once been the kind of guy to fuck an underage girl. Maybe he wasn't particularly an honest man.

She filled her cup and then turned to survey the tables once more. Definitely didn't want to sit anywhere near the moms with babies. Or the business guys. She eyeballed a table next to the reading woman. It was either that or a two-top table off in the corner, near where she and Ingrid and Liv had sat when they'd last come here together.

Last come here together? She almost laughed out loud. The only time they'd come here together. And that had ended in an argument.

She chose the table near the reading woman, because she didn't want anyone to see her sitting off in the corner with a man other than Nathan and assume anything. The woman looked up as Amber slipped by her table. Her smile was small, but sincere, and it warmed Amber just a little. She returned the smile and then moved on. Set her things on the table and then pulled a chair out. Hung her bag on the chair and sat down. She took a small sip of her black coffee and then reached to unzip her bag.

Pulled her iPad from the bag and turned it on. Wondered again if Kyle Carpenter was hipster. If he drank coffee or chai tea. If he'd be dressed business casual or in jeans. If he was a family man, or if he spent more time at work than with his wife and kids. If he'd ever cheated on his wife. If he'd be open to meeting Hadley or if he'd tell Amber to go to hell.

She took a small bite of her muffin and tapped her iPad screen. Synced with JI's wifi and then looked up. Saw him. She hadn't really worried that she wouldn't recognize him. After all, she'd seen his picture on Facebook. But still, she felt a jolt the moment her eyes found him at the counter. It unnerved her a bit that he'd walked down the waist high wall to her left and entered the café, all without her noticing him.

Had he seen her? Studied her when she wasn't looking?

Did it matter?

She watched him now. He was taller than she remembered. Dressed in khakis and what appeared to be a button down shirt. Blond hair, thinning a bit on top. She wondered now what about him had attracted her. Other than the fact that he was older, that he was a teacher, and that she'd known he'd been attracted to her. She'd known even then, at sixteen, that she had a powerful weapon with her body, with sex.

He was talking to the woman at the counter, and Amber wondered if he came here often. Or if he knew the woman. Maybe she was a friend of his wife's. Jennifer was her name, she thought. Jennifer was a petite woman with a dark chin-length bob. Amber wondered if she'd been one of those babbling, gushing moms that set her teeth on edge.

Kyle finally turned to the tables, steaming cup of something in his hand. Tea? Seriously? His brown eyes-she couldn't actually see their color from her seat, but she remembered them-surveyed the tables, the people. He wore wire-rimmed glasses with square lenses, and she wondered again why she'd been attracted to him.

She sighed softly. Wondered if she was disappointed in herself for what she'd done with this man fourteen years before. Or if she was disappointed in how he'd turned out. Which was dumb, really, because *she didn't care* how he'd turned out. She didn't care if he shuffled around the house on weekends in a bathrobe and slippers. She didn't care if he liked watching golf or boxing on TV. It didn't matter if he wore Wranglers and spoke softly or if his laugh was loud and obnoxious.

What mattered is what he would say about and to her daughter.

She knew the moment he noticed her. She saw him square his shoulders. Almost imperceptible. But she'd been watching for it, for some sort of reaction, and so she saw it. He smiled as he approached the table. For a moment, Amber thought about running. She could scale the waist-high wall and haul ass out to the Passport.

She didn't, though. She didn't want to admit, even to herself, the only thing holding her in her chair right now was Nathan. His comment to her the other night. That she only thought about herself.

Should she stand up? Offer Kyle her hand? What was proper etiquette for meeting someone for the first time after fucking him in the back of his car fourteen years earlier? She stood slowly as he neared, set his cup-it was tea-on the table.

"Amber." His smile seemed genuine. He stepped toward her and suddenly, they were hugging, and it was awkward, and Amber patted his shoulder and stepped away as quickly as she could without making a scene.

"Kyle." She returned his smile. Wished for a moment that she could throttle Nathan. For pushing her into this. Hadley. For asking about her father in the first place. Herself for what she'd done. If she hadn't had Hadley fourteen years ago, could she and Nathan have met and made love and created her?

No. Of course not. There could never be another Hadley. As much as she hated to admit it, this man now sitting across the table from her had as much to do with how amazing Hadley Williams was as she did.

"I was surprised to hear from you." He sat back in his chair and studied her face so intensely she almost squirmed. "Not often I get a coffee request from someone famous."

"My sister's the famous Williams," she told him.

"But you're the famous photographer."

"Doesn't hold a candle to best-selling author." She shook her head.

"That's a matter of opinion." He shrugged. Picked up his cup and took a sip of the tea. She shrugged and looked away. "It's good to see you."

She wondered how he would feel about that after she said what she had to say.

"You too," she lied as she looked back to him. "So. You're a college professor now."

He chuckled and shrugged.

"I teach algebra to college freshman," he told her. "Nothing too fancy about that. I don't take sabbaticals and do research and publish stuff in scholarly journals."

Amber laughed softly. She couldn't tell him she was glad to hear that. That she didn't want Hadley's father to be a stuffy, snooty scholar who understood quantum physics but not how to talk to his children.

"You're married."

"I am." He nodded. "Married Jennifer Columbus. Ten years ago. Do you know her?"

"No." Amber didn't remind him that she was ten years his junior and didn't know his friends or even acquaintances.

"She's a dentist." He picked up his cup again, but only held it. Didn't drink from it. "We have two boys. Shane is nine. And Payton is seven."

"Wow. I'm sure they keep you busy."

"They do. They both play travel soccer. We're always on the go."

Amber nodded slowly. If he'd known about Hadley, if he'd been around, a part of Hadley's life, would she have been a soccer player? If Amber had allowed it, would Hadley have experienced more exciting, more meaningful things than what Amber had been able to give her?

"How about you? Are you married?"

"No," she said quietly. "Never married."

He nodded. She wondered if he'd ever looked at her Facebook page. If he'd seen pictures of Hadley. Had he ever looked at her and wondered? Then again, he didn't have a reason to go trolling around on her Facebook page, did he? She'd only looked at his, through his pictures-his sons both had Hadley's nose and her sweet peaches and cream complexion-to see his kids.

Maybe, she thought now, she'd done it to see what sorts of life experiences Hadley had missed out on. Like the trip his family had taken two years ago to see Mount Rushmore.

"So." He cleared his throat. Amber recognized it as a *you're not very good at small talk, what do you want from me?* gesture. "What did you want to talk to me about? Looking to go back to school?"

A flash of heat stroked her shoulder blades, over her spine and down to her toes. For just a moment, she was back in that car with him, his teeth on her neck, her thighs straddling his. At sixteen, she hadn't known what good sex was, though she'd pretended to. Looking at him now, she couldn't imagine that he could make her feel much of anything. The heat she felt right now was uncomfortable, shame and embarrassment pumping through her body.

Amber took a deep breath and then pressed her lips together. Met his eyes.

"I got pregnant," she said quietly.

"I'm sorry?"

She almost felt sorry for him. Brows drawn, bewildered brown eyes studying her, he looked almost like a teddy bear or a puppy dog or at the very least, someone completely incapable of getting someone pregnant. Of getting her pregnant.

"When we were together." She kept her eyes on the table between them. "I got pregnant."

"You-" he started, but he closed his mouth and let silence, a pregnant silence-Amber almost lost the battle with her nerves and laughed out loud-settle over them.

She finally lifted her eyes to meet his gaze. Nodded slowly.

"She's fourteen." She swallowed hard. Hated every word she was saying. Hated that she had to say anything at all ever again to this man across the table. This stranger. How had they created a baby, when she and

Nathan had been in love for two years and there'd never been a baby? Why had she been so careful with Nathan after being so reckless with Kyle Carpenter?

"Oh." He took a deep breath. Leaned forward in his chair.

Amber hoped he couldn't read her mind. That he couldn't see inside her right now and see that she was wound so tightly, she might explode. What would he say? Would he tell her to go to hell? That he didn't care to know Hadley? That he wouldn't share this with his wife?

Then again, what if he wanted to know her? Wanted to meet Hadley? *Her* daughter?

"What's..." He started and stopped. Lifted his eyes from the table to meet her gaze. "What's her name?"

She'd be lying if she didn't admit to herself that it was the right question. If he'd demanded proof that Hadley was his child, if he'd led with that, she'd have hated him. Sure, it would be understandable if he did ask that. She'd been a wild sixteen-year-old, and now he had a family, a wife, and why would he jump in head first to hurt them? Without proof.

And yet, the fact that he'd asked her name touched Amber.

"Hadley Renee."

He winced and nodded. Sat silently for a moment. Probably trying to take it all in.

"Do you..." He breathed deeply and then raised his eyebrows. "Do you have a picture of her?"

Amber cleared her throat. "I do." She reminded herself to move. To sit back and to reach for her iPad again. She hadn't brought it with the intention of blasting Kyle with pictures of Hadley, but since he'd asked, she could pull up a couple.

She sat back further, touched the home button on the iPad and tapped the photo icon. Wondered if he'd noticed she was shaking. So far, he was asking all the right things, if Amber wanted him to want his daughter. If she wanted Hadley to get to know him.

She wasn't sure, though. Maybe Nathan was right about her. She wasn't sure she wanted Hadley to know him. She wasn't ready to share her daughter with Kyle Carpenter.

His eyes heavy on her, Amber selected a picture of Hadley she'd taken just a few weeks ago. They'd been on their way to dinner. Stopped outside to marvel at the snow in the trees. Hadley had turned her face upward toward the trees and the sky. Long shiny hair flowing down over her shoulders, the bright red scarf wrapped around her neck the perfect splash of color against the snowy backdrop. But what Amber liked most about the picture was the look on Hadley's face. Abandon. For just that moment, she'd let go of that teenager thing. She'd dropped the walls she'd started building around herself a year ago. And Amber had pulled her phone from her pocket and snapped the picture before Hadley had even known what was going on.

"She's beautiful," Kyle mumbled when Amber turned the iPad so he could see it.

The hint of a smile curved Hadley's pale lips. Just a hint. Just enough to make you want to know what she was thinking. Though the picture was cold and white, Hadley's cheeks were rosy red, and her hands were raised to the sky, almost in offering. Amber wondered if Kyle noticed that even Hadley's hands were perfect. Elegant. She had long, slender fingers. She always kept her nails bare, but neatly trimmed and shaped.

Amber nodded. What was she supposed to say to that? Thank you seemed wrong, since part of Hadley's perfection had come from Kyle's genes.

"I think so," she said softly.

Kyle continued to study the picture, though Amber wasn't sure if he was hungry for details about a child he'd only just learned about or if he was studying Hadley trying to find visible proof that she couldn't be his.

Finally, he sat back in his chair and blew out a long, hard breath. Let his cheeks fill up and deflate slowly. Stared at something far away over Amber's shoulder. Maybe he was remembering their afternoon in his car. She kind of hoped not. Maybe he was thinking about his wife. And his sons. About what Amber's bomb was going to do them.

"Why didn't you tell me? Sooner?" he asked after a long, uncomfortable silence.

Amber had assumed he would ask this. She'd practiced her answer, over and over actually, so she wouldn't be caught off guard. But nothing she'd rehearsed seemed right now. She hadn't kept Hadley a secret because she didn't want to inconvenience him. Maybe somewhere in the past fourteen years, that thought had crossed her mind. But it wasn't the truth. The real truth.

"Because I didn't want to," she answered honestly. "In fact, I wouldn't be here now if it weren't for Hadley. Asking."

He shook his head and frowned. "She's asked about me?"

Amber took her turn to breathe deeply. To settle the fire in her belly, but she only fanned the flames. She picked up her cup and took a sip of coffee. Because more caffeine was definitely what she needed. For just a moment, Amber thought again of the day she'd told Ingrid she was swearing off coffee. Only this time, she focused on Ingrid. Ingrid, whom she'd blamed for pretty much every bad thing in her life. Ingrid, who seemed to be trying to bridge the gap she'd left between them.

Amber wished Ingrid was here with her now. For support.

The thought scared her more than the man across the table from her.

"She asked about you when she was four…" Amber stared at the table, rather than meet his gaze. "Because I was with her on daddy's day at preschool. She asked when she was a little older-"

"What'd you tell her?"

Amber lifted her gaze to his, surprised to see his face painted with fear.

"Just that you weren't in our lives." Amber swallowed a mouthful of guilt. Maybe he hadn't been in their lives because she hadn't given him the opportunity. Maybe if she'd have told Kyle in the very beginning, he'd have been a part of Hadley's life.

The thought itself made her head spin. She hadn't wanted him to be involved. That's why she'd never named him as Hadley's father. Well, that and the fact that her parents might have had him arrested for statutory rape if she'd told them.

"She asked again…"Amber's words trailed off. She ducked her chin to her chest and rubbed the spot between her eyebrows. Her head was pounding suddenly. Her selfishness-pretty sure Nathan would have called a spade a spade here-was at war with the guilt she felt for denying Hadley a father. Denying Kyle the opportunity to know his daughter, if he'd wanted to.

She took a deep breath, disgusted with herself by the small sob that escaped.

"This past holiday season." She licked her lips. "She was asking about you. She's adamant that I give her your name."

"Did you?"

Amber dropped her hand to her lap and sat up straight again.

"I haven't." She shook her head. "Up until a few days ago, I never said your name out loud to anyone."

Their eyes met and held for a few long moments.

"So someone knows?"

"My sisters." Her voice was little more than a whisper. "My boyfriend."

For just a second, she hated that word. *Boyfriend.* Felt like maybe telling Kyle she'd discussed this with her husband would sound better. More mature. And then she hated herself for thinking that way. Why should she have to bend to society's expectations? She was happy with the way things were with Nathan. Why should they change anything?

Kyle leaned forward again, rested his elbows on the table. Covered his face with his hands.

"I don't..." Amber stopped to gather her thoughts. She stared at Kyle's hands. The wedding band on his finger. Just a simple gold band that meant so much. Gave him things that she would never have. For a moment, she envisioned the rest of Kyle's day. Going to his office. Trying to grade papers. Thinking about Hadley. Going home to his wife and kids. Telling his wife about a backseat romp fourteen years ago and the girl that romp had produced.

She raised her eyebrows and turned her head a bit. Stared at the napkin dispenser on an empty table to their left.

"I don't want anything from you, Kyle," she whispered. "I'm not asking for support. I just...it's been a hard time for Hadley. My dad passed away just after Christmas. We're all trying to...to...deal with Mom and Dad's estate, and we're trying to remember how to live around each other again, and I'm...I guess maybe Hadley's getting lost in the shuffle."

As soon as the words tumbled out of her mouth, Amber felt a jolt of dread. Why had she said that? Why tell him anything? It was one thing to say Hadley had asked about him. The rest of it wasn't his business.

"Okay." He nodded. Rubbed his face with his hands and then looked up at her. He cracked his knuckles and folded his hands on the table.

"Okay?" she repeated. "What does that mean?"

"I need..." He looked around and shrugged, as if he was trying to find the words to say to her. "I just...this is a lot to think about."

"I understand," she answered with a tiny nod.

"Does she...want-" He shook his head.

"I don't know. I don't know what she'll say. If I give her your name. I don't know if that much will be enough for now. If she wants to meet you. I don't..." Amber looked away from his inquisitive eyes. "I don't know."

"Okay."

"I just didn't want to give her your name. And have her just..." Amber started to close her iPad. "Show up on your doorstep. I know you're married. I know you have a family. I don't know if I wanted to protect you..." She shrugged. "Or Hadley."

"Can I see it? One more time?"

Amber pulled her hand from under his when he touched her. She cleared her throat and nodded and wiped the back of her hand on her jeans, like they were kids and he'd given her cooties just by touching her.

With her other hand, she pushed the home button again and suddenly there was beautiful, sweet Hadley on the screen, and Amber's heart hurt.

What had she done?

"I need to talk to my wife."

Amber wondered why married people did that. Why hadn't he just said he had to talk to Jennifer? Why did married people have to throw those labels around? Liv had just done it the other night. Wishing she had time to herself. Being surrounded by students all day and her kids and her husband in the evenings.

She watched him push the iPad at her. Felt a pang of guilt for what she'd just done to his marriage. Didn't compare to the hole she'd ripped in her guts by sharing this with him. The gaping hole that was Hadley shaped.

"Can I..." He frowned. She noticed a deep crease in his forehead. A mix of age and worry, she figured. Interesting to see the years piled on him now. And yet it just made her wonder again how she'd ever been attracted to him. "Is this a good number?" He held up his phone. "To reach you?"

"Yes."

"I'll be in touch." He stood up.

Was that a promise? A threat?

Amber looked up as he pushed his chair in.

"Amber."

Her chest was tight, and her throat ached, and she simply raised her eyebrows.

"Thank you. For telling me."

His words hit her in the gut. He could have been pissed. He could have raged at her. He could have told her never to contact him again. Any of the above would have devastated her, because of what it would do to Hadley.

Instead he'd thanked her, and she felt like he'd just eased a long blade into her lungs and robbed her of her breath. She nodded and dropped her gaze to the iPad, determined not to watch him walk away.

Fifteen

She'd waited, frozen at the table, for a long time before she stood up to leave. To make sure he was gone? To avoid running into him again? Or because she couldn't have moved? Because her feet had been cemented to the floor under the table? Because her stomach had felt leaden and heavy, and because she'd known when she tried to stand that her knees might give?

The moms she'd stared at with disdain were long gone by the time she'd stood to go. The two businessmen were gone. Only the lone woman reading a book and the man reading the paper were still there. Amber had packed her iPad back in her bag, found her keys, and walked stiffly out of the café and across the street to her Passport. She hadn't eyed the cars as she left. In case he was still there. Behind the wheel. Thinking about what she'd told him. Waiting to watch her leave. Stupid, she knew. He had to be long gone.

Once she'd started the SUV, she'd pulled her phone from her bag and glanced at it. Checked to see if Gretchen had left her a message. She'd been disappointed when she hadn't found one. She'd called Gretchen. Before backing out of the parking spot and heading to her studio, she'd called her. Left a quick, breezy message on Gretchen's voicemail. She'd wondered at the way she could sound so normal, when really, her world felt tilted and wrong, and she'd driven absently across town, wishing she could talk to Nathan.

She'd even gone so far as using Bluetooth to dial him. But she'd chickened out before the phone even started to ring. He'd either be driving. Or he'd be in a meeting. Or actually working. None of the scenarios was good for a conversation. Not with where they were at at the moment.

Hadley was probably still sleeping, but even if she wasn't, Amber couldn't go home to her. Not with how she felt right now. And Liv was at school. She'd just have to swallow the bitter pill she'd popped a while ago and get on with it.

It crossed her mind as she pulled into her leased parking space beside her small downtown studio on Maine that she could call Ingrid. Sure, she was working. But she was at home. She *could* answer. She *could* talk Amber down. But Amber wouldn't do it. She wouldn't bother Ingrid while she was writing or editing.

Or, probably, ever.

She hurried from her car to the studio and jumped right in. Pushed the dregs of her guilt and her fear-no, terror-down her throat, now with a bitter aftertaste in her mouth. And turned her mind off. Slipped into her safety zone. There was no room for anyone else in her dark room. No stray thoughts. No guilt. No sorrow.

Just her and her vision coming to life. Becoming the art that apparently other people loved. Amber had never been so shocked when her first photograph had sold to a parenting magazine. She'd lugged her camera with her everywhere, and she'd snapped zillions of pictures of Hadley, and she'd snapped a zillion more of the trees in the park and the waterline at the river and the bridge, but she'd never in a million years have guessed she'd make a career out of a hobby.

She jumped when she heard someone tap on the door.

"Just a sec!" she called. She washed her hands in the small sink on the western wall of the dark room. Pulled the door open and stepped outside, surprised to find Ezra leaning on the counter up front.

"Stranger." He grinned at her.

"Me?" She laughed and touched her chest. "You're the one hiding out all the time."

"What's going on?" he asked. The grin lingered on his face. Amber studied him silently, wondering if he'd painted it on before he walked in or if things were going okay right now.

She shrugged. "Same old."

"How's Hadley?"

Her heart skipped a beat. Who had told Ez about Hadley and Kyle? Did he know she'd met with Kyle earlier?

"Fine. Why?"

Ezra leaned over and rested his elbows on the counter. His eyes were on a black and white photo of an old Lutheran church in a small town near Quincy. Amber had lined her counter with photographs she'd taken and then had a specially cut glass laid over the top of them. She'd done it on a whim, but it had been a good idea. Everyone that came in ended up mesmerized by the array of pictures under the glass.

"Thought she had strep."

"Oh." She nodded. Backed up to sit on the black vinyl stool behind the counter. "Yeah. I think she's feeling a little better. She's been on antibiotics a few days now."

Ezra, still leaning on the counter, lifted only his eyes to look at her.

"What else would I have been talking about?"

He pinned her in place with his intense stare. Amber swallowed hard. She smiled sheepishly.

"She's kinda been a basket case lately, hasn't she? Sneaking out? Getting in trouble?"

"She snuck out again?"

"Not since the night she called Ingrid to come and get her," Amber admitted. "But I haven't talked to you in forever."

Ezra stood up straight. His turn to look chagrined.

"You doing okay?" she asked quietly.

"Yeah, sure." He nodded.

"Shay?"

"Mm." He lifted a shoulder in a lazy shrug. He didn't want to talk. He never wanted to talk. Amber worried that he would blow up one day. Just explode and there'd be bits and pieces of Ezra brain and liver and lungs splattered all over the place. It'd all be okay; she figured she could walk around it, and dodge the worst of it, except for the emotions he was always trying so hard to hold in. The resentment. Sadness. Anger. Who knew what else he swallowed down every morning with his breakfast.

"You shoulda brought Samuel in."

Ezra shot her a hard look. When she laughed, he rolled his eyes.

"I'm on my lunch break," he told her. "Couldn't pack him in the lunch box today."

Amber grinned.

"I miss him."

"I know."

"Come to the next family thing. 'Kay?"

Ezra stretched. "When's that?"

"No idea," she answered with a shrug. "Just promise me you'll come. I miss you guys."

"Yeah." He nodded. "I'll try."

"'kay."

Amber looked up when the bell above her door jingled again.

"Ezra Williams." Ingrid flashed a big grin at Ezra. "How are ya, stranger?"

Ezra turned his head to Amber and rolled his eyes.

"Wow." Amber hooked her feet around the bars of the stool. "I feel popular today."

"Thought I'd see if you wanted to get lunch."

"It's really lunch time?" Amber reached for her phone. She'd left it on the small shelf under the counter when she'd gone to work in the dark room. She was shocked to see that it was almost one o'clock. She noticed a text from Nathan, but she looked back at Ingrid.

"Got time?" Ingrid raised her eyebrows hopefully.

"Um." Amber sighed. "Sure."

"Ez?"

"Nope. On my way back to work." He lifted a hand toward Amber. "See you later."

Amber nodded.

"Hey." Ingrid punched him when he walked by her. "Come to the next family dinner."

Ezra glanced at Amber and grinned.

"When is it?"

"I dunno, but I'll let ya know when I find out."

"See ya," he called as he pulled the door open and stepped out. The ringing of the bell drilled painfully into Amber's brain.

"I hate that frigging bell," she muttered.

Ingrid took a few small steps toward the counter. Amber recognized the uncertainty, but she ignored it and looked at her phone.

I miss you.

The words poked at her already bruised heart. She tapped out a quick response. Just *me too* and then slid off the stool. She pushed her phone into her back pocket.

"Hang on." She slipped out from behind the counter and made her way back to the dark room. She took a quick look around. No reason, really. She'd finished up what she could do for now. Maybe she'd just needed to see it, to look at what was hers to feel grounded before leaving with Ingrid.

"This is so cool."

Amber jumped. Ingrid's voice was right behind her. She looked at her sister over her shoulder.

"What made you decide to do this?"

"Do what?" Amber flipped the light off and moved to leave the room. Ingrid scrambled to get out of the way. "Rent here? It was all I could afford then. I've never taken the time to do anything else since." She shut the door and pulled a key ring from her pocket. Locked the door and turned to Ingrid.

"No." Ingrid shook her head. Amber thought she saw disappointment flash over her face, but it was there and gone so quickly, she decided maybe she'd only imagined it. "That's not what I meant."

Amber grabbed her bag from behind the counter, felt the weight of the iPad and had a flash of Kyle's hand touching hers as he reached to touch the tablet. As he asked if he could see Hadley's picture one more time. She looked up to see Ingrid wandering slowly through her space, looking at her cameras and tools and the photographs she had on display.

"What'd you mean?" Amber asked impatiently. "Where do you wanna go?"

Ingrid looked at Amber over her shoulder. "I don't know. Is there something good around here?"

"Um." Amber narrowed her eyes in concentration. Java Infusion. That was out. She didn't care to ever set foot inside that place again. There were actually several small, trendy restaurants around, but she was stuck thinking about Java Infusion. "There're a lot of little places around...I'm just..."

"Is there somewhere quiet? Where we can just...talk? For a while? Or do you have...somewhere to be?"

"Um." Amber shivered as a chill climbed from her lower back to her neck. What could Ingrid want to talk about? Amber still woke in a cold sweat some nights, remembering that afternoon not long ago when she and Ingrid and Liv had been in the attic and Ingrid had told them about her outpatient surgery.

Their mom had died six years ago. Breast cancer. Amber had never given a thought to herself or her sisters. Not even when the cancer spread, and it was obvious her mom wasn't going to pull through. Now she couldn't shake the fear that Ingrid's doctor had made a mistake, and that she did have cancer, and maybe if she did get to know her sister again, she'd only lose her again.

"No." She shook her head. "I just need to check on Hadley."

"Oh." Ingrid nodded. "Well, do you wanna go home-"

"I'll just call her."

"Okay."

Amber figured anyone watching them or eavesdropping on their conversation wouldn't know they were sisters. At the moment, they were acting more like polite strangers.

"We could go to Carino's," Amber suggested.

Ingrid's eyes narrowed. Amber could almost see the wheels turning in her head as she tried to remember where Carino's was.

"Italian place by the river?"

"Sort of," Amber answered with a nod.

"Okay."

Amber's heels clicked on the floor as she crossed the big open room. A glance back told her Ingrid was still meandering slowly behind her. When Ingrid arrived at the front door with her, she offered Amber a small smile and stepped outside. Amber returned the smile, flipped the lights off, and then pulled the door closed and locked it.

"I'll drive," Ingrid offered. Amber noticed Ingrid's Subaru parked just across the street from her shop and nodded. They stepped up to the curb and waited for three cars to pass and then together, they stepped down and started walking. Amber admired Ingrid's black flats. Little bows on the toes. Simple jeans and a black leather blazer. Amber had gone for the same sort of grown up look today. Low-heeled boots, dark wash jeans, and a simple crème-colored knit shirt. She hadn't been trying to impress Kyle.

Had she?

No. She'd only wanted to assert herself. As the parent. As Hadley's one true parent.

So, if that was the case, why had she let that stuff come up? The whole thing with Hadley getting lost in the details of her father's death and the estate?

"Do you?"

Amber blinked when she realized Ingrid had said something to her. Something she'd apparently missed.

"I'm sorry." She shook her head. "What?"

Eyes on her, Ingrid stuck the key in the ignition and started the SUV.

"Do you? Do portrait photography?"

Amber grinned as she buckled her seatbelt.

"Why? You guys need a cheap session fee for your engagement pictures?"

Ingrid snorted and rolled her eyes.

"No." Amber shook her head. "I used to. I mean...I was a kid. With a kid. And no money. I was desperate-"

"Mom and Dad didn't help?" Ingrid looked over her left shoulder and eased out into traffic.

"Yeah, they did." Amber nodded. "But I...didn't want them...shouldering everything. Parenting Hadley."

"Did they? Parent her?"

"Um." Amber sighed. "Sometimes. Sort of."

Ingrid nodded.

"So you didn't like it?" she asked after a few minutes. "Portrait photography?"

"No." Amber frowned. She could hear music playing, and she thought she was listening to grunge, but she wasn't sure. She leaned over and turned the volume knob on Ingrid's radio. "Nirvana?"

"Lithium station." Ingrid shrugged.

"Wow."

"Stop that," Ingrid groaned.

"Stop what?"

"That thing you do." Ingrid turned right on Fourth and glanced at Amber. "Like I'm not allowed to like normal things-"

"What?"

"Music." Ingrid tossed her hand out at Amber as she drove. "You're always picking at the music I listen to. Jesus, at least I don't listen to the Eagles, like Liv."

"What's wrong with the Eagles?" Amber shook her head.

Ingrid sighed.

"And no." Amber tucked her hair behind her ear. "No, I don't."

"Don't what?"

"Like portrait photography!" Amber snapped. She shot Ingrid a look of frustration, but she had to laugh at the way her face was screwed up in a confused frown. Ingrid laughed, too.

"Why not?"

Ingrid swung the SUV left into the gravel-covered parking lot across the street from Carino's. Amber ignored Ingrid's question and sang along with Kurt Cobain to 'Come as You Are.' When Ingrid pulled her keys from the ignition and opened the door, Amber continued to sing.

"Don't quit your day job," Ingrid called to her as she slipped out of her seat and closed the door.

"Haha." Amber climbed out her side and pushed the door closed. "I was in love with him, you know?"

They met at the back of the Subaru and started across the lot.

"In love with who?"

"Kurt Cobain," Amber told her.

"You can't be in love with him-"

"I said I was-"

"He's been dead for years-"

"Aren't there some women who are still desperately in love with Elvis?" Amber shrugged.

"That's different," Ingrid argued.

"How's that different?" Amber leaned into Ingrid to nudge her with her elbow.

"I mean, Elvis!" Ingrid tossed her hands in the air and looked at Amber with a laugh.

"But Cobain." Amber did the same thing and winked at Ingrid.

"Really?"

"Yeah."

"Like you thought he was good-looking?"

"Yeah. No. I don't know. I just loved his music. I loved his...I loved him. Such a tragic guy."

Ingrid raised her eyebrows. "So's that why you said no to Nathan? Some deep, unrequited love for Cobain?"

"Yes." Amber looked away, let her eyes sweep the ground in front of them as they walked. She hoped Ingrid didn't notice that her heart wasn't in the laughter anymore.

"So. Why?"

They stopped at the curb at Third Street and waited while the southbound traffic rushed by.

"Really?" Amber frowned. "I dunno."

"No. I mean, why don't you like portrait photography."

"Oh." Amber arched her eyebrows. They wandered across the street, no hurry now that the cars had all zipped by. "Too many little kids."

"What?" Ingrid reached out to grab the door and pull it open, but she looked at Amber over her shoulder. "What does that mean?"

As they stepped inside, Amber looked around. Carino's always did a steady business, but she was happy to see open booths on both the north and south walls.

"I just..." She dragged her fingers through her hair and finally looked at Ingrid.

Ingrid was watching her, but she turned away when the hostess asked how many and then led them to a table. Amber felt her phone buzz in her bag as she followed Ingrid to the corner booth on the north wall.

Amber slipped into the booth and unzipped her bag. Pulled her phone out and remembered she hadn't called Hadley yet.

I'm sorry.

He wasn't, though, was he? Should he be? If this is what he really felt, if he really thought Amber was self-centered, shouldn't he say that? She sighed and texted back. Another *me too*. Asked him to call her later.

"Gonna call Hadley really quick."

Ingrid slipped her glasses on and picked up the menu. Eyes on the list of appetizers, Ingrid answered with a silent nod.

Sixteen

"She okay?" Ingrid asked when Amber ended her call to Hadley and dropped her phone back in her bag.

"Watching TVLand and sleeping."

"I loved a good sick day when I was a kid." Ingrid grinned. "Got to stay home. Watch TV. Eat good stuff all day. It was great."

"Yeah, except for being sick." Amber nodded. "Did you ever get strep when you were a kid?"

"Actually, no."

"It's awful." Amber rubbed at the skin under her eyes.

"I had a lot of sinus infections." Ingrid blinked and stared at her water glass. "Liv used to get ear infections a lot."

"Hadley gets strep at least once a year," Amber said on a sigh.

"So. You don't like portrait photography because of the kids."

Amber started to answer, but she stopped herself when she saw their waiter approaching their table. She hadn't even looked at her menu. Ingrid asked for a glass of chardonnay. Amber hadn't realized this was going to be a cocktail sort of lunch. Probably, she shouldn't have-with the headache that had been pounding at varying degrees all day-but she ordered a glass of pinot noir.

"It wasn't just the kids," Amber said when they were alone again. "What are you gonna get?"

"I think the salmon special sounds good," Ingrid answered without hesitation.

"Yeah? I think salmon belongs in a river, swimming upstream."

Ingrid snorted.

"I think I'll just get tortellini."

"You don't like salmon?"

"I don't like things that swim," Amber answered.

"Fair enough." Ingrid nodded.

Amber sat back in her seat and immediately regretted it, because she felt pinned in by Ingrid's stare.

"I used to hang out in the attic a lot."

Ingrid's eyebrows shot up quickly. "Really?"

"I don't know that I ever set foot in the basement before we started cleaning stuff up. But I hung out in the attic a lot."

"Alone?" Ingrid's tone needled its way inside Amber and threaded sadness through her heart. Her throat.

"Sometimes."

"Sounds lonely." Ingrid's voice was a little gruff.

"Sometimes," Amber repeated. Uncomfortable with the intimacy in the moment, she cleared her throat and broke the eye contact. "I found…an old camera in a trunk. When I was maybe…thirteen. Fourteen."

"What kind of camera?"

"A Konica C Thirty-five. Auto focus."

Ingrid laughed softly, and Amber shrugged and arched her eyebrows as if to say *what're you gonna do?*

"Did you know that? When you found it? Did you know what it was?"

"I knew it was a camera," Amber answered with a grin. "But, no. I mean, I used that one ten you and Liv had when you were at home."

"One ten?"

"The thin little blue camera you guys had?"

"Oh yeah. Yeah. I remember." Ingrid nodded.

"Okay. And I found a one-twenty-six in the attic, too."

"That's the one that took the perfect little square shots, right?"

"Yeah."

"I remember Mom and Dad using that one. When Liv and I were little."

"Well, I dug around a lot. In the attic. Found some interesting things."

Ingrid smiled. "I'm sure you did."

"The cameras interested me. I mean, I took pictures. Like you guys did. With my friends. When we went skating or sleepovers or whatever. But I liked to just take pictures...of anything. Mom would get so mad at me. She said I wasted film. I shot up a whole roll of film one time...pictures of her flowers...in the backyard. She grounded me when she saw that she'd paid five bucks for a whole roll of flower pictures."

"And look at you now."

Amber shrugged off Ingrid's words.

"Do you still have them?"

"The cameras?"

She did. For sentimental reasons, she'd kept all the old cameras she'd collected from around the house, including the attic. Most of them were at her studio.

"The pictures. Of Mom's flowers."

Ingrid's hope stretched through her like fingers, prodding to hold onto something.

"Yeah. I do."

"Can I see them?"

Amber nodded.

"I loved her flowers," Ingrid said quietly. "I mean...I didn't. When I was kid. At home. Or maybe I did, but I didn't know it until I was like thirty-something and the flowers were gone, and Mom was too sick to care about tulips and marigolds."

"Yeah. I know." Amber looked up as their waiter appeared and set their wine glasses on the table. She had to remind herself she had a headache and gulping down a glass of wine wasn't going to help it a bit. Instead she took a hesitant sip as Ingrid ordered. Asked for the tortellini when the tall, blonde looked at her in askance.

"So you were actually interested in photography? When you were that young?"

"Well." Amber pursed her lips. "I wouldn't say I was interested like I wanted be a photographer. I just thought the old cameras were cool. When…Hadley was born…I um…got a job."

"On top of being in school."

"I'm not a slacker, Ingrid," Amber said softly. "I've worked my ass off to support her."

"I'm sorry," Ingrid whispered.

"For what?"

"If I hadn't left, I could've helped you out."

"That's not the point, though. Mom and Dad helped. Liv and Wade helped. Even Ezra helped when he could. But I didn't want my mistake to be everyone else's burden."

"She's not a mistake."

Amber squeezed her eyes closed for a second. "No. She's not. But you know what I mean."

"I do." Ingrid nodded.

"I worked at McDonald's for a few months. And I hated it. God, it was so awful. I hated coming home to her, smelling and feeling so gross. I'd shower, and then I'd spend as much time with her as I could. And then I'd hit the homework."

"My first job was at the grocery store. I worked the checkout lane."

"I know." Amber nodded. "I remember."

Ingrid bit her lip, but she said nothing.

"So, anyway," Amber cleared her throat, "Liv and I were at the mall one day. And-"

"You and Liv were at the mall? Together?"

"Yeah." Amber nodded. "I don't even remember why. Maybe we were looking for something for Mom's birthday? I don't know."

Ingrid took a sip of her wine.

"Sears had a sign up. At their portrait studio."

"Oh." Ingrid grinned. "Gotcha."

"And since I had a thing about cameras, Liv suggested that I apply. Had to be better than burgers and fries, right?"

"Sure."

"So I worked at Sears until I was twenty."

"Hence the portrait photography and the dislike of said portrait photography."

"Hence." Amber flashed Ingrid a smile.

"It was okay. I mean...the little kids were cute, yes. But I was still going to school. And I was spending so much time with other people's kids. And then I'd have to smush all my time and energy for Hadley into this small space. Into what I had left over for her. Ya know?"

"Did she go to daycare? I mean, I know Mom watched her. But did she ever go to daycare?"

"No. Couldn't do it. It killed me to consider it. And I think if I'd have brought it up, Mom would have killed me."

"Mom was a wreck, Amber. When you were pregnant."

"What?"

"She was...beside herself. Somehow Liv and I had managed to escape adolescence with nothing bad happening. We were terrible. Of course we were. We were kids. We drank. We partied. We were lucky. You got caught."

"What'd she say?" Amber let her eyes roam over the room, noticed someone she'd gone to school with but didn't particularly want to speak to, and then looked at Ingrid. Looked away just as quickly. "About me?"

"She was just worried." Ingrid shrugged. "I mean, you were her baby. She was beside herself thinking about what you'd done to get pregnant-"

"She really thought you and Liv had never-"

"I dunno. We just never talked about any of that when Liv and I were that age. I mean, Mom had you and Ezra. When you guys came along, it was like..."

"Like what?" Amber sounded breathless. The conversation fascinated her, but it hurt, too. She rubbed her hand over her stomach, feeling the hollow there.

Filling with fear. The ache that she'd felt when she was a little girl and her mom left her at school alone. The ache she'd felt when she was a little girl and Liv and Ingrid left the house to go out with friends or dates.

"It was like Liv and I...like our childhood was done. Zip. Done. We had to grow up, because Mom and Dad were busy with you guys. I mean, babies need more attention than teenagers, right?"

"Do they?" Amber mumbled. She hadn't intended for Ingrid to hear her, but she saw the slight arch of Ingrid's brow, the small smile that played at the corner of her lips.

"Well. We all made the mistake of assuming Liv and I were grown up, and that you and Ez needed them more than we did."

"You turned out okay."

Ingrid snorted. "So did you."

"So." Amber blew out a deep breath. "After a while, I hated it. The job. The people I worked with. The-"

"Everyone ends up hating a job like that."

"I hated...fighting for smiles from babies. From little kids. I hated the crabby parents. The moms that were so damned determined to have the perfect baby pictures. I hated the crying and the screeching and being so...fed up with all of it...when I went home to my little girl."

"I get it."

"When Had was little, I took a picture of her. Just a snapshot. We were at the park, and she was holding Dad's hand. They were walking in front of me. They'd stopped. To look at a butterfly or a worm or something."

"A butterfly or a worm? Really?"

Amber grinned sheepishly. "I dunno. Anyway, I sat down. On the sidewalk behind them. And I took a few pictures. I didn't take a ton, because I was thinking how Mom would go nuts on me for wasting film. But I ended up with a shot...of Had looking up at Dad. Little fingers wrapped around his hand. Her hair was in pigtails, and you could see the curve of her cheek. The sun just behind her face, like it was there for her. To spotlight her. The whole world in her eyes."

Ingrid smiled sadly.

"Sure. She was looking at Pop."

Amber nodded.

"Yeah." She pulled her phone from her bag and glanced at it. Habit? She was no better than the other fifty people in the restaurant that checked their phones every fifteen minutes. Or was she checking to see if Hadley had called? Or was she hoping for another text from Nathan?

"I sent the picture to a parenting magazine. Just for the hell of it."

"Mom sent me about six copies when it came out."

"She did?"

"Mm-hmm. You love what you do, don't you?"

Amber blinked at the shift in subject, but she nodded.

"I do. I love everything about what I do. I love...the challenge of getting the right angle. The right lighting. Of making you feel what I feel when I see whatever I'm looking at."

"You do that well."

"Portrait photography is so...static. So stifling."

"Really?" Ingrid frowned. She sat back when the waiter approached and set her plate on the table in front of her. "I would think it would be the opposite."

Amber's stomach growled as she looked at her own lunch. She picked up her fork as the waiter walked away, but she simply held it and looked back at Ingrid.

"Portraits are fake," she said simply. "It's so much more challenging to take a candid shot and find something real, something raw..."

Ingrid considered Amber's words for several long moments. "I get that," she drew her words out slowly, "but...what about nature? What about the still shots you do?"

"Do you think you and I could take a picture of Had and they'd look about the same?"

"What do you mean?"

"If we sat her down on the front porch at Mom and Dad's. Told her to smile and snapped a picture. Would they look the same?"

"You're the professional-"

"All things equal...same lighting...same camera...same film speed. They'd look pretty much the same."

"Okay."

"But if you and I were at...Liv and Wade's...and we were walking around taking pictures of everyone just mingling, our pictures would be different. Because we see things differently. Different things strike us...what's important to me may not be important to you. Same with a barn or a church. You might like the windows in a church. What's not to like about stained glass?"

Ingrid nodded, either in agreement to Amber's question, or to show she was following Amber's train of thought.

"But maybe I like the way the wooden door is warped with age and light. Maybe in a shot of that church, I'd focus on the door, that you wouldn't even notice-"

"Okay." Ingrid took another drink of her wine. "Yeah. I see what you mean."

"So my challenge would be to sell you on why that door makes a better photo than the window, which of course is beautiful."

"That's...really...neat, Amber."

"Don't patronize me, Ingrid-"

"I'm not. Not at all." Ingrid poked her salmon with her fork. "I know exactly what you're saying. It's like writing."

Amber raised her eyebrows, inviting Ingrid to continue.

"Are you hearing the conversation at the table to our right?'

"Not really."

"I am. I'm hearing two women who might be sisters or maybe friends...talk about a third woman, who they think deserves better than how her husband treats her. He won't let her join a book club they're talking about. He doesn't like it when she goes jogging by herself. And he likes to play golf two nights a week."

"You heard all that? While I was talking?"

Ingrid nodded.

"And my brain is thinking of five different ways to spin that. You and I could sit here with pens and papers and write two completely different stories about what I just told you. It's my job to make my readers give a damn why it's bad that this guy treats this woman this way."

"Wouldn't that be my job, too?"

"Well, you could go with that. And we'd still have two different stories, because that's just the way we're made. We're two separate people, and our imaginations would go different ways. But you might write about him. Why does he treat women like that? Why does he have an issue with his wife-"

"What if she's not his wife?"

Ingrid grinned. "Exactly."

"Because maybe they didn't want to get married. Maybe they're only living together-"

Ingrid laughed now. "Yeah. Everyone brings something different to the table. No matter what meal they're sitting down for."

"This has to be the most boring lunch you've ever had."

"Why would you say that?" Ingrid asked quickly.

"We've just spent at least thirty minutes talking about photography. And me." Amber hadn't even eaten half of her lunch, and she was beginning to feel full already. "You said you wanted to talk about something. I highly doubt that was it."

"It's exactly what I wanted to talk about, Amber."

Seventeen

Amber eyed Ingrid suspiciously.

"What?" Ingrid set her fork down and sat back. "Did I do something wrong?"

"No. No, I just…"

"Just what?"

Amber sighed. She drained her glass and considered another. Might be hell on the headache. On the other hand, might help her take the edge off. Because that sharp edge around herself-she envisioned herself as a cartoon character with a silver aura around her, silver being the color of a sharp edged knife-was probably ninety-nine percent the cause of the headache.

"When you said you wanted to go somewhere so we could talk." Amber dragged her eyes away from Ingrid. She shrugged and shook her head.

"What?"

"I just…" Amber bit her lip. "I thought maybe you had…"

"I promised you it wasn't cancer, Amber."

"Yeah, I know. But."

They sat quietly for a moment.

"Have you found a doctor? Here?"

"I haven't," Ingrid admitted.

"Are you going to?"

"Gonna be hard to beat my doctor up there."

"So you're gonna take the train there? Take the train to Chicago when you need to see your obgyn?"

Ingrid laughed. "I could. Be a nice excuse to visit Julie and Rafe."

"Don't…" Amber held her breath for a second. "Just don't…wait too long. Okay?"

Ingrid cocked her head to study Amber's face.

"You're really worried about this, aren't you?"

"Kinda."

"Have you checked yourself? Since I told you?"

"No," Amber admitted in a whisper.

"But you're worried about me?"

Amber chewed on her lip. Counted to ten. She didn't want to gush about Ingrid. To say something stupid about how she'd waited all these years for her big sister to come home and she sure as hell didn't want to lose her now.

"Yeah. I guess I am."

"Amber..."

"I'd worry about Liv, too, if it was her."

"I was like that. Right after...everything happened. I mean...well, you know what I mean. I told you. But...I feel good about it now-"

"Okay, but just promise me that you won't wait too long. Find someone to see."

"Who do you go to?"

"Me?"

Ingrid raised her eyebrows and looked around their table.

"Nancy Graves."

"A woman?"

"Yep. She's a woman."

"And that doesn't bother you?"

Amber snorted. "God, now you sound like Mom."

Ingrid grinned. "You like her."

"Yeah. I've been seeing her since I was twenty-three."

"I'll have to think about it."

"She's a doctor, Ingrid."

"I'm not into the idea of a woman having her hands on me."

"But you like having a strange man's hands on you?"

"No. I don't like that either."

"Do you have blood work done very often?"

"It's been a few years," Ingrid said slowly. "Why?"

Amber shrugged.

"Thinking about Dad?"

"Yeah. I guess."

"Did he sing? In the shower? When you were a kid?"

"Um." Amber laughed. "I don't know? I wasn't around when he showered."

Ingrid rolled her eyes.

"Liv and I used to hear him singing in the shower. On the weekends."

"Hmm. Maybe he sang after he and Mom-"

"Don't even go there." Ingrid shivered.

"He always had to have the TV on. No matter what room he was in. No matter what he was doing. He always had the TV on."

"I remember that."

"Once when Ez was…I dunno…twelve? And I was nine…"

"What?"

"He instituted a no TV rule for Saturdays."

Ingrid raised her eyebrows and shook her head.

"How long did that last?"

"Two weeks? Maybe three?"

"That long?"

"Yeah. The first Saturday, he drug me and Ez out of bed at, like, eight. And we went for a drive. Went to Siloam Springs. And we walked the trails out there. All morning. Treated us to ice cream on the way home."

"That sounds fun."

"It was." Amber nodded. "The second week, Mom made us clean our rooms."

"Eh."

"No kidding."

"What about the third?"

"It rained like forty-six inches that Saturday…and Ez and I were dying to just watch TV. Or a movie. Or something."

"What'd you do?"

"Dad and Ez spent hours working on a model car."

"Really? Ez was into that stuff?"

"Are you kidding me? He loved it."

"What'd you do?"

Amber started to answer, but she frowned, trying to remember. "I dunno. Maybe that was a day I spent in the attic."

Ingrid winced, but before she could say something about how sad that sounded. Amber continued. "By the fourth week, Dad was going nuts with no TV. So the rule was rescinded. And we all watched *Star Wars* that night."

"I could live without a TV," Ingrid announced.

"Really?" When Ingrid nodded, Amber asked, "What would you do?"

"Read."

"You wouldn't write?"

"Well, yeah, but sometimes it just makes my brain hurt, so I have to do something to relax."

"Writing? Makes your brain hurt?"

"Sometimes."

"What do you mean?"

"Sometimes I waste hours staring at a blank screen. Sometimes I waste hours afraid to open the file and stare at a blank screen. And sometimes there's so much inside that I can't write fast enough. Anyway you look at it, it makes my head hurt."

"But you love it."

"I do." Ingrid flashed her a grin. "Hey. Um…Liv…finished that manuscript."

Amber laughed softly and rolled her eyes.

"What?" Ingrid asked quickly.

"It's not a big deal."

"What's not a big deal?"

"The manuscript." Amber tried to hold the eye contact with Ingrid, but she couldn't. Maybe the manuscript itself wasn't a big deal, but the fact that Ingrid had let Liv read it first was. In fact, in Amber's head it was kind of huge.

"You don't wanna read it?"

Amber's eyes flew up to meet Ingrid's when she heard the hurt in her voice.

"No." Amber reached across the table to touch Ingrid's hand. "No, I mean, yes. I do. But I just…"

"What?" Ingrid asked softly. "You acted upset. When you saw that Liv was reading it."

Amber took a deep breath and let it out slowly. She pushed her plate away and set her fork down.

"Ingrid, it's not the manuscript. It's…that you guys always remind me that I don't belong."

"What?" Ingrid snapped. "What? What do you mean you don't belong?"

"You and Liv were Mom and Dad's first family. You grew up together. I was just a tag-along."

"That's not true."

"It is, Ingrid, and really, it's not your fault. All those years when you were gone, Mom and Liv would talk about you, and I couldn't even be a part of that. Liv would clam up if I was around, or Mom would tell me to go do the dishes or something."

"What do you mean?" Ingrid licked her lips. "They talked about me?"

"Like if you'd called or something. I remember Mom talking once about some guy you were involved with. She was upset because you and Scott had split up-"

"I've dated like…four guys…in my life…Seriously dated. And that includes Scott and Luke." Ingrid frowned. "Sounds like she made me out to be quite the slut. Guess you all thought of me as the black sheep."

"She was a mom. It was her job to think that stuff."

"What did Liv say?"

"She defended you."

"She did?"

"Yep. I might have, too, but I wasn't ever supposed to know what was going on. Not even when I was older."

Amber pulled her billfold from her bag and unzipped it.

"It's funny what you can believe about someone. Without even knowing them. Isn't it?"

Amber stuck her thumb and index finger into her billfold and pinched the corner of her debit card. She pulled it out and finally looked up at Ingrid.

"Even family."

"I don't think Mom meant anything bad about it, Ingrid. She was just...concerned. She was afraid you were gonna get hurt."

"So." Amber reached for the ticket and pushed Ingrid's hand away when she tried to take it. "I got it."

"I can get it. I asked you to come with me."

"And I put you to sleep talking about myself and photography," she mumbled as she read over the ticket to make sure it was all correct. "Besides, I owe ya one."

"Thanks."

Amber lifted only her eyes to look at her sister. The headache had eased. Enough that she wished they could sit for another hour and have another glass of wine. But the sadness at the corners of her sister's eyes spilled over onto her, and Amber winced and looked away, knowing this time she'd done it. She'd hurt Ingrid, and she wasn't even sure if she'd meant to or not.

"So?" She hoped she didn't sound overly cheerful.

"What?" Ingrid opened her purse and dug around for her keys.

"Can I read it?" When Ingrid looked up at her, Amber ducked her head and shrugged. "The manuscript?"

"You don't have to."

"But I want to."

"You do?"

"Yeah." Amber nodded. "Did Liv like it?"

The waiter appeared from nowhere this time and took the black leather folder with Amber's debit card in it. Ingrid watched him walk away and then turned her attention back to Amber. She shrugged and picked up her water glass.

"She said she did."

"And what? You don't believe her?"

"Would she tell me if she didn't?"

"Ingrid."

"What?"

"We love your books."

Ingrid opened her mouth to argue, but she only raised her eyebrows and shook her head.

"It's not a thriller. And I think it sucks. Which is why it was buried in my stuff."

"Why would you think it sucks?"

Amber looked up as the waiter made his way back to their table. She figured a twenty percent tip, jotted down the numbers and signed her name, all the while glancing up at Ingrid from time to time.

"Ingrid," she coaxed as they stood up to leave together.

"Don't you ever doubt yourself?"

"Of course I do."

"So do I."

They walked straight into the street in the absence of traffic. Amber wished she'd have had the rest of her lunch boxed up, but she'd been thinking about Ingrid, about how this time she'd accidentally hurt her feelings, and she'd completely forgotten the leftovers.

"How was the salmon?"

"Good."

"Just good?"

"It was really good," Ingrid admitted quietly. She smiled as they rounded her Subaru to pull open their doors. Amber glanced at her phone as Ingrid started the SUV. "Can I ask you something?"

She took a quick breath, winced at the little jolt of pain in her chest. Looked up at Ingrid expectantly. Part of her had wanted to dump everything on the table earlier. To be able to cut loose and talk to Ingrid about everything. But part of her loved that they'd had a nice lunch with a (mostly) nice, civil conversation and she hadn't had to go into what was making her crazy these days. Talking about photography had taken her mind, her heart off Hadley and Kyle. And Nathan.

"What?" she asked when Ingrid still didn't say anything.

"Can I come down and look around your place sometime? Watch you work?"

"Me?" Amber arched her eyebrows. "Really? Why?"

"Research-"

"Yeah, I know, but why me? You're I.G. Arenson. You could ask anyone-"

"I'm asking you, Amber," Ingrid said simply.

Amber nodded and turned away to look out her window. "Yeah. I'd like that, Ingrid."

Eighteen

"But you didn't. You didn't stop. You kept backing up-"

"The guy was drunk!" Luke argued. "I wasn't gonna listen to a drunk-"

"You shoulda." Wade shrugged. His grin disappeared behind his Bud Lite bottle. "You shoulda. That's all I'm sayin'."

Amber moved her eyes from Wade to Luke, both of them laughing quietly. She glanced at Liv, who looked mildly amused, but as if maybe she'd heard the story a time or two. Ingrid was grinning, but she was flipping through Amber's pictures, the pictures she'd taken of their mom's flowers when she'd been a kid. Compared to her work today, they were boring, flat and amateur. Because they were pictures of something that had been special to their mom, Amber had treated them like they were precious since she'd come across them when she was eighteen or nineteen. She'd been digging through her dresser drawer looking for God only knows what, and she had no idea if she'd ever found whatever she'd been looking for. But with each passing year, she was more and more comforted to have the pictures of the flowers.

"So did you hit it?" Ingrid asked Luke.

"Nailed his ass," Wade told her. Ingrid snorted and shot a quick look at Luke for confirmation. He answered with a sheepish grin. "Seven hundred dollars worth of damage."

"Ouch." She flinched. She stacked the pictures together and slipped them back into the envelope Amber had brought them in. "Thank you," she said quietly as she pushed the envelope over Liv's black and sand marble-topped kitchen table.

Amber nodded. She watched Ingrid turn her attention back to the guys who stood at the peninsula counter across the room. Nathan sat at the end of the counter, hand wrapped around a Bud Lite. A minute ago, he'd been laughing with Wade and Luke. Now he was head to head with Charlie, both of them looking at Charlie's phone. Amber wondered if they were playing a game or if they were reading a text message. She wondered if Charlie talked to girls yet. If maybe a girl had texted him.

"Want another?" Liv asked Ingrid. Amber'd noticed Ingrid's beer bottle had been empty for quite a while. Not like Liv to miss that. Liv, like her mother, was a good hostess. Actually, Liv was a lot like their mother in a lot of ways.

"Um." Ingrid looked around the room. Amber dropped her gaze when Ingrid looked her way. Weird. Things had been good the other day at lunch until suddenly, they weren't that good, and Ingrid was upset about something-the only thing Amber could figure was that she'd upset her when she'd insisted that the manuscript hadn't been that big of a deal-and since then Ingrid had been quiet. Not aloof or cold. Just quiet. Withdrawn. "Sure."

"Wade." Liv called. Amber, feet propped on the chair to her left, turned to look at Wade. He'd had a few already. She could see it in the red in his face. What the hell? It was Friday evening. Time to cut loose and relax, right? "Wade."

"What, babe?" he asked. His eyes were on Luke, though, and now Charlie moved away from them, and Nathan was back to listening to the guys, throwing in his two cents when needed.

"Check the grill."

"Yep." He nodded, killed the Bud Lite, and set the bottle down, all the way laughing at something Luke had said.

Amber loved Liv's house. In fact, she'd be hard pressed to say whose she liked better, Liv's or Ingrid's. Both were beautiful and sprawling, more than spacious, and yet, still homey. Ingrid's had more of a rustic cabin atmosphere, though Amber figured you could fit a good ten cabins inside it, it was so big. Liv's house was modern and elegant. The kitchen alone was gorgeous. Amber loved the cherry cabinetry and the black appliances and the black and sand marble countertops.

She looked at Nathan again when Wade slipped around the counter and headed out to the deck to check the chicken kebabs on the grill. He'd come home earlier this afternoon. Thank God Hadley had gone back to school today, because Nathan had shown up just after one. Amber had happened to stop by the house on the way back to her studio. She'd run in, thinking she'd grab an apple and a granola bar for lunch.

Back to the door, she'd hesitated when she heard him come in. He'd come up from behind her, slid his arms around her waist and kissed her neck. Undressed her in the tiny kitchen-wouldn't it be more fun to make love in a gorgeous kitchen like Liv or Ingrid's?-and taken her on the floor and when they'd both been exhausted and sweat-slicked and panting for air, they'd picked up and moved to the bedroom where they'd spent the next hour.

They hadn't talked, though. Not enough. She'd told him she met with Kyle Carpenter, and he'd asked what she'd thought about visiting with him. Rather than ruin the moment with honesty and emotion, she'd simply said it was okay. That Kyle had said he'd talk to his wife and get back to her. She'd hated that. Making it all clean and tidy like that, because it was anything but tidy. But by that time it was after two, and she'd needed to get moving to get Hadley from school.

He loved her. She knew that. But his words still stung. She didn't consider herself self-centered. She was protecting Hadley.

"Where's Ez?" Ingrid asked Liv when she handed her a fresh beer.

"Said they'd be here," Liv answered with a shrug. "Amber?"

"Um." Amber picked her beer up and eyed it. "No, I'm good for a while."

Liv nodded and pulled the chair to Amber's left from under the table. She swatted at Amber's feet and laughed when Amber grinned and pulled them off the chair. Liv scooted onto the seat sideways.

"How come you're so quiet tonight?" she asked Amber.

"I'm exhausted," Amber answered, "and I'm not being quiet. Ingrid is."

"Why are you exhausted?" Ingrid took a long drink of her beer.

Amber shrugged. Probably because she hadn't been sleeping well. Too much on her mind. Maybe because she'd had a delicious afternoon romp, and rather than curl up with Nathan and sleep when it was over, she'd had to put her *mom* clothes back on and rush to get Hadley from school and take her home and then head back to the studio to put in a couple of hours in the dark room.

"You aren't getting sick, are you?" Liv sounded concerned.

"I'm fine."

Ingrid looked from Amber to Nathan and back to Amber. She arched an eyebrow at her as her lips curved up in a smile. Amber grinned and bit her lip. Ingrid gave her a thumbs up.

"What'd I miss?" Liv turned back to Ingrid.

The doorbell rang.

"The prodigal son!" Ingrid announced. "Let's hope he brought baby Samuel."

"I get to hold him first," Liv said as she headed out of the kitchen and down the hall to the door.

"No fair!" Amber yelled.

"House rules," was Liv's faint reply.

Amber conceded defeat. House rules. Liv's house certainly ruled. At least over hers. She sat up straight and stretched when Wade came back inside, meat platter piled high with chicken kebabs.

"There you are!" Ingrid was off her chair and around the table in two seconds when Ezra and Shay appeared in the kitchen. Amber watched her hug first Shay and then Ezra, a little bit jealous. Ezra was her brother first and then Ingrid and Liv's. She'd grown up with him; they hadn't. Then again, that sort of thinking on a wide scale was what continued to hold them each at arm's length from each other, wasn't it?

"Hey." Ezra squeezed Ingrid and then stepped away from her to hug Amber.

"I'm so glad you're here."

Ezra sighed. He pinched the bridge of his nose and frowned. "We almost didn't make it."

Amber looked at Shay over Ezra's shoulder.

"She okay?"

"I dunno." He shrugged.

"Wanna beer?"

"Better not." He shook his head.

"Where's Samuel?"

Ezra looked at her as if to say *really?* Amber snorted and nodded when Liv appeared a moment later with Samuel in her arms.

"House rules," she mumbled.

"What's going on with you?" he asked. Amber watched Ingrid and Shay cozy up to the back counter. Ingrid poured Shay a glass of iced tea. Liv, baby in her arms, moved to stand by Wade, who ducked down to say something to Samuel. Amber loved to see a grown man talk to a baby.

She turned her attention back to Ezra.

"Nothing. Why?"

"Amber."

She picked her beer and nodded for Ezra to follow her out to the deck. It was warmer, though she still felt a chill in the air. Staying light a little longer, too.

Supposedly it was spring, but as far as Amber could tell, winter still had her icy claws hooked into them and had no intention of letting go anytime soon.

"Guess what I did the other day." She leaned on the deck railing and studied Liv and Wade's immaculate backyard. She loved the berm and the evergreens at the west edge of the lawn. The feel of privacy, but the natural flow of the trees around the property. The deck faced a neighbor's deck, but it was partially hidden from view by the tree line to the south.

"Um. Photographed a nude session."

Amber snorted. "That's your fantasy, not mine."

"Waste of good equipment," he mumbled.

She dipped her head and studied her hands on the railing. Her right hand held the beer bottle. Her left, she'd curled around the rail. She stared for a long moment, oddly mesmerized by her bare fingers. Her bare ring finger. She'd never wear a diamond there. But then, she'd said that's what she wanted, right?

"Who says I've never taken nude shots of Nathan?"

"Thank you."

"I like the brief shots better anyway...ya know? I mean, what a pack-"

"Amber."

She looked up at him and chuckled.

"You asked for it."

"What'd you do the other day?"

She stared at him for a moment and then broke the eye contact. Looked at the trees again. Down at her hands.

"I talked to Hadley's father."

Ezra actually took a step back, away from her, as if she'd knocked him off his feet.

"Like you ran into him and you said *hey, how ya doin*?" Ezra asked hopefully. "Or..."

"Or." She nodded.

"Hmm." He'd been standing sideways, facing her, but now he turned and stood square to the rail.

"What? What are you thinking?"

He shrugged. "Why?"

"I wanna know. I wanna know what you think-"

"Why did you talk to him?"

"She keeps asking me about him." Amber took a deep breath, pleasantly surprised by the smell of spring in the air. The smell of rain mixed with the smell of the recently used grill was comforting.

"So. You told her? Who he is?"

"No." Amber looked up at Ezra. "No. I wanted to talk to him first."

"Okay." Ezra nodded his agreement.

"Can I ask you something?"

"It's different, Amber."

"What?"

"You're gonnas ask me if I would rather not have known. Aren't you?" When she didn't answer him, he nudged her gently with his elbow. "If I'd rather not have known that my father was Michael Seckman."

"How?" She took a drink and leaned over more to rest her elbows on the rail.

"I had Dad."

"Hadley has Nathan."

Ezra shook his head. "Not the same."

Amber swallowed hard and nodded. She'd known that. Still. Hurt to hear someone else say it. Especially Ezra.

"For the record," he said after a few moments of silence, "sometimes I wish they wouldn't have told me."

"Really?" Amber was surprised by Ezra's admission. "Why?"

The door banged open, and Ingrid waltzed out.

"What're you two brains plotting out here?"

Ezra smiled at Ingrid, clearly not intending to tell her anything. Amber turned to face Ingrid, the railing at her back.

"I talked to Hadley's father the other day."

"You did?"

"Mm." Amber took a drink of her beer.

Ingrid moved her eyes to Ezra. "Shay's looking for you."

"Yeah. Okay." He took Amber's beer from her and took a long swallow. "You okay?"

"Sure."

He nodded and then squeezed Ingrid's shoulder as he walked by her.

"They're *not*...happy. Are they?" Ingrid asked once she heard the door close, and she was certain she and Amber were alone on the deck.

"Not really. No."

"Why not?" Ingrid's words were so softly spoken they barely carried to Amber.

"Shay's..." Amber sighed. "Um. Post-partum depression."

Sure. That explained why things were rough right now. Amber wasn't sure what she'd lay the blame on for her brother's rocky marriage before his wife had gotten pregnant.

Ingrid winced and shoved her hands in her pockets. "I hate to hear that."

"He loves her so much," Amber said quietly. "But she just keeps pushing."

"Pushing?"

"Pushing him away. Pushing his limits." Amber shook her head. She swallowed hard, guilty for telling Ingrid Ezra's secrets.

"Don't worry." Ingrid must have read her mind. "I won't say anything."

Amber nodded.

"Those pictures." Ingrid smiled. She stepped forward and joined Amber at the railing of the deck. "Of the flowers."

Amber's laugh was self-deprecating. "At least we have them, right?"

"Are you kidding me?" Ingrid turned sideways to look at Amber. "I love them. I felt like I was standing in the backyard. Took me back, like, thirty years."

"Damn, you're old."

"Shut up." Ingrid chuckled. She poked Amber's leg with the toe of her boot.

"Another reason why I like photography."

"What's that? Because you're young enough to understand the new high tech equipment?"

"Well, no." Amber met Ingrid's eyes and arched her eyebrows. "But that's a good point."

"What else?" Ingrid ignored the gentle barb.

"A camera's a time machine."

"What do you mean?"

"Exactly what you just said. Pictures can take you back a hundred years. Place you anywhere in time, in space."

"Well." Ingrid nodded her head back and forth.

Amber shook her head.

"You okay?"

"Ingrid Grace." The door opened, and Liv leaned out to holler at them. "I sent you out to get Ezra and Amber. Dinner's ready."

Ingrid nodded without looking at Liv. "Be right there."

"Okay."

Amber was surprised Liv backed off and left them alone. Closed the door to give them a second. She didn't answer Ingrid immediately. In fact, she didn't answer her. Just swallowed hard.

"Amber?"

"I don't know."

Nineteen

Amber felt Nathan's eyes on her later, after dinner, when she was holding Samuel. She felt guilty for not helping Liv and Ingrid with the dishes. But she knew that more than likely, any minute, Shay would decide she'd had enough, and she'd be packing Samuel up and herding Ezra out the door to go home. She wanted her baby time just like Liv and Ingrid had theirs.

She caught Nathan watching her once. Samuel on her shoulder, sucking wildly on his binkie, she'd been rubbing his back, and then Nathan was watching her, and she thought of Hadley. She hadn't seen much of her daughter since they'd walked into the house hours earlier. Hadley and Grace had disappeared upstairs to Grace's room. She trusted Grace, though; it hurt her to admit, even to herself, that she wasn't sure she trusted her own daughter. She knew the girls had probably been listening to music or watching a movie. Talking, sure. Amber couldn't begin to police the things Hadley said or thought. She didn't even want to. But it was her job to observe Hadley's behavior. To guide her. To punish her when she had to.

Nathan had simply smiled at her, but she'd seen a flash of sadness there before he'd looked away. She dropped a quick kiss on Samuel's black peach fuzz hair when she saw Shay coming for him. Reluctantly, she handed him over, even helped her sister-in-law bundle him up and strap him in his car seat for the drive home.

She missed the baby days. The smell of baby shampoo and lotion on her daughter's skin. Hadley's huge blue eyes looking up at her when she rocked her to sleep at night. She'd even had enough time away from it to be able to think wistfully of holding her, breastfeeding her at two in the morning.

When Shay said goodbye to everyone else, Amber had thrown her arms around Ezra. Shaken for no apparent reason, she'd been afraid to let him leave. She'd made herself let go. Told him she loved him. Kissed Shay's cheek when Shay gave her a quick hug and then she'd watched them go.

Joined her sisters in time to help with clean up, after all.

"Vince Vaughn." Ingrid dried a plate and reached to put it in the cabinet. Amber wondered why they weren't using the dishwasher, but she only picked up the meat platter Wade had used to carry the meat inside and put it away in the cabinet by the refrigerator.

"Really?" Liv stilled her hands in the dishwater. "Really?"

"Yeah." Ingrid nodded.

"What's the question?" Amber asked as she reached for a handful of silverware. Ingrid was drying, but she didn't know yet where everything went so Amber set about putting things away. She noticed Ingrid watching her, probably trying to memorize things so she could do it next time. It made Amber sad that Ingrid felt like she had to catch up with her.

"Favorite actor," Liv told her.

"Mm." Amber nodded.

"He's not sexy." Liv directed this at Ingrid.

"First of all, he kind of is. And second, who says an actor has to be sexy? I love his movies."

"Really?" Liv shook her head.

"Oh my God." Ingrid snapped the dishtowel and hit Liv in the arm. "Shut up. You asked me."

"Liv's favorite is Matthew McConaughey," Amber guessed.

"She right?" Ingrid asked Liv.

"Yep."

"What? Because you liked him in *Magic Mike*?"

Liv snorted and laughed. She shook her head. "No. I did not like him in that movie."

Ingrid glanced at Amber and rolled her eyes. "How about you?"

"Um." Amber pursed her lips. "Bradley Cooper...Harrison Ford."

"Mm." Liv nodded appreciatively. "Amber, did you see *The Good Wife* this week?"

"No. But I recorded it, so don't tell me anything."

"Seriously?" Ingrid leaned a hip on the counter as she dried what appeared to be the last of the plates.

"Seriously, what?" Liv pulled the plug in the sink and let the water drain.

"You guys...what? Watch it and then check in on Facebook or something?"

"No." Liv frowned. She glanced at Amber and giggled.

"We usually text each other while we watch it."

"Oh my God." Ingrid rolled her eyes. "I can't believe my sisters are TV junkies."

"Same thing when we read-" Amber cut herself off. Her eyes flew up to meet Liv's.

"What?" Ingrid asked. "Let me guess. You both read Gaelen Winters' books. And you text each other about them?"

"No." Liv wiped the sink and the counter down. "We read your books. And text each other and talk about them." Liv raked her gaze over Ingrid and then glanced at Amber. "The biggest challenge is not reading them too fast. I mean, we have to wait a whole damned year in between books, and then we wanna just devour them, but we try to savor them."

Ingrid appeared to be stunned.

"Really?"

"You think I'm lying?"

Ingrid shrugged.

"Hadley's answer to having to wait so long for your books is to reread the old ones a hundred times each."

Ingrid swallowed hard and nodded. "Wow."

"So. I dunno. Maybe you can work a little magic and make your ass write a little faster."

"I do a book a year per my contract," Ingrid answered simply.

"So do something independent on the side," Liv told her.

"Do you guys read Gaelen Winters?" Ingrid asked. She'd put the dishtowel down now, but she was picking at her fingernails.

"Amber does." Liv moved down the counter and then over to the table. "I think he's too wordy."

Amber saw Ingrid look at Liv and nod. She laughed quietly.

"Who do you like to read?" she asked Ingrid.

"I read absolutely anything and everything," Ingrid answered. "But I really like Trinity Buchanan."

Liv carried the dishrag back to the sink and rinsed it out, nodding all the way.

"Love her," Liv agreed. She looked up at Ingrid suddenly. "Do you know her?"

"Oh God." Ingrid grinned. "Please don't go fan girl on me."

"Do you?"

"Not well, but I've met her."

"That is so cool."

"Hey. You never asked me if I know Ansel Adams."

"He's dead!" Liv turned to Amber with a frown and a frustrated laugh.

"What is it with you and dead guys?"

Amber pulled a chair out and flopped down at the counter.

"You gotta thing for dead guys?" Liv asked her.

"Only some."

Ingrid leaned on the counter across from her. Liv pulled a bottle of port from the wine cabinet behind the counter.

"Either of you guys driving?"

"Nope."

She held the bottle up in offering.

"If you get me drunk, Luke might take advantage of me."

"If you're against that idea, I'll take your place tonight," Liv suggested.

"Liv, do you and Wade ever do it in here?"

"What?" Liv reached up into the cabinet to their left. Amber watched her snag two wine glasses, set them on the counter, and then reach for a third. "In the kitchen?"

"Mm-hmm."

"Yep."

"Yeah?" Amber looked around the room, thinking again about her afternoon with Nathan.

"Oh my God, don't!" Liv smacked at her hand.

"Don't what?" Amber drew her hand away from Liv. She watched her pour the first glass.

"Don't..." Liv shivered. "Don't picture me and Wade having sex. That's just weird."

"I wasn't."

Ingrid smirked at Amber over the rim of her wine glass. "You and Nathan had kitchen sex today, didn't you?"

"Yep."

"And?" Liv handed her a glass.

Amber sighed and gave in. Took a small sip. She would regret this, and not because Nathan might take advantage of her. But because she'd already had three beers, and she didn't like to mix alcohol, and she didn't usually drink port.

"Good?" Ingrid asked.

"Yeah." Amber nodded. "Just wondering what it'd be like to do it in this kitchen. You know. State of the art."

Liv shot her a hard look. "We don't...use...any state of the art appliances, Amber."

Amber took another drink and met Ingrid's eyes. "Well, maybe that's your problem."

She giggled. Ingrid knuckled her across the counter.

"Well. Not in the kitchen, anyway," Liv amended.

"Yeah? You're more into the power tools in the garage?" Ingrid wiggled her eyebrows.

"Don't you guys use sex toys?" Liv asked them.

"Nothing that can be used in the garage," Ingrid answered quickly.

"You can't use your vibrator in the garage?"

Ingrid ducked her head and covered her face. Amber could see that she was laughing.

"I guess I could, but we haven't ever." Ingrid stood up straight and wiped at her eyes.

"Actually, Wade has these gloves. They're like butter. So soft-"

"Oh my God," Ingrid snorted. "Stop it."

"We also have a hot water spigot-"

"Stop!" Ingrid planted her hand on Liv's chest and gave her a gentle shove. "Dang it, I wanna ask Amber something. Something serious."

"Please don't." Amber shook her head.

"Amber?"

"What?"

"Have you ever taken nude pictures of Nathan?"

Liv stared at Ingrid, wide-eyed with surprise. But she quickly turned her face to Amber, anxious for an answer.

"If I say yes, are you gonna ask to see them?"

"No, I'm good with what I've got." Ingrid winked at her. "But have you?"

"I have," Amber answered with a slow nod.

"Thought you didn't like portrait photography."

Amber's laugh was loud and contagious. Suddenly, the guys appeared in the kitchen.

"What's going on out here?" Wade asked with a lecherous grin. "Because it sounds like fun."

"You're drinking port?" Luke asked as he sidled up beside Ingrid.

"Apparently, I am. Liv twisted my arm."

"Drink up." He kissed her cheek and looped his arm around her shoulders.

"Hmm." Wade stepped up behind Liv and kissed her neck.

"On that note." Amber stood up. "You ready, Nathan?"

"Really? You're not gonna at least finish that glass?"

Amber smirked and glanced at Ingrid.

"Babe, they're asking if I've taken nude photos of you."

"Oh." He grinned, but his face flushed a violent red.

"I'm not sure if they wanna see 'em, but I do." Amber snaked her arm around his waist.

"Why look at pictures when you've got the real thing?" Liv asked.

"Maybe they have a selfie stick," Wade suggested. "Maybe she's in the pictures, too."

Amber ducked her head in Nathan's chest and laughed. She felt the blush climb her neck.

"Goodnight guys." Nathan was laughing.

"Lemme go get Hadley."

"Can she just stay?" Liv asked Amber.

"I dunno. Is she gonna come downstairs and find you and Wade going at it with those buttery soft gloves on the counter here?"

"Buttery soft-"

Liv snorted. She rolled her eyes. "I'll bring her home in the morning."

"Okay." Amber nodded. "Thanks, Liv."

"Love you." Liv stepped around the guys and Ingrid to give her a hug. Amber squeezed her back and then leaned over to hug Ingrid goodbye.

Nathan linked his fingers with hers as they headed down the hallway.

"Do I wanna know?"

"Nope."

"Did you really tell them you took nude pictures of me?"

"No. But they did ask."

"You ever look at them?" He smiled suggestively as he grabbed their jackets from the coat rack by the front door.

"When you're gone, I do, sometimes."

"Okay." He cupped himself to readjust things. Amber smiled knowingly. "I'm gonna drive, like, eighty to get us home. Because that just blew my mind."

"Me looking at your nude pictures when you're gone?"

"The way you blushed when Wade suggested maybe we had a selfie stick." Nathan yanked her toward him as they crossed the sidewalk to the driveway. "That was beautiful."

"That was sincere," she answered.

"Yeah." He nodded. "That's why it was perfect."

Twenty

They were all over each other before they got inside the house. Nathan's kisses were so hot and demanding, Amber forgot they were on the back stoop, and there were neighbors in the alleyway and maybe even on Chestnut that could see them, not to mention the cars driving down Chestnut that might be catching the show. She'd managed to slow him down enough to jam the key into the lock and turn the knob and step inside. Her jacket hit the floor first. Blouse. Bra. All before they got through the dining room. She wanted him, but she wanted him in bed. If she had a house like Liv's, she might feel differently about making love in every room. Christening it, if you will. Then again, usually she was good with being with Nathan anywhere in her house. And it had been their afternoon together, that had started in the kitchen, and then sitting in Liv's kitchen tonight that had made her feel differently about the whole thing.

"Amber." He tugged on her hands and when she stepped closer to him, his hands were everywhere, and she shook her head.

"The bed, Nathan," she argued. "Make love to me in our bed."

It had taken another five or ten minutes, give or take, but they'd made it to the bedroom. With Hadley gone, they'd rocked the bed in a delicious rhythm, until it wasn't just squeaking but knocking on the wall, and then when they'd both come and they were spent and breathless, Nathan had climbed over her and dropped kisses, wet ones and chaste ones and half way in between ones, all over her body, with particular attention to her thighs and the backs of her knees and her breasts.

He said her name as he lay beside her and drew her in close to him. She turned to her side and rested her head on his chest. She hadn't had much port, but between the mix of alcohol and the family time and the time she'd had alone with Nathan, she felt like she and Nathan were floating, spinning just a bit in the bedroom. She wished she could grab onto the sensation and memorize it so she could pull it back sometime in the future if she might need it.

She awoke with a headache. A little too loud and obnoxious to be from drinking. She wasn't a lightweight. Her cell buzzed on the bedside table as she blinked the room into focus. When she stretched, she felt Nathan beside her in bed. With a groan, she picked up her cell, vaguely remembered it falling on the floor last night when Nathan had tugged her jeans off her and she'd leaned down and picked it up, set it on the table.

"What time is it?" She was hoarse. Assumed Nathan was still sleeping when he didn't answer her. Figuring it was Liv calling to see if they were up and moving, so she could drop Hadley off, Amber pushed up on her elbows and answered the call. "Hello?"

"Hey stranger!"

"Gretch." Amber laughed softly. They'd been playing phone tag all week. "Hey."

"What's going on? Is this a bad time?"

"I don't know. I don't even know what time it is." Amber squinted to look at the alarm clock on the nightstand.

"Oh wow!" Gretchen's bawdy laughter hammered at her skull. "It's nine-thirty! Big night?"

"Mm-hmm."

"Still…in bed?"

"Yep."

"Call me later."

"Mm-kay." Amber ended the call and half tossed, half dropped the cell on the nightstand. "Headache," she mumbled. Nathan had moved a second ago, when she'd admitted to Gretchen she didn't know what time it was, so she assumed he was at least partially awake.

When he didn't answer her, she turned over to look at him, surprised to find him sitting up, propped against the headboard.

"Hey. How long have you been awake?"

She reached for him, rested her hand on his thigh.

"Didn't sleep much," he mumbled.

"What's the matter?" She stroked her fingers up over his thigh and stopped at his hip. "You look upset about something."

Nathan dragged his eyes from whatever he'd been staring at across the room and looked at her. He stared at her for a moment, picked up his hand and brushed her hair from her face and then sighed. His face twisted like he was in pain.

"Amber."

"What's wrong?" She scooted closer to him and started to sit up, but she froze when Nathan slipped away from her and climbed out of bed.

"I don't know…" He started. She watched him wander across the room, eyes roaming over his naked back. Broad shoulders and slender hips. Tight ass, long and muscular legs. "I don't know how to say this."

A little stab of pain just below her heart took her breath away. She drew her legs up and rested her forehead on her knees, so he wouldn't see the tears in her eyes.

"I can't do this anymore."

Her stomach pitched at his words. She held her breath, waited for him to go on.

"I love you, but I want more from a relationship than convenient sex and a dinner partner-"

"Nathan-"

"I want marriage, Amber, and you know that. You've known for almost two years now that it's what I want, and you keep blowing me off-"

"I don't blow you off-"

"I want to come home from work to my wife. To my step-daughter. I want the two of us, no, the three of us, to find a house together. To start fresh-"

"We can do that without-"

"I want kids, Amber."

Stunned by this admission, she finally raised her head to look at him.

"What?"

"I wanna have kids. I'm crazy about Hadley, but I want to have a baby with you. I want to have two babies with you. I want to put my hands on your pregnant belly. I wanna feel my baby move in you. I wanna do the newborn stage and the terrible twos and-"

"I can't." Amber shook her head.

"You won't."

"I can't do that to Hadley," she argued. "I can't do that."

"What, exactly, would you be doing to Hadley? Giving her a family? A step-dad and brothers-"

"She's fourteen. There's no way she'd be a part of a family you and I made together. There's too much of a gap-"

"Everything you do is centered around Hadley. You're not just gonna change. You and I together can keep her involved-"

"No." Amber shook her head.

Amber felt his heavy stare on her shoulders. Down to her hips. He shrugged and shook his head. She watched him stalk back across the room and grab for his jeans, one leg of them caught on the corner of the bed.

"This is..." He stepped into them and then looked around for his shirt. "This is what I mean. I can't...I can't keep waiting."

The emptiness, the hole inside her yawned, spread through her stomach and up into her lungs. When he realized he wasn't going to find his shirt in the bedroom, he wandered out the door. Stunned, Amber sat still for a moment longer. When she realized he was in the living room, dressing to leave her, that he was really going to leave her, she scrambled out of bed and pulled the comforter with her. It trailed behind her like the train of a bridal gown as she walked out of the bedroom. Upset by the image, she held it together at her chest with one hand and reached behind her to gather the rest of it up in the other.

"Nathan."

Shirt and shoes on, he turned away from her and led her to the kitchen. She followed him and hovered in the doorway. Watched him opening and closing cabinets one after another, as if he was hunting for something.

"What're you doing?" she whispered.

"Looking..." He let his words trail off. "Trying to remember what's yours and what's mine." He pulled a couple of mugs from the cabinet and stared at them like he didn't recognize them as belonging to either of them.

"Please. Don't leave."

"I have to."

"But you love me."

"I do." He put the mugs back in the cabinet and then rested his hands on the counter. "I do, Amber. I love you so goddamned much-"

"Then don't go. We'll get a house together. You and me and Hadley-"

"Will you marry me?" He arched a brow at her. He leaned into the counter, palms flattened against the Formica.

"Why do you need that? Why-"

She watched disappointment paint over his face like a mask. Killing any emotion. He shook his head and turned away from her. Pulled open the silverware drawer and started rifling through it, again like he was desperately searching for something.

"I'm thirty-three years old," he announced. "I'm not getting any younger. I want a family. I want-"

"Since when have you wanted that? Since when have you wanted to have your own child?"

"Since the beginning." He looked up at her, eyes blazing with anger. "The first time I asked you to marry me."

"You never said anything." She stepped into the room, toward him. Felt a little jolt of pain when he backed up a step.

"Watching you with Samuel last night." He pressed his lips together and shook his head again. "Being with your family. I love that. I love being a part of that. But I need more, Amber. I need more from you."

She sniffled and rested her head on the cabinet. "I can't, Nathan. I don't have it in me. I don't have that to give you."

He nodded. Refused to say anything.

She watched him pull open and close a few more drawers. He shoved the last one closed finally and then threw his hands in the air and turned back to her.

"I'll…" He sidestepped her and slipped out of the room. She turned to watch him. "I'll come back…for my stuff."

"Nathan?"

He grabbed his jacket and pulled it on. Patted the pockets and apparently found what he was looking for. Cell phone, most likely. He slid his hand into his back pocket then, checking for his billfold. She imagined it had spent the night hanging upside down from the bed in his pocket.

"You're really leaving?"

He slowed down, finally. Stepped closer to her. Her body was shaking both from being cold and from the onslaught of fear and sadness.

"I love you." His voice cracked, and he cleared his throat. "I love you so much-"

"Nathan-"

"Amber, if you love me, you-"

"Please don't ask that of me. I can't do it-"

Eyes closed, she didn't see him reach for her so the touch of his fingertips on her face surprised her. She blinked and looked at him. Nathan cupped her face in his hands, brushed at her tears with his thumbs.

"You have to let me go." He dropped a soft, chaste kiss on her lips, and then he backed up a step. Two more.

"Please don't go-"

"I'll..." He hesitated at the door. Her knees buckled. She hung on his words, praying he'd change his mind. "I'll come and see Hadley. To tell her...goodbye."

"Why are you rushing this? What was last night about? Nathan, we're good together. Don't do this-"

"I'm not rushing anything. I asked you to marry me two years ago. You blew it off. I thought you'd change your mind. I thought there was time."

"Hadley and I aren't enough for you?" she whispered.

"That's not fair," he argued.

"You've been thinking about this. For a while. You've been planning to leave me."

"Two years, Amber!" he shouted. "Two goddamned years-"

"When did you decide?" She brushed at the tears on her face.

Hand on the doorknob, he sighed in frustration.

"I've thought about it for a while," he admitted. "I decided last night."

"Was that before or after you fucked me one last time?"

He swallowed hard. Amber saw the doorknob turn under his hand. She thought he would say something. But he pulled the door open and stepped outside. Amber waited. Watched the doorknob. Sank to her knees on the floor when she heard his car start. Lifted her head and listened to his tires crunch on the bits of gravel in the alley.

Twenty-One

When he was gone, she climbed to her feet. Let the goddamned comforter drag on the floor through the living room and into the bedroom. She tossed it to the floor at the foot of the bed. Considered ripping the sheets from the bed and tossing them in the washer. Saw her jeans tossed on the floor near the closet door and remembered she was now stalking around naked and decided she should probably shower in case Liv showed up with Hadley.

Her hands shook as she yanked the top dresser drawer open and fished around for clean underwear. She found the last pair, made a mental note to do laundry today and then pulled her robe from the closet and slipped it on. She glanced at the bed one more time. Thought about last night. The way he'd taken her to the brink time and again, and then he'd finally driven her over the edge and they'd fallen together. The gentle kisses she'd mistaken for I love yous, when maybe they'd really been goodbyes.

The bed was blurry now, and she blinked and felt warm sticky tears on her face. Frustrated, she dashed at them with her hand and then turned to walk out of the room. She locked the door and then locked herself in the bathroom. Turned the water on. The bathroom being no bigger than a glorified closet, it didn't take long for steam to gather in the corners.

Probably the hot water scalded her skin, but she didn't feel much of anything when she climbed into the shower. Little bit angry. Little bit hurt. Little bit stunned- the morning seemed to come out of left field, and Nathan's admission that it hadn't, that he'd been thinking of leaving her, somehow made it worse. Mostly, she was numb.

Maybe he would come back.
Maybe not.
Probably not.

Not if he really wanted the whole goddamned nine yards and then some. Not if he really wanted a wife and kids of his own. Like she and Hadley weren't enough for him. She shouldn't be surprised, though. She'd never been enough to keep anyone satisfied for too long.

So unfair of him to do this to Hadley, though. She'd been so careful through the years. Never letting anyone she'd dated get close to Hadley. Not that she'd even dated that many guys. Nathan had been different. She'd fallen for him so quickly, and she'd believed in him so quickly, she hadn't kept Hadley from him and now he was going to hurt her, and Amber hated him just a little bit for that.

Anger seethed in the pit of her stomach. Anger felt better than that all-consuming sadness that sometimes threatened to tear her apart. Anger, she could deal with. She'd run with that. High-octane fuel. She'd let her anger with Nathan get her through the next week or two. Surely, Kyle had talked to his *wife* by now. Surely, he had come to some sort of decision regarding Hadley. She wasn't sure she wanted a decision. She kind of wished she could hit rewind there and spin it all back to the day she'd met with him and pretend that they'd accidentally bumped into each other and said cool hellos and walked away. Rather than handing over the most precious part of her life. In effect, offering to share Hadley with him. All with Nathan's encouragement.

When she finally turned off the shower taps and dried herself off, she was hot and sticky and a little bit dizzy. She perched on the edge of the bathtub for a few moments and rested her elbows on her knees. Dropped her head and breathed deeply.

Her skin was hot and red. She studied her feet, decided she needed a pedicure. *Fuck you, Nathan Marquardt. Think I'm gonna lay down and die because you left me? Think again.*

Feeling the first pangs of hunger, just around the edges of the hurt-that big hole Nathan had ripped inside her-she finally stood and hung her towel over the shower curtain rod. Stepped into her panties and reached for her bra. The one that she'd hadn't thought to bring in with her.

She groaned out loud. Took her robe from the hook on the door and slipped it on again. She'd put the hook there herself after she and Hadley had moved in. She'd loved the house then. Perfect for her and Hadley. So what if the kitchen was tiny? So tiny they couldn't even fit a table in it? They had a dining room. Big ass dining room with a big ass table they didn't particularly need. But on the plus side, Amber's desk fit perfectly against the east wall. So what if that meant sitting with her back to the dining room table and windows and door? Not like anyone sat at the table anyway, and she sure as hell didn't have a view. An alleyway. And someone's aluminum sided garage. With mold growing on it.

She didn't know the neighbors, didn't know whose garage or mold was out there. Didn't care. The upstairs here had been perfect for Hadley. The living room was on the small side; in fact it would have been perfect as the dining room, and the dining room would have made a good family room. On the other hand, who needed a big family room when you didn't have a big family? She and Hadley fit in the living room on the couch. That's all that mattered.

She found her bra on the dining room floor. She'd forgotten about it earlier, when she'd followed Nathan out here. Desperate to hold him here. Not willing to beg. She leaned over and snatched a strap and carried it into her bedroom. Shimmied out of her robe, put her bra on and then turned to the closet to find something to wear.

What to wear to a secret broken heart party? Who the hell knew? She had no intention of talking about this.

Not to Liv. Not to Ingrid. And she figured she was in a for a day of both of them. They'd gotten through a few of those boxes last week, but they'd all walked out of the house that night and pretty much left it all sit. Easier. And not. Easy to walk away from a mess. Let it go for another time. And yet, the mess never really went away. Stayed on the mind, like a storm on the horizon.

She yanked a gray pullover from the closet and then went back to her dresser to find a t-shirt. When her fingers closed around a handful of Nathan's Nike and Adidas t-shirts, she slowed down. Stood for a long moment, head bowed. Tears burning her eyes. Dammit, but she hated to cry.

She swallowed hard, pushed Nathan's shirts aside- why the hell had he been digging through kitchen drawers and cabinets and not packing shit like this up-and found a pink Nike t-shirt to put on. Black yoga pants from the next drawer down.

Barefoot, she padded back to the bed and grabbed her pillow. Took the pillowcase off it and dropped the pillow to the floor by the bed. Tossed the pillowcase to the floor at the foot of the bed. She planted a knee in the mattress and reached for Nathan's pillow. Started to pull the pillowcase from it, but she stopped. What if he was really gone? What if this wasn't just him blowing off steam? What if he left, and all she had left was what he'd left behind? His t-shirts. A coffee mug or two. A bottle of aftershave in the bathroom. His scent on his pillow and the sheets and maybe the blanket.

She buried her face in his pillow. Breathed deeply. His scent was so strong it warmed her and broke her at the same time. She squeezed her eyes closed and thought about last night. Not the sex. But dinner. Hanging out at Liv and Wade's. Sitting with him at the table. Watching him talk to Charlie. Watching him with Samuel.

The doorbell rang. Amber set his pillow down on top of hers and then padded out to the door. Opened it so Liv and Hadley could some inside.

"Hey." Liv grinned. "This okay?"

"Yeah." Amber nodded. She hadn't taken the time to dry her hair. And she hadn't put makeup on. Both of them had seen her often enough in the natural state, but she worried that today her eyes would give her away. "How do you feel?"

"Okay." Hadley shrugged.

"Get any sleep?"

"Are you kidding? They were both asleep before Wade and I went to bed." Liv closed the door behind her.

"We were tired."

"Probably good for you," Amber decided.

"We grabbed some breakfast." Liv held up a McDonald's bag and shook it.

"You can't tempt me with McDonald's breakfast," Amber told her.

"Mom." Hadley gave her a gentle push and stepped around her to go to the kitchen. Amber stood for a moment and listened to Hadley banging around. She was making coffee. Liv was really going to hang around for awhile.

"You really chose McDonald's over staying in bed with your husband this morning?"

"My niece spent the night. We don't do any of that stuff when we have visitors."

"Uh-huh." Amber nodded. "You were half way there when we left you in the kitchen."

"Well." Liv raised her eyebrows. "They were sleeping."

Amber rolled her eyes and shook her head. She turned to go back to the bedroom. Liv followed her.

"Looks like you guys had a good night." Liv propped her shoulder on the doorframe and eyeballed the wrecked bed.

"Mm." Amber swallowed hard. "Yeah. We did." Because they had. Last night, they'd come home riding the high from the family evening, from their afternoon tryst, and they'd gone a little crazy, and it hadn't been until this morning when the wheels had come off, and Nathan had left her.

The words sent a little shot of pain through her. She felt her legs go weak again, so she moved. Made her body remember that she wasn't going to fall apart. She wasn't going to give Nathan the satisfaction.

"How late did Ingrid and Luke stay?" she asked just to shift the conversation off herself and Nathan.

"Um." Liv leaned her head on the doorframe, too, and closed her eyes. "I think they were there until midnight."

"Midnight?" Amber repeated. She and Nathan had left before ten. Maybe she shouldn't have asked. Maybe she shouldn't have left Liv and Wade's last night.

"We played cards." Liv cleared her throat. "And we killed the bottle of port."

"What?"

"Well." Liv bit her lip. "Wade had a glass, but Ingrid and I killed it."

Amber felt a burning in her chest. Like heartburn. Would they have done that if she'd stayed? Sat down and played cards together? Drank more together? Laughed more? No, because Amber threw a wrench in every goddamned thing Liv and Ingrid did. No, because they'd probably played Euchre and that was a four person game. No, because if she'd stayed, maybe Ingrid and Luke would have left.

She'd chosen to leave, she reminded herself. She'd come home with her boyfriend. Had explosive sex and then watched him walk out of her life. Maybe that was the problem with boyfriends. They could leave. Just pack up and walk out. Maybe marriage made that final decision just a little bit harder. Maybe if Nathan had been her husband, maybe instead of leaving this morning, maybe he'd have just said he thought they needed marital counseling.

"Amber."

Amber looked up at Liv as she leaned over to pull the sheet from the mattress.

"So you and Ingrid drank too much." She forced a smile. She did it often with her sisters; she wasn't worried Liv would see that she was pretending to think it was funny.

Liv answered with a lazy grin.

"It was fun. I wish you would've stayed."

"You do?" She forgot to sound annoyed or jaded or hateful. Even she heard the wistfulness in her voice.

"Yeah." Liv nodded. "I don't know how many times Ingrid picked up her phone to text you about something, but Luke wouldn't let her."

"Why not?" Amber asked softly. God, did he have something against her, too?

"He figured you guys were busy."

Amber snorted. She made a show of looking at the wall behind the headboard.

"We had that problem once." Liv rolled her head on her neck and raised her eyebrows. "Grace was maybe…nine…Charlie was seven." She shrugged. "They heard the headboard banging, and they came running to our room because they thought someone was at the door."

This time, Amber's smile was genuine, but she was quick to pull it back.

"So…drunk…and maybe a little hung over…hence the grease for breakfast."

Liv ducked her head, but Amber saw her sheepish grin.

"Mom?" Hadley appeared behind Liv. She cringed when she saw that Amber was pulling the sheets off the bed. "Oh man. That's so gross."

"Why do I have an audience?" Amber tossed her hands up and laughed quietly. "Get. You don't need-"

"You didn't need to do that-" Hadley shivered.

"Hmm...sometimes," Liv mumbled.

"Aunt Olivia!" Hadley rolled her eyes. "Yuck. Anyway. The coffee's almost ready. I'm gonna go change clothes."

"No shower?" Amber asked doubtfully.

Hadley shrugged. "Not going anywhere today. I have homework to do."

"Okay." Amber nodded. "Whatever."

"Don't eat my McMuffin," Hadley warned her.

"It's so safe with me," Amber promised. She squatted down and picked up the pile of sheets and carried it out of the room. Liv followed her.

"Care if I stay?" Liv asked her.

"Nope. Pour me some coffee?'

"Sure."

Amber hurried through the kitchen-two steps got it-and down the basement stairs. The basement was her least favorite part of the house, not much better than her parents' basement, really. It was smallish, and the walls were cement and dirt, and it was cool and damp, and Amber was convinced a civilization of daddy longlegs lived down here.

She dumped the sheets in the washer, turned the washer on and then tossed some detergent in. Shut the washer and stood still for a moment. So far, so good. An hour into her breakup, and she'd held it together enough that neither her sister nor her daughter knew.

On the way back through the kitchen, Amber grabbed a Pop-Tart. She found Liv at the dining room table, an egg McMuffin in front of her.

"That's not Hadley's, is it?" she asked as she sat down across from her sister.

"A Pop-Tart?" Liv ignored her. "Really?"

"Yep." Amber punctuated her word with a big bite of the frosted strawberry pastry.

Liv shrugged as if to say *whatever*.

"So." She took a drink of her coffee.

"How are you not…like…dying? A bottle of port, for God's sake."

"I didn't drink a bottle," Liv argued.

"One glass put me over the edge."

"I wish you would have stayed," Liv said again. Amber might have thought Liv was pushing that idea too hard for it to be sincere. But Liv's eyes were sad. "I keep thinking…"

"What?"

"I dunno. I keep thinking we're getting…that we're all getting closer…and then nights like last night happen, and I guess I just realize maybe we'll never all be close."

Amber pursed her lips, unsure what to say. She'd enjoyed last night. She'd enjoyed every minute of yesterday and last night. She'd had fun with her sisters. Maybe if she'd have stayed, instead of coming home when she had, maybe she'd have had more fun.

So why did Liv apparently consider last night a failure?

Amber swallowed another bite of her Pop-Tart, but her throat was dry and tight with emotion, and the Pop-Tart was sideways, and it stuck in her throat, and it hurt. She patted her chest and coughed, and decided it was best that she was sort of half-choking on the Pop-Tart so Liv would think that was the cause of the tears in her eyes.

"Where's Nathan?" Liv asked innocently.

"He left."

Twenty-Two

Liv hadn't asked. Where Nathan had gone. She'd just assumed he'd had to pack up and leave for business again. Because that's what Nathan did. Except that maybe now Nathan did other stuff, and Amber might never know. Maybe if Liv *had* asked, Amber would have caved and told her. As it was, she hadn't, so Amber didn't. She kept it to herself and let it burn inside her. She'd hoped he would call. That maybe by the time he'd gotten to his own place, he'd have changed his mind. His heart. That he'd call and say he was sorry.

No calls.

In the late afternoon, Amber had left Hadley, snuggled with a blanket again, on the couch, watching a Disney movie-*Hercules*, her favorite-and gone to her parents' house. She hadn't told either Liv or Ingrid she'd planned to go. Honestly, she didn't want company. She kind of wanted to wallow in self-pity; she didn't want distractions. She'd kissed Hadley goodbye and left with a huge heartache and a gut full of guilt for not telling Hadley yet, and she'd driven across town and pulled into the driveway-well, the ruts in the grass they'd all thought of as the driveway when they were younger. Parked right in front of the garage so maybe if her sisters or brother happened to drive by, they wouldn't see the Passport, and they wouldn't stop.

Rather than sit on the kitchen floor, she picked up two big handfuls of those old pictures and carried them to the table. Pushed the sleeves of her gray pullover up and then sat down at the head of the table, the chair Ingrid had claimed when they'd both been staying here in the days after Dad's funeral.

She'd looked at the top picture for at least ten seconds, trying to decipher it. Figure out the scene. The characters. And then she'd looked out the windows that surrounded the table. Thought about Nathan. The day she'd met him. He'd come into her studio. Friend of a friend recommended her to him. She'd been on the verge of turning him down, telling him she didn't do portrait photography when he'd asked if he could just browse the photographs she had on display. If they were for sale. She'd told him some of them were, and yes, he was free to browse.

And then she'd watched him for a minute or two. He'd looked younger then. She hadn't even realized he'd aged at all, but now that she thought about it, she recognized the years on him. Small squint lines around his eyes. The beard he'd started growing when they'd started dating. The slightest hint of a spare tire around his middle.

He'd purchased a sixteen by twenty that day. Black and white photo of a crumbling country bridge she'd seen on a drive to Springfield several years ago. The photograph was a gift for his best friend's wedding. Maybe that should have sent flags flying for her. His friends were married and responsible and maybe that would mean he would get there eventually. But then that friend and his new wife had moved to Texas, and Amber had forgotten to worry about it.

Her phone rang, startling her. She snapped out of her memories, realized she was still holding the photograph in her hands. She dropped it and reached for her phone. Saw that it was Gretchen and groaned.

"I'm so sorry," she answered with a laugh that sounded suspiciously to her like a cry. "I forgot."

"It's okay. I'm at the front door. Lemme in."

"I'm not at home."

"I know. I'm on your parents' front porch."

"Oh shit!" Amber laughed. "No kidding! Hang on." She was climbing out of her chair and around the table as she talked. "I'm coming."

"I'm hanging."

She jogged down the hall to the front door and pulled it open. Gretchen, dressed in running clothes, raised her arms for a hug.

"Please tell me we're not going jogging," Amber said as she stepped into Gretchen's arms. She gave her friend a squeeze.

"Oh, hell no." Gretchen shook her head as she backed up. "What's going on with you? Haven't seen you in ages."

"I know." Amber nodded. She stepped back to let Gretchen inside. "It's been...so...crazy. With Ingrid home. Trying to get the estate done." She felt a knot in her throat.

"I know, Amber," Gretchen said softly. "I know. Don't feel guilty-"

"Nathan left me, Gretch." The whisper came on a breath, followed by a sob. Gretchen might have thought she was bullshitting her at first, but when Amber folded, Gretchen stepped in again and put her arms around her.

"What? What happened?"

Amber buried her face in her friend's shoulder and let herself cry. Just for a minute. It felt good to finally loosen the gate on the emotion. But she couldn't lose herself. She still had to go back to Hadley. She had to figure out a way to stay strong for Hadley.

With a deep breath, she backed away again and rubbed at her eyes. Without a word, she turned to head to the kitchen and Gretchen followed her.

"He told me he couldn't do it anymore."

"Do what?" Gretchen watched Amber open the fridge and grab two beers. Really, the thought made her stomach turn. But she thought it might help her to talk. She straightened up and offered one to her friend.

"Waste his time with me." Amber found the bottle opener still in the drawer, though the silverware was gone now. The empty drawer hit her like a fist and took her breath away. Her parents' things were disappearing now. Amber's foundation, her childhood was vanishing, and she wanted to grab for it and hold it in her hands.

She stared at the handful of plastic forks and spoons, what they'd left in case any of them were there and ordered in while they were working. Picked up the bottle opener and handed it to Gretchen.

"You okay?" Gretch lifted her eyebrows as she popped the top off her beer.

Amber hadn't been aware she'd been holding her breath until she let it go on a soft laugh. She started to explain-the way that empty drawer just knocked the breath out of her, that opening a closet door and finding empty shelves made her sick to her stomach-but instead she only shook her head and tossed her hand in a half-ass way to the drawer where she'd found the bottle opener.

"No." Amber shook her head. "No. I'm not."

She considered her lead card. Losing Pop. Of course she'd talked to Gretchen since her dad had passed away, but it was still there. Still so huge inside her. Parents were just always supposed to be there. She and her dad hadn't had some incredible open relationship. They weren't the *Bravermans*, for God's sake. But he was *her dad*. And this was his house, and Amber's memories, good and bad, lived here in this house. She wasn't ready for them to go anywhere else.

Or she could tell Gretchen about Hadley. And Kyle Carpenter. That the guy she'd fucked in the backseat of a car when she was sixteen, the guy who fathered Hadley was so goddamned ordinary that it had made her sick with disappointment. That he wasn't tall and broad-shouldered and good-looking anymore. That he wore glasses over a kind, simple face that could have belonged to a priest. That his hair was thinning and already his pants bagged on him like he didn't even have an ass.

Or she could tell Gretchen that Nathan had told her this morning he wanted kids. That there was no way she could hold onto him now, because he wanted more than her and Hadley.

"Wanna talk about it?" Gretchen offered.

Amber opened her own beer and then dropped the opener back into the drawer. She took a long drink.

"No. Not really."

Was it too soon? Or had she been drowning for so long, she was tired of it? She took a deep breath, reminded herself that she'd come here alone for the express purpose of wallowing in self-pity. That didn't mean she had to dump it all on Gretchen, though.

"Okay." Gretchen nodded. Her sable-colored ponytail swung back and forth as she looked around the kitchen. Since they'd been college friends, Gretchen hadn't been over here often. Amber had lived at home to save her parents money, but she'd tried to balance Hadley and homework with being out and active on campus. She hadn't loved the idea of bringing any friends to her parents' house. Because she hadn't wanted her two worlds to cross. "What're you working on?"

Anyone that had been through a move, whether because of a death in the family or a change in jobs or just a move to a bigger house, was familiar with the mess in Amber's parents' kitchen. Amber wasn't embarrassed for Gretchen to see the boxes and the piles of detritus that had come from the boxes.

She was simply overwhelmed.

"Believe it or not, I am currently on picture duty."

"Picture duty?" Gretchen repeated. She raised her bottle to her lips, but she hesitated. Finally she looked around again and then back at Amber. "You mean, like…you're documenting…the…you're taking pictures-"

Amber blinked and stared at Gretchen silently.

"No." She shook her head. "But…that's an interesting idea."

Gretchen grinned and shook her head. Waved the idea away.

"You don't have time for that." She finally took a drink. "What's your picture duty?"

Amber filed the thought away and led Gretchen to the table.

"This is picture duty." She dropped into the chair she'd been sitting in when Gretchen had called.

"Oh." Gretchen sat down in the chair to her right and reached for one of the perfectly square snapshots. So far, that was all Amber had been able to ascertain from the photographs. They were perfectly square, meaning they'd come from a one twenty six camera. Beyond that, it was anybody's guess what these photos were and who they belonged to. "I love old photographs."

"Well, yeah," Amber shrugged and nodded, "but this is different. This is weird, because I'm the youngest damned one in the family, and I don't know who these people are. I was born in the thirty-five millimeter time zone. Color film. Automatic flash."

"Yeah, but look." Gretchen set the picture down and pushed it across the table toward Amber. "Look at the hair styles. And the bell-bottoms."

"I can't get past the plaid to see the bell-bottoms."

Gretchen grinned and leaned back in her chair.

"You're smiling."

"Am I?" Amber widened her eyes and covered her mouth. "Oops. Won't happen again."

"Please let it happen again," Gretchen said softly. "You're gorgeous when you smile."

"And I'm not otherwise?" Amber teased.

"No, you're scary as hell when you don't smile."

"That's me. Scary as hell Amber."

"How's Hadley taking it?"

Amber took a deep breath. Turned her face away and stared at what appeared to be an old bird's nest outside the window. She wondered how long it had been there. If her dad had ever seen it. If it had been there on a morning when Hadley had been here having breakfast with Pop.

That thought led to memories of her and Ezra sitting here, alone together, at a table for eight, eating Fruit Loops and playing Eye Spy.

"She's not," Amber said softly, "because I haven't told her yet."

"Amber."

Amber avoided Gretchen's eyes, but she shook her head violently.

"Too soon."

"When? Did he leave?"

"Right after you and I got off the phone this morning."

When Gretchen didn't answer her, she finally turned to look at her friend. She braced herself. Gretchen didn't lecture. She didn't judge. And yet, the moment was so full of possibility, Amber assumed she would launch into some sort of tirade. Or maybe that was what Amber thought she deserved. Her family would blame her for this, that was for certain.

"I'm sorry, Amber." Gretchen was sincere. "I thought you guys would be together forever."

Right there would be a good place for her sisters to jump in and tell her she and Nathan could have been together forever if she'd just given in and married him. Thank God Gretchen was different.

"Me too."

"Maybe…" Gretchen sighed and shrugged. "Maybe he'll come back. I know he misses you. He's probably as miserable right now as you are."

Amber gave herself twenty seconds to think that way. To believe Nathan would come back. She shook her head, though, and met Gretchen's eyes.

"He really wants the whole family thing. Marriage. Babies." She shook her head. "Hadley and I aren't enough."

Again, this was where Liv and Ingrid would tell her to marry him and have his babies. Gretchen simply raised her eyebrows.

"It's his loss." She sat forward again. "You and Hadley are precious."

Amber ducked her head as her eyes filled again. She breathed deeply through her nose; her throat was so tight, it hurt. Gretchen laid her hand on Amber's arm. Squeezed gently.

"Let's look at these pictures," she suggested. "We need some Elton John or BeeGees to set the mood."

"I could sing." Amber laughed. She wiped at her eyes as she reached for another photo.

"You don't really wanna do that to me, do you?"

"You're awesome."

Gretchen gave her a sly grin. "So I've been told."

Twenty-Three

Nathan had come back. To talk to Hadley. Amber had never had anything against Mondays, but being that he'd come by Monday evening and broken her daughter's heart, she hated them now. Kinda hated him just a little bit. Hated herself. Kinda hated the world.

Turned out, Hadley kinda hated her. Blamed her. Amber should have known. Everything in Hadley's life that turned out wrong was Amber's fault. Hadn't been enough to have to see him when he'd come by. To notice that even though he was a little pale, even though his eyes were bloodshot, he looked good. When she'd opened the door to him, she'd noticed his forearms. He'd looked apologetic, maybe because at first glance, Amber's heart had soared, and she'd mistaken his visit for him coming back. And it had probably shown on her face. And so he'd sort of shrugged and tucked his hands in the pockets of his jeans and she'd noticed his wiry, muscular forearms and then she'd let her eyes climb up over his chest to his shoulders. She loved his shoulders. His neck.

He'd asked if Hadley was home, and then it had hit her. Why he was there. And probably that had shown on her face, too. She'd probably looked foolish at the least and crushed at most, and she hadn't trusted herself to speak, so she'd simply nodded and stepped back to let him in. She'd hovered for a moment in the living room, wanting to protect Hadley from what he was going to say. It had even crossed her mind that she should stay to defend herself to Hadley and Nathan, because she'd already thought that Hadley would blame her.

She hadn't, though. Stayed. She couldn't just stand there, heart exposed and take more of Nathan's honesty. She couldn't hear him say he loved her, but not enough to stick around if she wasn't going to give him marriage. Children. Instead, she'd gone for a walk. Of course now that her life was falling apart around her, nature was flirting with springtime and sunshine, and

Amber thought if she ever came face to face with Mother Nature she would have some choice words for her.

Nathan had still been there when she'd come home. Ready to leave, but hanging out with Hadley. Probably, he hadn't wanted to leave her alone after what they'd just talked about. Part of her loved him for that. Part of her hated him for doing it to her in the first place. When she'd come back inside, she'd seen him give Hadley a kiss and draw her in for a desperate hug, and then he'd left and Hadley had launched herself off the couch and taken her apart limb from limb.

She'd reminded herself that Hadley was just hurt. Sad. She hadn't meant to be so hateful to Amber. Well, she'd meant it, but only because of how much it hurt her that Nathan had chosen to leave them. Didn't help, though. Hadley had even gone down the road of her father's identity. Told Amber that if she didn't want to tell her who her father was, she'd just pretend it was Nathan. That she'd rather live with Nathan because he wasn't selfish and cold like she was. Amber had given up trying to defend herself. She'd stood with her head bowed, tears on her face, and let Hadley vent. When Hadley had finally quieted, she'd looked up at her daughter. Seen the hurt in her bloodshot eyes, in the tears on her swollen, red face. She'd tried to console her. She'd taken the first step toward Hadley, intending to take her in her arms, but Hadley had read her intentions and screamed at her to leave her alone, and she'd turned from Amber and run upstairs to her room.

That had been two days ago. Hadley hadn't spoken a word to Amber since. They'd lived around each other since Nathan had left. Amber had always considered herself tough. She'd watched her older sisters share their teen years, their secrets and their love affairs and their laughter and tears, and she'd been treated either like a sweet little baby girl or a pain in the ass tagalong. She'd watched her brother walk away from her, from their family one weekend a month since she could remember. She'd always known he was spending time with his other family, though at that tender age, she hadn't understood what that meant. She'd gotten pregnant at sixteen, handled her parents' wrath and disappointment. Her classmates' ridicule. She'd worked her ass off with a newborn at home. Kept up an A average, though by God, there had been times that had been hard.

She'd raised her daughter on her own. Struck out on her own after school and launched herself a hell of a career. Maintained good relationships with her parents, even though she'd never felt safe enough with them to confess Kyle's name to them.

Tough, yes. Invincible, apparently not. Her shoulders hurt. She worried that they might eventually break.

She'd picked Hadley up from school earlier and driven her home. Sometimes, she'd call it quits at the studio then. Just stay home with Amber. Sometimes she worked from home; sometimes they ordered pizza and watched movies. TV. Sometimes they curled up on opposite ends of the couch with books and popcorn or candy. She'd considered ordering pizza tonight. But Hadley had announced that she didn't want Amber to pick her up anymore from school.

"What do you mean?" Amber had asked her after a moment of shocked silence. She wasn't sure if she was more shocked by what Hadley had said or just from hearing her voice after almost two days of punishing silence. "How're you gonna get home?"

"I'll figure it out."

"You're not getting a ride from-"

"I didn't say I was," Hadley snapped. "I'll figure it out."

"Hadley."

"It's nice out now, Mom. I can walk."

"You've been sick-"

"I'm fine. It's not that far. It's warm."
"Had-"
"I wanna be alone."

Amber had pulled into the alley by the house and into her parking spot behind the house.

"Are you ever gonna forgive me?"
"No." Hadley had answered immediately. "No. I'm not."
"Had, I love you. I'm trying to protect you-"
"Funny way to protect me, Mom." Hadley had sneered at her. "Making sure I don't have any dad in my life."
"Hadley-"
"Just lemme alone."

Amber had watched Hadley scramble out of the car and around the back to the backdoor. She'd sat for a moment. Not because she thought Hadley would have a change of heart and come back out to talk to her. But because she'd been so shaky, she didn't think it was safe to drive.

She picked up her phone now. Wondered about Kyle. If he'd talked to his wife. Would it be a step in the right direction? To be able to tell Hadley her real father's name? Could she ever offer that as an olive branch?

No texts or calls. It had been over a week now since she'd talked to him. Told him about Hadley. Sure, it was a lot to take in. A lot to explain to your wife, your preexisting family. But it was a lot for Hadley to wait on. It wasn't fair for Hadley to have to wonder like this.

Then again, Amber had been the one to put Hadley off forever. Amber had made Hadley wait for this piece of information. She couldn't blame Kyle. Actually, she could. Petulant and immature as it was, she *could* blame him, and she did.

She'd been busy this morning. Actually had some foot traffic. Sold a few pieces. It had been slow enough lately that she could have just stayed home with Hadley.

She hadn't, though. Not after that scene in the car. Honestly, she didn't want to be alone with Hadley. Not right now. Hadley's claws were too sharp, and her intentions even more so, and so Amber had come back to the studio. She'd cleaned up a bit. Cut some of the photos she'd taken and developed the week before.

In the absence of phone calls or texts, she tapped the photo icon on her phone screen. Studied the first picture to pop up on the screen. She'd taken it Sunday night. Sitting with Gretchen at her parents' kitchen table. They'd poured over the photos for over an hour. Crushed a couple of beers each. Talked more about Nathan. Gretchen had talked about work. Being irritated with one of the girls who worked at the clinic with her. Amber had told Gretchen about Hadley just coming off of strep throat. Gretchen had told Amber about cutting her foot a few weeks before. The story behind the cut had been so wild-involving a hammer, Gretchen trying to hang a shelf in her closet for belts and purses and scarves, Gretchen dropping said hammer on her bare foot and the claw side cutting her and a trip to the ER-that Amber had demanded Gretchen take her shoe off and show her. Gretch had told her she'd only been able to start wearing a shoe again two days ago, and Amber had shriveled up in sympathy when she'd seen her friend's foot.

Swollen and black and blue. A deeper purple zipper of a cut across the top of her foot, only an inch away from her toes. The zigzag lines of the stitches still there, though the stitches themselves were long gone. Before Gretchen could object, Amber had snapped a picture with her phone.

"Ew." Gretchen had looked up at Amber with a frown. "What's that for? Gonna frame it for Halloween décor?"

"That's a thought," Amber had answered with a nod. She studied it now, though. Paid attention to detail. The puffy area around the cut. The base of Gretchen's toes, also black and blue. Even taken with her phone, it was a visceral, ugly shot, and it made Amber's stomach pitch and nearly quiver in sympathy. The same way you felt that almost electric jolt singe through your body when you saw a little kid who was flat out running fall and skid across pavement, trading skin for blood and even dirt and rocks embedded in the knees.

Stomach still a little queasy, she stood up and wandered around the studio. She didn't want to go home. To Hadley. Without Nathan. Arms folded over her chest, she moved from framed photo to framed photo on her walls. Studied her productions. Her skill. Tried to decide if she'd improved over time, or if she'd stayed the same. Thank God, her trained eye noticed improvements, because she didn't want to be static. Mediocre in the face of the serious competition out there in the big wide world.

Maybe she could just throw herself into her career. To hell with personal relationships. She'd sucked at them as long as she could remember. If Hadley were older, Amber might travel more. She'd considered Rome for a while now. The only way she'd go now was if she took Hadley with her. Normally, not a problem. The thought of her and Hadley on a plane, a long flight, in a foreign country together now was hell. As angry as her daughter was right now, she'd have Amber shredded to bits before they got to the airport to leave.

She was almost finished with the current book, her part in it, anyway. She had a few more photographs to get, but Amber was confident she'd wrap it up within a week or two. Per contract, she was done after this one. Normally, not a big deal. She'd take a walk, snap some pictures, and pitch a new idea. Right now, the way her luck had run out, she worried she might end up penniless and homeless, burning her framed pictures for heat next winter.

Really, she should go home. It was almost five. And it was more than pathetic that she was afraid to go home to her daughter. Fear of rejection couldn't get in the way of parenting. If nothing else, she needed to get home and check on Hadley. Wasn't that long ago the kid was sneaking out and meeting a seventeen-year-old boy to go to parties. She'd even confessed to Ingrid that she liked Kesh, and that they'd made out a time or two, and Amber knew Ingrid was right. She needed to keep an eye on that. Hadley was too young, too immature to be with Kesh. And Amber knew all to well the dangers of hanging out with older boys and doing anything to hold their attention.

Even if Hadley was at home on the couch or in her room, Amber still needed to get home and check on her. Make sure she was doing her homework. Be there just in case. Just in case Hadley broke down. Just in case she decided to forgive Amber.

She'd worn her Nikes today, but now she missed the click of her heels on the floor. The professional persona she usually strapped on in the morning before she left the house. Today she'd been exhausted, and she'd opted for jeans and Nikes and a black pullover hoodie. She was supposed to meet Ingrid and Liv at the house tonight. Then again, they didn't know she'd been over there until after ten Saturday night. She'd stayed even after Gretchen left. Sorted through tons of photos, though when she'd checked the box again on the way out, she'd found tons more still buried.

After a quick check of her dark room, which she locked, and grabbing her purse and phone, Amber headed to the front door. She flipped the lights off and pulled the door closed behind her. Locked it. Eyed the big glass windowpanes that fronted her studio. Decided she needed to wash them. Or have them washed. Maybe she'd do it tomorrow. Physical labor sounded like a good idea right now.

She beeped her SUV unlocked and opened the hatch. Double-checked her equipment. She liked to have her cameras with her, just in case something caught her eye. Satisfied that she had what she wanted, she reached up to close the hatch. Not paying attention, she jammed her finger.

She hissed and pressed it to her lips as she pulled the hatch closed with her right hand. Climbed into the driver's seat and examined her hand. Nothing broken. Not even bruised. Just sore. She started the SUV, eyes still on her hands. Traced with her fingertip the scar from where she'd cut herself when scraping wallpaper with her sisters. Ingrid had been so worried about it. Worried that it might affect her ability to take pictures. She'd cleaned it for her and put a Band-Aid on it, and Amber had thought it was nice to have someone take care of her now and then.

Just a scar now. Kind of ugly, but actually pretty faint. Nothing like what Gretchen would have on her foot.

She put her Passport in reverse and looked over her shoulder. Nothing anywhere around her. She backed slowly out of her parking spot and then put her blinker on for a right turn. Waited for a cop car to pass and then she pulled onto Maine.

She supposed not all scars were ugly. The ones on her ankle? Ugly as hell. She'd broken her ankle playing basketball when she was in high school. She hated looking at her foot. At the white lines from the surgery it had taken to put her back together. The scar on her hand, though. That was nothing. Mom's scars from her surgeries. They'd bothered Mom. Probably the same as Ingrid's scar bothered her. But to Amber, those were beautiful. They were evidence of character. Of staying power. Of winning a battle.

As she drove, she decided she should call Gretchen later and see if she wanted to get together this weekend. Maybe for coffee. Or lunch. Not dinner. Amber wasn't up to being out like that. Around people.

In the evening when people went out for dinner and drinks.

What had Gretchen asked her the other day? Picture duty. If she'd been assigned the task of taking pictures of her parents' house. Sure, they all had pictures taken there, snapshots that chronicled family events, holidays, school dances, what have you. But what about pictures of the house? Of the walls that had housed them. The shell of their childhoods, empty and nearly ready for abandonment.

She raised her eyebrows as she cruised down Maine, mindful of the cop in front of her. She could snap a few. Just for the hell of it. See what they looked like. Nothing in the basement. Or the garage. Jesus, who needed a reminder of how ugly and damp the basement was? Amber had had a nightmare shortly after they'd started the basement shift. Something about a rat and a spider as big as her hand and she wasn't sure, but she thought there was some mold.

Wouldn't be a project she'd pitch. But maybe an offering of some sort to her siblings. Maybe a little bit of comfort to her as they prepared to invite total strangers in to trample their memories and wipe away any residual *Williamsness* in the house.

Twenty-Four

Hadley was on the couch when she got home, but not curled up with blankets and pillows and stuffed animals. Gone was the sweet, snuggly girl that tended to only come out when she was sick. The smartass teen was back, and she was still mad as hell at Amber.

"What're you doing?" Amber had asked her as she walked through the living room to her bedroom. Hadley hadn't answered; that would have been too easy. Instead Amber felt the evil eye on her shoulders. It was warm enough that she was hot in the hoodie, so she yanked it off over her head. Tossed it on the bed. Looked away before her mind had a chance to sucker her in for some of those poison memories of Nathan.

"I said what are you doing?" She stepped back into the living room. Hadley, eyes on her phone, finished typing something before she looked up at Amber. The TV blared some ridiculous people's court show. Amber hated the shit Hadley watched most of the time. Disney movies were okay; beyond that, she sometimes wished they didn't own a TV.

"Texting someone. What's it look like?" Hadley rolled her eyes.

"Who are you texting?"

"Just someone."

"Hadley?"

"Tiffany," Hadley groaned.

"Yeah? If I took your phone right now, I wouldn't find any texts with Kesh?"

"You're not taking my phone." Hadley slid it between her leg and the couch.

"I will if I want to," Amber reminded her. Probably, she should. But she didn't want to. Not right now. She'd always heard the phrase *pick your battles*, but she hadn't ever put it into practice in her own home until Hadley had become a teenager.

"What do you want for dinner?"

"Already ate." Hadley glued her gaze to the TV screen.

Amber felt a pang in that big open hole inside her. She was tired of being alone. She missed Nathan, but she missed Hadley just as much.

"What'd you eat?" She hoped her voice didn't give away her hurt feelings.

"Warmed up some ravioli."

"I thought we'd order pizza."

Hadley tore her eyes away from the TV for just a second. Long enough to look at Amber like she must be stupid.

"I'm sick of pizza," she announced.

Amber sighed. She dragged her fingers through her hair.

"Do you have homework?"

"Just have to read for English."

"What're you reading?"

"Same stupid thing I was reading last week."

That was helpful. Amber nodded. She put her hands in her pockets.

"I'm supposed to meet Liv and Ingrid at the house. But I can stay-"

"I don't care what you do," Hadley said coldly. This time she didn't bother to even look at Amber.

"Hadley, he hurt me, too," she whispered.

"All you had to do was marry him, Mom." Hadley looked at her and shrugged her thin shoulders. Amber saw sadness flash over her face, but it was gone quickly. Replaced with that hard, bitter look that didn't belong on any teenager's face.

"He knows I don't believe in marriage-"

"Yeah, I get it. You were okay with shacking up." Hadley nodded. "You know what I wish? I wish I could live with him. I really do. I'd rather live with Nathan, and deal with being by myself when he's out of town, than live here with you."

Amber blinked and closed her eyes. Covered them with her hand when the tears started to fall.

"Hadley, he wanted-"

"Just go away."

Amber dropped her hand to find Hadley back on her phone. A huge smile spread over her face, but Hadley pulled it back when she looked up at Amber.

~

Ingrid was outside when Amber pulled into the driveway. She let the SUV idle for a few moments, actually considering pulling back out and driving away. She was in no mood to talk to either of her sisters; no mood to deal with anyone right now. And she knew herself well enough to know any attempt either of them made to pull her into any conversation was going to get ugly.

Ugly. Again. Everything about her life these days was ugly.

When Ingrid threw a glance in her direction, she figured that was her cue to get moving. She turned the Passport off, tugged her keys from the ignition and climbed out of the SUV. Not sure she was ready for any questions about anything that might involve her camera and the house, she left all of her equipment in the SUV and carried only her purse and her keys up to the house. Ingrid was dressed like she was: t-shirt, jeans and tennis shoes. Deep in the garage, though that was relative because the garage wasn't particularly deep, Ingrid only looked up and waved at her as she hurried up to the backdoor. Amber wondered if maybe Ingrid had a bug up her butt, too, since she hadn't hurried out to gush anything at her or give her hell for taking so damned long to get here.

She didn't care, though, and she pulled the screen door open and hurried inside. Liv was on her knees at this end of the counter, two different piles at her sides. One looked to be nuts and bolts and screws, mostly greasy and dirty or rusted and bent. The other pile appeared to be a dismantled robot or maybe a chainsaw or even a wood chipper. Amber wondered why Liv hadn't taken that particular mess outside, as it seemed more and more likely they'd be shelling out the cash to replace the flooring in the kitchen.

Liv glanced at her as she stretched her legs to step way over the top of a box. She nearly missed and put her foot in the middle of the pictures she was supposed to be looking at-to what end, Amber didn't know, but if it kept her from tearing apart old oily machinery, she was happy to continue to play along. She came down hard on her right foot, felt a little flash of pain, and wondered at Liv's grunt of a greeting. Had she and Ingrid gotten into it before she'd arrived?

Her ankle throbbed a bit as she hobbled to the table. She muttered a string of cuss words that actually did very little to make her feel better. Tossed her purse and keys on this end of the counter and propped her hands on her hips as she surveyed the piles of pictures on the table. Happy to see they didn't appear to have been touched, she started toward the table, but stopped when she heard her phone beep.

Figuring it was Hadley calling to rip her to shreds yet again, but wishing it was Nathan calling to say hi, she stepped back to the counter and dug her phone out of her purse. A glance at the caller ID sent a wave of nerves through her body.

Kyle Carpenter. Why the hell did he have to call now?

"Hello." She spoke quietly, since to actually get privacy would be to jump back over the big ass box and possibly hurt her other foot and draw Liv's attention to the fact that she was indeed on the phone.

"Amber."
"Yes."
"I um…"

Amber felt her stomach squeeze and turn. She'd scarfed down a cold cut sandwich and an apple before she'd come. Wasn't what she ate or the fact that she'd stood alone in her tiny kitchen to eat that caused her stomach to be so jumpy. It was the situation that had been morphing, going from bad to worse for days.

"Is this a good time?" he finally asked.

Amber almost pulled her phone away from her ear to examine it. *Really?*

"Yeah, it's fine."

"Okay. I just wanted to touch base with you."

Again, she found herself ready to snap at him. *Just say it!*

"Okay." She sat down at the table and hunched her shoulders.

"My wife and I are talking...we haven't made any decisions. I just wanted to let you know where things stand."

Amber closed her eyes and rubbed her fingertips over her forehead. She cleared her throat and willed herself to calm down.

"Okay. Thank you. For calling."

"Have you talked to her? To Hadley?"

"No." Amber ducked her head and shoved her fingers up through her hair. "No, I haven't."

"Thank you."

As if she was considering his feelings and not Hadley's.

"I'll call you the first of next week."

Amber wondered about that. If he and his wife were talking, trying to make decisions, how could he just give her a random date that he would call her? Or was he going to give his wife an ultimatum? Or was there something else going on in their lives that severely impacted the amount of time they'd had together to talk about this?

"That sounds good." She nodded. "Thanks, Kyle."

She ended the call and sat for a moment, her cell in her hand. Her head hurt. Pounded right between her eyes. And at the base of her neck. She opened her eyes and tapped the texts icon on the screen. Looked at the threads there: Hadley, Ingrid, Liv, Gretchen. Nathan. She reread his last text; he'd sent it last Friday when he'd been on his way home. Before their afternoon tryst. Before the family night at Liv and Wade's.

On my way. Love you.

She wondered how you loved someone that way on a Friday and then just turned it off on Saturday.

"Kyle?"

She pushed the home button on her phone when she heard Liv's voice. Closed her hands around it and held it to her chest when she heard Liv stumbling over the box and coming closer.

"Yeah."

"*The* Kyle?"

"Yeah."

"Ingrid said you mentioned seeing him."

"Mm-hmm." Amber took a deep breath. She moved suddenly, stuck her phone in her back pocket and then reached for the nearest pile of pictures. Gretchen had suggested sorting them based on color versus black and white. Size, though the majority of this bunch were the perfect square products of a one twenty six camera, and then by possible subject. Amber couldn't say who most of the people in the photos were, but after studying them closely, she'd been able to pick out familiar faces within this bunch, and she'd sorted them by people present in the photos.

"When?"

Amber sighed. She sensed Liv over her shoulder, possibly looking at the pictures, but she didn't look at her.

"Um. Earlier last week."

"How'd it go?"

"Don't know yet."

Amber felt her shoulders fall when the screen door banged and then Ingrid made her way over the boxes. She wondered why they didn't move them out of the way.

"How long'd you say we have the dumpster for?"

"Jesus, Ingrid, I took a three minute break," Liv muttered.

"I just asked."

"You rented a dumpster?" Amber didn't remember seeing it out there. Then again, she'd made a point of hustling her ass inside so she wouldn't have to talk to Ingrid, so it was totally possible she'd missed it.

"A week."

"Okay." Ingrid sounded agreeable. "Hey Amber."

"Hi."

"I like what you started there. With the pictures."

"Okay." Amber tried to decide how she felt about Ingrid having looked at her work in progress. Decided she didn't give a damn. If they'd been her photos, viewed and studied before she was ready, she'd have been pissed.

"Looks like you've put some time in on that," Ingrid commented.

"Yeah. Came by over the weekend."

"So what do you mean, you don't know yet?" Liv poked her shoulder.

"I mean, I don't know yet."

"Why not?"

"About what?" Ingrid asked. She wasn't standing as close as Liv, but Amber could tell she was on this end of the counter.

"Meeting Kyle."

"He's talking to his wife."

"Oh."

"What does that mean?" Amber snapped. She pushed her chair back, no doubt startling Liv, and stood up. "What does that mean? *Oh?* Like his wife is just-what, Liv? Gonna shut it down? If his wife doesn't want him to meet Hadley, he'll come back to me, tail between his legs, and tell me he can't? Because his wife is his fucking boss?"

Liv raised her eyebrows. Amber seethed with anger when she saw Liv look at Ingrid.

"No." She shrugged. "Didn't mean anything by it."

Amber felt a flash of guilt as Liv turned and made her way back to her own mess on the floor. Ingrid stared at her a moment longer and then she turned and climbed back over the box. Amber sat down again, looked at the pictures, and then stood up to grab herself another handful. Because sorting through these pictures, these god-awful displays of plaid and stripes and bandanas and wide ties was far more important than figuring her own shit out.

Twenty-Five

Because Liv would be at school all day and because Ingrid was probably tucked away in the office at the house she now shared with Luke-or maybe, because the sun was out, she was outside with her laptop and a cup of coffee-Amber dropped Hadley off at school, musing that it was funny how she was good enough to drop her off early in the morning when it was still a little chilly or Hadley was still tired but not good enough to pick her up in the afternoon to take her home, and headed straight to their parents' house. She parked down by the garage again, in an attempt hide from anyone who happened to drive by. Noticed the big blue dumpster as she climbed out of the Passport and went around to the hatch to get her camera out.

A slight breeze stirred the dead leaves in the backyard under the tree. The Maple she used to climb. The Maple Ezra had fallen out of. Amber felt the same breeze tickle the ends of her hair as she stood at the back of the Passport attaching her smaller lens to the body of her Nikon D5000. She'd decided to go with the digital on this shoot. It was a personal endeavor. She might take as few as five shots, and she might shoot five hundred. She could still play with the effects using the digital. Just seemed a bit more economical to go this route. Or maybe it was the memory of her mom finding that she'd shot up a whole roll of film on nothing and giving her hell about wasting the film and the money it had cost them to develop the pictures.

Amber felt a smile playing at the corners of her mouth. Lens firmly attached, she picked up her bag, other lens inside-though she couldn't imagine needing it-and closed the hatch. Beeped the locks shut. She'd left her purse on the floorboard of the passenger side, but she'd stuffed her phone in her pocket. Mad or not, she couldn't ignore her phone on the off chance that Hadley might need something.

She stepped around the back of the Passport and stared at the dumpster for a few moments. Wondered how much junk her sisters had tossed into it last night after she'd left. If she climbed up there now and dropped inside it, could she put the puzzle pieces together and reconstruct her adolescence? Probably not, she decided. After all, they'd bagged up anything worth saving several weeks ago and delivered all of it to the Catholic Charities.

Still. There was junk in the dumpster that had once been her mom and dad's junk. Maybe her junk, though probably not much of it was hers, since it had come from the basement, and she'd avoided the basement like a pit of vipers.

What the hell?

She walked over to the backdoor and set her bag down on the step. Turned around and studied the dumpster. She looked down, twisted the power disc on the camera and then took a few steps away from the door. Lifted the camera to see through the viewfinder and took a few shots. Her idea had been to record the memories. The good, the bad, the *happy to be finished with it*, the *can't let it go because it hurts too much*. The dumpster with the corner of the garage in the background might be considered *happy to be finished with it* or *can't let it go because it hurts too much*.

Probably, if the neighbors were home, they thought she was crazy. Most people didn't spend thirty, forty minutes walking around a huge blue dumpster snapping pictures right and left. She didn't care, though. They still owned the house; she had every right to be here, and if she wanted to spend the whole goddamned day walking circles around the dumpster, she would.

When she was satisfied, at least for now-for the time of day and the lighting in the backyard-she wandered back through the yard, down the side of the garage. She'd worn her hiking boots today, as she'd planned to do exactly this, and she'd thought the yard might be a little muddy and the leaves no one had raked last fall a little slimy. She stopped at the back corner of the yard and turned to look at the house. Leaned back on the fence. Stood up straight and looked back at it. It was rotting. She wondered if it would hold her. Figured it wasn't that far to fall if it didn't and turned around again to lean.

The alley behind the yard was quiet. Then again, there'd never been that much traffic out there. Bicycles, maybe. Skateboards. Kids running around, but never too many cars. She craned her neck around and looked at the houses across the alley. Doubtful any of the same neighbors were still around from when she was a kid. *Well.* Maybe the older folks, but Amber assumed the kids-they would be her age give or take-were probably all gone. She saw the houses through tree limbs still mostly dead, though some were beginning to bud. The houses were old, but Amber felt a stirring inside. Old but beautiful. Like her parents' house. The one directly behind them, though, that one was like the castle on the block. Well-kept. Yard was always well-tended. Even now. She turned again to eyeball the place. Doctor Morgenstern and his wife had lived there when she was a kid. They had five kids. All boys. Two of them had been, like, five when Amber was eight or nine. Real pains in the ass. One of them had been Ezra's age. In fact, Dom had been one of Ezra's best friends when they were kids. She had no idea if Ezra still talked to him. One of the brothers had been a year older than Ez. He'd been the proud owner of beautiful blue eyes and two gorgeous guns and a solid muscular chest. Brian had been Amber's Kesh. She'd found herself alone with him a few too many times. She'd been happy to make out with him, only a little bit embarrassed that he had to have known she was a virgin. She'd only been thirteen or fourteen at the time.

Amber's cheeks warmed as she thought of the things he'd taught her. They'd never had sex, but they'd become pretty well acquainted with each other's bodies. She'd learned enough that she probably seemed pretty experienced by the time she'd lost her virginity when she was sixteen, not long before Hadley was conceived.

She turned back to her parents' house, embarrassed all over again for the silly girl who'd thought Brian Morgenstern had loved her. Humiliated again like it was only yesterday that she'd found him with a girl from school. She'd been skipping-skipping, for Christ's sake-up the sidewalk through his backyard. Thinking about the way she'd kissed him the last time they were together. How he'd guided her, told her what to do. And then she'd heard it. A giggle. And she'd looked up and seen Brian and the girl-Amber later learned her name was Kasie-lounging on the patio. Brian was on the chair, Kasie was on Brian, Brian's hands were on Kasie. Even to Amber, who thought then that Brian had loved her, it was obvious what was going on. Kasie had a class ring on, and suddenly it had all clicked in Amber's lovesick mind that Brian was going steady with Kasie and using Amber because she'd always been willing. Brian had been whispering something in Kasie's ear, and Kasie had been laughing, and Amber had known they were laughing about her. She'd skipped right on around the house, as if Brian would believe she'd come over to see his brothers, and once around the front of the house, she'd hauled ass all the way back around the block to get home. And then she'd done her best to never run into Brian again until he left for college.

She wondered where he was now. She'd think he was an asshole, but then she'd been stupid. She'd never said no. Her eyes took in the perfect house-the trim appeared to be freshly painted, the mortar perfect without pockmarks-and the neat yard. She sighed and turned her back to it. Decided it was a rite of passage. He'd hurt her then. Embarrassed her. But really, he hadn't done it to be mean. He'd done it because he was a teenage boy who was probably horny twenty-four seven. And because she'd been a willing student. Just the same way Blake Keshing was a horny teenage boy, and Hadley was apparently willing to be his student.

Her parents had kept the swing set in the opposite corner of the yard. Not the one they'd had as kids. It had been fresh and shiny for Liv and Ingrid, and it had been rusty and faded from red, white and blue to a pale reddish pink, a slate blue, and a dingy white for she and Ezra. The trapeze bar had hardly moved for them, and when she was ten, she'd been consumed with jealousy over the fact that probably Liv and Ingrid had hung from their knees on it and flipped off it a million times a day. The slide had been cracked when she and Ezra had inherited the damned thing. In fact, Amber had cut the back of her thigh on it when she was younger, and she'd cried like she was going to bleed to death. Her parents had gotten rid of that monstrosity when Liv and Wade announced they were expecting a baby.

Now, even this swing set-Amber supposed it was more appropriately called a jungle gym-was old and forgotten. Grace and Charlie had played on it. Amber remembered that. And Hadley had played on it, too. Amber remembered sitting Hadley at the top of the slide and then holding her chubby little hand and walking beside the slide as Hadley came down. Catching her and sweeping her up in a big hug. Dropping kisses over her sweet little upturned face.

It hurt to think about it. Because Hadley hated her right now. Because baby Samuel would never get to play on it. Because Amber would never have another baby to play on a swing set.

Where the hell had that thought come from? She gave herself a mental shake and lifted the camera again. Snapped off several shots of the jungle gym. Moved closer. Studied the rusty screws. The trampled brown winter grass under the swings. As if the damned thing had been played on recently. She knelt down next to the slide and changed her mind. Scooted closer until her knees were almost touching the faded red plastic and shot a picture up from the bottom. She knew it would suck, so she leaned over to lie on the slide itself. Shot another up from the bottom.

She flipped over to lie on the slide on her back. Winced with the discomfort of having the slide edges in her shoulders. Apparently she'd grown some since she was a kid. From that viewpoint, she took a few pictures of the trees. She found the limbs with their delicate blooms fascinating against the bright blue morning sky.

Several pictures later-she'd covered every piece of the jungle gym, even hanging upside down from that trapeze bar, with a moment of panic when she'd had a hard time wiggling herself back up and wiggling her fat ass out of the trapeze-she moved on to the garage. Shots that showed the whole mess. Close-ups of the broken trim boards around the outside. Water stains. The gutter, filled with leaves. Crossed her mind she could be working for a lawyer documenting a case of neglect. Why hadn't they paid more attention to the house? They could all have helped Pop out. Well, all of them except Ingrid, who'd left them all and not just Pop.

She was thirsty when she came around the front of the garage. She considered going inside. Grabbing a bottle of water. Starting on shots there. But she opted to wait, and instead she pulled her keys from her pocket and unlocked the small door at the side of the building. She coughed as she flipped the light on and stepped inside. It was musty and damp in here, much the same as it was in the basement. Ingrid had made only a small dent in the loads of stuff here, but Amber found that she was happy about that. Gave her more to work with.

She worked without pause. Pictures of old lawn tools. Shears for pruning the bushes. A rake and a hoe that looked like they'd been brought over on the Mayflower. Pop's old self-propelled push mower. Once a bright red, it almost looked pink now. She zoomed in on the gas cap and the pull start. The front left wheel that looked more oblong than round. She climbed up on Pop's work bench at the risk of getting splinters in her butt and took a picture of the ceiling, complete with cobwebs and even a spider or two. That gave her the willies, but at least it wasn't a mouse. She wasn't naïve enough to believe there were no mice here. She just figured if they kept their distance, they'd all be fine. At least long enough for her to get what she wanted. She spun around on her butt and took close ups of Pop's tools on the bench. When he'd been younger, he'd been meticulous with his stuff. But the years had slowed him down, and Amber figured losing Mom-*really losing her*-had handed him a little dose of blasé, and cleaning his garden tools and any other tools, for that matter, had probably seemed unimportant in the big scheme of things.

She set her camera down for a moment. Picked up the old blue bike pump and turned it over in her hands. Thought about that last night at Liv and Wade's house. The bottle of port. The teasing with Liv and Ingrid. The fact that Ingrid and Luke had stayed until midnight. Wished she'd been asked to stay. Thought about that and decided no, she didn't wish that. She wished that it was such an everyday thing-her hanging out at Liv or Ingrid's-that she wouldn't have to be invited, that it would be *expected* of her.

Maybe if she hadn't rushed out last Friday to be with Nathan-*wasn't that pathetic*-maybe she'd have been expected to stay. Maybe it was unfair of her to make everything Liv and Ingrid's fault.

She put the bike pump down and jumped off the bench. Brushed her hands together but they still felt a little grimy. She picked up her camera, intending to head into the house, but she stopped short when she saw her bike. Half covered with a tarp, she'd almost overlooked it. So she wouldn't drop the camera, she moved back to the workbench and set it down. Rubbed her hands on the seat of her pants and walked back over to her bike. Studied it for a moment. Decided she liked it half-hidden by the tarp and went back for the camera. Snapped off a few shots and then put the camera down again. Leaned in to pull the tarp from the bike. Grinned from ear to ear when she saw the ten-speed handle bars. The black tape around the bars had begun to peel away even back when she'd still ridden the bike. She took a close up of the tape. Made the mistake of touching it and getting sticky residue on her hands. Held the camera in one hand to wipe the other off again. And then switched. She climbed over a scooter-who it belonged to she had no idea-and twisted around to get a close up of the silver jagged pedal. Realized Ezra's bike was just behind hers and took a few pictures of it. Decided probably Liv and Ingrid's bikes had long since disintegrated if they'd been left in the garage and finally moseyed back out and locked the door.

~

She'd busied herself until after lunchtime. Still not finished with what she'd wanted to accomplish, she'd decided to call it quits for the day. She still had the last few photos to choose for her latest submission so she'd grabbed a salad at Wendy's, which was really a pain in the ass long drive out of her way, but she didn't care. She'd considered stopping at the house to eat, but she'd decided she didn't want to so she'd gone on to the studio.

She hooked the Nikon on up to her Mac and perused the photos from her morning shoot while she ate the salad. It was good, but the pictures were perfect. Amber was stunned at the flood of memories that assaulted her as she studied picture after picture. Imagined some of them in black and white. Others, she thought were perfect with the morning sun peeking through the treetops and the decayed grass a good contrast. Some of the pictures, the close ups of the rusty screws and the broken trim boards on the garage, whispered to her, though they could have been any rusty screws or trim boards and nothing to do with her family home, with her life.

She'd save them. Might come in handy some day for something.

When she'd finished the salad and a bottle of water, she'd turned the Nikon off and made her way to the dark room. She'd lost hours at her parents' house, and it was the same in the darkroom. She thought it had been around one-thirty when she'd flipped the closed sign and stepped inside. As always, she'd become completely involved with the chemical process. Studying the negatives, watching the pictures emerge on the photo paper. Choosing immediate favorites, immediate nos from the photos she hung to dry.

When she left the dark room, it was close to four. She'd taken Hadley at her word. Hadn't gone to pick her up. She'd kept her phone with her while she worked, but Hadley hadn't called. She had double-checked with her this morning to make sure she had a house key. Naturally Hadley had snapped at her the second time she'd asked.

She'd been preoccupied with her creations, but the second she stepped out of the darkroom, she'd been overcome with guilt. Worry. What if Hadley hadn't made it home? What if she'd walked and someone had picked her up? Irrational, but there ya go. Didn't every mother entertain completely irrational scenes, exhibit neurotic behavior at least once a day?

Not expecting an answer, she texted Hadley. Just asked if she was home. She set her phone on the counter. Checked her Mac to look at her schedule for the next few days. Sometimes she listened to music when she worked, but today she'd been so consumed with the home place pictures she hadn't even thought about it. When she heard the insistent knock on her front door, she nearly jumped off the stool behind the counter.

Her stomach dropped, almost tripped her up as she walked around the counter. What the hell was Ingrid doing here now? Hadley hadn't texted back, so now she was a mix of worried and angry. Even though technically it had only been about four minutes since she'd texted her.

Amber turned the lock and pulled the door open.

"What do you want?" she asked before Ingrid could get a word out.

"Jesus, Amber, what the hell is your problem? I swear to God you're schizophrenic."

"That's a little politically incorrect, isn't it?" Amber folded her arms over her chest.

"What if it is?" Ingrid shrugged.

"Ingrid, I'm busy. I need to get out of here. Get home to Hadley."

Ingrid, half inside the door, eyed Amber like she was worried she'd go ahead and close it. Cut her in half. She groaned and dropped her head back.

"Remember last week? When we did lunch? You said I could browse?"

"Now? Not now! I told you I have to-"

"Not now." Ingrid's voice was cool and smooth. "I was gonna call you earlier. But I've been wandering around downtown, and I thought I'd come in and see you for a minute."

"What're you doing downtown?" Amber asked quickly. She flattened her hand on her throat and rubbed gently. Blinked. If Ingrid had been wandering around downtown, why hadn't she stopped in earlier? Why hadn't she asked Amber to join her?

Ingrid took a breath and started to answer, but she only shook her head.

"Tomorrow. Will you be in?"

"Um." Amber raised her eyebrows. She'd planned to go back to the house.

"Forget it. Too much trouble-"

"No. It's fine. I'll be here."

"What time do you come in?"

"Um. What time do you wanna come in? I can do whatever."

"Nine?" Ingrid suggested.

"Sure." Amber nodded.

"Great. Thanks." Ingrid turned without another word, without making eye contact again, and stepped back onto the sidewalk. Amber started to call out to her, to stop her, but if she did, she didn't know what she'd say anyway. Instead she stood with one hand on the door and one hand on the frame and watched silently as her sister walked away.

Twenty-Six

Amber's phone beeped on her drive home. She waited until she was stopped before she picked it up to look at it. Hadley, saying she was home. Nothing more. Amber felt a little bit relieved just knowing that Hadley was home safely. A little bit ridiculous for getting worked up over it. After all, Hadley had walked home from school before. She also felt more than a little bit nervous about having to go home and deal with Hadley ignoring her all night, but she swallowed that down and tried to ignore it. Little bit like trying to forget an ulcer, though, because the past week with Hadley burned inside her. Either Hadley would continue with the cold shoulder or put it aside long enough to tear into her again about how it was her fault that Nathan had left them.

She didn't text back. Just tossed her phone on the seat and drove the rest of the way home in silence. She might have missed the music earlier at the studio, before Ingrid had come in. But right now, her head was pounding and even the quiet inside the Passport, Amber supposed it was only the sound of her own breathing, was killing her.

The living room was quiet and dark when she opened the door and stepped inside. Amber tossed her keys and purse on the dining room table as she walked through. She stopped at the foot of the stairs and listened. She didn't hear Hadley, but she heard Hadley's music. Something gut-wrenching. Zedd? She wondered. 'Clarity' maybe. She stood for a moment staring up the steps, seeing only the light in Hadley's room, wondering which of her daughter's personalities would greet her. Wondered if Hadley was really up there. If she was alone.

Only one way to find out, she supposed.

She made her way upstairs, no particular hurry. She wasn't exactly careful to be quiet, but it just happened that she didn't hit any of the creakier steps. The music changed when she was half way up. Florence and the

Machine. Amber found herself nodding enthusiastically at the improvement.

When she hit the top step, she found Hadley sprawled over her bed, an open text book under her nose. She took advantage of the moment, drank in the sight of her daughter in repose. Her hair was pulled back in a loose, messy ponytail, her face sweet and soft. One leg was stretched toward the end of the bed, foot curled around the edge of the side of the mattress and the other was bent at the knee, foot bobbing in the air, though not in rhythm with the music.

Amber felt a little flash of guilt for intruding, but before she could say anything, Hadley did.

"I'm studying."

Amber waited for Hadley to lift her eyes from the book. When she did, Amber nodded.

"'kay."

"I'm hungry."

"Did you walk?" Amber ignored her comment.

"Yeah. Walked part of the way with Tiff."

"You were alone then?"

Hadley looked back at her book, but she nodded. Amber hated to think of Hadley walking home alone. Not necessarily because she was worried. More so that alone time invited thinking time. Not to mention that they'd all taken long walks all over town before Nathan left.

Amber watched her struggle to avoid looking at her, saw the moment when she caved and finally, blinking rapidly, glanced at her again.

"Still hate me?" Amber asked softly.

"Kinda." Hadley nodded.

Amber took a deep breath. She'd expected as much. Still hurt to hear it. She rubbed the back of her neck and turned back to the steps.

"I'm hungry."

"What do you want, Hadley?"

"Wings."

"Wings?" Amber repeated. "Why can't we-" She cut herself off when she saw the cold mask fall back over Hadley's face. "Okay. Fine."

Hadley stared at her a moment longer.

"Anything else?"

"Salad."

"Wanna ride with me?" Amber asked hopefully.

Hadley stared at her long enough to roll her eyes. "No."

Amber waited for her to say something else. To change her mind. When she didn't, she simply nodded and mumbled that she'd be back and headed downstairs.

She retraced her steps, arguing with herself. She was spoiling Hadley. Then again, kind of too late to worry about that, wasn't it? She snatched her keys and purse from the table and headed back out to the Passport. Dialed the number of Buffalo Wild Wings as she climbed inside. When they asked if they could put her on hold, she mumbled a yes and then dropped her head back to rest on the seat until the girl came back on.

Amber asked for the small order of spicy garlic wings and two garden salads with ranch dressing. She nodded as the girl totaled her order and then hung up and dropped the SUV into reverse. Eased down the alley to Chestnut and then zipped down the street, irritated to find herself alone in her SUV again.

Alone. Alone. Alone.

She reached out and punched the radio power button. Commercial for a local appliance outlet. She rolled her eyes and tapped the first preselect button. She sighed and let her hand drop to her lap when she heard Jason Aldean singing. She wasn't particularly a country music fan, but she didn't feel like spending the entire drive searching for something worthy.

At Eighteenth, the music had changed to something by Eric Church, she thought. Rather than continue listening, she turned the radio off again. She thought she heard someone honk at her as she coasted down Chestnut between Twenty-Sixth and Thirtieth. Too tired to care, she didn't even bother to look around. She slowed to a stop at the T at Thirtieth and Chestnut, looked to her left and when she saw that it was clear, she made a right hand turn and hit the gas. Hit a red light at Broadway and sat in silence, thinking about Nathan.

Had he even thought about her? It had been almost a week since he'd left her, and except for him coming over to break up with her daughter-to tell her daughter *sorry, I'm not going to be in your life anymore, either*-she hadn't heard a word from him. Was she that forgettable?

She followed a white minivan through the intersection on the left turn signal and then zoned out again as she drove Broadway out to Buffalo Wild Wings. Thank God the lot wasn't too packed. Hopefully she could get in and grab her order and get out quickly. She swung into a parking spot reserved for carry out customers, cut her engine and climbed out, pocketing her keys as she did so.

Just as she was about to reach to open the door, it flew open and a young guy and a little boy hurried out. The guy, who carried their paper bags, was chuckling at the little boy, who apparently was trying to be the *Incredible Hulk*. Amber laughed softly when the young guy looked up at her, and she sidestepped them and slipped inside. It took a moment for her vision to adjust when she stepped inside the restaurant. The sun was still bright outside, and it was darker, of course, inside. She blinked and then stepped up to the counter. Gave the girl there her name and was asked to hang on a second.

Of course it wasn't ready yet. Amber wandered over to the eating area and looked up at a big screen TV. She flinched and dragged her gaze away. Nothing like MMA fighting while eating. Another TV showed a college lacrosse game. She sighed and let her eyes roam the tables quickly before looking up at yet another TV screen. NBA.

Marginally better than MMA fighting, anyway. But her eyes wouldn't cooperate, and she was looking over the tables again.

Her heart beat painfully hard, and then the hole in her stomach yawned just a bit bigger, and Amber wondered how much of herself she could lose this way before she simply vanished. If she were to unbutton her blouse right now, would her abdomen still be there, all in one piece?

Nathan. And a couple. And.

Another woman. Sitting with him. On his side of the booth. Amber tried to look away before he noticed her. But she couldn't make herself do it. The woman-girl? She looked pretty damned young-was pretty. A short brown wedge cut, pretty eyes from what Amber could tell and then shit! Nathan looked up and saw her.

Maybe she hadn't truly believed it. Not until right at this moment. Maybe she'd harbored the hope that he was thinking it over and that he would change his mind and come back to her. Maybe even though her brain had denied that, her heart had secretly believed it. Almost paralyzed with hurt, she backed away and stepped closer to the counter. He'd made a move to stand up. Amber fixed her eyes on the girl at the counter and prayed that she'd get her order ready now.

"Hey."

She didn't look at him. Instead she opened her billfold and pulled her debit card from it. Handed it to the girl-her nametag said Chelsea-and stood completely stiff, waiting for the girl to finish the transaction. Waiting for Nathan to leave her alone.

"Amber."

She looked at him then. Mistake number two hundred and twenty-three maybe? Her eyes filled. She blinked and looked away. He looked upset, but then he was the one with the date, so he couldn't be that upset, could he? He'd left her, so it wasn't like he was cheating.

He just wasn't hers anymore. Owed her absolutely nothing.

The girl-Chelsea-oblivious to the tension on Amber's side of the counter handed her the bags and her debit card. Amber didn't even bother to put the card away. She mumbled a thank you to the girl, though it came out more like a warped whisper, so she didn't know if the girl had heard her. Without a word to Nathan, she turned to walk out. He followed her. Even had the nerve to get the door for her.

She couldn't get to her keys now, with the bags and her billfold in her hands. Nathan took the bags for her. She pulled the keys from her pocket, unlocked the Passport and tossed her billfold and debit card in. Nathan lifted a hand to stop her before she could take the bags from him.

"You're already seeing someone else?"

The sharp words came out sideways. Their eyes met, but his were so kind and so warm, that she had to break the connection. Embarrassed for him to see her crying, she covered her eyes with her hand. Turned away from him.

"It's just-Amber." He touched her shoulder.

"Who is she?"

"Nicole." He sighed. "Her name's Nicole."

She shook his hand off. "How long have you been seeing her?"

"No, Amber, it's not like that," he argued. "Will you look at me? Please?"

She took a quick breath and turned to look at him. Took a step away from him when he reached for her again.

"It's a blind date. That's all."

Maybe those words should've made her feel just a little bit better. Maybe it shouldn't hurt as bad if he hadn't been cheating on her. Still hurt like hell, though, that he could end it with her last weekend and be out with someone new tonight.

"I mean…" He floundered. Looked around, as if he was casting about for the right words to come to him out of nothing. "It's not even a date. I tagged along for dinner. And she tagged along…"

"Yeah. Sounds like a blind date." Amber nodded. She swallowed hard. Stared at Nathan for a moment. "I gotta go. Hadley's waiting on me."

"How is she?"

He cared. She knew he honestly cared about Hadley. But still, it hurt to know she was going home to her daughter who had been crushed when Nathan walked out, to more verbal abuse or maybe back to the silent treatment, and Nathan was going back inside to friends. To an attractive woman. To a fun evening. Maybe they would ask who he'd been talking to. Amber hadn't paid enough attention to see who the other couple was, but odds were she'd been out with them if they were Nathan's friends. Maybe Nathan would tell them, and they'd all get a laugh at her expense. *Ex-girlfriend.* Even that sounded somehow less deserving of all the heartache she was carrying around than *ex-wife* might.

After all, being that they weren't married, Nathan had apparently moved on pretty quickly.

"She hates me, Nathan." Her voice was hoarse. "My fault you left her-"

"I didn't leave her. I promised her I would always be there for her-"

"Yeah?" Amber took a swipe at her eyes. "She wants to move in with you. Because she hates me. Because I'm selfish."

The word hung in the air between them.

"Did you say that to her?" she finally asked. "I know you think that of me, but did you say that to her?"

"Of course I didn't."

Amber shrugged. She swallowed another knot of tears.

"Maybe you did." She looked over his shoulder, wondering if his friends were looking for him. "I don't think you ever loved me," she whispered. "Not if you can walk away and be out with someone new this soon."

"I told you it's not really a date. It's just dinner."

She couldn't hold it in any longer. The sob exploded out of her with her next breath. Nathan reached for her, but she put her hands up to hold him off.

"Maybe I'm selfish, Nathan," she whispered, tears on her lips, "but I loved you so much." She shook her head. "So much."

"Amber." He reached for her, caught her hand. But she shook him off and climbed into the SUV. He stepped back, but he stood at the curb and watched her drive away.

She glanced at the to go bags as she pulled out of the lot. Easier to look at the food that would now be wasted than to watch him get smaller in the rearview mirror.

Twenty-Seven

Hadley met her at the door and took the bags. Either she didn't notice Amber's tears, or she simply chose not to acknowledge them. Amber stood in the kitchen and watched Hadley put her wings on a plate and grab a can of soda from the refrigerator. Normally, she'd at least try to talk her out of sitting in the front of the TV to eat. Hadley met her eyes boldly, obviously a challenge, as she walked out of the kitchen with her food, but Amber didn't say a word. She was still standing there staring at the fridge when Hadley came back for her soda.

"Aren't you eating?" Hadley finally asked. She nodded at the salad on the table. The half of the wings order she'd left for Amber.

"No." Amber shook her head.

"Why not?"

"Not hungry."

"But you ordered food." Hadley eyed her suspiciously. "What happened?"

"Nothing." Amber's voice was heavy with anger. "Just not hungry."

Hadley nodded and finally shrugged. "Whatever."

Amber watched her walk out of the kitchen again. She leaned against the counter, nowhere to go. She'd have to go through the living room to get to her bedroom. Pass by Hadley. She wasn't in the mood for it. She wasn't in the mood for anything.

Still stunned that Nathan was already dating, Amber took a deep breath and went outside. She stuck her hands in her pockets and wandered around to the front of the house. Saw through the living room window that Hadley was watching some game show. Glad she hadn't gone through the living room-she couldn't imagine the inane chatter on a game show right now-she stepped up onto the front porch and grabbed a folded lawn chair that had been propped against the house for the winter.

She unfolded it, eyed it carefully to make sure it would hold her, and gingerly sat down. When the chair seemed firm, she relaxed into it and turned her attention to the street in front of the house. What the hell was she doing here? The place was a dump. She could do better. She'd found it when she was just getting started in the business, and it had been affordable and comfortable, and she'd never given a thought to change.

She could start looking for something new. But she wasn't sure how Hadley would feel about it. Wasn't sure she wanted to talk to Hadley right now to find out how she felt about it. Wasn't sure she was ready to deal with anything like a move, anyway. Not right now.

Nicole. Nicole with a cute haircut and pretty eyes.

Amber wondered how long he'd really been seeing her. If it was all just an innocent set up tonight or a really honest to God planned blind date or if he'd been seeing her for a while. Maybe he'd found Nicole a while back, and he'd started a fling with her, and Nicole had just suddenly let him know she was open to more than blowjobs and kinky sex. Maybe Nicole had suddenly decided she wanted kids, and maybe two months from now Nathan would have a baby on the way.

She rested her head on the back of her chair when she felt tears dripping from her chin. Before Nathan, she'd guarded her heart. Guarded Hadley from the guys she'd dated, guarded her own heart from them. Why had she fallen so hard for him? Why had she allowed it? Like she could have stopped it from happening. They'd gone to dinner for their first date. Dinner, not hot wings. He'd taken her to Pier Nineteen, and they'd gotten the giggles over a man two tables away.

Amber couldn't really even remember what they'd found so funny. Seemed like the guy had said something that sounded stupid, but Amber had been in the middle of saying something to Nathan, and they'd both looked at the guy-funny, she could remember he was wearing a red knit shirt and black Dockers, but she couldn't remember what about him had made them laugh-and Amber had stopped midsentence, and they'd looked at each other and lost it.

They'd shared a bottle of chardonnay, and Amber hadn't been much of a wine drinker until then, and the wine or Nathan had gone to her head and her heart. She'd ordered crab cakes, and Nathan had linguini, and they'd held hands when they walked outside after dinner. He'd asked about her as they walked.

Tell me one thing you like about yourself.

She'd opened her mouth to answer him, but she'd had to stop and think. It wasn't often she thought about herself like that. About what she liked about her life. Obviously Hadley was the best thing she'd ever done, but she hadn't wanted to share anything with him about her daughter. Not then.

She'd finally told him she liked that she was ambitious. That she'd established a good career even after a teen pregnancy. When she looked up at him, he'd smiled and nodded, like he approved of her answer.

"What about you?" she'd asked him.

"Um." He squeezed her hand as they crossed into the park to the south of Pier Nineteen. "I like that you radiate energy-"

She laughed and reached with her free hand to touch him. Splayed her fingers over his arm and shook her head.

"About you? What do you like about yourself?"

"That I'm holding hands with you right now."

"Nathan."

They'd laughed some more, and then finally, he'd nodded and put on a serious face. "Okay. I like where I am in life. I like what I do." He'd told her over dinner that he was a contractor and did a lot of big construction jobs. Hence the nice arms and shoulders, she'd decided.

"Do you like the traveling?"

He considered her question and finally nodded. "I do. Right now. Can't say I wanna do it forever, though. What about you?"

"Dunno yet," she said with a straight face. "I'll let ya know what I think of your traveling after we have another date."

He grinned.

"Traveling. I'm guessing you travel some for your career."

She pursed her lips. "I do. Sometimes too much. I don't like being away from my daughter." On the rare occasions Amber went out of town for business, Hadley had either stayed at Pop's place or with Liv and Wade. Even knowing she was well-cared for at either place, Amber didn't like leaving her. "And sometimes I wish I could travel more."

"Would you take her with you? Your daughter?"

"I'd love to." Amber had nodded.

"Okay. One thing you'd like to change."

"Oh man." She'd stared at him with wide eyes. Laughed nervously. "I wish...I had more to give Hadley. A family-"

"That's not you. One thing you'd like to change about yourself."

"Um." She frowned as they walked. "I'd like to lose ten pounds."

"Where exactly could you afford to lose ten pounds?" He'd stopped walking suddenly and when she'd kept going, he pulled her back to him. Slipped his free hand over her waist and rested it on her back. Eyes locked on hers, he'd shaken his head. "Nothing physical. What would you change?"

She'd noticed then that his eyes weren't really just brown. They were a warm brown with flecks of gold in them. The intimacy between them a little overwhelming, she'd dragged her eyes from his only to realize she was staring at his soft, full lips. Thinking she'd like to kiss them.

"I'm not a very forgiving person," she'd finally said. "I wish I could change that."

Amber blinked Chestnut into focus now. She'd forgotten that. She'd told him that on the first date. Just before he'd leaned into her and kissed her. A soft, sweet kiss that touched her lips and her heart and hinted at so much more to come.

He was a first date kisser. She wondered now if tonight had really been a first date for Nathan and Nicole, if he'd kissed her goodnight. If it had been that same sweet kiss he'd given her that first night. Or if he'd changed. If they were at his place right now, burning up the sheets.

She hadn't changed much. Maybe she'd dropped the ten pounds she'd wanted to lose, but she was still unforgiving. Still selfish. Still scared to let herself go and be happy.

No wonder he'd left her.

~

Sleep hadn't come easy, but that had come as no surprise. She'd tossed and turned and finally dropped off well after midnight. But she woke up around three and lay awake until after five. Turned her alarm off and climbed out of bed. Hadley had been glued to the TV while she had her dinner last night, and then she'd stuck her head outside and grunted something about studying and disappeared up to her room. Most of the time if she was studying for a test, Amber would check on her. Ask if she wanted a snack. If she wanted her to quiz her on anything. Last night, Amber hadn't moved from the porch until after nine.

At least Hadley had taken her stuff to the kitchen. Amber had figured she'd come inside and find Hadley's plate and soda can on the coffee table, or worse, the couch. She'd found them in the sink. And left them there to deal with now. When she found the mess in the kitchen, Amber reminded herself that leftover heartache was no better than fresh. She should've just cleaned everything up last night so she wouldn't have had to walk into the kitchen to find the mess she'd left.

She'd wanted sweats and Nikes today when she got out of her shower. But she wouldn't let herself do it. Couldn't let herself do it. She was her own boss on a day to day basis, and she was feeling low enough right now to let everything get away from her. Best to try and keep her professional life separate from her personal life. She'd tied an apron on over her lightwash jeans and black blouse. Laughed at herself for having an apron; she'd never actually used it for cooking, because mostly she didn't cook, and right now, she would be hard pressed to say where she'd even gotten the damned thing.

While she worked, she heard Hadley come downstairs and take her own shower. Too late, she realized she hadn't made coffee and sure enough, within thirty minutes, Hadley-dressed in jeggings and an American Eagle sweatshirt (Amber envied her the comfort clothes)-appeared in the kitchen bitching that there was no coffee made. Amber had largely ignored her, but when they had made eye contact, she'd only shrugged and turned away, because honestly, she didn't give a damn that Hadley didn't have coffee this morning before school.

The drive to school had been painfully quiet again, but this time, Amber was so wrapped up in the thought of Nathan with another woman-she had him married to Nicole by the time she got up this morning-that she didn't even notice Hadley's hateful anger directed at her. She'd only nodded when Hadley had told her she'd walk home from school again today, and then Hadley was gone, and the silence in the SUV at least became less threatening.

Head pounding from too little sleep, she leaned forward and looked around the floor of the SUV for her sunglasses. Not finding them, she muttered something about the sun, but quickly took it back being that it was finally beginning to feel like spring. She gave up her search for the sunglasses as she drove westward on Maine. Pulled into her parking spot and climbed out of the SUV. She smoothed her jeans down and then reached back in for her purse. Closed the door and walked around to the hatch. She'd intended to get her camera, but she thought better of it, and beeped the locks before she went inside.

Running on no sleep, Hadley's anger filling her from head to toe, and wondering if Nathan had kissed that girl last night, if anything else had happened, she was in no mood to deal with Ingrid today. It wasn't going to go well, and if Amber was willing to recognize that over an hour before Ingrid was even there, it seemed like a particularly bad idea.

She unlocked the studio door and stepped inside. Flipped the light on, but kept the closed sign turned to the street. She didn't officially open until nine, and that, of course, was on days when she was actually in the studio and not on a shoot. Her heels clicked on the old, warped wooden flooring as she crossed the room to toss her purse and keys on the counter.

Restless, she drummed her fingers on the counter. Took a moment to look at the pictures under the glass. Found one of Ezra and Shay that she'd completely forgotten she'd taken. Just a candid shot from a night out before they were married. Shay looked beautiful. More than that, she looked happy. Amber had almost forgotten there had been a time when her sister-in-law was ever happy.

What she wanted to do right now, instead of twiddling her thumbs while she waited for Ingrid to get here, was go to her parents' house and get back to her project. But she'd have about an hour, and she knew better than to rush any picture session, whether for a book or a personal project. She was tempted to leave. To go take some pictures. It had helped yesterday. Being at the house and taking pictures had helped take her mind off Nathan. And Hadley. She knew without question that being there alone would be soothing. Being there alone, working on the pictures, the memories she wanted to share with her siblings would go a long way toward calming her down.

But she could already imagine the phone call. Ingrid would call her to see where she was. Maybe she'd assume Amber was out grabbing coffee or something, and she'd call to see how long she was going to be, and then Amber would have to tell her she was busy working and couldn't come today. Ingrid would be pissed. After all, she had probably taken a day away from writing or editing or whatever it was she was doing right now, and she'd be pissed losing a day for no reason.

Amber sighed. She went to the back of the studio, to the corner where she kept a small table and two folding chairs. A coffee maker. No fridge, no microwave. She didn't want a mess there, but there were days when she desperately needed the caffeine and so she'd allowed herself the table and coffee maker. She assumed Ingrid would want coffee, too, so she made eight cups. Thought about Hadley. Wondered how she was doing. She hated that she was hurting through this, and she hated even more that she was angry with Amber and wouldn't let her in.

Hated that right now her heart hurt so much, it was so fucking hard to breathe that she could hardly feel for Hadley. It made her stomach hurt, the guilt for not keeping Hadley first in her mind, in her heart. Then again, maybe she was drowning, and she had to save herself first and then find a way to help Hadley.

Either that or she needed to find help for Hadley.

Instantly, Kyle's face was in her mind, and just as instantly, her stomach heaved, and she thought she might throw up. Except that she hadn't eaten since that salad she'd eaten from Wendy's yesterday afternoon.

What if Kyle decided to step up? What if his wife allowed him to step up? And he came rushing in and saved Hadley from heartache, like a knight in shining armor. Hadley had never really been the shrinking violet princess type. Then again, if ever she had a reason to be that damsel in distress, this was it.

She turned on her computer and sat down. Tucked her chin to her chest and rubbed the back of her neck. Without looking, she curved her hand over her mouse. If she couldn't be over there right now taking pictures, she could at least go over what she'd done yesterday. Maybe start sorting the pictures out. First sort might be the possible pictures she could use for her siblings versus the ugly stuff. Then maybe she could sort garage, yard, exterior of the house, and the swing set.

Finally looking up at her screen, she moved the mouse to the blank box to type in her password and then tapped it in. Started to move the cursor to the new file from yesterday, but a knock on the door made her jump.

She groaned out loud as she stood up. Considered praying for strength to get through the day with Ingrid, but she figured God or fate or whoever was in charge up there wouldn't particularly want to hear from her either. Not these days.

"Hey." Ingrid flashed her a smile when she pulled the door open to let her in. "Luke and I went for breakfast. Do you mind if I'm early?"

Amber shook her head, but she bit her lip to keep from saying anything. Because what she was thinking was that if Ingrid was here early, maybe she would get out early, too.

"Where'd you go?" she asked as Ingrid stepped inside.

"What?" Ingrid's cheeks were a little pink, and Amber could smell cold air and sunshine on her. A little bit jealous, Amber stepped around and flipped the lock again. Ingrid wore the look of a gorgeous woman in love, and Amber turned away and walked back to the counter before Ingrid could even answer her.

"Breakfast?" Amber heard the sharp edge in her voice. Almost cringed, waiting for Ingrid to hear it and remark on it.

"Java Infusion." Ingrid set her purse on the counter and slipped her jacket off her shoulders. Amber was thankful her back was to Ingrid, otherwise she'd have seen the color drain from her face. God knew, Amber had felt it.

"Oh." Amber looked at Ingrid over her shoulder. "I...made coffee."

"Good." Ingrid nodded. "I had juice."

"Juice?" Amber repeated. That didn't sound like her sister. "What? Are you cleaning things up so you can get pregnant?"

Ingrid drew back as if Amber had taken a swing at her.

"Or are you already pregnant?" Amber nearly choked on her own sarcasm.

"Never been pregnant in my life, Amber," she said softly, and Amber winced and looked away, because obviously never having been pregnant in her life was a sore spot for Ingrid.

She glanced at her computer, relieved to see the screen had gone dark. Stupid, as she hadn't even clicked on her file yet. But it was her business, and she wasn't ready to invite Ingrid inside.

"Do you want-" She started back to the table, but she spun around to look at Ingrid as she walked.

"Please." Ingrid nodded.

Amber's hands shook as she grabbed two mugs and flipped them over. Ingrid had gotten really pissed at Hadley not long after she'd come home. Not long after Pop's funeral. Hadley had apparently been nosing through Ingrid's email and text messages. Amber supposed Ingrid had a right to be angry about it. She'd laughed it off with Ingrid, but she'd laid into Hadley later that day.

She poured the coffee and then picked up the non-dairy creamer she kept by the coffee maker. Ingrid stepped up beside her and took it from her.

"How's Luke?"

"He's good." Ingrid smiled. "Still talking about that trip to Colorado."

"Do you really think his daughter wouldn't like you?"

"I have no idea what to think about it," Ingrid answered honestly. "Never dated anyone with kids of any age."

Amber took a sip of her coffee and wondered again how the hell she was going to get through an eight hour day side by side with Ingrid.

"So. Walk me through a typical day."

"Really?" Amber frowned. "It's not too exciting."

Ingrid shrugged.

"You gonna have a character be a photographer? Do I at least get to be the killer?"

Ingrid lifted only her eyes from her mug to look at Amber. "You wanna be the bad guy?"

"Seems fitting."

"I dunno, Amber. I just…this is what I do."

"Gather intelligence and then assimilate it and decide what you're gonna use."

Ingrid considered Amber's summary of her research process and nodded.

"Um." Amber looked around and shrugged. "Some days I spend here. Some I'm out doing the fun stuff."

"So the taking of the pictures is the fun stuff?"

Amber almost said yes. "Well. Some days…yes. I love being out on my own. Um…especially the…nature shots. The architecture shots-"

"You don't like people."

"I don't." Amber laughed. "I do. I like candid shots of people. Look." She forgot herself, forgot who she was talking to, and laid her hand on Ingrid's wrist. "C'mere."

"Coming." Ingrid nodded. Amber led her back to the counter. Located the picture of Ezra and Shay she'd been looking at only a few moments ago.

"They had no idea I was standing so close or that I had the camera."

"Mm." Ingrid nodded slowly. Amber wondered what she was thinking. "That's a beautiful picture." She looked up at Amber. "I mean, I totally get what you're saying. Catching a moment of honest emotion rather than a fake, posed shot."

"Exactly." Amber bit her lip.

"But…" Ingrid tapped the glass. "She looks so real there."

"Real?" Amber repeated.

"Yeah. I mean…you look at her now, and she's like a shadow of that woman. What happened to her, Amber?"

Amber raised her eyebrows when she realized Ingrid was seriously asking that question, hoping Amber would answer.

"I dunno," Amber lied. "Anyway. I love being out…in the field. Taking the pictures."

"But?"

"There's something…magical…about developing the film, too. Seeing the images come to life while you're watching. Seeing proof that the shot you just knew was going to be perfect really is perfect."

Ingrid nodded.

"When you're here, do you do anything else?"

"Well, I sort through any digital work on the computer. I do the not so fun stuff like payables and receivables and-"

"I hate that stuff. The business side of things."

Amber perched her butt on the edge of the stool behind the counter.

"Do you ever do shoots here? Like…you don't do portrait photography, but do you do shoots here?"

"What do you mean?"

"Well…" Ingrid shrugged. "Like if you're doing a book on kitchen utensils, would you take pictures here of that stuff?"

"Sometimes. Sometimes, I'd use my stuff. Or Mom's stuff. Or my neighbor's stuff. Or Gretchen's stuff."

"Do you do photo shoots for advertisements?"

"Like local businesses and products?" Amber asked.

"Yeah."

"I used to."

Ingrid took a drink of her coffee. Amber watched her wander away, leaving her cup on the counter. There was nothing in the studio that Ingrid shouldn't see, nothing a client or customer off the street wouldn't see if he or she wandered in to look around. Like Nathan had.

And yet, it made Amber uncomfortable to sit and watch Ingrid perusing her place, to think she was making mental notes about Amber's routines. Maybe Amber herself. Maybe Ingrid's character would be a snotty little sister type who wished bad things to happen to good people.

The silence in the studio felt awkward, and Amber tried to think of something to say to her sister. Anything she thought of would probably come off as forced or fake. Small wonder.

"So…" Ingrid was looking at a poster print Amber had framed and Nathan had hung on the wall. Amber watched Ingrid study the print, her arms folded over her chest. Amber had taken the picture when she and Nathan were in Sedona together, maybe a year ago. The

Red Rocks Church, taken at an odd angle, so it sort of felt like you were falling as you looked at it.

Amber leaned over and rested her elbows on the counter. Rubbed her eyes. Waited for a question about the picture. Maybe just Ingrid asking if she'd taken it. If it was indeed the Red Rocks Church. When she'd gone to Arizona.

"What's the status with Kyle Carpenter?"

Twenty-Eight

Stunned by Ingrid's question, Amber stared at her silently for a moment. She glanced at the poster, over Ingrid's shoulder, still warm with that connection to Nathan. Felt the cold steal in as Ingrid stared at her.

"What?" Amber sat up again and rubbed her elbows. Reached for her coffee mug, found it nearly empty, and scooched off the stool.

"Really?"

Amber ignored Ingrid as she went back to the corner table to pour herself more coffee.

"It's…"

"Can I ask you something?" Ingrid sounded uncertain.

Amber raised her eyebrows and turned to look at Ingrid.

"Why are you asking permission to ask me something? Most of the time, you just aim and fire."

"Aim and fire," Ingrid repeated. "Nice."

"What?" Amber took a sip of her coffee as she came back to the counter. She perched on the edge of the stool. "I met with Kyle…last week. He's supposedly talking about…this…about Hadley…with his wife."

Ingrid, hands in her pockets now, wandered back to the counter. Met Amber's eyes boldly, yet Amber could see it cost her. Her shoulders were hunched a bit, as if to protect herself. Apparently, from Amber.

"Do you wish I wouldn't have come back?"

"It was so weird-" Amber stopped talking when she realized what Ingrid had asked her. Confused, a little hurt and not sure why, Amber shook her head. "What?"

"Would you be happier if I was still in Chicago?"

"No."

"I mean…did my coming home…mess you and Liv up?"

"No."

Ingrid nodded slowly, but she didn't look convinced. She took a deep breath.

"Have you ever…" Amber switched her brain back to Kyle, needing now, to talk about it. To share her fears with someone. With Ingrid. "I don't even know…what I wanna say…just…been disappointed in yourself?"

Ingrid trailed her hand over the glass as she edged her way down the counter, eyes on the pictures under the glass.

"You're so hot and cold, Amber," she whispered. "You make it so hard for me to read you."

Amber caught her breath. Felt her throat getting tight. She swallowed hard, dragged her fingers through her hair.

"I mean…when I was sixteen," she continued, scared of confronting Ingrid, and still wanting to confide in her. "He was…so…hot…ya know? And the other day…I mean…it was like…he looked like someone's dad. He looked like the neighbor dad or the dad who sits in front of you at mass and wears boring clothes and has no ass, so his pants bag on him and wears those cheap ass fake loafers with the comfortable sole instead of a real dress shoe. I couldn't believe…" Amber shook her head. She didn't look at Ingrid, wasn't even sure if her sister was listening. "I couldn't believe I'd been with him…that he was Hadley's father."

"I don't regret moving back." Ingrid cleared her throat. "But I guess…I guess I thought we would be past this awkward part. This stop and start thing."

Amber chanced a peek at her and then found herself drawn in, drowning in the emotion in Ingrid's eyes.

"I mean…sure, it's gonna be…it's like we're getting to know each other again, but don't we have a safety net? We're family."

"It makes me sick to think that way about him." Amber licked her lips. "To be disappointed in who he became. In myself for being with him. Because I wouldn't change a thing about Hadley, and I feel like the regrets I have about what happened take away from what I feel about my daughter."

"Do you talk to Liv? I mean, if I weren't around, would you have told her? About meeting Kyle?"

"No." Amber stood up. She balled her hands into fists and squeezed her eyes closed. Swallowed down the surge of emotion. "No. I don't talk to Liv. I don't talk to anyone, Ingrid."

"Your friend? Gretchen?"

"Not really." Amber shrugged.

"I mean…you warm up a little with me, and I'm…ecstatic. I'm so happy to spend time with you, and then while I'm walking around thinking things are good, you turn around and-"

"I'm talking-"

"But you didn't want to. When I first asked, you looked at me like you wanted-"

"Ingrid." Amber dropped her head to her hands and sobbed. "Please stop? Please?"

"I'm not gonna leave. But if you want me-"

"He left." The words slipped out on a whisper. Her shoulders shook as she gulped for a deep breath, still crying. "He's seeing someone else."

"What?"

Amber felt Ingrid's hand on her shoulder.

"He left last weekend, and he's already seeing someone else, and she's pretty-" Amber hiccupped. Face still hidden in her hands, she wouldn't look at Ingrid. "She's young. He wants more…than I can…he wants babies, and she looked so young. He'll never come back-"

"Amber."

Suddenly, Ingrid was on her side of the counter with her. She pulled her up, off the counter where she'd leaned when the sobbing had robbed her of energy. Ingrid turned her in her arms, so that Amber leaned into her.

Face still in her hands, Amber let the past week come back to get her. Now that she was safe, she could cry.

Ingrid said nothing. She only smoothed her hand over her back. Let her cry. Amber thought to worry about Hadley, but she remembered it was early in the day, and Hadley was at school. It crossed her mind that she was falling apart in her place of business, but the door was still locked. No one could wander in at the moment.

She didn't know *how* to talk to Ingrid. She'd never been one to confide too much to anyone. Gretchen, sure, but she'd never been emotionally naked in front of Gretchen, even, and even though Ingrid hadn't said anything at all-let alone anything judgmental-Amber was afraid to look at her.

When her knees buckled, Ingrid went down with her. Slowly. Still with her arms around her, protecting her from the real world. Once Amber's butt hit the floor, Ingrid moved to her side, arm still around her shoulder, her other hand closed around Amber's wrist, now in her lap. Amber shriveled under Ingrid's intense stare.

"I'm sorry." Ingrid's whisper was a little gruff.

Amber shrugged. Didn't matter if Ingrid was sorry that Nathan had left, because Nathan had left. Nothing would change that. Didn't matter if Ingrid was sorry because she'd been pushing about their relationship because nothing mattered anyway, with Nathan gone.

"Nathan?"

Amber nodded.

"God, Amber, I'm so sorry." Ingrid leaned into her and rested her forehead on the top of Amber's head. "Does Liv know?"

She started to say no. But her voice wouldn't work, so she simply shook her head no.

"You haven't..." Ingrid sat up straight and then cocked her head to see Amber's eyes. "You haven't told anyone?"

She'd told Gretchen, but in her heart that didn't count. Because she'd refused to give in to this tidal wave of emotion.

Ingrid still watching her closely, Amber shook her head.

"Why?" Ingrid squeezed her wrist gently. "Why would you go through this alone? This is what Liv and I are here for."

Amber finally looked up. "To judge me? To lecture me? Tell me it's my fault that he left?"

A surge of guilt rushed her. Zipped through her lungs and took her breath away when she saw Ingrid's face fall, fold in on itself. Ingrid let go of Amber's wrist and took a swipe at her eyes.

"Is that what you really think?"

Amber pressed her lips together and took a deep breath through her nose.

"I don't know what I think about anything anymore," she admitted.

"Why's it your fault that he left?" Ingrid reached for Amber's hand again, and this time she covered it and entwined her fingers with Amber's. "What happened? You guys were so cute Friday night."

"Don't." Amber shook her head.

"What happened?" Ingrid asked again. "Amber, let me listen. I can listen."

"We…" Amber took a deep breath. "We were crazy, Friday night. When we left Liv's."

The corner of Ingrid's mouth tipped up just a bit.

"I'm jealous." She bit her lip. "We stayed, and I drank way too much and felt like hell Saturday."

Amber stared at her silently.

"Which was better. Than what you…" Ingrid shrugged helplessly.

"When I woke up, he was already awake. Apparently, he'd been awake most of the night. Thinking."

"I hate that word."

"Me too."

Ingrid moved her left hand from Amber's shoulder and played with her hair.

"He said he couldn't do it anymore."

"Couldn't do what?"

"Waste his time with me."

"Mmm." Ingrid winced and squeezed Amber's hand again.

"He wants marriage. He wants babies. Hadley and I aren't enough."

Ingrid chewed on her lip for several long seconds. Finally, she sighed, and Amber figured she was going to launch into her lecture.

"Honey, he loves you." She shrugged. "He loves you, and he's crazy about Hadley. Anyone can see that."

Amber lifted a shoulder and raised her eyebrows, and then looked away when she felt more tears.

"'s not enough." She shook her head. "He thinks I'm selfish. That I only think about myself. He thinks that in every relationship I'm involved in, I only think about myself."

"I think we all have a little bit of that in us." Ingrid stared past Amber, lost in thought. "Self-preservation."

"I saw him last night with someone else." Amber's chest hurt. She couldn't breathe. She ducked her chin to her chest and closed her eyes. "I can't believe he's dating already. What if he's been seeing her, Ingrid? What if he's been seeing her for a while? Trying to figure out how to get rid of me?"

Ingrid shook her head. "I don't believe that."

"I saw him with her."

"I don't believe for a second that he was seeing her while he was with you."

"No?" Amber looked up at Ingrid. She hated the hopeful note in her voice.

"No."

"But still, Ingrid." Amber pushed her hair back from her face. "It hasn't even been a week, and he's seeing someone."

"How's Hadley?"

Amber tried for a sarcastic laugh, but it didn't stop there. Ingrid dropped her arm around her shoulders again and scooted closer.

"She's devastated."

"I'm so sorry," Ingrid said again.

"She hates me."

"What?"

"My fault he left. She wants to move out and live with him."

"You know what?"

"What?"

"She knows you love her enough to forgive her for hating you."

"I do." Amber nodded. "Of course I do. Doesn't make a goddamned thing any easier…"

Ingrid leaned forward again and dropped a kiss on Amber's head.

"I just…I don't get why you'd try to do this alone."

"Pretty much how I do everything." Amber's voice broke. "Just one of the things that Nathan doesn't like about me."

"But why? You know Liv and I love you. I mean, if you don't wanna talk to us, I know Ez would listen."

"Ezra's got his own thing to deal with," Amber mumbled.

"What-" Ingrid stopped when they heard something vibrating. "Someone's ringing."

Amber watched her climb gracefully to her feet. Ingrid reached across the counter for her purse.

"Not me. Where's your phone?"

"My purse."

Ingrid twisted around and then moved quickly when she saw Amber's purse by her computer.

"Can I?" Ingrid gestured toward it. Amber nodded and watched Ingrid dig around her in purse and finally pull her cell out. She glanced at the screen and then looked at Amber. "Kyle."

Amber groaned. "Let it go to voicemail."

"Hello?" Ingrid pushed the home button and put the phone to her ear. "Amber's indisposed at the moment. Could I take a message?"

"Indisposed?" Amber frowned. "Jesus, Ingrid, that sounds like I'm in the bathroom or something."

Ingrid spared her a glance, but she was obviously paying attention to Kyle and not Amber.

"I'll give her the message," she finally said. Amber looked away from the smile on Ingrid's face, not knowing how to decipher it. Was she just smiling because it was polite to be friendly and speak with a smile on a phone call? Or had Kyle said something funny? After having coffee with him last week and seeing who he'd become, Amber doubted he had a funny bone in his body.

Maybe Ingrid was thinking about the future. About Hadley meeting her father. Having another family. A dad who played soccer with her-again, after seeing who he'd become, Amber couldn't imagine Kyle practicing soccer, or any sport, with his sons-and it hurt Amber to think someone else could give Hadley something she couldn't, so she didn't want to see Ingrid's smile.

"What's the message?" Amber asked when Ingrid ended the call and moved to sit down by her again.

"What time do you open?"

"Nine." Amber leaned her head back on the shelf behind the counter. "But it's not a big deal if I'm not open, because I could be out on a shoot."

Ingrid nodded, but she looked around the studio.

"What're you doing?" Amber whispered when Ingrid stepped over her and around the counter. She heard Ingrid's footsteps cross to the door and then the lights went off, and Ingrid came back to sit with her again.

"So. Kyle said he would like to talk to you again. And he suggested Java Infusion. Monday morning."

"Great." Amber closed her eyes. "Why didn't you just let it go to voicemail?"

"Why? Did I handle it wrong?"

"No, but..." How could Amber tell Ingrid that it had bothered her to see that smile on her face, and that she needed to know what it meant. If Ingrid really believed Hadley was going to be better off with Kyle and his wife than with her. Ingrid wouldn't get that. Jesus, even Amber knew she was half ass crazy on this stuff. No one was going to understand how she felt. Rather than try to explain herself, she let her thought go and only shrugged.

"I thought it was too important to let it go to voicemail. There's a lot at stake with him."

"I know," Amber whispered.

A few moments of silence passed between them.

"Thank you."

Even with her eyes closed, she could feel Ingrid looking at her.

"For what?" Ingrid finally asked.

Amber opened her eyes and stared at Ingrid. She shrugged.

"Didn't think I had it in me to listen? Without lecturing?"

"I wanted..." Amber started and stopped. "I wanted to talk to you. That day."

"When Nathan left?"

Amber winced and looked away. Even though she'd spent the last six days without him, even though she'd seen Nathan with someone else last night, Ingrid's words hit her like a sucker punch.

"The day I talked to Kyle."

"Why didn't you?"

"I figured you were working."

"I would've listened."

Amber raised her eyebrows and looked away. "You helped anyway."

"I did?"

"You asked me to lunch."

"You talked to Kyle the day we went to lunch together? And you didn't tell me?"

"I didn't have to, by then. You were quizzing me about other things-"

"I wasn't quizzing you-"

"Research, whatever-"

"Amber, I just want to get to know you. The adult you."

"You mean you really aren't going to write a book with a badass photographer? I don't get to be the bad guy?"

Ingrid smiled sadly. "Yes. No. I don't know." She shrugged. "But really, I just wanna know what I missed out on."

Twenty-Nine

"What about you?" Amber reached for Ingrid's hand. "What've I missed in your life?"

Ingrid laughed softly. "Not much."

"Don't do that." Amber shook her head. "Tell me something. Anything." She ignored the way the words sounded a lot like Nathan's words to her on their first date. They way it kind of hurt her to say them.

Ingrid pressed her lips together and stared at Amber's hand on hers.

"I told you and Liv my biggest fear was the whole cancer thing."

"Yeah, but tell me something else. Now. Something I don't know about you."

Ingrid offered her a small smile.

"It was hard…after Scott and I split up."

"Really?" Amber was surprised. "But you said it was all amicable-"

"It was." Ingrid nodded. "We figured out together that it wasn't working. That we were great as friends, but not as…a couple. And we were friendly through the whole thing. But still…" Ingrid shrugged. "I mean, we'd been the best of friends for so long, and then we were married, and intimately involved, and then that part went away and we were friends again. But…"

"What?"

"I still lost something," Ingrid said softly. "I mean…I failed, yes. But more than that, I lost…a piece of myself to Scott. To the experience."

Amber considered Ingrid's words.

"Nothing like what you feel," Ingrid continued. "Nothing at all like that. Nothing at all like I would feel if I lost Luke now."

"I get it."

"I think it was more that I'd lost my friend."
Ingrid twisted around to lean back on the counter like

Amber. "Too much changed to go back to the way it was before."

"I miss him," Amber whispered. "It's not even like he's around all the time, but I miss him now."

Ingrid, head resting against the shelf like Amber's, turned to look at her.

"Because I know he's not coming back."

"He might," Ingrid said softly. "Maybe he just needs a little time to figure things out. Maybe-"

"I keep wondering if he kissed her goodnight-"

"Who?"

"The girl he was with last night." Amber shrugged. "He kissed me on our first date."

"And you're sure he was with her?"

"He said it was a blind date."

"You talked to him?" Ingrid sat up quickly, lost her balance and almost bumped her head. "Damn."

"He came up to the counter while I was waiting for our order."

"So he came to you? Amber, doesn't that say-"

"He asked about Hadley."

"Mmm." Ingrid winced. "I'm sorry."

"I talked to him...about Hadley's father. Before...everything happened."

"What'd he say?"

"He thought it was a good thing. Telling Hadley the truth. Talking to Kyle to...pave the way. I was so scared about it. That's when he called me selfish."

"You're not selfish."

"You thought I was when you first came back home."

"I think we were all thinking bad things about each other then." Ingrid sighed. "It was a bad time."

"It just...it feels unfair. He wanted me to do it. To tell Hadley. So I set things in motion, and then he walked out."

"Too soon to remind you that you're beautiful? That it's his loss, and you'll-"

Amber nodded. "Too soon."

Ingrid rubbed her hand over the toe of her boot. Amber watched as she tried to smooth a knick in the leather.

"So what about Kyle? What were you saying about him earlier?"

"When you were giving me the beat down for not being able to answer right away?"

Ingrid looked up at Amber with a little grin.

"I don't know why you're afraid to talk to me."

"I'm afraid to talk to anyone," Amber whispered, "and sometimes, you get so full…of that hurt. Ya know? And it expands inside you and pushes your air out and you can't say a damned word, because you're suffocating…"

"Yeah." Ingrid nodded. "I know."

They stared at each other for a long moment, and finally, Amber tore her eyes away from Ingrid.

"He's…" She needed the perfect word. She only had one shot to say it perfectly. For Ingrid to get exactly what she was saying. "Ordinary."

"Ordinary," Ingrid repeated.

"Yeah. I had the whole thing…so…blown up in my head. Ya know? In my memory…he was…the whole thing was incredible-"

"Was it good? Did you like it like that?"

"No." Amber shook her head. "But I was sixteen. I didn't know what was good. I didn't know what I was supposed to like."

"Scott was good." Ingrid bit her lip. "He knew exactly what he was doing."

Amber smiled sadly. "I didn't get that until I was…twenty-something."

"Still." Ingrid shrugged. "Now we know the difference, right?"

"Yeah," Amber agreed. "But in memory, Kyle was...what he was supposed to be. And to see him the other day...looking...so...normal. I just couldn't help but wonder what it was about him that had attracted me to him in the first place."

"He was an older guy, interested in you when you were just...finding yourself. Figuring that stuff out."

"And now he's just an older guy. Who has two sons that play travel soccer. Who teaches algebra at the college. Drinks chai tea."

"But he might be a firecracker in bed," Ingrid told her. "You never know."

Amber laughed and rolled her eyes. "I don't wanna know."

"I know." Ingrid nudged her with her toe. "Just teasing."

"I'm scared, Ingrid."

"What are you scared of?"

"That she'll love him. That she'll be crazy about him." Amber swallowed hard. "What if she likes him better than me?"

"Amber, you're her mom." Ingrid reached for her hand again. "Girls always need their moms."

"I miss Mom," Amber whispered.

"Oh God. Me too, Amber, me too."

"She'd get so damned mad at me. At some of the stuff I did, but I just-"

"She was so proud of you," Ingrid told her. "For working so hard. For being so good with Hadley."

"Really?"

Ingrid nodded. "Really. I just never wanted to hear it."

"Why?"

"I dunno. I think part of me didn't want to know what I was missing. I came home a lot more when Gracie and Charlie were younger."

"Why not when Hadley was little?"

Ingrid shrugged. "I don't know. But I'm really sorry that I didn't."

Amber rubbed her eyes. "Me too. I wanted her to know you."

"Am-"

"That's not true," Amber confessed. "I wanted you to come home...for me. I missed you."

"Amber-"

"See? This is what he was talking about. Everything I want is for me. I can pretend it's all about Hadley, but it's always me. A man like Nathan can't love a woman like me."

"Why can't you be looking out for both of you?"

Amber took a look around the studio.

"God. I'm a wreck. I know this isn't what you had in mind when you asked if you could hang out-"

"So that's it? For the day? You're done talking to me."

"We're not solving anything."

"There's no easy solve for heartache, Amber. You love him."

"And he doesn't love me-"

"He does. He loves you."

"Well, according to him, if I love him, I need to let him go. To find what's going to make him happy."

Ingrid arched her eyebrows.

"And you know you can't be that person? To make him happy?"

"I don't wanna get married."

"Why-"

Amber held her breath and stared at Ingrid.

"'Kay. This is the part you don't wanna talk about. The part where I lecture you."

"Do you...wanna go out and take some pictures?" Amber suggested.

"Watch you shoot?"

"No. You take them. You develop them."

"Oh." Ingrid grinned. "Yeah. That sounds kinda fun."

Amber took a deep breath. Bit her lip.

"Mind if I stop by the house first?

"Course not."

Amber pushed herself up from her sitting position and then watched Ingrid do the same.

"Ingrid."

"Hmm?"

"What you said earlier…"

Ingrid raised her eyebrows in askance.

"I love you, too," Amber whispered. "I'm sorry I keep pushing you away."

"That's your way of saying you're gonna keep doing it, isn't it?"

"It's what I do."

"Do you do that with Nathan?"

Amber drew back and frowned at Ingrid.

"You do." Ingrid nodded. "You love him, but you hold him out here…away from your heart."

Amber stepped around her to grab her purse.

"Why?" Ingrid tried again.

"I grew up alone, Ingrid," Amber reminded her. "It's what I know."

Thirty

Somehow, the rest of the day seemed easier. Easier, at least, to be with Ingrid. In fact, a few times Amber had been so caught up in the moment with Ingrid that she forgot about Nathan and that he was gone, and it would only come back to her when she'd take a breath and wonder about dinner or remind herself she needed to stop at the grocery store on the way home to pick up a six pack and the pretzels that he liked.

Even that, though, was so hard that the easy wasn't worth it. So hard when it would just hit her so suddenly. Like a knife in her throat. She hadn't wanted Ingrid to see it, when it hit her, but seemed like each time it did hit her, and it hurt, and she'd almost gasp for air, Ingrid would notice. Touch her shoulder, slide her arm around her and squeeze. Just something. Amber was thankful Ingrid had let the conversation go. That she hadn't pushed on the whole marriage thing.

They'd wandered around downtown forever. Trading the camera back and forth, Amber coaching Ingrid on lining up her shot. Making sure the light was right. Finally, they'd gone back to the studio, and though at first, the ghosts of all the words Amber had said earlier in the morning rushed at her and robbed her of her voice, Ingrid had been quick to flip the lights on and announce that she was starved. And just like that, the words, the emptiness of the morning abated, just a little.

Rather than go out, Amber suggested delivery. When Ingrid agreed and told Amber she trusted her to order something, Amber called and ordered cheeseburgers and fries from the bar on Ninth and Ohio. Damned good greasy bar food. Felt right. Amber kind of wished it was evening, so they could drink a cold beer.

Ingrid had asked Amber about her digital work, so while they waited for their late lunch delivery, Amber booted up the Mac again. She was careful to stay away from the new file she'd started, the pictures from Mom and Dad's. Instead she opened a file of pictures she'd taken of Hadley when she'd turned fourteen.

She supposed Ingrid was more interested in the process. In Amber's criteria for keeping a photo or deleting it. But Amber was struck by the changes in her daughter. In the pictures, her face was still sweet and young. In real life, Hadley's cheekbones were a little more prominent, as were the hollows just below them. Her eyes, though pretty, didn't pop in the pictures, the way they did now.

For a moment, she was overwhelmed. Seemed like just a week or two ago, she was walking next to a three-year-old Hadley, riding her shiny red tricycle. Suddenly, Hadley was almost finished with her first year of high school. She'd turn fifteen in the fall. Amber was proud; Hadley was beautiful by anyone's standards and more so by Amber's. She felt a flash of desire. Need. To share that with someone. To share that gut-bursting feeling of pride. And hope. Hope for Hadley's future.

Nathan. She'd grown so used to Nathan being a part of her and Hadley's family, it was inconceivable to her that he wasn't anymore. Nathan had fallen so hard for Hadley. He'd been her dad in every way but biological for the past couple of years. She wondered if he missed Hadley more than he missed her, and before that thought was gone, she hated herself for it, because it only reminded her that Nathan was right.

Kyle? If Kyle's wife had given him the go ahead on meeting Hadley, on forming a relationship with her- Amber shivered at the thought-would she share her pride with him? After all, he was part of who she'd become, wasn't he? She didn't want to, though. She didn't want to share her pride or her dreams for Hadley with Kyle.

"You okay?" Ingrid dropped her hand on Amber's knee, but she didn't look at her. "You totally zoned out there."

Amber nodded, though Ingrid still wasn't looking at her. "She's all grown up."

"No. She's not." Ingrid squeezed Amber gently. "She looks like it, but she's still just a kid. And she still needs you."

"Do women ever outgrow needing their moms?"

That made Ingrid look at her.

"No." Ingrid shook her head. "I don't think most of us do."

Amber ducked her head and rested her elbows on her knees. She buried her face in her hands and rubbed her eyes.

"Maybe that's why we have sisters," Ingrid said softly. Amber felt Ingrid's fingers in her hair.

"Maybe."

"Speaking of sisters."

"Hmm?"

"Liv texted. She wants to do a girls' night."

"Yeah?" Amber finally lifted her head and looked at Ingrid. "Like more basement box duty?"

"No. A night away from all of that."

"You told her, didn't you?"

"I haven't talked to her all day. You know that."

"Did you text her?"

"Do you wanna look at my phone?"

Amber thought about calling her bluff, but she shook her head.

"Besides." Ingrid looked up, sat up straighter in her chair. "Lunch is here."

"Besides, lunch is here?" Amber stood up as the door opened. The delivery kid had been to her studio before, though she didn't really know him. He offered her a smile, she handed him cash for the food and he set it on the counter. Mumbled a thanks and left the way he'd come.

"He was cute."

"Please. He looks like he's, like, twelve."

"Now you sound like Mom."

Amber shrugged. "So. Besides?" She unfolded the brown paper bag and reached inside.

"Are you really not gonna tell Liv what's going on?"

Amber set the food out on the counter, folded the bag up and realized Ingrid was staring at her.

"Of course I'm gonna tell her." She shrugged.

"So what does it matter if I did?"

"You did."

"I didn't!" Ingrid groaned. "I did not tell Liv. I have been with you all day, Amber. I just…she'd wanna know."

"Okay."

"Should we-?" Ingrid looked from the food to the table in the back corner of the room.

"Yeah."

They each picked up their burgers and fries, Amber tucked the bag under her arm.

"Don't do that. You'll get grease on your shirt."

"Sorry, Mom."

Ingrid laughed. "What are we drinking?"

"Soda machine, outside to the left."

"Okay. What do you want?"

"Diet Coke."

"I'll be right back." Ingrid found her purse under the counter and unzipped it. Dug in for her billfold. "Don't steal any of my fries."

"Might." Amber shrugged. "No promises."

"I'll know if you do," Ingrid warned her as she headed for the door.

"How's that? Eyes in the back of your head? Like Mom?"

Ingrid snorted and ducked out the door. Amber sat down at the table, but she only stared at her cheeseburger. Stood up and went to the counter to find her phone. She'd purposely ignored it earlier, when she and Ingrid had been walking around. Now she couldn't stand it. Like if she waited one more second to see if he might have texted, she'd come unraveled and her skin would start peeling off.

As she wandered back to the table, she tapped the text icon. Tiny little rush of happiness when she saw that Liv had texted her, too, about a girls' night. Crashed a little inside at the silence from Nathan.

"Hey." Ingrid pulled the door open and stepped inside. "Don't do that."

"What?" Amber waited until Ingrid could see her and then she took a fry from her pile and popped it in her mouth.

"Well, that, but that, too." Ingrid waved her hand at Amber's phone.

"Can't help it, Ingrid." Amber's voice broke, and she took a quick breath and counted to ten. "I just...I wanna talk to him."

"Can I tell you something?"

"Yeah." Amber sat down. Ingrid handed her a bottle of Diet Coke. "Thank you."

"Julie's pregnant." Ingrid set her billfold on the table and sat down. Amber watched her twist the top off her own Diet Coke.

"Julie. Like...your friend...Julie?"

Ingrid nodded.

"Isn't she..."

"Old? Like me?" Ingrid arched an eyebrow at Amber and laughed and nodded. "She is."

"That's kinda scary."

"Yeah. I think she's a little shell-shocked."

"Well. I mean, she knows how that happens, right?"

"Yep. And I think they've been pretty hot and heavy since Rafe moved back home."

Amber took a bite of her cheeseburger. "Does it bother you?" she asked around a mouthful.

"Does what bother me?" Ingrid avoided Amber's eyes. Ate a few French fries.

"That she's pregnant."

Amber waited for Ingrid to shrug the question off, surprised when Ingrid finally met her gaze.

"Yeah." She nodded. "Kind of."

Amber blinked at her, unsure of what Ingrid meant and unsure how to answer her.

"What about Luke?" Amber finally forced herself to speak.

Ingrid's eyes went wide, and she shook her head. "No. No, no, no. It's not Rafe."

"You guys are just friends."

"Yes. We're friends. We had like fifteen minutes of more than friends, and it shouldn't have happened."

"A lot can happen in fifteen minutes."

Ingrid frowned. "Yeah, but I like to take things a little slower."

"Ingrid."

"It didn't happen, Amber. It did *not* happen."

"Okay." Amber nodded. "Because Hadley happened in less than fifteen minutes."

Ingrid turned away from her. Made a show of picking up her cheeseburger.

"So, that's it." Amber took a drink of her soda. "You're upset that Julie's pregnant."

"I'm not upset," Ingrid argued. "I just wish…"

"Wish what?"

"I wish I'd have met Luke sooner. That we'd met when we were younger."

"Because you wanna have a baby with him?"

"I wish I could," Ingrid answered quietly. "I know…it would be a huge risk, and I'm not even sure what he thinks about it. I just…I regret that I missed out on that one."

"Being a mom," Amber clarified.

"Yeah." Ingrid smacked her lips together and nodded. "But. Whatever. At least I have two nieces and two nephews. Maybe if I work hard, I can establish favorite aunt status with at least one of them."

Amber grinned, but her mind was reeling. She was shocked by Ingrid's confession.

"I thought you just didn't want kids."

"I don't think I knew that I did until it was too late."

"You could. It would be high risk, but you could talk to-"

Ingrid shook her head. "No. I don't wanna be sixty when my child's graduating from high school. Besides, maybe there's a reason why I've never...had so much as a pregnancy scare."

Amber slouched in her chair. Would she feel that way when she was in her forties? True, she had Hadley, but would she regret never having another child?

"So." She cleared her throat and nodded at her phone. "Liv texted me, too."

"Yeah?" Ingrid's smile lit up her face. "So you wanna do it? Girls' night?"

"I guess."

"We could take Liv to Skinny's."

Amber snorted and covered her mouth.

"No way."

"Why not?"

"She'd be floored-"

"I know!" Ingrid nodded. "That'd be the best part."

"I'm not going to Skinny's."

"Why not?"

"I'm not going to a strip club. You have someone to go home to. Liv has someone to go home to. I'm not gonna go watch a bunch of chicks grind a pole and go home alone."

"Turns you on, huh?"

Amber laughed and blushed. "Well, no…but…kind of…puts you in that frame of mind."

"That it does," Ingrid agreed. "Makes you make bold claims, too."

"What?"

"Luke claimed he could eyeball a chick and guess her bra size."

"Yeah? How'd he do with you?"

"I dunno. His hands were on me before he made a guess. Told him he was disqualified-"

"I'm still a little jealous that Liv walked in on you and Luke-"

"Keyword. Me. Sisters. You don't watch-"

"Yeah, but Luke Ashley's bare ass in motion…"

"Just remember my hands were on it," Ingrid winked at her. "He's mine."

Amber laughed softly, but she felt her eyes fill.

"Do you think he kissed her? Last night?"

"I don't know if he kissed her." Ingrid shook her head. "But I bet if he did, he was thinking about you."

Thirty-One

Hadley dragged downstairs the next morning as Amber was filling her coffee mug and getting ready to head out.

"What're you doing up?" Amber asked her, forgetting that communication with them had been spotty at best for the past week. She'd slept somewhat better last night, though she'd dreamt of Nathan. And woke up feeling sad. A shower had helped, but mostly she was desperate to get out of the house and get over to her parents' place. Jonesing to get back to the pictures, to her project.

"Can I go to a movie later?"

Amber frowned. She looked at the clock-ten after seven-and back at Hadley.

"You're up at ten after seven to ask if you can see a movie later?"

"Can I?"

"With who?"

"Grace."

"Grace Girard?"

"Do I know another Grace?" Hadley snapped.

"When did she ask you? I mean...did she just text or something?"

"She asked last night. Like, after midnight."

"What movie?"

"I dunno. Does it matter? Jesus, Mom, you trust Grace more than you trust me."

"Language, Had."

Hadley rolled her eyes. "Can I?"

"I guess."

It crossed Amber's mind that maybe she shouldn't let her go. After the way Hadley had behaved toward her the past week. And yet, Hadley had a reason for her behavior, didn't she? She was hurt, and Amber was a huge part of why she was hurting.

"Thank you." Hadley snagged Amber's coffee and took a drink. "Where are you going?"

Amber watched Hadley with her coffee, waiting for her to give it back. "Shoot."

"On a Saturday?"

Amber shrugged uncomfortably. "Kind of a personal project."

Hadley arched an eyebrow at her. "Like what?"

"Personal, kid. You know what that means?"

"You doin' a nude session with some hot dude?"

Amber stared at her silently.

"Sorry," Hadley mumbled. She stuck her hand out, offering Amber the travel mug.

"Hadley, I love him so much," Amber whispered. She took the mug from Hadley and stepped closer to her. "You know that."

"Sure, Mom." Hadley shrugged.

"I miss him, too."

Hadley took a step away from her, toward the door.

"Do you remember the day we all went to Siloam Springs together? Hiked those trails. And then we went for pizza?"

Amber nodded. "Didn't we watch a movie later?"

"*Parent Trap.*" Hadley nodded.

"And we ended up piling in the car and going for ice cream. We had to hurry because Dairy Queen closed at ten."

"Yeah."

Amber noticed the tears clinging to Hadley's eyelashes.

"Best day. Ever."

As words go, in general, those shouldn't have hurt. Hadley hadn't used a snarky tone. She simply sounded sad. Which is why the words hurt Amber so. She watched helplessly as Hadley left the kitchen. Heard her hurry up the stairs.

Feeling her daughter's pain as keenly as she felt her own, she considered staying home. But to what end? Hadley didn't want her here. If she changed her mind, she'd call her or text her. And Amber was itching to get over to the house. Wander the halls and the rooms and feel something a little different. Pain. Sorrow. But that pain and sorrow were a dull ache inside her that she'd carried for so long she'd made her peace with it.

Or had she?

Tired of second-guessing herself, tired of wallowing, (funny, because what was wandering the halls of her deceased parents' house, of her childhood home but wallowing in a past that could never live again) she grabbed her keys and her phone and walked out. She'd tucked a twenty-dollar bill and her license in her pocket. Decked out in jeans, a Game of Thrones t-shirt and Nikes, she didn't give a damn about what she looked like. She just needed to get out of the house. To put her brain on autopilot and let her camera do the thinking for her.

There wasn't much traffic at this hour, so it didn't take long to get there. Like the other days she'd done this-and no, she didn't feel guilty for sneaking around, not at all-she pulled her SUV all the way into the drive and down by the garage. Took a long wistful look around the backyard before she let herself in the backdoor. Eventually, they'd sign some papers and stick a *For Sale* sign out front. And they'd get an offer, and Amber doubted they'd get what they wanted out of the place because you can't put a dollar amount on a family, on lives lived in a house and a yard, and eventually, they'd sell the house and this-*all of this*-would be gone.

And once this was gone, Amber would never have anything like it again. Even if she did move. If she and Hadley found a newer place, with bricks or new siding and a kitchen big enough to change their minds in, and a big, sprawling yard instead of the slice of dead grass next to the alley they had now, she'd never have *this*. A backyard where her family would live. Grill hamburgers. Play on a swing set. Climb trees. Play wiffle ball. She'd never have that, because it was only the two of them, and Amber knew that soon she was going to blink, and Hadley would be off to college.

Knowing Hadley, she'd make her way, and she'd blaze her own trail. And she wouldn't look back. Amber wanted everything in the world for her daughter, but thinking about Hadley leaving hurt her already.

The house felt a little warm when Amber unlocked the door and stepped inside. She set her keys down and walked over to the window above the kitchen sink. Stood on her tiptoes and opened it. Took a deep breath and then got caught up, looking, again. The Maple in the back. They'd climbed it. Well, Ezra had tried and failed, but she'd climbed it. Her sisters, she figured, had climbed it. But she'd forgotten until this moment, that it had been their base. When they'd played hide and seek or kick the can or ghosts in the graveyard, what have you, that Maple had been base.

For a moment, she was breathless standing there, remembering her preteen self hauling ass back up through the alley and the backyard and lunging for the tree before her friends or Ezra could tag her. She'd hit the tree too hard on more than one occasion. Left skin on the trunk. Walked away with bruises on her arms and legs.

She gave herself a mental shake and went back out after her camera. Snatched her keys from the counter on the way by. With a look around, she opened the hatch on the Passport. Noticed a pothole, if you could call it a pothole since the driveway wasn't a paved driveway at all, about four feet behind her. She unzipped her bag, took her camera out, grabbed the smaller lens and attached it.

Wandered over to the hole in the ground and snapped a picture of it. The grass around it was ragged and brown. A mean looking weed grew next to it, but stopped just short of falling into the hole. She squatted down and took another picture, all the way remembering how she and Ez would fly up and down the gravel ruts on their bikes. She looked down the length of the driveway and then back at the hole and decided it would be an ugly picture. She'd taken quite a few of them lately. She wasn't sure what the appeal was, but something about it made her feel just a little bit good.

Back inside, she moved slowly through the first floor. Not thinking, really. Not remembering. Taking pictures. Recording so much more than furniture and wallpaper and flooring. Maybe to anyone else, the pictures would be nothing but junk. To Amber, it was her life.

Hadley texted at noon and said Aunt Liv had invited her to lunch with her and Grace. Asked Amber if she could go. Amber wondered again if Ingrid had told Liv about Nathan leaving but decided it really didn't matter. Sooner or later, Liv was going to know. And it wasn't as if Amber wanted to tell her herself. Wasn't like she relished the idea of going through the whole damned story again.

She had no idea what kind of time had passed when Hadley texted again. Asked if she could stay at Aunt Liv and Uncle Wade's house. Again, Amber worried that Liv knew something was going on. She hesitated with her yes, this time, if for no other reason than wondering how things were between Liv and Wade. In the end, she'd told Hadley she wanted to talk to Liv first. Figured she'd pissed Hadley off with that comment but didn't care.

Settling herself on the floor of her old bedroom, she stared at her phone for a moment. Wished Nathan would call. Told herself to get over it.

She imagined her teenage self sitting in this very spot on the floor, cordless phone in hand, talking to her friends. About boys. Talking to boys. Too tired to laugh, she settled for a little smile and tapped out Liv's cell number on her phone.

"Hey." Liv answered within a couple of rings. Amber wondered what Hadley had said to her, if maybe Hadley had told her what was going on.

"Hey. What's going on?"

"Well, lunch was good. And the movie…well, the girls watched the movie. I shopped."

Amber nodded. Decided a shopping trip sounded kind of fun.

"Grace asked if Hadley could stay over again tonight."

"You don't have to do this, Liv."

"Do what? Grace asked."

Amber rubbed her forehead and then dragged her fingers through her hair.

"I know. But…it's an inconvenience-"

"It's not. It's not a problem at all. I think they had fun together last weekend."

Amber sunk her teeth into her lip and bit down hard to keep from saying anything.

"Okay."

"Good. What're you doing?"

"Hmm?"

"What're you doing? Ingrid said she saw your car at the house."

So much for being sneaky.

"She was here?"

"Drove by."

"Why didn't she stop?"

"She was on her way to lunch with someone she used to know. Someone from school or something."

"She drove by here on the way to lunch? Where was she eating? The neighbor's house?"

Liv made a small noise, like maybe a laugh or a murmur of agreement, maybe?

"I don't know. I drive by a lot when I don't have to, too."

"Yeah." Amber nodded. She had to admit she did, too.

"So?" Liv asked. "What are you doing?"

"Um-"

"Pictures?"

For a second, Amber couldn't breathe. How did Liv know? And then it hit her. Liv was asking if she was going through more of their parents' old photographs.

"Yeah," Amber mumbled. Little white lie like that couldn't hurt.

"Are you by yourself?"

"Yeah, I'm fine."

"Okay." Liv said something, apparently to one of the girls.

"How's Hadley?"

"Fine," Liv answered in a way that sounded completely natural. Apparently, Hadley had pulled it together. Even that hurt Amber. Hadley shouldn't have to pull her shit together and pretend that everything was good. Kids shouldn't have to hide their feelings.

"Okay. Thanks, Liv."

"What about that girls' night?"

"Tonight?" Amber yelped. "No."

"No. But maybe soon?"

"Yeah. Soon." Amber nodded.

"Catch up with you guys in the morning," Liv said. Thankfully, she ended the call, because her reference to Amber and Nathan, as a couple, sliced through Amber and left her bleeding and speechless.

After the phone call, she didn't even have the heart to take pictures. Instead she wandered from room to room. Missing even the days just after Pop had died, when she and Hadley and Ingrid had all been staying here. At least she'd been only lonely then, not alone and lonely, both.

She found herself in the attic, and the lighting was awful, but she had a flash and so she took pictures of the trunks and the clothing and the stacks of magazines and the toys. She'd thought they'd hauled all of this stuff away, and while she could see they'd made a dent in the mess, there was still so much more to do. Good thing Ingrid had decided to stay in Quincy. She'd hate to be here indefinitely, without Luke, without a place of her own.

Night fell around the house while she was upstairs. A little bit knock-kneed with hunger-she was running on the coffee and two granola bars she'd munched on through out the day-she'd finally climbed to her feet and made her way down to the second floor. Hungry. But no appetite. Hell of a thing. She stood in the doorway of her parents' room, trying to tell herself something sounded good. Maybe a couple of tacos. Frozen pizza. A bowl of cereal.

She rested her head on the doorframe and closed her eyes. She should just tell Liv. Actually, she should just man up and tell them all. Liv and Wade. Luke. They were all going to find out, and they would all realize eventually that it was her fault, and probably one of these days, one of them would see Nathan out with someone else, anyway.

She heard someone knocking on something, but she didn't process the sound. Still with her eyes closed, resting against the doorframe, she was thinking about going home. Maybe she'd take a long, hot bath. Wouldn't compare to Ingrid and Luke's hot tub, but maybe it would be nice to just have some alone time.

Kidding herself. She didn't want to be alone. Here or home. She didn't want anything, but Nathan.

The knocking faded, and then she heard the doorbell. It didn't startle her. Maybe on some level, she'd heard the knocking and figured one of her siblings had dropped by only to realize he or she had forgotten a key. Maybe she'd processed it and ignored it, because she didn't want to see anyone.

Pretty hard to ignore the doorbell, though. With a sigh, she stood up straight, flipped the light off in the master bedroom, and made her way slowly down the steps. The house was dark; she'd left the kitchen light on, but it had only served to chase the shadows further down the hall to the front, where she now stood in varying shades of dark.

She turned the porch light on without looking outside, unlocked the door and pulled it open. She was working on a reason she couldn't hang out and talk or go out to eat or whatever Ingrid or maybe Ezra asked her to, and so when she realized Nathan was standing on the porch, she could only stare at him.

After a moment, he half-shrugged and asked if he could come in.

"What do you want?" she asked, but she backed up a few steps so he could come inside. She kept her hand on the doorknob, because she figured whatever reason he was here, he wouldn't stay long, and rather than hope otherwise, she stayed where she was, ready to show him out and lock up behind him.

"What're you doing?" He made a show of looking around the dark front room.

"What do you want?"

"I went by the house-"

"My house?" she asked sharply.

Nathan sighed. "I went by the house to see Hadley. She's not there."

"I know."

"Is she with you? Is she here?"

"She's with my sister."

"Doing what?"

"How should I know? She went to lunch with Liv and Grace, and then they went to a movie. Was I supposed to tell her she couldn't stay overnight there because you might come by to see her?"

"No." Nathan shrugged. "Of course not. I was...I worried that-"

"That she might have snuck out?" Amber interrupted him.

"I just...I'm worried about her," he mumbled.

Amber nodded. "Yeah. Well, she's not your worry anymore. Remember?"

"Amber."

"You need to go," she whispered.

"Can I see her tomorrow? Maybe she and I could go to lunch or something?"

"You need to go," she repeated. "This isn't fair. You left me, Nathan. I can't see you like this-"

"I left you, not Hadley."

Amber turned away from him and rested her forehead on the door.

"How was your date?"

"What?"

"The blind date Thursday. How was it?"

"Amber-"

"Did you kiss her goodnight?"

"I'll call Had. Tomorrow-"

"You did, didn't you? Did you sleep with her?"

"And see if she wants to do something-"

"I miss you." She tucked a chunk of her hair behind her ear. "I miss you, and you're already out fucking other women-"

"I didn't fuck her, Amber. Nothing happened."

Forehead still resting against the door, Amber looked at him with one eye.

"Nothing?"

Nathan winced and looked away.

"I kissed her goodnight."

Amber nodded. "I figured. You're a first date kiss kind of guy."

"It wasn't..."

Amber shook her head. "Just go. I'm busy. Go and-"

Without a word, he reached for her hand. Lunged after her when she tried to dodge his touch.

"Kissing her was nothing like kissing you."

She caught her breath when he settled his hands on her hips and pressed her up against the door. They pushed it to the threshold, not quite shut completely.

"Is that a good thing?"

In the darkness, still only in the shadows from the kitchen light and a tiny spot of porch light through the front door, Amber looked up at him and met his gaze. She squirmed against him, trying to push him away.

Instead, it seemed to make him more determined to hold her in place. She lifted her hands to his chest to push, but he grabbed both of her wrists in his left hand and raised her arms over her head.

She realized when his gaze dropped to her lips and his erection stirred and pressed against her middle he was going to kiss her. His fingers wrapped painfully tight around her wrists, he leaned in, lifted his other hand from her hip and pressed his thumb to her upper lip.

Frustrated that he'd done it, that he'd put his hands on her when she was still reeling from the things he'd said to her a week ago, angry that he held her hands in a vise grip, and she couldn't push him away or pull him closer, she opened her mouth and scraped her teeth over his thumb.

"I wanna fuck you, Amber Williams. Right now."

"Couldn't drum up anything better than me?" She nipped at him again.

"There's a lot of women out there, ready and willing, but none of them are you."

His eyes stayed on her lips, but he moved against her now. Grinded his hips against her. Amber's knees were weak. Still, he didn't kiss her.

"Do it." She closed her eyes.

"Do what?"

"Fuck me, Nathan." She lifted her hips from the door to meet his.

When he still didn't kiss her, she opened her eyes. Watched him lower his free hand to cover her breast. She strained against him, still unsure if she wanted him to walk away or tear her clothes off.

Still holding her wrists, he dropped his other hand to her waist and pushed her t-shirt up until he could see her bra.

"Have you been with anyone?" he asked gruffly.

"What?" She looked up to meet his eyes. Felt her throat tighten. "No. I don't want-"

He covered her mouth with his. Caught her off guard, stroked his tongue inside her lips, dragged it over hers. Amber imagined that she tasted Nicole on him. She heard a soft hum, a little mew catch in her throat as he slipped his fingers inside her bra and slid them over her nipple.

"Nathan."

He pulled away from her. Pressed his open mouth over the corner of her lips, across her cheek and down over her chin.

"Are you wet?"

"Please?" She wiggled her fingers and felt the pins and needles starting to stick her. "Please."

Finally, he let go, and she wrapped her arms around his shoulders and found his mouth with hers. He whipped her shirt off over her head and pushed her bra up out of his way. Shoved her against the door; Amber felt it give and latch. Hands cupping her ass, he leaned over to suck her nipples into his mouth.

When he reached to unbutton her jeans, she fought him. Just enough to get her hands inside his shirt. Impatient, he grabbed the back of the collar and pulled it off over his head. Unbuttoned her jeans, worked her zipper and shoved everything down in just seconds.

"Nathan." She jumped and moved with him when he touched her. Felt her tears slide when he pulled his hands away and worked his belt buckle, shoved his own jeans out of the way. Moving so fast, she felt like she was stumbling drunk, she kicked her left shoe off. He pushed the left leg of her jeans down over her foot and then he slid his fingers up the back of her naked thigh, lifted her and drove into her, smacking her head against the door.

She moved with him, grabbing desperately to hold onto him. Her hands seemed to move of their own accord, claiming his shoulders and his arms and his neck and finally into his hair. When he turned, still holding her in his arms, she shook her head.

"Here."

She had no idea where he was going to take her, but she couldn't wait. He turned back to the door, rested her against it and then eased them both to the floor.

It was over before Amber really got started. She lay on the hardwood floor, panting, sweaty and desperate for him to touch her again. For him to kiss her. Put his hands on her breasts. Her thighs.

"What're you doing?" she asked when he moved away from her and climbed to his feet.

"I head out Monday," he said as he pulled his jeans back on and situated himself so he could zip them. "Gonna go home and pack so I can spend some time with Hadley tomorrow."

"You-Nathan-but-"

"I needed to be with you," he said unapologetically. She felt the hot tears slide off her face and into her hair. Watched him yank his shirt back over his head. "This doesn't change anything."

She sat up as he reached for the doorknob.

"Yeah," she whispered. "It kinda does."

Thirty-Two

"My treat," Kyle insisted.

"No, thanks, Kyle, I've-"

"Really, Amber, it's coffee."

Amber raised her eyebrows and glanced from Kyle to the woman behind the counter at JI.

"Sure." She nodded. No need to cause a scene. "Thank you."

The woman processed the transaction, handed Kyle his change and his chai tea and Amber an empty coffee cup. Rather than find a table, Kyle followed Amber to the coffee bar across the room.

"Beautiful weekend," he announced.

Amber's hands shook slightly, and she spilled coffee on her fingers.

"Fuck," she mumbled and quickly raised her eyes to see if he'd heard her. Either he hadn't, or he was ignoring her. He stood with his back to her, surveying the tables. He wore jeans today. A navy pullover with a gold, white and light blue *LA Galaxy* embroidered on the left chest. Amber looked him over, checked out his ass in his jeans (much better than the baggy Dockers) and then looked back down at her coffee cup. Her fingers were red from the splash of coffee. She grabbed a napkin and wiped her hands off. Tossed it in the trash can under the bar and picked up her cup.

"Did you do anything fun?" he asked.

Friendly and comfortable Kyle was nauseating. Or maybe it was simply that the only thing fun she'd done over the weekend was a five-minute desperation fuck on the hardwood floor in the front room at her parents' old house. Or maybe it was watching Nathan show up at her house the next day and speak to her politely-for Hadley's benefit, as if nothing had happened-or maybe it was all of the above.

End result: Amber desperately didn't want to be here today. Discussing her daughter with Kyle Carpenter.

"No," she finally answered when Kyle glanced at her. She thought of last Friday, spending the day with Ingrid, and decided that had been sort of fun. But she wouldn't share any of that with him. She was about as likely to tell him the whole story as she was to tell the guy at the drycleaners. Wasn't like they were close just because they'd created Hadley.

"No?" He led the way to the same table they'd shared the last time they were here. Amber's stomach hurt when she sat down with him. Last time had been hard. But she'd called the shots. And she'd had Nathan to go home to and now she was so fucking miserable she hated everyone she looked at, and she had to do this. She had to have this conversation with this man right now.

"Busy." She shrugged.

"What're you working on?"

Her eyebrows shot up, but then she realized he meant professionally and she shook her head. "Busy, yeah, but mostly right now, my siblings and I are just...trying to get our parents' estate...taken care of."

"Sign with a realtor yet?"

"No." She took a drink of her coffee and felt it burn all the way down her throat and into her stomach. "I thought we were about ready, but I was in the attic Saturday and saw that we still have a lot of stuff up there to get rid of."

"You could hire someone, you know. To handle that part of it. Throw stuff out. Clean it up."

She nodded slowly.

"We could. But..."

"It's emotional," he supplied for her.

"Well." She raised her eyebrows. "It's all sentimental stuff, and yeah, that gets emotional."

"How many siblings do you have?"

Amber wondered how long she was going to have to do the small talk game. Her heart hurt so badly right now. Nathan had done a number on her Saturday and every part of her body had hurt yesterday and still, today and maybe every day from now, her heart hurt.

"Two sisters and a brother."

Kyle nodded. Took a drink of his tea.

"What's LA Galaxy?" She couldn't help herself. Stupid to ask a question that would only encourage more idle chit-chat, and yet the words were out before she could stop them.

"Soccer," he answered with a grin. "Jen and I keep talking about taking the boys to LA for a game."

"Really?" Amber wondered if they did that often. She didn't know many people that enthralled with soccer. She wondered how good his boys were.

"Yeah. LA Galaxy's won the cup five times."

Amber shook her head. "Lost on me. The only thing I know about soccer is Beckham."

"He played for LA." Kyle nodded.

"Hmm." Out of her league and almost out of patience, Amber shifted in her seat, ready to talk about Hadley. Or not. Maybe she could just walk out. "So."

"How is she?"

Amber blinked at Kyle silently. His words were a little reminiscent of Nathan's the other night and for just a second, she was on the floor with Nathan, matching him thrust for thrust.

She looked away from Kyle, hoping her face didn't give away her thoughts. What the hell right did he have to ask after Hadley like this? Why wouldn't she be okay, as far as he knew?

"She's fine."

"Have you talked to her?"

"Not yet."

He twisted his cup in a circle, and Amber decided he was a pansy. She wondered if Jen had told him she wanted nothing to do with his bastard daughter, and she thought maybe he should grow some balls and man up.

"Jen was upset, of course," he started. "We're very...we have a good marriage-"

Amber didn't give a damn about his marriage. She wanted the bottom line.

"It hurt her...that..."

"That Hadley exists?" Amber offered.

"That I never told her."

"You didn't know."

"That you and I..." He shrugged.

Amber considered that. A little bit of relief. What had happened in the backseat of his car when he was twenty-something and she was sixteen and he wasn't married to Jen shouldn't matter at all. Sure, Amber had told Nathan, but that was different. She'd given birth to Hadley and raised her. Nathan had been a part of Hadley's life. Kyle shouldn't have thought twice about that afternoon until last week.

"You tell her about every...girl you were with before you were married?"

He stared at her silently. She nodded when she guessed that was a yes. She wondered if he'd left her out because she was sixteen, and what he'd done was illegal. Or if she was just that forgettable.

"We'd like to meet her."

Amber sucked in a sharp breath, winced at the pain in her throat.

"Just you."

"Jen and I do everything together-"

"Just you. The first time. I don't want to overwhelm her."

He thought about it for a moment and agreed with a reluctant nod.

"Okay."

She was ready to run. Get the hell away from him and the hope in his eyes. She needed to cry. To scream. To break something. She eyed her coffee cup, but again reminded herself she didn't want to cause a scene.

"When can we do this?"

Shit. Details. She'd forgotten the wheres and whens.

"Um. Next weekend?"

He winced like he wasn't happy to put it off for so long.

"Kyle, she's in school. She's just coming off strep throat." Okay, that was a stretch, but he had no way of knowing that. "We're still dealing…with Pop's house. And we've got…"

"Got what?" He pushed.

"Next weekend," she said again.

"Okay."

"What if we met at the park? The farmer's market."

"Washington Park?"

"Mm." She nodded.

Kyle looked over his shoulder now, as if he could see the park through the front of the building.

"Okay."

"Nine?" she suggested. Wondered what Hadley would say about having to be somewhere early on a Saturday morning. Thought about Hadley being awake last Saturday at seven. Thought about Had staying with Liv. The way Amber had ended Saturday night.

"Great." He nodded. He pushed his chair back to stand. Looked at her expectantly.

"It's okay." She tried to smile. "I'm just gonna…"

"Amber?"

"What?" She sighed.

"Thank you."

She wanted to ask him what he was thanking her for. To let him know that there was a limit to what she would give him with Hadley. To let him know that she'd never let him take Hadley on a family vacation. That Hadley wouldn't magically morph into a soccer fan. That she might hate Jen and Kyle's sons. But Amber didn't, because what if Hadley did? Decide she liked soccer? Decide she liked having little brothers?

She thought about telling him not to thank her, because Hadley was a fourteen-year-old girl with an attitude. That he had no idea what he was getting himself into. But she didn't. Because attitude aside, Hadley was an amazing kid, and Kyle had missed out on fourteen years of that.

Instead of saying anything, Amber simply nodded. She didn't look up when he walked away. She stared at their table. Prayed that no one was looking at her too closely, because they would see her fault lines. They would see that she was crying silent tears.

After several long moments had passed and she was sure he was gone, she lifted her head and noticed he hadn't finished his tea.

One more swallow of coffee, she picked up her purse and walked out of the café. Crossed the street. Thought to herself that she still didn't know what he drove. Unlocked the Passport and looked out at the park. There were a few people wandering around, perfect day to be outside. Again. In fact, seemed like the more fucked up she felt inside, the nicer the weather was.

Her eyes caught on a small pile of clothing beside one of the park benches. Intrigued, she put her purse in the hatch and grabbed blindly for her camera bag. Unzipped it, grabbed the camera and lens and then closed the hatch. She pocketed her keys and then wandered up over the curb and across the sidewalk.

No one around, Amber stopped a few feet away and studied the pile. It was an old winter coat. Faux fur, white with black spots. Made her think of *Cruela Deville*. Tossed down in the mud, the coat was dirty. Matted, of course, with mud and simply dingy. Peeking out from under the coat was a pair of dull pink Crocs, one of them missing the ankle strap.

Amber looked around for a few moments. No one hovered nearby. Then again, why would anyone feel the need? Who would steal something like this?

The ugly spoke to her. Loud and clear, she heard it. She squatted down, perhaps a foot away, and snapped a picture. Two more. Three more. When she finally stood, no one rushed at her. No one told her to leave his or her things alone. No one shooed her away, insisting she had no right to take a photograph of anything.

Emotion pounding in her throat, she headed back through the park to her SUV. Wondered if she'd ever find anything as ugly as she felt inside.

Thirty-Three

Liv had called her later, when she was driving home. Standing in the kitchen, flipping through the mail-mostly junk mixed with a few bills-Amber listened to her voicemail. She didn't call Liv back, though. She had more important things on her mind than a girls' night.

She'd picked up takeout for dinner. Actually, she'd driven out of her way to Panda to get dinner. Made sure she had Hadley's favorites: Chinese spare ribs, chow mein, and eggrolls. She'd even brought home a large Mountain Dew, and honestly, she hated when Hadley drank so much soda.

"Hadley?" she called as she made her way to the steps. "Can you come down?"

She stood at the foot of the steps and listened. Music. Sounded like something Hadley listened to all the time, but not something Amber could name. She waited a few minutes and decided she heard Hadley giggling. Curious and yet dreading what she would find, Amber climbed the steps, this time being as quiet as she could.

She blushed when she found them. Hadley and Kesh, in various stages of nudity, hands nowhere to be seen.

"Hadley."

"God, Mom!" Hadley half sat up, but realizing or remembering or something that she didn't have a shirt on, she tried to duck underneath Kesh.

"Get your clothes on and get downstairs. Now." Amber's voice shook with barely controlled anger. "And you, Mr. Keshing, do not set foot inside my house. Ever. Again. Do you understand me?"

"Yes, ma'am."

Amber squeezed her eyes closed and shook her head. She turned to go back downstairs, but she looked back at them. Saw enough to notice Kesh's jeans were open at the waist.

"Two minutes."

Her daughter ignored her, but Kesh, eyes averted, nodded. Amber moved slowly down the stairs, listening for any complaints. For a suggestive squeak of the bed. Slowed, almost missed a step when she heard a big squeak and a banging noise, but kept going when she realized it was probably the kid getting off her daughter. She marched to the kitchen and waited. Counted out a hundred and twenty seconds and stepped out into the dining room, ready to go back after him. Kesh appeared first. Avoided her eyes as he hurried across the dining room to the front door. Slipped outside, still tucking his shirt in.

Hadley looked a little green. Embarrassed maybe? Ashamed? Guilty?

"What in God's name do you think you're doing?" Amber asked without preamble.

"He just came over."

"Just came over. Even though you are grounded from any sort of communication with him, he just showed up."

Hadley, eyes on the floor, nodded and shrugged.

"And I don't give a goddamned how or why he showed up. I want to know what you were doing with him in your bedroom."

To her credit, Hadley didn't say a word.

"What do you think I should think, Hadley? You're fourteen years old-"

"I'm almost fifteen."

"And that makes it okay?" Amber snapped. "You've got no business inviting that kid in. Taking him to your bedroom. Taking your clothes off for him. Are you kidding me, Hadley? Haven't I taught you more than this?"

"He cares about me, Mom."

"No, Hadley, he doesn't. He cares about what you've got in your pants. He's a kid. He wants sex anywhere he can get it, and you're willing."

"We didn't have sex."

"You're were heading that way." Amber shook her head. She ducked into the kitchen and grabbed the Panda bag. Carried it to the dining room table. "Do you not understand that? Kesh is older than you, bigger than you. He could take advantage of you-"

"Why would that be such a bad thing?" Hadley looked up defiantly.

"You're too young for this, Had. Save it. Save something for when you're older. When you meet someone you-"

Hadley shook her head. "Don't say love."

Amber set the bag down and stared at Hadley.

"You can't begin to compare what you were just doing with that kid to me and Nathan-"

"You know what?" Hadley yelled. She wiped at her eyes and smeared her mascara over her face. "At least he's here. At least he wants to be with me for something."

Amber swallowed hard. She dropped into a chair and stared at Hadley. Tried to catch her breath.

"What does that mean?"

"You're always gone. Since Nathan left, you're never here-"

"You don't want me here!" Amber shouted. "When I am here, you don't want to spend time with me-"

"That doesn't matter!" Hadley sobbed. "You're my mom, and you're not here. I don't know what you're doing. If you're fucking somebody else already or if you just-"

Amber stood up, hand raised. Hadley stared at her wildly, eyes bloodshot, face streaked with black.

"Don't you ever…" Amber lowered her hand. "Ever say that to me. Again. Do you understand me-"

"Are you, Mom? Is there someone else?"

Amber's knees gave out. She sat down again, buried her face in her hands.

"No."

"So you just don't wanna be here. With me."

She couldn't fight it. The rush of tears, the sobs that shook her shoulders.

"You know…" Hadley's voice was small. "This is so unfair. You weren't married to him, so I can't even choose him. No divorce, so I can't choose him. Typical you."

"What?" Amber looked up at Hadley. "Hadley-"

"I hate living here. I hate you. I hate what you did to him-"

"I didn't do anything to him, baby. I love him-"

"If I knew my real dad?" Hadley tilted her head and studied Amber's face. "I'd live with him. I'd leave. And I'd never come back to you."

Stung, Amber watched Hadley spin around and march back to the stairs.

~

Her first instinct had been to walk out. Not to leave Hadley alone. But to work off the anger. The intensity of Hadley's hatred. She hadn't, though. If Hadley needed her to be in the house with her and needed to hate her at the same time, Amber would stay put. She'd torn the house apart, though. Cleaning. Scrubbed out the fridge. The stove, even though it was rarely used. She'd dusted and vacuumed and scrubbed the bathroom until her elbows hurt.

She'd left the food sit on the dining room table, and at some point while she was cleaning, Hadley had come downstairs and snatched it. When the house was spotless enough to eat off any surface, Amber had gone down to the godforsaken basement and done every last stitch of laundry. She'd found a few of Nathan's shirts, and she'd sat alone in the dark, damp basement and suffered through an ugly crying jag.

Thought again about looking for just one thing uglier than who she was inside. When she'd come upstairs, she'd texted Gretchen. Asked if she could use the picture of her foot for something.

Gretchen had thought she was kidding.

When Amber had said she was dead serious, Gretch had asked if she was doing a medical book or something. Amber had answered with an *or something*, glad they were texting, because Gretchen had no idea which way to take her. Gretchen had, of course, given Amber permission to use the picture.

She'd wished for her computer at the studio. At the very least that she'd put some of her pictures on a memory card and brought them home so she could work with them on her laptop. Since that wasn't an option, Amber went outside after her camera and then come back in and snapped at least twenty pictures of the ugly parts of her house. Like the basement. Nathan's shirts, piled with her laundry. The scuffed linoleum in her kitchen, where the uneven basement door dragged on it when you opened or closed it. A water stain in the corner of the bathroom ceiling.

She went to bed without telling Hadley about Kyle Carpenter. Stayed awake thinking about how she'd set the wheels in motion on that piece of machinery and how now she had to tell Hadley and how maybe Hadley would just decide to move in with him, even though he was a complete stranger to her.

It nagged at her, and she tossed and turned most of the night. Also crossed her mind that she was searching for something uglier than herself inside her own home. Maybe tomorrow, while Hadley was in school, she'd go hunting. Looking for something atrocious.

She fell into a deep sleep just before the alarm went off. Woke up on Nathan's side of the bed, hugging his pillow. Rolled to her back and closed her eyes again. Thought of the other night. When he'd fucked her. She'd asked for it. But she'd naively thought it was the first step in fixing things. That maybe after doing it, they'd scoot closer to the wall and sit up together and lean on it and talk.

Even now, she didn't know what she'd say to him. To make things better.

When she dropped Hadley off at school, she told her she'd be there to pick her up. Arched her eyebrows when Hadley started to argue. Told her she'd be taking her phone when she picked her up. Watched her walk up the sidewalk to the huge wooden doors. Heart in her throat, she hoped the hate would go away. Some day.

She'd wondered, too, in the slowest moving early morning hours, if anything else had happened with Hadley and Kesh. If she'd stopped it before it happened. Or if they'd already done it, and they were in the process of dressing so he could leave. So Amber wouldn't catch them.

Her phone buzzed as she let herself into the studio. No longer in a desperate hurry, hopeful that Nathan would call or text, Amber set her purse down and calmly reached in for the phone. She was still hurt, still sad about Nathan, but she was angry, too, at him and at herself, and even if it was Nathan, she wouldn't gush to him. Take a swing at him, maybe.

Ingrid. Asking if she and Hadley would like to come for dinner.

No. Amber had no desire to pack her kid up and go to her sister's for dinner. But she had no desire for a repeat of last night, either. She wasn't sure how much longer she could stand sitting by herself in that house.

Before she could answer, Ingrid texted again and said Liv was coming. Liv and Grace. A bit weary, Amber texted back. Asked if this was a girls' night.

Sorta. But not like…the…girls' night.
Amber sighed.
Bring your suit.

What the hell? She stared at her phone for a moment like it would explain. She jumped when it lit up and started buzzing.

"Hey."

"Hey." She sighed. Leaned on the counter and closed her eyes. Exhaustion tugged at her eyes, her hips, her knees.

"Will you come?" Ingrid asked.

"I guess."

"You don't sound too excited."

"Bad coupla days, Ingrid."

"What happened?"

Amber let her eyes roam over the walls of her studio. Tried to breathe through the ache in her chest.

"Not a good time," she sniffled, "to talk."

"Okay. So tonight. You could talk to me and Liv."

Amber swallowed hard. "Maybe."

"I was thinking we could sit in the hot tub for a while. Have a glass of wine or something."

"Yeah." Amber nodded. "Sure."

"Luke won't be here. Wade's not coming. Just us girls."

"Do you want me to bring anything?"

"Just you and Had. Okay?"

"Okay."

Amber started to pull the phone away from her ear, but she heard Ingrid say her name.

"What?" Her voice jumped an octave. Her emotions had been ready to rip out of the gate when she thought she was done with the phone conversation.

"Come whenever. Okay? Come as soon as you get Hadley after school. If you want."

"Thanks, Ingrid." She ended the call before Ingrid could say anything else.

Thirty-Four

Amber wondered how Hadley had been able to act as if nothing was wrong when she'd spent last Saturday with Liv. Tonight, she had no qualms letting the world know how much she hated her mother. Ingrid had fixed lasagna. Salads. Garlic bread. Amber couldn't remember the last time she'd eaten, and she hadn't eaten anything good in a damned long time. She'd wanted to forgo dinner, because she wasn't interested in food or really, anything, but her stomach had started growling as soon as she smelled the garlic in the kitchen.

Hadley and Grace had sat at one end of the table, whispering and giggling about something Amber didn't even want to know about. She and Liv and Ingrid sat at the opposite, sipping a dry red and talking. Well, Liv and Ingrid talked. Amber pretended to listen.

When the girls finished eating, they carried their plates to the sink and disappeared into the living room. Ingrid waited until she heard the TV come on, the surround sound speakers come alive.

"Do you remember what it was like to be that age?" she asked as she stacked her and Liv and Amber's plates.

"Mm." Liv smiled wistfully. "I do. Freedom. No responsibilities at all."

Amber dragged her fingers back through her hair. Ironic. She couldn't stand being at home these days. Alone. Alone with Hadley. But she couldn't stand this either. Feeling alone with her sisters right across the table.

Ingrid carried their plates over to the counter.

"Let us help." Liv drained her glass and stood to help Ingrid with the dishes.

"Not too much to do," Ingrid said with a shrug. Amber stood and carried her glass to the counter. Watched Ingrid fill the sink with hot, soapy water. Liv scraped the leftover lasagna from the glass-baking dish into a Rubbermaid container. Amber picked up a towel ready to dry whatever Ingrid washed.

"So?" Ingrid glanced at her. "What happened?"

Amber fought to control herself. Shook her head.

"What's going on?" Liv asked. Amber, eyes brimming with tears, looked at her and then at Ingrid.

"I haven't said a word," Ingrid said quietly.

"Amber?" Liv tapped the spatula on the edge of the dish and then dropped it in the sink. "What's wrong, hon?"

The kindness was her undoing. She sobbed out loud. Threw the dishtowel down and slipped out of the kitchen to the deck. Within minutes, she heard the door open. Turned to find Liv step outside with her.

"Tell me."

"Nathan left me, Liv," she whispered. "He's been gone almost two weeks."

Instead of giving her hell for keeping it to herself, instead of asking why, Liv hurried to her and wrapped her arms around her. Amber was glad for her strength, because maybe without it, she'd have fallen apart on the deck. Broken into tiny pieces.

"I'm so sorry." Liv rocked her, smoothed her hand over her back. For just a moment, Amber thought of their mom. Quick to get angry, to reprimand. But just as quick to love, to soothe.

"Where's Ingrid?" Amber dashed at her eyes and stepped away from Liv.

"Finishing up in the kitchen."

Amber nodded. Waited for Liv to ask why she'd told Ingrid everything and said nothing to her.

"I have an idea."

"We slash his tires and trash his house?" Amber asked hopefully.

"Close." Liv grinned. "Let's put our suits on. Get a bottle of wine, get Ingrid and sit in the hot tub. Talk about this."

Amber frowned and eyed the hot tub suspiciously. "I thought that was the sexiest seat in the house."

"He's not here," Liv said with a wink.

Amber laughed softly.

"C'mon. Ingrid just had to wash the lasagna dish and wipe the table down."

Amber allowed Liv to lead her back inside. As Liv had said, Ingrid was wiping the table off. She turned to them with a small smile, eyebrows raised.

"Done. Grab a bottle. Let's go."

"Um." Liv winced. "Suits?"

Ingrid snorted. "Right. Forgot that. Don't usually need one out there."

"I've never had sex in a hot tub." Liv shrugged and nudged Amber's arm. "Have you?"

"Swimming pool, but not a hot tub."

"Really?"

Amber nodded.

"Nath-"

She shook her head and cut Liv off. Ingrid grabbed for their hands. Amber let herself get caught up in the rush with her sisters. The wine with dinner had been good. Another glass sounded nice. She wasn't sure how much talking she could do, but she'd try it. It was either that or maybe explode one of these days.

Ingrid slipped into the bedroom she shared with Luke. Liv disappeared into a spare room, and Amber claimed the main bath. The only suit she had was a bikini Nathan had bought for her when they'd gone to Florida last summer. Hadley had pretended to gag when he'd picked it out, but later, she'd told Amber she looked good in it.

Amber moved slowly. Unwilling to see herself. Naturally, she'd opted to change in the bathroom. Complete with a giant mirror that took up half a wall. She couldn't help but notice the faded bruises on her back, on her shoulder blades. Slipped the bikini bottom up over her hips, thankful they hadn't done it on carpet. At least she wouldn't have to explain away rug burn.

The black and royal blue bikini left her feeling horribly exposed. She hated looking at her pasty white skin. The way the top sagged a bit. Of course if she was going to lose weight because of stress, it would have to be in her boobs.

She stood for a moment, staring at herself in the mirror. Remembering the first time she'd worn the bikini for Nathan. The way he'd kissed her. Through the material. Pulled the suit and her nipple into his mouth. Slid the tiny scrap of material between her legs aside.

Breathless, she jumped when someone pounded on the door.

"Let's go. Wine, Amber. Concentrate."

Let it go, she told herself. Don't concentrate. At all.

She opened the door to find both Liv and Ingrid in the hall waiting for her. Both of them wore simple black one piece suits.

"Damn." Liv whistled. "Ingrid, did you know our little sister had a hot little body like that?"

Amber rolled her eyes. "It's the only suit I have."

"I had no idea she had such big boobs." Ingrid shook her head. She stepped closer to Amber and tugged gently at the top. "Are those real?"

"Can I have that wine now?"

"Are they?"

"Yes." Amber blushed.

"Where do you hide them?" Liv asked as they walked back out to the kitchen. Amber heard the girls talking over the TV in the living room. She watched Ingrid grab a fresh bottle of cabernet sauvignon, she'd already opened it, and pick up her glass. She and Liv grabbed theirs and followed Ingrid outside.

"I bind them down as tight as I can-"

"Like in the olden days? When girls wanted to be seen as boys so they could help on the farm or go to war?"

Amber stared at Liv silently. Finally nodded. She turned to Ingrid as she stepped into the hot tub and carefully eased down into the water.

Liv poured the wine.

"C'mon. Luke and I don't have sex in here all the time."

Amber snorted.

"Sometimes we do it on the deck." Ingrid took a drink of her wine. "Pretty much right where you're standing."

Liv laughed, but Amber looked away.

"So?" Ingrid said softly. "What's going on, Amber?"

Amber climbed into the hot tub, groaned out loud as she sat down.

"Really? Like you feel it? Just by getting in the water?" Liv eyed Amber curiously.

"That's sick." Ingrid poked Amber's knee with her toes.

"I didn't say it."

"What happened?"

Amber watched Liv slip down into the water. Waited until she was comfortable. Leaned her head back and closed her eyes and started talking. Ingrid jumped in now and then, when Amber slowed down to breathe. To cry. But she listened silently when Amber added the last part of the story. The meeting with Kyle. The desperation fuck at their parents' house. Finding Hadley with Kesh. The last huge blow out between them last night.

"Why don't you call us? When this happens?" Liv asked.

"What can you do?" Amber shrugged. "You're here. I'm there." She glanced at Ingrid.

"But it helps just to talk, Amber," Liv insisted. "It would calm you down."

"I can't let her see me get that upset."

"You can. Maybe you need to. Yes, you're the parent, but maybe she needs to see you break down. You're trying so hard to be strong for her, she doesn't see how deeply you're hurting."

"What're you gonna do?" Ingrid held her glass, poised at her lips, but she waited for Amber to answer before she took a drink.

"I don't know. I have to talk to her about Kyle."

"You do," Liv agreed.

"It could be a good thing, Amber-"

"I'm not looking to lighten the parenthood load-"

"I didn't say that," Ingrid argued. "Didn't mean that at all. Just saying it might be good for Hadley. To meet her father. To see more of the world-"

"So you think I should just let her go? If he wants to-"

"No. No, no, no. I just meant....maybe it would be good for her to see how another family lives. Interacts. Maybe she'll find things about him that she likes. Things she doesn't like. Maybe-"

"Maybe she'll appreciate you more when she sees other people. Other families." Liv pursed her lips.

"Exactly." Ingrid nodded.

"What if it works out so well, she's living with him next year at this time?"

"Won't happen." Liv shook her head.

"What if this is it for me?" Amber didn't expect an answer. "I had a chance with Nathan. And I blew it. What if I lose her, too?"

"Why are you so afraid of being alone?" Liv asked her. "It's not gonna happen, Amber. Hadley's always going to love you. Need you. And you'll always have me and Ingrid."

"Nathan's a jerk for what he did."

"I asked for it."

"Well, okay, it was a stupid move for both of you. And yet, sounds like you both needed...it..." Ingrid took another drink and set her glass down on the short drink table next to the hot tub. "So, as your sisters, we're gonna help you scheme to get him back."

"Slashing his tires and trashing his house?"

"No." Liv shook her head. "No, I don't think so."

"What are we gonna do?" Amber looked at Ingrid. "Are we getting him back? Or are we getting back at him?"

"Do you want him back?" Ingrid asked.

Amber dropped her gaze to the bubbling water and nodded.

"Yeah. I do."

"Then we're gonna get him back."

"How?"

"Let me think about it."

"Amber?"

Amber looked from Ingrid to Liv.

"Hmm?"

"Why don't you wanna marry him?"

"Show me a marriage happier than the way he and I were happy."

"But you weren't. Not if he left because of this."

Amber leaned back. Closed her eyes. The words were inside her. Always before, the thoughts were there, pushing her heart up into her throat. Making it hard for her to breathe. Impossible for her to say anything, much less bare her soul to anyone, even her sisters.

"I don't...want to do that...to Hadley."

"Hadley is crazy about him," Ingrid reminded her.

"But what happens when Nathan and I are married...and I get pregnant? What then?"

Liv shook her head, a deep crease between her eyes.

"Hadley gets a baby brother or sister," Ingrid said simply.

"Yeah. Hadley, who's fourteen now, gets a baby brother or sister."

"And?" Ingrid shrugged.

"She's not gonna want a baby to compete with. She'd be embarrassed for people to know Nathan and I have sex. She'd be ready to get a job, to start dating and I'd be changing diapers. She'd be my daughter. A new baby would belong to me and Nathan."

"Liv and I were working and dating when you and Ez were babies."

"Exactly." Amber nodded. She swallowed hard and tore her eyes away from Ingrid's gaze.

"I don't get it, Amber. What are you trying to say?" Ingrid leaned forward. "Liv and I don't carry scars from our childhood."

"You and Liv had a different childhood. You were the first family."

"But we loved being around you and Ezra."

"And then you left."

"Oh my God, really?" Ingrid groaned. "Amber, I thought we were past this-"

"You left," Amber whispered. "One day, Hadley will leave."

Ingrid stared at her silently.

"You're not worried about hurting Hadley." Liv shook her head. "You're worried about a baby you could have with Nathan."

"No-"

"You're letting him go over a baby you aren't even carrying yet?" Ingrid reached for Amber's hands. Amber started to stand up, but Ingrid and Liv both reached for her.

"Honey. Don't do this."

"You're so afraid to have a child grow up the way you did, you'd choose to lose Nathan?"

Amber let the tears go. Pushed her hair off her face. Closed her eyes and covered her face with her hands. Still felt their eyes on her.

"He said I was selfish."

"I told you before, we all have a little of that inside us."

"Well, apparently, I got more than my fair share."

"What...what happened, Amber? When you were little? What happened to hurt you like this?"

Amber shrugged. Shook her head.

"I did it?" Ingrid asked quietly. "Did I do this to you?"

"I was..." Amber took a deep breath. "I was just...when I was little, I felt closer to you than I did to Mom. I mean...she was always busy. With Ezra. With mom things. Doing laundry. Cleaning the house. Dealing with you guys. With your schedules. The car. Dates. I just...when I needed Mom, I went to you."

"Amber-"

"I mean, I was...three...I just...knew you were fun. You took the time to read to me. To play games. Time Mom didn't have."

"Amber, Mom loved you so much-"

Amber held her hand up to stop Liv. "I know. I do. And I loved her. I miss her. It's just...I don't know...my earliest memories...you were...you were always there, Ingrid. And then you weren't."

"Oh man." Ingrid rubbed her face. "I'm so sorry. I had no idea. I never-"

"I know." Amber nodded quickly. "I know. I'm not trying to...make you feel bad..."

"But this is it?" Ingrid asked her. "This is what you're afraid of with Nathan? That you might have a baby who would feel this way?"

"I don't know. It's all just a tangled mess inside. What I feel for Nathan. Hadley. The thought of marrying him and having a family with him."

Liv wiped at her eyes. "If this wasn't...a factor...if you didn't have this...abandonment issue-"

"Thanks, Olivia," Ingrid mumbled.

"Would you want to marry him?" Liv ignored Ingrid.

Amber combed her hair away from her face and stared at the surface of the water. Ashamed to look either of her sisters in the eye.

"Yeah." She held her hair at the nape of her neck with one hand. Rubbed at her eyes with the other. "I think so."

"Really?" Ingrid asked quickly.

"I've thought about it so much lately. Looking at you and Luke. At what Liv and Wade had-"

"Wait." Liv reached for Amber's hand. Linked their fingers. "I made a mistake, Amber. A big one. But I love him. I'm still in love with Wade, and I don't ever want that to end-"

Amber shrugged and nodded.

"I wish I had the courage to try." Amber licked her lips. "I wish it wasn't too late to tell him that."

"What about Hadley?" Ingrid asked her. "Have you ever talked to her about any of this?"

"No."

"Maybe you should. Tell her why you've hesitated. What you're afraid of."

"And if she still thinks I'm self-centered? If she still hates me?"

"What if she understands? What if she's open to the idea of a new family? Of babies?"

"What if I'm too old for-"

"You're not too old for this." Ingrid shot down that argument before Amber could spit it all out. "Julie Webb's too old-"

"What?" Liv asked quickly.

"Long story." Ingrid shook her head, but she didn't spare Liv a glance. "Don't wait, Amber. Because there's nothing sadder than knowing you waited too long and the time to do it has come and gone."

Amber rubbed the tip of her nose and took a deep breath.

"It doesn't matter anyway. Remember? Nathan left."

Thirty-Five

Alone on the highway, Amber goosed the gas and watched the speedometer climb past seventy. Felt her heart rate spike as it slipped upward past seventy-five. Eased off. She'd taken some pictures of wrecked vehicles today. Didn't mean she wanted to see what kind of damage she could do to her own SUV. She wasn't normally a *wind in her hair* kind of girl, but today she had her window more than a little bit cracked and the fresh air had helped keep the headache at bay.

She'd bared her soul to her sisters two nights ago. She'd never before let her fears solidify into words. She'd never truly acknowledged her fears. Saying them out loud had left her a little raw. Liv and Ingrid had been good to her. They'd listened. They'd coaxed her into her confessions, argued gently against her reasons to stay alone, to stay lonely. She'd appreciated the kid glove treatment. But all in all, she'd walked away from Ingrid's a little bit more exposed and everything about her hurt.

Nathan hadn't called. Hadley hadn't forgiven her. The only thing that had changed, maybe, was Amber, and she wasn't sure it was a change for the better. Amber had felt the flame of wanderlust lick her heart, her soul last night. When she'd called Ingrid and asked if she could pick Hadley up from school and hang with her until she got home, Ingrid had agreed without question or comment. Hadley had overheard her and sneered at her. Insisted she didn't need a babysitter. Amber had simply said that until she proved she could be trusted, she needed a babysitter and would have one.

She'd driven to Jacksonville. Considered going on to Springfield, and she decided she might still do exactly that. For today, Jacksonville had been enough. She'd wandered around a gas station where wrecked vehicles had apparently been towed and taken pictures of the most twisted, bent up pieces of metal there. Those most unrecognizable as vehicles. She'd walked through the park, through residential areas and captured some ugly on film.

Nothing to match her insides, yet, but she wasn't done looking.

On the drive back to Quincy, she turned off on a gravel road. She was near Griggsville. Drove through back roads, hungry eyes taking in everything they could as she drove. She found her way to Highway 104. There was no draught this year. No onslaught of rain, either. Then again, maybe it was too soon to say on either count. It was only April, after all.

No dilapidated barns, but then she'd just shot that barn for the book she'd recently submitted. She didn't particularly want to repeat a subject, even for a different project, different idea.

She had to tell Hadley. About Kyle. She was running out of time. Not a good idea to show up at the park Saturday and say *oh by the way…*

They'd talk about Kyle. Probably nothing else, because Amber was yellow and didn't have the guts to share her innermost self with her daughter. It still kind of surprised her she'd been able to put that huge feeling inside into words. That she'd said those words to her sisters.

She honestly hated what she'd done to Ingrid. Again. Intellectually, she knew that Ingrid's leaving had nothing to do with Amber. And yet, sometimes hearts didn't listen to brains, and she'd hurt Ingrid, and she hadn't meant to this time.

The last of her drive disappointed her. There was ugly stuff in the world. How could it be that Amber could only find it in herself right now? She considered her options as she drove through Liberty and brought 104 around the curve at Five Points. Crossed her mind that there might be something worth looking at at the state park. And yet, the thought of the day she and Nathan and

Hadley had spent-Hadley's best day ever-kept her from turning off there to pick up the Kellerville Blacktop.

Maybe another day.

She found Ingrid and Hadley at the house. Front porch. Feet up on the railing-didn't matter, it was chipping paint, rotten in spots-talking about someone named *Blue* and someone named *Gansey*.

"Soap opera?" Amber asked as she stepped up on the porch with them.

"I don't watch soap operas." Hadley rolled her eyes.

"Books," Ingrid told her.

"You watch those stupid court TV shows. They're worse."

Apparently, Hadley couldn't disagree with her, because she looked away.

"Thank you." Amber stroked her fingertips over Ingrid's shoulders.

"Absolutely."

Amber felt a twinge of guilt when Ingrid stood up and smiled at her. Right now, she thought Ingrid might offer her a kidney or even her heart if she needed a transplant. Amber didn't want her to feel like she owed her something. They were adults now. Everyone had adjusted. Ingrid had lived away and come home.

Then again, if Amber had adjusted well, then maybe she'd be married to Nathan by now and none of this would be happening.

"Girls' night this weekend," Ingrid announced.

"Like dinner? At your house?'

"Like dinner out. Invite Gretch."

"Really?"

"Julie's gonna be in town. She's coming."

"Is Liv bringing a buddy?" Amber arched an eyebrow.

"Beats me. I'm trying to talk Shay into coming, too."

"Good luck with that."

"Okay. I gotta go." Ingrid kissed Amber's cheek and then stepped off the porch. "Call me. If you need anything."

Amber watched her go, again overcome with guilt. She dropped into the lawn chair Ingrid had been sitting in.

"I resent that you don't trust me."

Amber looked at Hadley. "Really? I resent that you break every rule I set."

"You never specifically said I couldn't lay with Kesh in my bed."

"No, I just said you weren't to communicate with him in any way, shape or form. I think what you were doing could be classified as communication."

"I have homework." Hadley stood up.

"Sit down." Amber shook her head. "We need to talk about something."

Hadley sat back down. Drew her knees up and curled her toes around the edge of the chair. The chipped pink polish on her toenails reminded Amber that no matter how quickly Hadley wanted to grow up, she was still just a kid.

"Nathan?" Hadley's voice squeaked a bit, Amber knew with hope, and she hated to shake her head and douse that little flame inside her daughter.

"No."

Hadley sighed. "What then? Am I in trouble again?"

"Did you do something to be in trouble again?"

"Told a guy that sits behind me in history class to fuck off."

"Hadley."

"You didn't get a phone call?" Hadley asked in disbelief.

"No."

Hadley groaned. "He wouldn't leave me alone."

"What was he doing?"

"Started out pulling my hair. Then he snapped my bra."

Amber bit her lip. "Okay. I'll give you a pass on that one."

Hadley almost smiled, but she caught herself. Looked away in case it got out of hand again.

"So what do you want to talk to me about?"

Amber sat silently, staring at Hadley, uncertain as to how to begin.

"Mom?"

"Mmm. Hadley…"

"Please just forget about it, Mom."

"Forget about what?" Amber asked quickly. Had Hadley figured out she'd been talking to Kyle Carpenter? Who had told her?

"Me and Kesh. I mean…everybody fools around. Either I'm a freak because I don't, or I'm easy because I do."

Amber opened her mouth to say something, closed it again and asked herself if she wanted to tackle that issue tonight. She didn't. She didn't want to poke it with a ten foot pole.

"It's not about that."

Amber noticed the color fade from Hadley's face. "Aunt Ingrid?"

Again, Amber wondered what exactly Hadley knew about Ingrid.

"You've asked about your father."

Hadley stared at Amber, clearly taken aback by Amber's words.

"You're gonna tell me?"

Amber answered with a hesitant nod.

"I'm…" Hadley took a quick breath. "I'm scared."

"To know?"

She nodded. "You know what I wish?"

"What?"

"That it could be Nathan. Like that you guys knew each other when you were younger. And he got you pregnant-"

Amber shook her head. How could this beautiful little girl in front of her, who had sweet daydreams like this, think it was okay to take her clothes off for some guy who claimed to be her friend?

"It's not, Hadley. I'm sorry."

Hadley pressed her lips together. Turned her face away from Amber. She nodded. Said in a tiny voice, so unlike her, "I know."

"His name is Kyle. Kyle Carpenter."

"Kyle Carpenter," Hadley repeated. "It feels weird. To say it."

"It feels weird to hear it in your voice."

"Does he know about me?"

"He does now."

Hadley whipped her head around to stare wide-eyed at Amber.

"You told him?"

"A while ago"

"What did he say?" Hadley dropped her gaze to her feet.

"Well. He's married. So he said he wanted to talk about it with his wife-"

"Was he married then?"

"When we-?" Amber asked. Hadley nodded, but she wouldn't look at her. "No."

"Did he talk to her? His wife?"

"Mm-hmm. They'd like to meet you."

"Really?"

When Hadley finally lifted her eyes to look at Amber, they were glassy, ready to spill.

"Yeah."

"Are you doing this to get rid of me?"

"What?"

"I said I wanted to live with him. Do you want that?"

"Hadley." Amber touched her chest, rubbed her hand over her heart. "God, no. I'm scared to death about this. I would never do anything to get rid of you-"

"But I've been so horrible to you."

Amber lifted her chin, trying to keep her tears from falling.

"You have. But I understand. You're hurting. You-"

"Did you ever think about it?"

"About what?"

"Aborting me."

"No."

"Honestly?"

"I never considered it. Why would you ask me that?"

Hadley shrugged. "I just think sometimes your life would be easier without me."

"Do you know how empty my life would be without you? You're the reason I get out of bed every morning."

Hadley eyed her suspiciously.

"But you waited until now…until Nathan's gone…to tell me about my father."

Amber reached her hand out to touch Hadley, but their chairs were too far apart for her to each her.

"Nathan and I talked about this before he left. If telling Kyle was the right thing. If you were ready for this."

"And Nathan thought it was? He thought I was ready?"

"Yes."

"Because he didn't want to be my father? Is that why he left?"

"Honey, Nathan's crazy about you. You know that."

"Why did he leave, Mom?"

Amber cleared her throat. "Kyle wants to meet you Saturday."

"This Saturday?" Hadley yelped.

"At Washington Park."

"That sounds creepy."

"I'll go with you."

"What's he like?"

"He's..." Amber faltered. How did she tell Hadley that her father was ten years older than Amber? "A college professor."

"Something cool?" Hadley asked hopefully. "Philosophy? Psych?"

"Algebra." Amber rolled her eyes.

"That's not cool."

"He's not cool, Amber. He's just a guy. Living his life."

Hadley scrunched up her nose. "He has kids. Doesn't he?"

Amber wished she could lie. But there was no point. Hadley would meet him in two days. And he'd tell her the truth.

"Yeah. He does." She nodded. "Two sons. Both younger than you."

"What if I don't wanna meet him?"

"You don't?"

"What if I don't?"

"Then I guess I'll tell him that." Amber leaned forward and scooted her chair closer to Hadley. "What's wrong? You don't want brothers?"

Hadley shrugged. Turned her face away from Amber. "From you."

Amber's heart lurched and left her feeling a little dizzy, out of breath.

"They play soccer. Sounds like they do a lot of family vaca-"

Hadley shook her head and held her hand up.

"Too much?"

"'s a lot." Hadley cleared her throat.

Amber stared at Hadley, wondering if she'd made a mistake. If Hadley's questions about her father were just questions. Just something to let Amber know she wasn't happy. Just a scab to pick to get attention.

"I still wish Nathan was my dad."

Amber watched Hadley stand up and slip by her. She heard the door open and close. Swallowed the knot of emotion in her throat.

"Me too, Hadley."

Thirty-Six

The sad settled deep into her bones, and Amber wanted to push it away. Ignore it. Fight through it. Wallow in it. Whatever it was she'd been doing since this all started. And yet, she'd been reminded recently that her coping techniques weren't working, and so when she went inside and found that Hadley had gone upstairs to do God knows what-homework, maybe-Amber called Ingrid.

She hesitated twice on the dial. Guilt made her fingers hover just over her phone screen. She'd already bothered Ingrid enough today. Dragged her away from working, and Amber hated to be interrupted when she was working on something. Figured Ingrid felt the same way. She hadn't really had a chance to talk to Ingrid before she left, either, and Amber knew Ingrid and Hadley had had a rough start when Ingrid had first come back for Pop's funeral. She had no idea how Hadley had behaved with her sister.

Guilt made her hesitate, but the need to talk to someone, to Ingrid, had her fingers twitching over her phone screen. She decided she would call and just ask if things had gone okay. If Hadley had been respectful. And then if Ingrid wasn't busy, she'd tell her the rest. She lifted her eyes from her phone, stepped out of the kitchen and into the dining room. Decided she'd be better off outside, in case Hadley came back downstairs for anything.

She sat down again in the lawn chair on the porch. Considered her ugly project and decided maybe she needed people. Not ugly people. Amber didn't believe a person was beautiful or ugly, not by sight alone. Cliché as it sounded, it was what was inside a person that made him or her attractive to Amber or not.

Which wasn't too say she didn't find Nathan Marquardt gorgeous and sexy as hell.

She needed other people's ugly truths. To erase her own.

Something inside her shifted. Opened up. The tightness in her chest eased. Purpose. Her project had just redefined itself in her head, and now she saw the purpose, and though her own ugly would never be far away, as she carried it inside, she felt a new little jolt of energy. Intensity.

Fueled by the revelation, she dialed Ingrid's cell and put her phone to her ear. Watched a squirrel scamper around the base of the big Oak tree in the easement in front of her house.

"Hey."

Her eyebrows jumped up at Luke Ashley's sexy voice in her ear.

"Hey, Luke." She laughed softly. A nerve or two lit up inside her. Maybe she'd worn out her welcome with Ingrid. Maybe Ingrid didn't want to deal with her any more tonight. "Is Ingrid busy?"

"Hang on two seconds," Luke told her. "She's finishing an email."

"Great. Thanks."

"I'm told Wade and I missed a great night here. Relaxing in the hot tub with a bottle of wine."

"Three sexy chicks," she told him. "You forgot that part."

"Best part," he answered.

"Exactly."

"I'm sorry about Nathan, Amber."

She winced. His words had hit her right in the solar plexus. Took her breath away.

"Thanks." She swallowed hard.

"Hang in there. He's gonna figure out he can't live without you."

She had no idea what to say to that. *Thanks* didn't seem to be fitting. *Doubtful* was fitting, but it would make her cry to have to say it. Before she could decide what to say, if anything, Luke spoke again.

"Here's Ingrid."

Amber started to thank him, but then her sister's laughter was in her ear, and Ingrid said something to Luke about dinner, and then there was another peal of laughter, and Amber let the sound pour over her and soothe her.

"Hey." Finally Ingrid was talking to her.

"Hi."

"Sorry I kept you waiting."

"It's okay. I got to talk to Luke of the sexy-"

"Hey, hey." Ingrid laughed. "No need for that kind of talk."

"Are you busy?"

"No." Ingrid sounded sincere. "Just figuring out what to do for dinner. What do you think? Salmon steaks or pork chops?"

"You're kidding me, right?"

"Eh. That's right. You don't do salmon."

"Nope."

"How's it going? How's Had?"

Amber lifted the phone away from her mouth so Ingrid wouldn't hear her sigh.

"Um. How was she? Today? When you picked her up?"

"Fine." Again, Ingrid sounded sincere. Amber thought she'd probably say if it was otherwise, as Ingrid had lectured her on more than one occasion about her daughter's behavior. Then again, after the big reveal the other night-Amber hated feeling that way, thinking of sharing her secrets as a big outing, as if her secrets, her feelings were important enough that everyone needed to know about them-she wondered if Ingrid would suck it up and deal with whatever Hadley threw her way. "We got Icees and sat on the porch and talked."

"Icees?" Amber repeated.

"Yeah. Like we used to get at Kmart. Remember? They had that little deli stand by the checkout lanes. Dad got lunch meat there, and sometimes Mom would let us get Icees."

"Um. Yeah. I never got Icees. She musta liked you and Liv better than me."

"You've never had an Icee?"

"Slush Puppies."

"Nope. Not the same."

Amber frowned at the crunching sound on the other end of the phone.

"You haven't lived if you haven't had an Icee."

"What are you eating?"

"A carrot."

"Seriously?"

"What? You don't do carrots, either?"

"Not unless I have to," Amber answered.

"No wonder you're so skinny," Ingrid decided. "Anyway. We talked about some books. Talked about her English class. I'm supposed to go talk to her class next week. Next Friday."

"You don't have to do that, Ingrid," Amber said quickly.

"I don't mind. I want to."

"Really?"

"Well, I hate speaking things, but I wanna do this for Hadley."

"Okay." Amber nodded. "And she was okay for you? Promise?"

"Absolutely. She recommended a few books for me to try."

"Good."

"You okay?"

Amber sighed again and then chewed on her lip. "I talked to her. About Kyle."

"Oh. How'd that go?"

"I think I scared her. Like she thinks I'm gonna make her live with him and his wife, because she's been giving me such a hard time."

"But you told her that's not true-"

"Of course I did," Amber answered. "I just...I can't keep up with her, Ingrid. She's upset. She's not sure she wants to meet him now."

"It's a lot for her to handle, Amber."

"I know. I just wish...I could do something. Something to help her with all of this."

"She's confused. She's sad. But she'll work her way through it."

"She said she wishes Nathan was her dad."

Ingrid must have sucked in a quick breath, because Amber heard the whistle of the air between her teeth.

"I'm sure you wish that, too." Ingrid's voice was gentle. "Just be there for her, Amber. Whatever she needs."

"I will."

"And if the only thing she needs right now is to beat up on you and hurt you so she can feel better, then remember I love you, okay? You're not alone."

Amber's eyes burned with unshed tears.

"Thank you," she whispered.

~

Hadley had slept well Friday night, even if she was nervous about meeting Kyle. They'd hung out Friday night, made homemade macaroni and cheese-possibly the only thing Amber cooked that didn't involve opening a package and dumping it into boiling water-and watched movies. Amber assumed Hadley's clinginess was all nerves, and that come Sunday, maybe even Saturday afternoon, Hadley would hate her all over again. But she'd decided she'd take whatever reprieve Had would give her, and though she hated that Hadley was so scared, she loved being there to comfort her.

When they'd watched the last movie-*Jurassic Park*- there'd been no question that Hadley would sleep with Amber. Neither of them worried about dinosaurs plaguing their dreams, but every second that ticked by on the clock filled both of them with dread. Even though it was well after midnight, they'd lain awake together, talking first about Nathan and how much they missed him. How mostly they missed the little things-Hadley missed talking to Nathan about movies, (She hated action movies, but she watched anything Nathan wanted to watch and never complained.) and Amber missed the way he'd trail his fingers over the back of her neck when she was curled up in the corner of the couch, reading. With Saturday morning bearing down on them, conversation had turned to Kyle, and Hadley had asked Amber so many questions about him. Most of them Amber couldn't even answer, because she hadn't known much about him when they'd conceived Hadley, and she didn't know much more now.

When Hadley had finally drifted off to sleep, back pressed against Amber's chest, Amber's arms around her, protecting her from anything that would try to take her away or hurt her, Amber had lain as still as she could and listened to the soft, steady rhythm of her daughter's breathing. She'd wondered a hundred times if she'd made a mistake. Telling Kyle about her. What if Hadley didn't like him? What if she didn't want anything to do with him? Did he have legal recourse to come after Amber? Hadley? Could he take Amber to court for visitation or something? Would he?

In her heart of hearts, she didn't believe he would do it. But even just one percent of uncertainty was like sand in her eyes, burning and keeping her awake. Things had been hard between them lately, and Ingrid had come home at a bad time, had experienced Hadley for the first time at a really bad time, but Amber loved Hadley fiercely and would do anything for her.

And maybe that was part of the problem. She'd always done everything for her, starting when she was just a little girl. Bending over backwards, trying to compensate for Hadley not knowing her father. Maybe Amber had given Hadley too much, let her get by with too much, because she felt guilty for raising her without her father. Trying to discipline her and show her a little tough love now was an uphill battle.

When Hadley had stirred in her sleep and scooted away from Amber, she'd loosened her arms and let her move. But she'd still watched her sleep, torn between envying Hadley her youth and needing to hover over her so nothing bad would ever happen to her again.

As far as that part of parenting went, Amber felt like an epic fail. She'd been so careful with Hadley, so careful to keep Hadley separate from anyone she dated. But she'd been so in love with Nathan, so quickly, so smoothly, it had been the most natural thing in the world to invite him in and let him be a part of Hadley's life.

She'd been awake at seven, so she'd turned the alarm off and slipped out of bed. Tiptoed around the end of the bed to find clean clothes and go take a shower. What if Hadley absolutely refused to go today? What would she do? Call Kyle, she guessed. She wouldn't force the issue, if Hadley decided she wasn't ready.

Under the hot shower, her thoughts turned to Nathan. She wondered what he was doing. If he was even in town right now. She wished she had plans with him tonight. The *snuggle on the couch and watch movies and eat popcorn with Hadley* kind of plans. Probably a night out with her sisters and friends would be fun, but Amber was so exhausted, so emotionally worn, she wasn't sure she could go through with it.

Then again, maybe the next couple of hours would push her one way or the other. If meeting Kyle was a bust, and Hadley hated him or Hadley showed him her teen angst, then maybe she wouldn't go. Period. Then again, maybe that sort of fail would drive her to drink. If Hadley and Kyle clicked, if she came home with stars in her eyes and spent the rest of the day talking about Jen, and talking about Kyle's sons, maybe she'd need a drink.

She dressed in her go-to jeans, a pair of BKEs from the Buckle that she'd had forever, worn smooth and easy around her hips and her butt-had Ingrid said something about her being skinny last night?-and a scoop neck black t-shirt. Hit her hair with the dryer and some mousse, brushed on a bit of makeup. Surprised herself with the results, considering she really hadn't slept well.

They could grab coffee at JI and then walk over to the park to meet Kyle. Maybe Hadley would eat a muffin or something. Or maybe she should let Hadley sleep a little bit longer, and she could just make coffee here at home. They could take their to go mugs, and just show up at the park and walk around until they found him.

Still trying to be quiet, she nearly yelped in surprise when she found Hadley in the kitchen. Sitting on the counter, eyes on Mr. Coffee, as if he was the last man on earth, Hadley was a pathetic little heap of sadness and nerves. Dark circles framed her eyes, but the rest of her face was startlingly pale. Amber actually moved close enough to her to touch her forehead, wondering if the strep had come back.

Hadley twisted away from her.

"What're you doing?"

"You look pale. Do you feel okay?"

"Are you kidding me, Mom?"

Amber winced and let her hands rest on the counter, on either side of Hadley's legs.

"It's gonna be okay, baby." Amber leaned in and kissed the top of Hadley's head.

"How do you know that?" When Hadley looked up, her eyes shimmered with crocodile tears.

"Because no matter what happens, it's you and me." Amber kissed her again and then moved closer and put her arms around her. "I promise you I will always be here."

"Swear?"

"Absolutely."

"What if he wants me to...visit...them or something?"

"Honey, it's all up to you. I would never force you to do anything-"

"I just can't help but feel like you're doing this to punish me," Hadley whispered. "To scare me. Like if you don't like my attitude now, you can just send me off to be with him-"

"I would never do that, and you know it." Amber took Hadley's hands in hers and leaned in so they were forehead to forehead. "We have never needed anyone else. Always been you and me, and I would never use something like this as a threat, Hadley."

"We had Nathan."

Amber tried to breathe around the knife in her throat. She nodded. Worked to calm herself down, tears would ruin the half-ass decent make up job she'd managed to drum up.

"We did. And we loved him, and he loved us. And I'm so, so sorry that I messed that up for us. For you. Please believe me, Hadley. I didn't want it to be this way-"

"Is there someone else?" Hadley asked her.

"What?"

"Is there?"

"It was just a blind-"

"Do you have someone else? Is that why he left?" Hadley turned her face away from Amber to avoid her eyes. "Were you cheating on him?"

"What?" Stunned by Hadley's question, Amber drew back to stare at her.

"I'm just asking-"

"No." Amber interrupted her. "No. Never. I would never have done that. He didn't do that. It wasn't like that at all."

"So. You seriously broke up because you won't marry him?"

"Is that what Nathan told you?"

"Is that why you split up?" Hadley pushed.

Amber sighed and answered with a slow nod.

"Why don't you wanna marry him?"

Amber blinked, trying again to get herself under control.

"Can we...talk about this later?"

"Mom."

"I promise we'll talk about it, Had. I promise. But it's getting late. And I don't wanna...get into this...I can't let myself...feel...this right now. When we have to go meet your father."

"Please don't say that. Don't say it like that."

Amber eyed Hadley carefully.

"Sweetheart, if you don't want to do this, we don't have to. I'm not forcing you. I just thought this is what you wanted-"

Hadley shook her head quickly and reached up to touch Amber's mouth with her fingertips.

"I want to." Her voice was hoarse. "I'm just...I'm not ready for...that. I'm not ready to think of some guy I'm getting ready to meet...as my...father."

"Okay. Okay." Amber nodded. "Anytime you need to walk away, you say the word, kid. Okay?"

Hadley pursed her lips and raised her eyebrows when the coffee maker beeped. A giggle rumbled up from her belly.

"What word? Do we need a code word?"

Amber grinned, thrilled to see a smile, to hear her daughter laugh.

"You pick out a code word."

"How about *telegnosis*?"

"What?" Amber took her turn to laugh. "I don't even know what that means."

"Clairvoyance."

"Yeah?" Amber raised her eyebrows. "Well, if we had clairvoyance, we wouldn't need a code word, would we?"

Hadley linked her fingers through Amber's.

"That's ESP. Not the same thing."

"Why do you know this?" Amber squeezed Hadley's fingers. "And how are you gonna slip *clairvoyance* or *telegnosis* or whatever into a conversation to use as a code word?" She rested her other hand on Hadley's bare knee, stroked her fingers over her soft skin. "Go get a shower. Let's do this."

"Mom, don't say that," Hadley said with a shiver and an eye roll as she hopped off the counter.

"What?'" Amber watched her slip out of the kitchen. "Isn't that the cool thing to say? *Let's do this*?"

"It is," Hadley called, "but you're not."

"I'm not cool?"

"No. You're my mom."

Amber stood for a moment, alone in the kitchen, trying to decipher the meaning behind Hadley's words. She looked up when Hadley ducked her head around the door.

"I'd rather you be my mom than cool," Hadley said quietly.

Amber arched her eyebrows in surprise. Hadley was gone again before she could answer her.

"I'm gonna hold you to that!" she called just as Hadley closed the bathroom door.

Thirty-Seven

Amber parked on Maine, as if she was going to Java Infusion. As she and Hadley climbed out of the Passport, she sort of wished she could rewind time and go back to meeting Kyle. Not because she was enthralled by him, but because she could put this off for Hadley. Because the first time she'd met Kyle here had been before Nathan had left her.

Hadley waited impatiently at the back of the SUV as Amber pieced her camera together. The daughter of a freelance photographer, Hadley was used to her mom packing the camera pretty much everywhere she went. Better to carry it around for nothing than to miss the perfect shot.

It was twenty 'til nine, and Amber wondered if Hadley felt the same way she did. If she felt more confident, if getting there first made her feel more in control of the situation. They wandered through Washington Park, walking close, heads ducked together as they talked to each other in hushed tones.

Amber had told her that Kyle was older. Hadn't been an easy thing to admit. Didn't sound so bad, even, saying it that way. But having to admit to Hadley that Kyle had been a teacher, albeit a sub, had been hard. She still felt a little ashamed of herself for only being able to confess that part last night after they'd gone to bed. In the dark. Where she wouldn't have to see the look on Hadley's face, whatever it might have been.

"Is this why you worry about me?" Hadley asked her now.

Amber, viewfinder at her eye, camera pointed at the fountain-not yet turned on as it was only April-and the two young boys playing there, lowered the camera and looked at Hadley in question.

"What?"

"With Kesh?"

"I worry about you with anyone, Had," Amber said with a shrug. "But, yes, definitely with Kesh."

"Because you don't want me to get pregnant." Hadley fisted her hands and buried them in her royal blue jacket pockets. "And have to live like you did."

Amber opened her mouth to argue with Hadley, but she thought better of it. Pressed her lips together and thought for a moment on exactly what to say.

"You know what?" she asked as she reached for Hadley's hand. "I wouldn't change you. Not for the world. I meant it the other night when I said you're the reason I get out of bed every morning. I can't imagine not having you in my life."

Hadley struggled to hold the eye contact, but she finally blanched and looked away. Amber tugged gently on her hand and led her to a bench on the west side of the fountain.

"What I would change is giving you a real father. It would have been so much better for you if I'd have waited, and gotten pregnant by someone I loved. If I would have married your father. If I could have given you a real family-"

"Mom-"

"I don't want you to end up pregnant, no," Amber continued. "Of course not. I want you to be involved in school stuff. In everything. Not just working your butt off to get through your classes. I want you to go to college. To do something you love."

"But you do. Something you love. Right?"

"I do." Amber nodded. "But I want more for you. And besides, it's not just about getting pregnant, Hadley. You're so young. Don't do that to yourself. Don't do something like that-"

"Because everyone will think I'm a-"

"Because you're young. There's no hurry. It's not going anywhere. Besides that, it's not great when you're a kid. Everything's better when you're-"

"Mom."

Amber knew she was making Hadley uncomfortable, but she took a quick breath, prepared to continue. Hadley nudged her leg and nodded to the right.

"Is that him?"

Amber felt a zap of electric energy trail down her throat and into her stomach. She turned to see Kyle wandering toward them with a hesitant smile on his face.

"Mm-hmm." She touched Hadlye's knee and then stood up. She was glad to see Kyle had chosen jeans again, because he looked normal, younger in jeans, and Amber hadn't wanted Hadley to see her biological father for the first time in khakis or Dockers and decide he was a nerd, that she wanted nothing to do with him.

She noticed he wore the same *LA Galaxy* pullover. Wondered if Hadley would know what it was, or if she'd wonder about it.

"Hey." She smiled at him as he approached, but she sort of felt like she was going to throw up. She'd never in her wildest dreams have thought this moment would happen, and even since knowing it would, she hadn't had time to prepare herself. Maybe a hundred years wouldn't have been ample time to prepare herself to maybe share her daughter with someone else. With this stranger.

"Hi Amber." He nodded at her, and then she was enclosed in his arms in that loose, awkward hug from the first day at JI. She patted his back as she had that first day and stepped away as quickly as she could without seeming rude.

"Kyle, this is my daughter, Hadley." She wondered if it was rude to introduce her as her daughter. Decided she didn't care. First and foremost, Hadley was her daughter, and she'd drill that into his head repeatedly to make sure he understood she'd do anything for Hadley. "Hadley, this is…Kyle Carpenter."

That had thrown her, and she almost felt dizzy as she stood there between them. Should she have said *this is your father? Could* she have said those words?

"Hi Hadley." Kyle turned his attention to Hadley, offered her a small, but friendly smile.

Amber felt her heart rate spike, saw the telltale flinch and the way Hadley had to try twice to get her mouth open to say hi. Her stomach hurt for Hadley. She wanted to tuck her under her arm and run with her back to the SUV and climb in and drive away from this guy, who just happened to be the one who fathered her.

The introductions were followed by a healthy dose of awkwardness, and Amber wondered what she should do. Possibly, Kyle would feel more comfortable talking to Hadley if she wasn't tagging along. If he was more comfortable, maybe he could draw Hadley into conversation, and they could begin the journey to make up for the past fourteen years. Then again, Hadley had told Amber she didn't want to be alone with him, and so Amber couldn't just throw her to the wolves and wander away.

"So." Kyle pointed at Amber's camera. "What're you working on now?"

Amber glanced at the camera, at the red and gray striped strap around her neck and then looked back at Kyle. He was trying to ease them into something comfortable. Possibly something Hadley knew something about, something Hadley enjoyed. But Amber wasn't ready to discuss what she was currently working on. Not the project for her siblings, and not the ugly stuff.

"I just wrapped up a book on the simple things in life. Barns. Farmhouses. Fire pits." She shrugged. "Haven't really started anything new, yet."

She saw Hadley's sharp look. She was never without a project, and Hadley knew that. So she knew she was lying. Then again, Hadley knew she wouldn't discuss an idea until she had everything lined up and ready to defend her pitch.

"I liked your black and white rivers," he told her. She stared at him silently for a moment, unaware that he'd ever followed her work, uncertain what to say now that she knew he did.

"Thank you."

"Kind of a wanderlust," he mumbled. "I'd love to see every river in the United States."

Personally, she'd rather venture to the coasts and see the oceans. She'd been west to the Pacific and she'd seen the Gulf of Mexico, but she'd never gone to the east coast, never seen the Atlantic.

She glanced at Hadley, wondering what Hadley thought. From what she'd seen on his Facebook page, Kyle and his family traveled a lot. Sure, Hadley had been a few places, seen a few things with Amber, with Amber and Nathan. But maybe she could see a lot more if she had a relationship with Kyle and his wife.

"Swim in them?" she asked, desperate to keep the conversation going, for Hadley's sake.

"No." He shook his head.

"Do you swim?" Hadley asked him, and Amber felt torn between relief and betrayal that she was going to talk to him.

"Yep." He nodded at Hadley. "How about you?"

She looked at Amber, and Amber wondered if she was asking permission to talk to him. Helpless, mesmerized by the interaction, Amber only gave her the slightest nod of encouragement.

"Yeah. Mom taught me when I was little."

Somehow, they'd started moving, and now the three of them were walking aimlessly around the park.

"Do you ever go white water rafting?" he asked Hadley. "Current River?"

"No." Hadley shook her head. "But Mom and Nathan and I took a dinner cruise on the Mississippi last year."

Amber felt a little pang in her chest. They'd had a blast, the three of them. Sure, it was a shabby old boat and no dinner anywhere could rival Nathan's cooking, but they'd had a blast. It had been a little chilly, and they'd all been bundled up against the October wind. They'd laughed at little things, and they'd talked about where they would vacation this summer, and Amber was hurt now by the way Nathan had simply walked away.

She wouldn't apologize for Hadley mentioning Nathan, but Kyle didn't even seem to notice.

"How about a Disney cruise?" Kyle asked, and for just a moment, Amber imagined he was inviting Hadley to join his family on a cruise, rather than asking if she'd taken one, and a glance at Hadley confirmed that she'd heard it the same way.

"No," Hadley said quietly.

Kyle shrugged and smiled.

"What do you like to do? With your free time?" Kyle directed the question at Hadley, so Amber kept her mouth shut. Wondered if Hadley would tell him she had a lot of free time on her hands these days because Amber kept grounding her.

"I read a lot," Hadley told him. "And I like music."

"Favorite author?"

Hadley looked at him as if to say *really?*

"I.G. Arenson."

To his credit, he smiled at her and nodded. "Of course. She's very good."

"Do you like to read?"

Amber raised her eyebrows when Hadley asked her own question.

"I do. I like historical fiction."

Hadley shot her a look, almost an eye roll. Probably thinking about him being a college algebra professor who liked to read historical fiction.

They walked the park two or three times, Amber mostly quiet, as Hadley and Kyle lobbed questions and answers, sometimes a little idle chit chat back and forth. Once, Amber trailed a bit behind them, took a few pictures of the old marquis at Washington Theater. Any photographer worth a nickel had taken pictures of Washington Theater and the marquis at least once, and Amber had her share, but it always called to her, spoke volumes about the history of Quincy, and it gave Hadley and Kyle just a moment together, hopefully without making Hadley uncomfortable.

Later, when they'd left the park and Amber drove home, Hadley talked in stops and starts about the morning. She spoke as if she'd sort of liked meeting him, but she'd also compared him to Nathan more than once. There was no comparison for Amber, between him and Nathan, but he was something different to Hadley, so Amber understood her need to hold him up against the only real father figure she'd had in her life.

They'd said casual goodbyes. No hugs. No handshakes even. Amber was glad Kyle hadn't made any overtures toward Hadley, in pretense of emotion. They'd simply agreed it had been fun-in the way jamming your toothbrush into your gums was fun, Amber thought-and Amber had told Kyle she'd be in touch, and they'd parted ways.

Even though Hadley was talking, Amber noticed she was careful only to repeat to Amber the things he'd said, the things he'd asked her. Amber was curious about how Hadley felt about the morning, what she really thought of him, but she knew it was too soon to push. So she drove quietly, happy to listen to Hadley talk. She swung out of her way and dropped into Pagano's thinking she'd grab some lunch for the two of them, and they could head home.

"Can we just eat here?" Hadley asked her.

Amber looked at her as she pulled the keys from the ignition. "Sure."

Hadley led the way into the small pizza and subs shop. Only three tables were occupied; it was still early. Amber followed Hadley to the corner booth, the one she chose every time they came here. The waitress appeared- Amber didn't know her name, but she knew her by sight, and the waitress knew their usual orders-they simply nodded and said *the usual*. Hadley would eat a personal sausage and pepperoni pizza (she only liked Pagano's sausage) and Amber would eat a sub. The waitress clucked away at both of them, something about how nice it was to see them out on such a beautiful spring day, and Hadley unzipped her jacket and slipped if off, as if she was reminded by the comment that she was a bit warm.

"So." Amber knocked on the tabletop and took a deep breath.

"Don't do that."

"Do what?" Amber asked with a frown.

"Knock on the table and act like it's natural. It's weird. You never do that. Just ask."

Amber laughed and shrugged. "How was it?"

"I don't know yet."

"You didn't have to use the code word."

Hadley giggled.

"Did you like him?" Amber tilted her head. "At all?"

"Um." Hadley shrugged her lips. "Yeah?"

"*Yeah?*" Amber repeated. "You sound less than enthusiastic."

"I just...I don't know yet, Mom."

"Okay. But Had?"

"What?"

"Don't hold back. For me. Okay? Don't worry about me."

Hadley stared at the table for moment and then dragged her gaze up to meet Amber's.

"What do you think they're like?" The words gushed out, and Hadley sank back in the booth, as if she was relieved to have said it.

"His family?"

"His sons."

Amber licked her lips, a little sad that Hadley had asked, but determined not to let Hadley see that.

"I dunno. Sounds like they're very active. On the go a lot."

"Do you think..." Hadley suddenly looked every bit the scared fourteen-year-old she was. "Do you think they would like me?"

"I don't know why they wouldn't."

Hadley looked up and sat up straight. The waitress set her Mountain Dew in front of her and then set Amber's Diet Pepsi at her place.

"I just wish..." Hadley let her words trail off.

"What? What do you wish?"

Hadley shook her head. "Nothing."

"It's okay. You can tell me." Amber assumed Hadley wanted to say something more about Kyle. Or his sons.

"I just wish...that if I was going to have brothers or sisters, they would be your kids..."

"What's the difference, Had? I'm sure you'd like Kyle's sons."

"No, I know." Hadley nodded. "I just...wish me and you and Nathan were a family. That if I had to have little brothers or sisters, that they were you and Nathan's...kids."

"Hadley." Amber rubbed her forehead. Tried to soothe away the headache.

"And that...there wouldn't even have to be a Kyle." Hadley stared at Amber sullenly. "That it could just be...Nathan..."

Thirty-Eight
"What're you doing here?" Amber asked without preamble. She leaned against the door and watched Nathan look at her. Take stock. She was dressed to go out; in fact, she'd assumed Nathan was Gretchen when he rang the doorbell.

"You look..." He raised his eyebrows appreciatively. "Um...do you have plans?"

She'd been hot and cold all afternoon, since coming home from Pagano's with Hadley. She'd been all but ready to call Ingrid and beg off when Hadley remembered that Ingrid had told her they were having a girls' night. Hadley had dragged her into her bedroom and found clothes for her, as if she were just a Barbie doll.

Because Hadley had been excited to dress her, Amber had relaxed and enjoyed it. Talked to Gretchen for a few minutes on the phone and told her just to come to the house and they'd go from there. A few different outfits had Amber feeling either slutty or middle-aged, but she approved of Hadley's final selections: skinny-legged Miss Me jeans, a sparkly black tank, and a fitted red blazer. Hadley had insisted on at least choosing Amber's makeup when Amber told her she would apply it herself. Hadley had chosen well. She'd also picked out Amber's black heeled boots for her, and big silver hoop earrings, which showed tonight because Hadley had told Amber to wear her hair up.

"Why are you here?" Amber asked him again.

He shuffled uncomfortably on the porch. Stuck his hands in his pockets and rocked back on his heels.

"Um. I just wanted to see Hadley."

Amber sighed. Was this good? Letting him see her? Letting Hadley see him? Continuing their relationship when *she and Nathan* didn't have a relationship?

"Are you going out?" His question interrupted her thoughts.

"Yes."

"Damn." Nathan nodded. "You look...incredible."

Amber's voice kind of stuck when she tried to say thank you.

"Is...like...a date?"

"Is it Gretch?" Hadley's voice floated down the stairs as Amber heard her footsteps. "Or it is Uncle Wade-"

Amber sighed. She knew the minute Hadley walked up behind her, because she saw Nathan's gaze shift just a little.

"What're you doing?" he asked Hadley. "When your mom goes out?"

"Going to hang out at Uncle Wade's. With Charlie."

"Where's Gracie?" Amber asked, surprised by the change in plans.

"I guess she had plans before. Uncle Wade knew, but Aunt Liv didn't."

"So you're gonna hang with Wade and Charlie?" Nathan asked her.

"Yep."

Nathan looked back at Amber. "Can I stay? With Hadley?"

"You wanna hang out with my brother-in-law?" Amber smirked.

"Had and I could grab dinner. And hang out. I came by...to see if she wanted to hang out tomorrow."

Amber folded her arms over her chest.

"You don't have a date tonight?"

Nathan frowned. Hadley tugged at her sleeve.

"Can we do that, Mom? Can I just stay home and hang out with Nathan?"

"What about Uncle Wade?"

"I'll call him."

Amber lifted her eyes when she saw Gretchen's Rav 4 crawling down the alley. Gretchen waved and flashed her a big smile as she crept by. Amber sighed and nodded.

"Fine. I guess."

"Thanks." Hadley put her arm around her shoulders and kissed her cheek.

"Pizza?" Nathan suggested to Hadley.

"Um. Had pizza for lunch."

"Okay." Nathan shrugged. He stepped inside when Amber moved to let him in. "Whatever you want. Your choice."

"Let me go change!" Hadley called as she hurried back toward the steps.

"You don't have to do this," Amber told him as soon as Hadley was out of earshot.

"I want to," he said simply. "I miss her."

Amber swallowed hard. Wondered if he had any idea how much it hurt her when he said he missed Hadley, but never her.

"Where ya going?" he asked. Reached out to touch her arm, but he let his hand fall to his side. "You look beautiful."

"Hadley dressed me." She grinned in spite of herself. "I feel like a Barbie doll."

"It's a date, isn't it?" He looked sad.

"No. Going out with the girls," she said simply. Pointed at the door when the bell rang. "That's one right there."

"Lucky girls," Nathan mumbled. Amber only shook her head and moved to let Gretchen come in.

"Hey Nathan," she offered him an uncertain smile. Glanced at Amber with arched eyebrows. Amber shook her head.

"Nathan's staying with Hadley."

"Oh." Gretchen nodded. "Okay."

"Speaking of which, I'd better call Wade, because Hadley will forget."

"What will I forget?" Hadley bounded down the last of the steps and appeared in the dining room.

"To call Uncle Wade."

"Nope. Just talked to him." She looked from Amber to Gretchen and hurried over to give Gretchen a hug.

"Okay." Amber shrugged. "You have your key-"

"I have mine," Nathan interrupted her. Amber picked up her purse, a small black leather cross body bag big enough to hold her phone and debit card, and turned to look at him.

"Why do you still have a key?"

He opened his mouth to answer her, but apparently he thought better of it and shook his head.

"I'll...leave it...when we come back."

Amber nodded. "Good idea."

Hadley hugged her goodbye. Gave her an extra squeeze and then looked at her uncertainly.

"What's wrong?" The look surprised Amber. She'd assumed Hadley would be thrilled to be going out with Nathan.

"You look too pretty to go out," Hadley whispered. "Without Nathan."

Amber caught her breath, embarrassed for Hadley to have said it, especially right in front of Nathan. She avoided his eyes, kissed Hadley goodbye and glanced at Gretchen.

"Ready?" Nathan tore his eyes away from Amber. Looked at Hadley for an answer and mumbled a goodbye to Amber and Gretchen. Amber watched them go.

"She's right," Gretchen told her. "You look incredible. Did you see him? He was green, thinking about you going out like that."

"Yeah, well, it doesn't bother him enough to change anything," Amber said quietly. "You ready? We're meeting everybody at Carino's."

"I'm ready." Gretchen followed her out the front door and waited on the porch while Amber made sure the door was locked.

"It sucks, Gretch." Amber led the way to the back of the house where their cars were parked. She opened her door and climbed inside the SUV. Gretchen beeped the lock on the Rav 4 one more time as Amber put the Passport in reverse and pulled out of her spot. "I mean, Hadley's crazy about him, so I'm glad he comes to see her. But it sucks that every time I open the door to him, my knees go weak and I'm so stupid, I think he's changed his mind, and he's come back to me."

"Maybe he'll come back after tonight. He was seriously all moony-eyed over you."

"Whatever." Amber rolled her eyes.

"Had really dress you?"

"Yep."

"Underwear too?"

"What?"

"Well?"

"No."

"Because, you know, if you're planning to hook up with someone, wouldn't be good to let a fourteen-"

"I'm not planning to hook up with anyone!" Amber reached across the front seat to smack at Gretchen's shoulder. "How's Steve?"

"Okay."

"Okay? That's it?"

Gretchen lifted a shoulder in a lazy shrug. "I told you this one's fun...I like him. Don't love him. Don't think I ever will. How do you know you aren't gonna hook up-"

"Because I'm old and responsible. I have a daughter at home-"

"Oh yeah…with your ex. You're not gonna be able to bring anyone home-"

"Gretchen!" Amber laughed. "I'm having dinner with my sisters and friends. End of story."

Gretch gave her a look as if to say *that's what you think.*

Amber turned the radio on and switched the stations until she found a Blake Shelton song.

"Really?" Gretchen asked when she dropped her hand back to her lap, okay with the song choice.

"Gettin' my country on."

"Save a horse and ride a cowboy."

"Oh my God! Stop!" Amber laughed. "I don't have a cowboy to ride these days. You're not being fair!"

"I could share Steve."

Amber heard her phone beep. Before she could ask, Grethen dug it out of her purse and offered it to her.

"Can you check it?"

"Sure." Gretchen pushed the home button and then tapped the text icon. "It's Ingrid. Says the reservation is in Liv's name."

"Okay." She was glad to hear they had a reservation. Carino's did a steady business on a weeknight. It was hard to get in on a weekend, especially with a big group.

"Can I ask you something?"

Amber decided she hated when people asked her if they could ask her something. It always led to a question she didn't want to answer.

"I guess."

She turned right on Broadway, already tired of the country station, but unwilling to give in and turn it. Apparently, her life was a little messy right now if she felt she had to remain in control of a radio station.

"If Nathan wanted to come back, would you reconcile?"

"Yes."

"Hmm."

Amber looked at her friend from the corner of her eye.

"What? What does that mean?"

"I'm just surprised you answered so quickly," Gretchen admitted. "I thought you'd tell me you're over him. That you don't want him back."

"I'd do anything for him to come back, Gretchen," Amber said softly. "But he won't."

The song had changed from the Blake Shelton tune she was okay with. Some sort of country rap talk noise that grated on Amber's last nerve. She made a left on Third and found a spot at the curb down just a bit from the restaurant.

She and Hadley hadn't had that conversation. Not yet. But she'd promised Hadley they would, and after some of the comments Hadley had made today, Amber felt like she owed it to herself and maybe to Nathan, too, to discuss the future with her. The only problem being that the discussion would be too late.

Amber supposed it would just be good to know for sure how Hadley felt about things, maybe good for Hadley to understand how Amber felt about things, even if the future wasn't going to be a problem for them. Nathan was gone, already seeing other people. And Amber had no intentions of falling in love again.

She and Gretchen climbed out of the SUV. Amber hurried around the back end and stepped up on the curb.

"This is fun." Gretchen reached for her hand. She gave her a gentle squeeze and then let go. "It's been way too long since we've done something like this."

"I know."

"Hey." Gretchen threw her arm around Amber's waist as they walked. "Don't feel guilty. I'm just saying I miss you."

"Me too."

"Hey!" Liv called as she and Shay crossed the street. Amber looked back at the parking lot, wondered if Ingrid and Julie were here yet. She wondered what mountain Liv had moved to get Shay to agree to come out with them. "Lookin' hot tonight, ladies!"

"Look at you guys!" Amber gave Liv and Shay the once over. Shay wore a crème-colored maxi dress with a cropped denim jacket. Amber thought her sister-in-law always looked exotic, but tonight there was a sparkle in her eye she hadn't seen in quite some time. Again she wondered what Liv had said to talk her into coming out. Liv, on the other hand, wore dark wash jeans and a royal blue blouse. Her jeans tucked into her low-heeled brown boots and her eyes heavily made up, Amber thought she couldn't look less like a high school English teacher. Supposed maybe the boys in Liv's class might like to see her now. Decided that was horribly inappropriate, given the way she'd spent her day, and gave herself a mental shake.

"Ingrid and Julie are already here," Liv told her. "Probably bellied up to the bar."

"Whatever." Amber gave Liv a playful shove. "Julie's probably guzzling white milk."

"You know it." Liv nodded.

"You, Shay Williams, look gorgeous!" Amber hugged Shay, happy that she had come along. Hoping that Shay didn't exact too high a price from Ezra for going out with his sisters tonight.

"Wade texted. Said Had's with Nathan."

"Mm." Amber raised her eyebrows. "Yeah. She is."

"Please tell me he saw you looking this drop dead gorgeous."

"He saw me looking this drop dead gorgeous." Amber nodded.

Gretchen laughed as she pulled the door to Carino's open.

"I love it. Let's get this party started, ladies!"

Thirty-Nine

Dinner was, of course, delicious. Amber had never had a bad meal at Carino's. Well, Amber had never had a bad experience at Carino's, whether it was a drive-by on the way south out of town or dinner and drinks. Tonight was special, because even though it hurt to give those thoughts and feelings she'd buried even just an inch, it was surreal to sit here with her sisters and friends. She'd been out with Shay a couple of times, and of course, she'd been out with Gretchen. But she'd never been out for a relaxing night with her sisters.

That couldn't be right. She held her wine glass for a moment, lost in memories, trying to decide if that could be true. She'd had lunch with Ingrid-here-not that long ago. She and Liv had grabbed lunch a couple of times. Hell, she and Liv had gone to dinner a few times through the years. But nothing to this extent. How sad that she would turn thirty in a few months and this was the first time in memory that she and her sisters had dolled up, invited friends, and gone out for no reason other than fun.

"Stop it." Ingrid nudged her with her elbow.

"Stop what?" Amber asked quickly.

"Thinking."

Amber answered with a small, guilty smile. She took a sip of her wine and looked back at Ingrid.

"I'm not even thinking about what you think I'm thinking."

"Um." Ingrid frowned. "What?"

"I'm thinking that this is the first time we've done something like this."

Ingrid frowned, and Amber had to laugh because now Ingrid had that serious look on her face.

"We went out for breakfast. To talk about me and Luke."

Amber nodded. "Uh-huh. And you totally shorted us on the details. But it's not the same."

Ingrid leaned closer to her. "The details would so...blow you...away." She shook her head. "I can't be responsible for that."

Amber snorted.

"Hey." Liv, to Amber's right at the circular table, just on the other side of Gretchen, tapped her water glass with her fork. "No secrets."

Ingrid lifted her hands in surrender.

"The kid just reminded me I shorted you guys on details about me and Luke's first romp."

"You did." Liv shrugged.

"I think she's bluffing us," Amber announced.

"Oh, Amber, I wish." Liv laughed. "I heard those bed springs on the first floor. I'm surprised they didn't break the bed."

"Wait." Julie, seated to Ingrid's left, shook her head. She looked from Liv to Ingrid. "What? You heard them?"

"I didn't just hear them." Liv shook her head. "I saw them."

"Jules, if you were in the house, and you heard someone-"

"Banging," Liv interrupted Ingrid. Amber laughed and glanced at Gretchen.

"Upstairs...doing something-"

"Banging," Liv repeated.

"Would you go up to look?"

"Um." Julie took a deep breath, seemed to consider Ingrid's question, and then grinned. "Having met Luke, yes, I absolutely would have gone upstairs to look. Mighta just stayed there to watch the finale."

"You saw Ingrid and Luke?" Shay asked with a giggle.

"Oh, I did," Liv answered with an enthusiastic nod. "Let me tell you, he's got a nice-"

Julie laughed out loud, but she covered her mouth when Ingrid shot a look of mock warning at her.

"Ass." Liv polished off the wine in her glass.

"Ssh!" Ingrid looked around. "You can't talk like that in a nice place like this."

Liv shrugged unapologetically. "He does." She directed her whisper to Julie.

Shay yawned and took a sip of her water. Still breastfeeding Samuel, she drank only water and caffeine free Pepsi.

"Tell me something," Amber said to her. Shay tilted her head, ready to field Amber's question. "Did Ez ever find out about that night you and I were out until three?"

It was kind of a gamble, reminding Shay of that night in particular. Reminding Shay of Ezra at all. But Amber missed her sister-in-law, the woman she'd been before she married Ezra, and she thought maybe it was worth the risk of asking.

Shay threw her head back and treated them all to a deep-throated bellow of a laugh. Amber had always been amazed by the power Shay packed in her petite little body.

"Um." Shay wiped at her eyes, still smiling. She hiccupped another small laugh. "No. No, he didn't."

"Wait." Ingrid touched Amber's hand. "Wait. What? When were you guys out until three in the morning?"

Amber and Shay locked eyes over the table, and both of them were lost in laughter.

"Oh." Gretchen nodded. "Yeah. This was the time-?"

Amber looked at her with a big grin.

"Lemme guess." Liv held up a hand. "Involves alcohol."

"That's amazing, Liv. How do you do it?"

"Amber and I went to a music festival."

"Here?" Ingrid frowned. "A music festival here?"

"Yes." Shay nodded. "Little festival with some home grown bands. Outskirts of town. Had a blast."

"We did," Amber agreed. "Drank a little too much…but the music was great."

"And?"

"Well, we had to pee. First time we were okay." Shay rubbed her fingertips under her eyes. "Second time, we snuck off into the fields, and some guys followed us. So we kept going."

"Some guys followed you to go pee?" Liv asked.

"I dunno." Amber shrugged. "Maybe they were weird. Or maybe they thought we were smokin' pot. Anyway, we kept going into the fields…decided after a while that we'd lost the guys."

"So we took care of business. And then we realized we were lost."

"Were you in…I dunno…a corn maze?" Ingrid asked with a frown.

Amber and Shay exchanged another glance and giggle.

"No. Just…you know…it was dark. We'd been drinking. We walked in a few circles. Ended up coming out around Forty-Eighth…close to State."

"Which was great," Shay said with a nonchalant shrug. "Except the car was way the hell away on Broadway."

"So what'd you do?" Ingrid asked.

Gretchen snorted and took a drink of her wine.

"What was there to do?"

"Well, you didn't call Ezra for help."

"Oh no. We went back into the fields. Decided we were good to go. Had it figured out. We'd come that way. Couldn't be that hard to retrace our steps."

"Oh my god." Ingrid rolled her eyes. "Really?"

"Oh yeah." Amber nodded.

"We found our way out."

"An hour later…got chased by a fox or something."

"I think it was just a dog," Shay argued. "Then again, he didn't answer to Rover or Fido, so maybe not."

"Stepped on a snake."

"How do you know? If it was dark?"

"Felt it slither under the heel of my boot."

"Oh Jesus." Julie shivered. "That's a nightmare."

"Least it wasn't a skunk."

"Once we finally got back to the car-"

"Who was driving?"

"I was," Shay told Ingrid. "We were hungry."

"Tell me you didn't drive drunk."

"I was *get lost in a random field* buzzed. Not drunk." Shay shrugged. "If I had to do it all over gain, I wouldn't have driven."

"We went to the Barn and Grill," Amber continued. "And we had breakfast."

"What?" Liv winced. "Like what? What for breakfast?"

"Cinnamon rolls."

Ingrid rubbed her face. "Did you barf?"

"Hell yes." Amber nodded. "We snuck Shay home around three."

"Ez was out. Sleeping like a baby. Didn't bat an eyelash when I slipped in bed beside him."

"We should do that again sometime." Amber smiled sadly. They wouldn't. Shay wouldn't go out much anymore. It was like having Samuel had flipped a switch inside her and changed her personality. They got glimpses of the old Shay, like maybe the switch was short-circuiting and the real Shay would fade in and out, but Amber didn't think things would ever be the way they used to be.

Not to mention that it had all happened before Nathan. Before she'd fallen so damned in love with him and before he'd walked out on her, and she figured her own switch had been flipped, and she might never be the same either.

She wouldn't blame Shay for whatever it was she felt, but then, Shay had Ezra and so Amber didn't totally get it. Maybe she never would.

Maybe because she felt sad suddenly, tired, ready to get back home, maybe it showed on her face, and Ingrid noticed it.

"On that note, let's get out of here. Go for a drink somewhere."

"We just had a drink." Amber nodded at her empty wine glass.

"That was dinner. Let's go get a drink."

Amber looked at Gretchen in askance. She grinned and nodded.

"I'm not gonna let you go home until you give someone your phone number."

"Well, then I guess we're gonna be out late, because I'm not out to give someone my phone number."

"Nah." Ingrid winked at Gretchen. "We don't have to deal with phone numbers. Let's just find someone to kiss the lip gloss off her face." Ingrid looked at Amber. "You look gorgeous, by the way."

"Kiss the-what? No! I'm not going out for-"

"Trust me. It'll be fun." Ingrid slipped her arm around Amber's shoulders.

"I like it." Liv nodded her approval. "We're in. It'll be like a scavenger hunt. For the perfect kisser."

"No-"

"Ooh yeah!" Ingrid laughed. She moved away from Amber and reached for her purse. "That's good."

"Best kisser gets her number," Gretchen suggested.

"Wait." Amber reached for her own purse. "Do I get a say in this?"

"Well, you can say yes or no to whomever we pick out for you."

Shay nodded slowly as she blinked at Amber. "Yeah. I like that. If he's skanky looking, you can say no. If he's at least a five-"

"By whose standards?" Amber laughed.

"I got it." Ingrid covered Amber's hand with hers when she pulled her billfold out.

"You don't have to-"

"I want to, and besides, then you'll feel bad for rating guys under a five, and you'll be more likely to join in the fun."

"Oh my God, really?" Amber sat back in her chair and laughed.

"Your standards," Shay decided. "But if one of us thinks he's cute, then we vote. We can overrule you."

"I could be at home right now with Had."

"Wouldn't be having quite this much fun, though. You already said this is fun," Liv reminded her.

"Yeah, before you guys decided you were gonna loan me out to strangers."

"Just good-looking strangers," Gretchen reminded her.

"And just for kisses," Ingrid said with a shrug. "Go with it. It'll all be good."

Amber ducked her head and rubbed the back of her neck. "This is crazy. You guys are all crazy."

"Think of what it's gonna do to Nathan to see you've been so thoroughly kissed."

Amber flinched. "Yeah, but I kinda just wanna kiss Nathan."

"We're working on it, kiddo."

Forty

Two hours and three bars later, Amber still wasn't feeling much other than wishing she was at home with Hadley. And Nathan. Sure, it was nice being out with Ingrid and Liv and the girls. It was fun; *they* were fun. But it was too soon for her to be able to even think about anyone else. Of course going home looking thoroughly kissed might get to Nathan, but as much as she wanted to make him jealous, to make him want her back, she didn't want to play games.

Thankfully, they let it go, only occasionally pointing out a good-looking guy to her. She had to admit they had good taste, and if she wasn't miserable over losing Nathan, she might be all in. As it was, they teased her only mildly, trying to cajole her out of her sad mood.

She drank her first few beers quickly, thinking the only way she'd be able to kiss a stranger would be with the help of alcohol. When her stomach began to protest, both from the alcohol and the anxiety over kissing a stranger, she slowed down. Nursed her last two beers. Listened to Julie talk about how things were mostly better with her and Rafe-Amber hoped to hell they were mostly better, since they were expecting another baby-and Gretchen talk about work. Being an accountant, there wasn't too much exciting stuff she could share, except office romances. She shared enough about those that it sounded like she was talking about a soap opera. Amber laughed with everyone else, heartache in check, thinking Gretchen could be a comedienne and that she needed to get out more and spend more time with her.

She noticed that Ingrid was more of an observer. She listened to everyone; Amber figured she probably heard everything that wasn't said just as clearly as what was said. Probably Ingrid noted body language and tone as much as the words people said. Not to write about this particular situation but to bend details and stories and fictionalize them. Amber watched Ingrid as she listened to

Gretchen, noted the far away look in her eyes, and yet Ingrid was totally in tune with Gretch, nodding at the right places, laughing when she was supposed to, saying the right things.

If this was how Ingrid worked, Amber could only applaud her. She loved reading Ingrid's books, and like Liv, wished Ingrid wrote faster.

By the end of the night, Amber was exhausted. Liv had tried to talk them into going to Skinny's. Apparently everyone was game except Amber. She'd had to promise Liv she'd go another time. It had made Amber giggle, that her oldest sister was determined to go to a strip club, featuring female pole dancers. Amber figured if things were good at home, if she and Nathan were still together, she'd have gone. The whole night would have been better, more fun, knowing that Nathan was at home waiting for her to come to bed with him, not at home hanging out with Hadley while she was gone.

When they'd left Carino's, they'd all piled into Ingrid's Subaru, at her insistence. Ingrid had driven from Carino's to the first bar, but after that, Julie offered to drive. Now they all filed out together and moved slowly to the Subaru.

"I'm sorry for ditching you guys," Amber mumbled. Instead of feeling better, she almost felt a little guilty for not being the party girl they'd wanted her to be.

"Are you kidding?" Liv asked around a yawn. "It's midnight. I can't stay awake."

Amber grinned. There was a tiny part of her that hoped they wouldn't keep the party going once she went home. But mostly, she didn't care.

"I just wanted you to have fun," Ingrid told her. "And I feel bad that we didn't find you even one kiss."

"I'm so good with not even finding one kiss." Amber laughed. "Trust me."

"But that one guy." Julie elbowed her and grinned.
"Which one?"

"With the low rise jeans...and the shirt sleeves rolled up." Julie wiggled her eyebrows.

"Mm." Gretchen nodded. "Nice shoulders."

"He was pretty dreamy," Ingrid agreed.

"Are you kidding me? He looked like he was sixteen."

"Not with shoulders like that, he didn't." Gretchen shook her head enthusiastically.

Amber laughed as they all piled into the Subaru. Shay and Liv climbed all the way to the back, Amber and Gretchen took the second seats, and Ingrid sat in front with Julie driving.

Julie offered to go back to Carino's to get the other cars, but Amber didn't want to deal with it tonight, and apparently Liv didn't, either. Amber rested her head on the seat, half listening to Shay and Gretchen talking about Samuel, half zoned out. She was tired. It had been a long day, the worst of it being the morning. Hadley's nerves. Her own volatile mix of nerves and fear.

She wasn't looking forward to having to see Nathan when she got home. She supposed it was nice that he'd offered to stay with Hadley, good for Hadley anyway. But finding him on her doorstep earlier had hurt her more than she'd wanted to admit. She sucked in a deep breath when Julie pulled the Subaru into the alley beside the house. No other way to deal with this tonight. Just plunge right in, say thank you, say goodnight and watch him go.

She and Gretchen climbed out of the back doors and started to wander away; Gretchen to the Rav and Amber to the house. Ingrid hollered at her, though, and stopped her. The buzz she'd acquired through the night had dulled to just a tiny bit tipsy, but she was still careful of her step as she moved back to stand by the passenger door.

"Hey. Call you tomorrow, okay?"

"Thanks, Ingrid." Amber nodded.

Ingrid leaned out the window and reached for her. Kissed her cheek and then grinned.

"Couldn't let you go inside without some kind of kiss."

Amber snorted.

"That's great, but I'm sorry. You're not as hot as the guy with the shoulders."

"I want kisses, too!" Liv called from the back of the SUV.

"Maybe we should all kiss her. Imagine her walking inside with lipstick all over her face."

Amber leaned her head in Ingrid's window.

"I dunno. That's almost intriguing, but not really," she called to Shay. "Thanks for the offer, though."

"That might get us all more than we bargained for," Ingrid mumbled.

"Well, I am pretty hot." Amber nodded as she stepped back.

Ingrid laughed softly and shook her head.

"Goodnight."

Gretchen draped her arm over her shoulders as they watched Julie ease slowly down the alley.

"Lunch. This week."

Amber turned to Gretchen and nodded.

"Promise."

"Awesome." Gretchen gave her a squeeze and kissed her cheek. Amber laughed as she stepped away.

"Cool. I can tell Nathan I got kissed by two pretty girls."

"Maybe you should at least smear your lip gloss a little bit."

"Whatever." Amber rolled her eyes. "My lip gloss has been gone since we ate dinner."

"What? Like you ate it off?"

"Eew. No." Amber took another step backward toward the door. "I just can't eat with something on my lips. I had to wipe it off."

"Really?"
"Yes."
"That's weird."
"Goodnight, Gretchen."
"Night."
"You okay to drive home?"
"Why? You want me to come in and-"
Amber snorted. "No. Goodnight."

The house was quiet when she slipped inside. She could hear the TV, but barely. Apparently, they weren't watching movies anymore. Amber walked carefully through the small kitchen trying to make as little noise as possible. Maybe it was dumb, but she didn't want Nathan to come out to the kitchen or dining room to talk to her.

She set her purse on the dining room table as she walked by. Stepped over to the door to the stairway and listened. She could hear music coming from Hadley's room. Again, barely audible. Quietly, careful not to step on the creaky stairs, she slipped up the steps, relieved to see Hadley alone and asleep in her bed.

Amber considered turning her lamp off-Hadley would sleep better-but she'd have to make it all the way across the room to her dresser and all the way back without waking her. She'd let it go tonight. She took one last long look, noticed a book half under Hadley's pillow, and wondered what time she'd come upstairs.

They would talk tomorrow. Hopefully, the truce would last, and Hadley would still talk to her, and they could move forward at least a few more steps.

Then again, Hadley had spent the evening with Nathan. It was entirely possible, and maybe even a little bit probable, that Hadley would hate her all over again in the morning. Amber moved back down the steps, dodging the noisy stairs as if she was playing hopscotch, and ducked into the bathroom. She'd gone at the last bar before they'd left, but already she had to go again. Unfortunately, she'd had enough that she'd probably need to get up through the night. As hard as it had been to sleep lately, she dreaded the thought of finally going to sleep, only to have to get up and stumble to the bathroom to pee again, just because she'd had a little too much to drink.

Business taken care of, she slipped through the dark dining room into the living room. The TV was on, turned to Netflix, but there was nothing actually playing at the moment. Apparently, Nathan had been watching *House of Cards*. Now he was asleep on the couch.

Amber's first instinct was to rouse him and kick him out. But as she stood and watched him sleep, watched his chest rise and fall as he breathed, she realized she didn't want to. Really, what she wanted was to wake him and tell him to come to bed. Or even just lie down beside him on the couch, rest her head on his chest, and sleep with him.

She'd let him sleep, she decided. Chances were, he'd be gone in the morning when she got up. No telling how long he'd been sleeping. Decision made, she had no reason to stare at him any longer. She couldn't help herself, though. When she realized she was reaching toward him, thinking about stroking her fingers over his chin, his lips, she almost jumped back. Shoved her hands in her jeans pockets.

Even in the dim light from the TV screen, she could see dark shadows under his eyes. For a moment, she wondered why. What was bothering him. And then she didn't. Because she had her own issues, and he'd walked out on her and he'd chosen to stop talking to her, to stop loving her, and so she turned on the balls of her feet and looked around for the TV remote.

She found it at the foot of the couch, and she had to reach around Nathan's leg to grab it. Sort of felt like she was playing that old board game-Operation-grabbing the remote control and not touching Nathan. Remote in hand, she turned back to the TV and turned it off. Nathan had pulled the throw they'd always kept on the end of the couch over him, and she resisted the urge to pull it up over his chest. To fidget with it in any way, as an excuse to be closer to him.

He didn't stir as she moved away from him. A little bit disappointed, she stepped into the bedroom and closed the door. She needed to wash her face, but she decided she'd rather not go back out there. She didn't need to see him again. Because maybe this time she'd cave and lie down with him on the couch or wake him and ask him to come to bed with her.

Instead, she crossed her fingers that she wouldn't break out because she skipped her normal cleansing routine once. Undressed quickly and pulled her nightshirt on, all the while terribly aware of the man she loved out there in the other room on the couch. She slipped into bed, tired and yet wired enough that she might not sleep. Her head hurt, and now that she was lying down, her stomach hurt. She decided if she felt this bad, she should have just had a little bit more. Maybe then the night would've been a damned good time, instead of just a nice night out with her friends. Didn't seem fair to her that she'd stopped drinking so she wouldn't come home drunk on her butt, and now she was home and not feeling well and she doubted the morning was going to be much better.

She tossed and turned for a while, fell asleep at one point. Woke up again not long after. She was hot. Sweaty hot. And of course, she had to pee. Again. Rather than get up, she turned to her side, hoping to relieve the pressure on her bladder. Dozed off for what felt like minutes, but when she looked at the clock this time, it was almost four. And she still had to pee. She gave in, climbed out of bed and padded barefoot to the door. Wondered if Nathan was still here, or if he woke up and left since she'd come to bed.

Irked her to realize that she wanted him to still be here. She eased her door open and peeked out into the dark living room. Thought she saw him still on the couch, but she wasn't sure. It was dark, and from where she stood peering into the room, the dark form she was looking at could simply be the couch and the throw tossed down on it.

She took a few silent steps into the living room, stopped with heart in her throat when Nathan snored loudly and turned over to his side. She took a deep breath and stood still for a moment. She wanted him here, but only if he was sleeping.

Brilliant, Amber.

The house was a little cold as she hurried through the living and dining room to the bathroom. The door squeaked when she closed it, and she stood still for another moment, praying that he hadn't heard anything. When no one hollered for her, no one knocked on the door, she flipped the light on, glanced at herself in the mirror and quickly looked away. She looked like hell, everything pale and made more so because of the rings of black around her eyes. She'd known better than to sleep in her makeup.

Head pounding, she moved quickly to take care of business, washed her hands and avoided another look in the mirror. No need for that. Might end up making her headache worse. After being in the brightly lit room, the rest of the house was darker than dark, and she picked her way slowly across the floor so as not to run into anything. At the doorway to the living room, she hesitated. She should take some Advil. It would do a lot for the headache now, but it would help head it off when she got up again, too.

But stumbling around in the dark or worse, turning on a light, might wake Nathan up, and she most definitely didn't feel up to a confrontation. Instead she hurried back through the living room, past Nathan, and into her bedroom. Shut the door. Made sure she heard it click and then moved back to her bed. Stubbed her toe on

the foot of the bed as she neared it, covered her mouth to keep the groan of pain inside and flopped into her bed.
    This time sleep took her almost instantly.

Forty-One

Amber awoke to music, though she didn't immediately recognize it. And the smell of coffee. Head hammering, probably from too little sleep as much as too much to drink, she squeezed her eyes closed and buried her face in Nathan's pillow. Actually, now that he'd been gone for a couple of weeks and seeing that he'd never officially lived with her, it probably wasn't Nathan's pillow anymore.

Didn't matter to Amber. She might think of it as his pillow until she was old and gray or even dead. Or until maybe Hadley graduated from high school and moved away for college and Amber got a dog to sleep with.

The coffee smelled good. Finally she blinked her eyes open and looked around the room. Her windows faced north and west, so there was no direct sunlight right now. The music wasn't particularly loud; in fact, Amber almost had to strain to hear it. To actually make it out.

Eric Clapton? Or was it Cream? Sounded like 'White Room.'

She decided it was great that Hadley was up and moving, that she'd made coffee. Might be a good sign. But what would be even better would be if Hadley brought her a cup right now. She even considered grabbing for her phone and texting Had to ask her for that, but she hesitated. Something was stuck, not necessarily in the back of her mind, but pretty close. Something she'd just thought...

Cream? Hadley didn't listen to Eric Clapton or Cream or Derek and the Dominos. Amber pushed herself up on her elbows and tried again to blink the room in to focus.

She jumped when she heard someone knock on her door and then before she could answer, she saw it opening, and Nathan stuck his head in. The music swelled just a little bit louder, but he'd been considerate of her still sleeping and kept the volume pretty low. Considerate or else he'd wanted to completely ambush her as he'd just done.

"Hey." He stopped just inside the door, two mugs in his hands. Amber wasn't sure if he was enjoying the view (even the thought was heavy with sarcasm) or waiting for her to give him permission to come further inside. She didn't. She only groaned out loud and dropped back on the bed.

"Go away," she mumbled when he approached the side of the bed.

"I didn't hear you come in last night," he said as he sat down. She scooted away from him. Watched him set her coffee on the nightstand on his side of the bed. Or, she corrected herself, the other side of the bed. The one that wasn't hers. Or Nathan's.

"Where's Hadley?"

"Doing homework."

"Where?" Amber cleared her throat. She planted her hands on the bed and pushed herself up to lean against the headboard.

"Upstairs. We had breakfast-"

"You had breakfast?"

"Mm-hmm."

She finally looked at him, disgusted to find him just as attractive in the morning, without a shower, still a little soft from sleep. He'd always been able to roll out of bed and be adorable, with just that one little piece of hair sticking up at the back of his head. Amber, not so much. In fact, she squeezed her eyes shut when she remembered the glimpse she'd had in the mirror around four this morning.

"Why are you still here?"

"Coffee?" He nodded at the cup like she needed the invitation. She stared at him a moment longer, and then reached, begrudgingly for the mug. Sipped it appreciatively and looked at him again. "Have fun?"

"Um." She took a deep breath. Watched him suspiciously as he shifted his weight on the bed and leaned a little toward her. He reached into his pocket and grinned when he pulled out a couple of Advil. She stared at him silently when he offered them to her. Reached out and scooped them up from the palm of his hand, loving and hating that her fingertips scraped his skin. "Yeah."

"Where'd you go?"

Amber looked around. She'd thought about texting Hadley before, but it suddenly occurred to her that she hadn't brought her phone in here to charge it. Probably, it was still in her purse out in the dining room. Dead or close to it.

"What's the matter? Need water?" Nathan asked her.

"Why?" Amber looked back at him. She bent her knees and pulled her legs up away from him. Ducked her head and brushed her hair off her face. Left her hand across her forehead, deciding it was a good place to hide from him. Nevertheless, she looked at him with only her eyes. "Why are you still here?"

He shrugged and lowered his gaze. "Hadley was up. We fixed pancakes."

Amber sighed. "What time is it?"

"Not quite eleven."

Damn. She'd almost slept the morning away. She shook her head, irritated with herself.

"Okay." She dropped her hand and lifted her head to look at him boldly. "You can go now."

"Amber."

"What? I'm serious. You don't need-"

"Tell me about last night."

She stared at him silently. Took another drink of coffee and then rubbed her eyes. She winced when she remembered that she still had makeup on and looked like a raccoon.

"We had dinner."

"That's it?"

"We had dinner. And drinks."

"Where at?"

"Carino's."

"Oh. " He nodded enthusiastically. "Let me guess. You had-"

"No. I didn't." She cut him off before he could ask if she'd ordered her regular. "I actually had lasagna."

They stared at each other silently for a moment.

"Sometimes change is good," she told him.

He shrugged and looked away.

"Where'd you go from there?"

"I don't know, Nathan. We went barhopping. Julie was driving. No idea where we ended up."

"You don't remember?" He looked back at her, apparently thinking she'd been drunk when she'd come home.

"I do. I just don't know why you need to know."

He shrugged again. "Guess I'm just wondering exactly who looked at you last night."

She shook her head and raised her eyebrows. "I didn't take names."

"You looked beautiful."

She took a deep breath. Looked away.

"How was Hadley?"

He grinned and then eased it down to a wistful smile. "Good. We went to The Cove-"

"Pizza?" That surprised Amber since they'd had lunch at Pagano's, and Hadley had eaten pizza.

"No. Shared some nachos."

"Mm."

"And then we watched *Parent Trap*." He took a drink of coffee, and so he missed the way Amber sort of folded in on herself and almost sobbed out loud. "And then we binge watched some *House of Cards*."

"Awesome."

"She um…" Nathan eased himself further onto the bed and crossed his right leg over his left leg. Amber watched him and wondered what gave him the right to do so. "Told me."

Amber shook her head when he looked at her. Playing dumb, mostly, because she assumed Nathan meant that Hadley had told him about meeting Kyle Carpenter. But he could be talking about the way she and Hadley had been getting along lately. Or maybe Hadley had told him about her best day ever or that she wished he was her father.

"About yesterday. Meeting Kyle."

Amber leaned her head back on the board, unsure how she felt about that. It was probably natural that Hadley talked to him about it; he'd been her father figure for two years, give or take. But he wasn't part of their family anymore, and so, yes, it bothered her that Hadley had confided anything to him.

"Things have been hard for her," she said quietly.

She took a drink and lowered her eyes to his hands, wrapped around his mug. Remembered the things those hands used to do to her, back when he belonged in this bed with her.

"I really wanted to kiss you last night." His gruff voice threaded a delicious mix of nerves and desire through her belly.

"But you didn't."

"Did anyone else?" he asked uncertainly. "Kiss you?"

Amber laughed sadly. "Yeah." She nodded. Almost wished now that she'd gone fishing for at least a few kisses. Maybe the guy with the shoulders. Now all she had was two pecks on the cheek, one from a friend and one from her sister.

"Can I kiss you now?"

She tensed up when he moved closer to her. Hated that she looked like hell. Wished she could at least brush her teeth, and then Nathan set his coffee on the nightstand and leaned into her. She melted when he slid his hand around and cupped the back of her neck. Stared at him silently when he lowered his head and kissed her. Just a soft, sweet kiss. He stroked his fingertips over her neck. Amber moaned softly when he touched her face with his free hand. She closed her eyes to lose herself to the sensation, but blinked them open again because she needed to see him.

Mindful of her own mug still in her left hand, she lifted her right to touch him. To frame his face.

"Who kissed you?" he whispered. "Should I be jealous?"

"Are you?"

He pulled away from her then and studied her face.

"The thing is..." He sighed.

"What?"

His kiss had been so soft, so sweet and now backing away like that, those words-that *the thing is*...it was like a bucket of cold water in her face. She'd lied to herself. She'd wanted him to stay last night, but she'd hoped he'd come to her like this. To her bed. At least to talk to her. Maybe to kiss her.

Maybe to tell her he still loved her and that he wanted to come back. Now she wanted him gone. She kind of wanted to punch him in the face.

"What, Nathan?" She dropped her hand to her lap. Curled her fingers into a fist, already missing the feel of his beard. What was *the thing*? Another woman? Another blind date? Or had Nicole been more than that? *Had* he been seeing her for a while now, while he was seeing Amber, too?

"I have to leave."

It hurt him to say it-she could tell from the look on his face-but she wasn't up for cutting him any slack.

Not after the time she and Hadley had had trying to deal with him being gone.

She let her gaze fall away from his and nodded. "Of course you do."

"It's only Indiana, but it's...I'll...it's a long job."

Long job or not, he *could* come home. He'd worked in Indiana two or three different times. Wasn't like he'd have to pay for airfare and hop a jet to come home and see her. See Hadley.

So, really, he'd only wanted to kiss her. Maybe he was hard up, and he'd hoped that she'd be ready for another rough, quick roll. At least this time could have been in her bed, saved her some bruises.

She wasn't, though. Ready. Up for it. Interested. Because being with him like that and then watching him walk away had left her in pieces. She wasn't so sure she'd found them all and put them all back together the last time it had happened. Maybe once more would make her lose just a little bit more of herself. Amber wasn't sure how much she had left to lose, but she had to draw the line somewhere. Hadley needed her, even if no one else did.

"Hadley and I talked about it. I told her to text me. Or call me-"

"How long are you gonna be gone this time?" She held her breath. Because she felt it coming. This was going to be different. Had she just told him change could be a good thing? Because *this* wasn't going to be a good thing.

"I'm...leaving...a week from tomorrow."

"And?" She shook her head and looked back at him. "You'll be back...when?"

"I don't know. It's...all..." He shrugged.

"Indefinite. You're leaving indefinitely." She pressed her lips together.

"Amber."

"Is there someone there? Someone else?"

"No."

"Then how can you-"

"It's my job, Amber."

She nodded. Her vision blurred, but she refused to let the tears fall.

"Why did you just sit here and ask me if someone kissed me last night? What does it possibly matter?"

Nathan turned sideways on the bed and put his foot down. Rested his elbows on his knees and covered his face with his hands.

"I don't want anyone touching what was mine."

"I'm not yours, Nathan. Not anymore."

"Were you ever?"

She shook her head. Set her mug on the nightstand and dragged her hair back away from her face.

"What does that mean? I loved you. I always loved you."

"Just not enough."

She took a deep breath. They'd had this argument time and again. And they'd done the break up and make up sex and here they were back at this argument again. To what end, she wondered.

"I thought you were a stand up guy."

"What?"

"My daughter desperately wants you in her life. She begged me to tell her who her real father is, and I finally told her," Amber brushed at the tears on her face, "and it's not what she wants. Not at all."

Nathan's shoulders heaved.

"She just wants you. She wishes you were her father."

"What do you want me to do, Amber? Quit my job? Stay here for her? I would stay for both of you. I would do anything for both of you. But I need more than an ex-girlfriend and her daughter."

"Why do labels mean so much to you?" Amber's voice was hard, but she was ready to break.

"Why are you so against them? Why are you so against marrying me?"

She shook her head. Wanted to say it wasn't him. It was marriage itself. But she couldn't speak around the knife in her throat, and then suddenly Hadley was at the door of her room, and Amber saw just from a glance at her that she'd heard at least part of their argument, and Nathan stood up.

Amber watched helplessly as he hugged Hadley goodbye. Dropped a kiss on the top of her head. And walked out. She arched her eyebrows hopefully, but Hadley only stared at her. Turned and walked out without a word.

Nathan had left her again.

Third time's a charm, she decided.

Forty-Two

"Hey." The backdoor swung open. Amber flinched when it banged the wall. She hunched her shoulders, but kept her eyes on the piles of photographs in front of her. "How long have you been here?"

"Few hours," she mumbled low enough that she knew Liv couldn't possibly have heard her. She glanced at her watch. It was after eight. She'd walked into the house around five. Gone home from the studio just after three-thirty. Found Hadley at the dining room table, algebra book open, left hand on the book, right hand and pencil flying over a piece of loose leaf paper.

She'd seen the way Hadley tensed up as she neared her, but she'd ignored it-or tried to-and dropped her hand on her shoulder. Leaned over to kiss her. Hadley had only grunted some sort of greeting Amber hadn't been able to make out.

When Amber set her purse and keys on the table, Hadley had looked up. Actually made eye contact with her.

"What're you doing home?"

"I'm gonna go over to Pop's tonight," Amber had answered. "Thought we could eat early."

Hadley rolled her eyes. Amber wondered if she was tired of Pop's house, the fact that it wasn't really Pop's house anymore and yet it seemed to eat up more time now than before, or if she just didn't want Amber around.

"It's not even four o'clock."

"Well, it will be by the time I get supper ready."

Hadley stared at Amber like her hair had just turned green.

"What are you making?"

"I put a ham steak in the fridge this morning. Thought we could have that and...rice? Does that sound good?"

"No."

"How about noodles?"

"Not really."

"Well, I'm going to make it and if you're hungry, you'll eat it."

Amber had thrown the ham steak in the broiler, put a pot of water on to boil and gone to her bedroom to change clothes. She'd raked her eyes over the bed, but she hadn't given her brain time to process Nathan sitting there yesterday, talking to her, telling her he was leaving. Instead, she'd changed her gray blouse for a t-shirt and grabbed a hoody and yanked it off a hanger.

Hadley was still working on homework when Amber hustled back through the dining room. Amber wanted to ask about her school day. About her Saturday night with Nathan-they hadn't talked yesterday after Nathan had left. But Hadley wouldn't even lift her eyes from her paper, and Amber was in a hurry to get to Pop's house. Not true. Amber was in a hurry to get nowhere fast, just so much easier to avoid the fight Hadley desperately wanted.

It had nagged at her while she watched the butter noodles in the pot on the stove. While she'd plated their dinners and carried them in to the table. While Hadley ate hers and kept her attention riveted on the algebra. They were going to talk about this. About Nathan. The whole *what if she and Nathan had kids* thing. Amber kind of wanted to talk about it. To feel Hadley out.

But if Nathan was going to be gone indefinitely, it seemed kind of pointless. And an indefinite move could lead to a definite move, and the thought made Amber's chest hurt so badly, she'd set her fork down and pushed her half-eaten dinner away.

She'd cleaned the table off. Rinsed the dishes off and loaded the dishwasher. Wondered if there was a chance of stopping him from going. Propped herself in the doorway and watched Hadley work for several long, silent minutes.

"What?" Hadley had finally snapped. She'd thrown her pencil down and dropped back in the wooden chair-hard enough to bang her head-and stared sullenly at Amber.

"You know how we were gonna talk about this stuff?" Amber raised her eyebrows hopefully. "About me and Nathan? But we were getting ready to go-"

"What's there to talk about? If he's leaving?"

Amber felt the same way, but it made her mad to have her feelings tossed back in her face.

"I just..." Amber sighed. "Would you have been okay? With it?"

"With what, Mom?"

"Me. And Nathan."

Hadley shrugged and shook her head.

"You and Nathan what?"

Amber had cleared her throat. Almost chickened out, but made herself stand there. Made herself say the words.

"If we'd had a baby."

"Like it would have mattered..." Hadley had sat up and reached for her pencil. "Why would you care what I think?"

Amber's heart had slipped a bit in her chest. Dropped. Twisted. Hurt. God, her heart hurt.

"I care a lot what you think, Hadley," she'd whispered. But Hadley was done talking; she'd turned back to her homework.

"What're you doing?"

Amber looked up now, as Liv joined her at the table. She eyed her closed file folders protectively and then looked at the piles of old photographs on the table.

"I don't know." Amber shook her head. "Wasting time, I guess."

"What do you mean?" Liv leaned over Amber's shoulder, over the table to get a better look at the photographs.

"Not wanted at home."

"Not wanted at-" Liv, still draped half way over the table, turned to look at Amber. "What?"

Amber swallowed hard and looked back at the closest pile of pictures.

"I think these are the only ones that I can actually identify anyone in." She pushed the pile toward Liv. "Maybe Aunt Cheryl…a few of them even look like maybe…Mom's aunts."

"Okay." Liv nodded slowly as she dragged her eyes from Amber's face to the pictures. "I wonder who would know…for sure."

Amber shrugged. "The rest of the piles…" She blinked and reached for the next closest one. "Like this one…um…neat…settings. Like…the old shopping center….Santa's house."

"Oh wow." Liv grinned. "Santa's house. I remember going there."

"I don't," Amber said simply. The fact that Liv did and Amber didn't, that Liv was sixteen years older than she was, kind of drive home the point. The one that had Amber dragging her feet on the whole getting married and having kids thing. The one that Hadley thought had nothing to do with her.

"The old JC Penney store," Liv said appreciatively. "Remember that?" She leaned closer, again, to the table, to eye the picture. Even though Amber didn't remember the building, she understood Liv's need, desire, to expand that picture, to make it bigger, so she could climb inside and walk around in the past. Explore the memory somewhere other than inside her head.

"Nope." Amber reached for Liv's hand and poked her wedding ring. Twisted it around so the diamond was visible, as it should be. Liv curled her fingers absently, rubbed her thumb over the bottom of her ring, and finally looked at Amber again.

"What?" she asked softly. "What happened?"

Amber smiled sadly.

"Were you and Ingrid here yesterday?"

"Ingrid spent the day with Luke's family. They did a cookout or something for his dad's birthday, maybe? I came over here, and Ezra showed up. We got the rest of the boxes and stuff out of here."

"Noticed that when I didn't have to do the obstacle course to get to the table," Amber said with a nod.

Liv hooked her foot around the leg of the chair next to Amber's and pushed it back from the table. She sat down, let her eyes roam over the table again.

"It was kinda nice."

"Finally getting something done?"

"Little bit of stuff left in the garage." Liv shook her head. "Hanging out with Ezra."

"Mm." Amber tilted her head and nodded. "I'm sure it was."

"Shay came by late. She had Samuel with her."

"So you got cuddle time with my nephew. Is that what're trying to say?"

"I did, yes." Liv grinned. "We need more babies. I can say that to you, but I can't say it in front of Gracie and Charlie."

Amber frowned.

"Well, I'm not saying I want grandbabies. I just want more babies to snuggle."

"So. I'm wondering..." Amber stretched and yawned. "Wait. Why are you here so late?"

"I had a meeting earlier...and I went to the grocery store. And I drove by the house and saw your car."

"Mm." Amber rested her elbow on the table and propped her chin in her hand. "I'm thinking we got most of the junk out..."

"Most?"

"Still stuff in the attic," Amber reminded Liv.

"Damn. I forgot about that."

"What're we gonna do with the furniture?"

"Auction?" Liv rubbed at a spot on the back of her hand. She flicked her eyes up to look at Amber, but she dropped her gaze quickly.

"What're you doing?" Amber covered her hand with hers. "Quit."

"What do you think?"

"An auction?" Amber rolled her eyes. "Because everyone needs the lovely brown flowered velour eighties sofa."

"You don't think so?"

"I think you'd be lucky to get fifty cents out of it."

"Hmm." Liv looked up and shook her head. "I dunno. I guess we can see if any second hand furniture stores want it. See if…anyone wants it. Put an ad in the classifieds. Some of it's not in bad shape."

"No, I know," Amber agreed. "I just…I look at it as part of the house. Because to me…it's part of the house. But it's gonna have to go."

Liv took a deep breath and sighed. "Yeah. You're right."

"So." Amber turned her attention back to the pictures on the table. "What do you wanna do with these?"

"I dunno," Liv said again. "Do you want 'em?"

Amber did want them, but she thought her sisters might think she was crazy. They were old. Faded. Worn. Corners torn off. Some of them creased beyond repair. But they were history, and some of them, though simple and actually awful compared to today's standards, were striking, and they spoke volumes to Amber where they might not even whisper to Ingrid or Liv.

"Do you care?"

"Of course not."

"Do you think Ingrid would?"

"No."

Amber nodded.

"What're you gonna do with them?"

"I don't know yet, but…" Amber reached for a couple of stacks. "I like them. It's…interesting…looking at them."

"Then take them." Liv nodded.

Amber looked over the many piles and hesitated. "I'm gonna leave them here one more night. Find something to keep them in so I don't get them all mixed up again."

"That's fine." Liv's gaze fell on Amber's two file folders. "What're those? Did you find them here, too?"

"No. They're mine."

"Oh. What are they?"

"Just…" Amber shook her head and waved her hand as if to tell Liv they weren't important. "Some ideas."

"Can I see?"

It hit Amber then that Ingrid had never given her the manuscript Liv had supposedly found in her stuff after she'd moved. For just a second, the old jealousy revved up inside her, but she tamped it down. The last time the manuscript had come up, Amber had shrugged it off. Like reading it wasn't important to her. She'd hurt Ingrid's feelings.

"Um." Amber pursed her lips. She reached for the top folder, but she pushed the other one-the one with pictures from the house-to the side. "I guess."

"What's that one?" Liv asked immediately. "Why'd you move it away from me?"

Amber laughed softly. "It's…it might be a surprise…"

"For me?"

"Maybe."

"It's not my birthday."

Amber shook her head, and Liv nodded.

"Just because I'm your favorite sister, right?"

"Ingrid didn't give me that manuscript."

"Really?" Liv cocked her head and stared at her. "The one I read?"

"Yeah."

"She said she was going to."

"I think I made such a big deal out of not needing to see it just because she let you read it that she thought I didn't wanna read it."

"Because I am a teacher, I followed that." Liv laughed. "Well, you need to get it from her."

"It's good?"

Liv had started to open the folder, but she stopped with it half open, and looked at Amber.

"Are you kidding me?" She frowned. "I laughed. I cried. I didn't know what to do with myself."

"Why's she so being so weird about it?"

"Because it's totally different from her thrillers."

"Mm." Amber nodded. She glanced at the folder in Liv's hands. Understandable that Ingrid would be skittish about sharing something different. Right now, Amber's heart was hammering so hard she felt like her teeth were beating, too. Like Liv could *see* it.

The pictures in that file were different from her usual style. Different. And yet the same. Amber saw the difference, as well as the similarity. But the whole concept was hers. What if Liv didn't get it?

She watched, lungs and heart and stomach in her throat, as Liv lingered for several long silent seconds over each of the pictures. They were only a sampling of what she wanted to do; she had so much more to do to complete the project. But she'd developed a few, printed a few of the digital shots. Call her crazy, but when she was beginning a project, it felt good, almost inspirational, to carry a part of it with her everywhere she went.

Maybe that's how Ingrid felt about her Mac. And any files, any story ideas she stored on it. No wonder she'd been like a barracuda protecting the Mac from

Hadley. Wasn't necessarily the thing with Rafe and Julie, although Amber knew that was a huge part of it, but it was her imagination and her vision she was fiercely protective of.

Liv studied the picture of Gretchen's foot-the angry red wound, the tracks from the stitches that would eventually become a scar. She flipped it up and then stared at a picture of a silver BMW with the whole front end smashed in to complete ruin. Amber had even captured the stains the color of rust on the driver's seat. She didn't know, but she assumed the accident had been fatal. The next picture was the warped, broken trim board on the garage.

Amber tried to swallow when Liv closed the folder and slowly lifted her eyes to look at her.

"You okay?"

Amber blinked, surprised by Liv's question. By her lack of response or emotion.

"You don't like them."

Liv raised her eyebrows. "They're stunning, Amber. Raw."

Amber scooted her chair back when Liv stood up. "And?"

"They make me hurt," Liv answered simply. "Are you okay?"

Liv wandered around the table to the window and stared out to the backyard.

"They make me sad." Her voice was a gruff whisper.

"Good." Amber nodded, though Liv wasn't looking at her. She'd wanted to make people hurt with this one. Honestly, she'd wanted to dig in and make people bleed. She'd heard the phrase misery loves company a hundred times or more. Right now, she was living it.

"The eyes are the window to the soul."

"What?" Amber asked when Liv looked at her over shoulder. Apparently, they were in a book of cliché sayings right now, but they weren't on the same page.

"Your camera has always been the window to your soul."

Amber winced. Liv's words stabbed her right in the heart. Liv *did* get it. Amber stared at her silently, ashamed to have her demons on display. Right here on the table for her older sister to scrutinize. Judge.

Liv stood at the window a moment longer and then came back to sit by her.

"You're gonna..." She looked at the file. "Is that your next proposal?"

Amber nodded.

Liv reached for her. Linked her fingers through Amber's.

"I hate that you feel this way, Amber."

"Yeah. Well." Amber shrugged. "Suck it up and move on, right?"

"What happened? The other night? Did he see you come home?"

"He's leaving town," Amber announced.

"What? Where-"

"I don't wanna talk about it, Liv." Amber shook her head. "I really...don't...wanna talk bout it. I can't."

Liv squeezed her fingers and nodded.

"Okay." She lifted her other hand and brushed Amber's hair back from her face. "If you're okay..."

She wasn't. They both knew it. But it was late. Hadley was home alone. And nothing either of them said here tonight would change anything.

"I'm okay."

Liv's eyes brimmed with tears.

"I love you."

Amber nodded. "I gotta go." She lifted her butt from her chair, leaned over to hug Liv and then grabbed her folders and walked away from the table. She snatched her keys and her purse from the counter and headed to the backdoor.

"Amber!"

Amber stopped, hand on the screen, but she didn't turn to look at Liv.

"Is Hadley-?"

Liv could have been asking a million different things. Is Hadley home alone? Is Hadley going to see Kyle again? Is Hadley still sneaking around? But Amber assumed Liv wanted to know if Hadley was okay.

"No."

When Liv didn't answer, Amber cleared her throat and gave the screen door a shove. Stepped outside. Caught the scent of rain in the air as she walked to the Passport. It was time to man up. Nathan wasn't going to be around to do it. So Amber would have to step up. Get over it. Take charge. And start herself and Hadley on the journey to something new. Maybe one day Hadley would appreciate it.

Forty-Three

"Hey."

Amber had heard the bell on the door, but she hadn't turned to look to see who'd come in. She'd been at her computer for-she glanced at the screen and saw that it was after ten-a couple of hours, making progress on sorting out the digital shots she didn't want. Of the house.

She'd talked to her agent yesterday. *Simplicity* was going to print, though it would take a while before it was ready. She'd pitched her latest idea, *the ugly stuff*, and though Kevin had agreed to look at it, she'd heard the reluctance in his voice, in the way he'd hesitated before answering her.

She didn't care. Come hell or high water, she'd do the book.

She closed the file on her computer as she stood up and turned to Ingrid.

"What're you working on?" Ingrid asked. She pushed a cardboard tray of paper coffee cups-the navy blue Beans, Leaves & Love ones-across the counter in offering. She nodded toward Amber's computer.

Amber shook her head.

"Is it the surprise you have for Liv?"

Amber stared at Ingrid silently. Her sister was dressed in jeans and a purple blouse. Amber studied the blouse closely and then looked at the purple streak in Ingrid's hair, thinking they looked like the exact shade. She carried her messenger bag-the worn brown leather bag she carried her Mac in-over her shoulder.

"For me?" Amber touched one of the cups.

"Yeah." Ingrid nodded. "Of course."

"Thanks."

"What surprise are you working on?" Ingrid asked quietly. She accepted the cup Amber handed to her. "I wanna see it."

"Well, you can't," Amber said simply. She pulled her cup from the tray and then tossed the tray in the trashcan behind the counter.

"Why?" Ingrid arched her eyebrows.

"When did you talk to Liv?"

"Yesterday."

"Why aren't you working?" Amber took a drink of her coffee and smacked her lips together appreciatively. Caramel mocha.

"Um." Ingrid adjusted the bag on her shoulder. "Needed a change of scenery. I was gonna hang out at Beans, Leaves, and Love, but it's so crowded. I felt like a dog on a school playground. Wasn't sure who to watch, which conversation to eavesdrop on."

Amber grinned. "Why do you need a change?"

"Just do sometimes." Ingrid shrugged.

"You and Luke are okay?"

"Yeah. We're good."

Ingrid looked around the studio again. Amber noticed her eyes were drawn to the poster again, the one of Sedona.

"Do you wanna work here?" Amber suggested.

"Um." Ingrid turned back to her.

"You brought me coffee to butter me up for something."

Ingrid's grin made her look like a little kid.

"Yeah. I wanna see the surprise."

"Not showing you the surprise." Amber shook her head.

"Did you do shots of the kids?" Ingrid asked. She slipped the bag off her shoulder and set it on the counter. Amber noticed it was packed so full, the buckle on the front was strained. "Neither of them has said a word! I can't believe-"

"No."

"Amber." Ingrid laughed. She reached across the counter with her right hand and grabbed Amber's hand. "Tell me."

"Can't."

"Why not?"

Amber heard it. The tiny little note of envy.

"Because it's for all of you guys."

"All of us?"

"Yes."

"Like-"

"Drop. It." Amber shook her head. "Just forget you know anything about it."

"Yeah, you know I was the kid that went digging through the house looking for Christmas presents, don't you?"

Amber snorted. "Yeah? I did that, too. Ezra used to get so pissed at me for that."

Ingrid unbuckled her bag, but she kept her eyes on Amber.

"Liv told on me."

"Rat."

"Exactly." Ingrid nodded. She pulled a huge stack of papers, rubber banded together, from the bag. Amber's breath hitched when she realized it was the manuscript. "Please don't feel like you have to read this-"

Amber snatched it away from Ingrid before she could change her mind.

"Awesome." She grinned and glanced down at the manuscript. "What's it called?"

Ingrid pointed to the top of the first page. "Untitled."

Amber snorted.

"Thank you." She nodded.

"Just…be honest? If you hate it? Tell me?"

"I will, but I won't," Amber answered quickly.

"What?"

"I'll be honest." Amber turned and set the manuscript by her computer. "But I won't hate it."

Ingrid shrugged. "Maybe you will."

"You can work here, if it won't bother you having me around for a while."

"Do you talk to yourself?"

"Um. No?"

"Do you mind if I do?"

"Do you ever say anything funny?"

"Have you talked to Kyle again? After the other day?"

Amber deflated. She'd forgotten that stuff. For the past five minutes, it was just her and Ingrid teasing about the surprise, taking a short trip down memory lane.

"Yeah. He texted yesterday. Said he really enjoyed meeting Hadley. And he wondered if she'd like to hang out again."

Ingrid nodded, but she sort of cringed. "You okay with that?"

"Don't I have to be? I set the wheels in motion here."

"You tell Had?"

"Yeah. She…they're…gonna have pizza Saturday. Doing lunch together."

"You weren't invited?"

"Not really." Amber shrugged. "She doesn't wanna be alone with him, but she made it clear that she doesn't wanna be with me, either."

"What happened?"

Amber chewed on her lip. Ingrid knew Nathan was leaving. If she'd talked to Liv, if she knew about the surprise, then she knew Nathan was leaving.

"He spent the night Saturday-"

"Really?" Ingrid asked quickly.

"He was sleeping on the couch when I got home. Left him there."

"And what? Before he left, he ducked in to tell you he was moving."

Amber sucked in a quick breath. *Moving* sounded so much worse than *leaving*. *Leaving indefinitely*. Probably a hell of a lot closer to the truth. Which is why it hurt hat much more, Amber realized.

"He um…" She swallowed hard. "Brought me coffee. Advil. Kissed me, and told me he hated the thought of anyone else doing that, and then he said…he was leaving."

"Jerk," Ingrid muttered.

"He's not." Amber shrugged. "I mean, he is, but he's not."

"I know, sweetie," Ingrid agreed. "It just-I hate this. For you."

"Me too. I hate it for Hadley."

"Kids are resilient. She'll bounce back."

"Maybe," Amber mumbled. "Just sucks that this is all happening just when I tell her about Kyle."

"You're still worried she'll like him more than you? She'll get comfortable-"

"Not much to like about me right now."

"Yes, there is," Ingrid argued. "Everybody gets down, Amber. Everybody's a little hard to love sometimes."

"Ouch."

Ingrid smiled sadly. "Hard for Hadley. Not me."

Amber tucked her hair behind her ears and took a deep breath. "I kind of want to see him. Before he leaves."

"Why?"

"Because I was…so angry the other day. So hurt. And we fought. Again. And I just…I don't want him to remember me that way. Ya know? I want him to remember something fun. Something happy. About us."

"So, then, see him."

"But what if I do? And I'm angry again, and we fight again? I don't think I can ignore…the way I feel…I can't…pretend I'm happy for him."

Ingrid's gaze lingered on the counter between them, but Amber saw the frown she wore.

"I think you should see him. I think if you don't, you'll always regret it."

Amber gave herself a mental shake. "Maybe. Maybe he won't wanna see me anyway."

Ingrid cleared her throat. "Liv said you're working on a new book idea."

Amber had wondered if Ingrid would ever get around to that. If she knew about the surprise and that Nathan was leaving, odds were Liv had told her about the pictures. She nodded, but she avoided looking at Ingrid.

"What'd she say about it?"

Ingrid pursed her lips. Shrugged. Looked away when Amber finally made eye contact.

"She said the pictures were striking. Haunting."

"Not haunting," she disagreed. "Ugly. Hard to look at."

"Can I see them?"

Amber had a bigger file of them on the computer, but she wasn't ready to share all of them. Not with anyone. Not yet. Instead, she dug through her own bag next to her desk, and pulled the same file from it. Handed it to Ingrid. She took another drink. Too nervous to watch Ingrid look at her work, to wait for a verdict, she wandered the studio.

Ingrid closed the file when she wandered back to the counter. She looked up at Amber and arched her eyebrows.

"Trainwreck," she said quietly. "You can't look away."

Amber felt a little wash of relief. Both of her sisters had said the right things. Apparently, she'd pulled a stroke of ugly, of truth from both of them. And yet, she was still nervous about what they thought. About the idea.

"Brilliant photography." Ingrid nodded. "To make something so hard to look at so necessary to see."

Amber shook her head. "I just needed to stop seeing everything wrong…everything ugly…in my life."

Ingrid nodded appreciatively. "I get it." She fingered the file again. "Do you have a working title?"

"*Other People's Ugly*," Amber said simply.

Forty-Four

Amber stepped out of her studio and shielded her eyes from the sun. She hiked a leg up to climb into the Passport. Days like this, when she was dressed for business professional-dressy crème-colored slacks and a brown silk blouse-a car would be nice. Something simple. She hated having to toss her purse into the Passport and climb into the SUV when she was dressed up. Then again, most days, the SUV was better suited to her needs than any car could be.

As she started the SUV, she heard her phone buzz in her purse. She assumed it would be Ingrid or Liv, so she strapped her seat belt on and leaned over to root around in her purse. She closed her fingers around it, tapped the accept button absently and put it to her ear.

"Hello?"

"Amber."

She sucked in a quick breath and curled the fingers of her free hand around the steering wheel.

"What?"

It was Wednesday. Nathan would be gone in four days.

"Are you busy?"

She rested her head on the seat and closed her eyes. "No. Just left the studio.

"I was…um…"

Funny. There'd never been a time when Nathan couldn't talk to her. He'd always been the voice of reason in their relationship.

"What?" she whispered gruffly.

"Um. Are you busy? Friday? Friday evening?"

She opened her mouth to answer him, but she couldn't make a sound. Couldn't breathe.

"I just wondered…if you'd wanna have dinner…you know. Before I go."

Before I go. She flinched.

"I mean," he continued. "I'd like to be able to talk…about Hadley…square some things away…"

She could remind him that Hadley wasn't his daughter. That they didn't need to set ground rules for Hadley to call him or visit him. That once he left, it was done. But she wouldn't. Maybe Nathan wasn't Hadley's father. But the fact that Hadley wished he was said something.

"Um." She swallowed hard. "Yeah. Sure."

She wound a piece of hair around her finger. Heard the huge rush of air on his end of the phone. Had he sighed? In relief?

"Where do you wanna go?"

"You pick," she answered. "I don't care."

Didn't matter if it was Carino's or McDonald's. Saying goodbye was going to suck. Maybe she needed to get Liv or Ingrid to come and snap a picture of them. At the moment, seemed like nothing could be uglier.

"Lloyd & Jones?"

She raised her eyebrows. He wanted to take her to the fanciest place in town to break her heart one last time? Bleeding hearts don't discriminate. Wasn't going to hurt any less in a dimly lit room with silver and black leather chairs and silver cloth napkins and waiters in black ties.

"Okay."

"I'll pick you up at six."

She nodded. Wondered, as she swiped at her eyes, if the tears would ever run out. Seemed like she cried all the time now.

"See you then." She barely got the words out before her voice broke and the tears began to fall.

She tossed her phone on the passenger seat but didn't put the SUV in reverse yet. Sat for just moment to pull herself together. She'd put her sunglasses on, but she still ducked her head when she saw a couple walking toward her. She hated for anyone to see her cry.

Maybe if she put something of her own in the new book. Something of her own ugly. Wasn't a page she'd ever have to look at again. But how could she ask other people to participate if she wasn't willing to herself?

She swallowed a knot of emotion. Probably some snot, some tears. Pushed her sunglasses up and rubbed her eyes again. Decided she'd go home. It was almost five. Hadley should be home. She could work there. Or just crash. Take a nap on the couch, maybe. Find something she and Hadley could eat for dinner.

Except she wasn't hungry.

Then again, she still had to feed Hadley.

She drove with the stereo off. Listened to the silence in her vehicle. The sounds of traffic just outside her windows. Thought again about moving on. Wondered how she was supposed to do that. If she could just find the first step. The first step away from the heartache.

Ingrid's Subaru was parked behind her house. Amber felt a little ping of guilt. She'd only read two chapters of the manuscript last night; she'd been so exhausted she couldn't keep her eyes open. And of course, when she'd turned her lamp off to go to sleep, she'd been wide awake.

Hadley sat on the kitchen counter when Amber went inside. She eyed Amber carefully, but she didn't greet her. Ingrid leaned against the doorway to the dining room.

"Hey."

"Hi." Ingrid flashed a smile at her. "You look nice."

Amber raised her eyebrows and attempted a smile. Though there wasn't any evidence she'd had a near crying jag in her parking spot at the studio, she didn't think she looked nice.

"Tell your mother hi," Ingrid instructed Hadley.

"Yeah." Hadley glanced at Amber again, but she didn't say anything.

"What's up?" Amber asked Ingrid.

"Mm. Nothing. Spent part of the day working at Java Infusion-"

"Didn't like the digs yesterday?"

Ingrid laughed softly. "And I thought I'd swing by and see Hadley before I went home." She finished her sentence. "I didn't wanna bother you again."

Amber smiled sadly. "I'm sorry. I only got through a couple of chapters-"

Ingrid shook her head quickly and held her hands up to stop Amber.

"No. Don't. I don't expect you to read it every night. I mean...whenever, Amber. Don't apologize for being busy...or tired..."

Amber nodded.

"What's for supper, Mom?" Hadley asked.

Amber glanced at Hadley and shrugged. "I don't know. What do you want?"

"Can we go out? For Mexican? Aunt Ingrid could go, too."

"Maybe." Amber slipped past Ingrid and walked on through the dining room. "I'm gonna change clothes."

"Tell me when we leave!" From the sounds of it, Hadley jumped off the counter. Amber looked over her shoulder and watched her skip through the dining room to go upstairs.

"Was she talking to you?" Amber asked Ingrid.

"About school." Ingrid shrugged. "Remember? I talk to her English class Friday."

"Mm." Amber did remember. She dragged her eyes from Ingrid to the stairs, wondering what, if anything, Hadley was up to.

"Have a good day?"

Amber sighed and set her purse on her nightstand. "I don't know anymore what a good day is."

"Okay day?" Ingrid wiggled her eyebrows at her.

Amber smiled sadly. She unbuttoned her blouse and slipped it off her shoulders. Tossed it in the dry clean pile in the closet and then pulled a black Nike pullover from a hanger.

"So do you wanna?"

Amber slipped her arms in the pullover and then yanked it over her head.

"Wanna what?"

"Go out to eat."

"Um. Sure?"

"Let's ask Liv."

"What about Luke and Wade?"

"Can we ask them, too?" Ingrid asked. "Or…"

"Don't baby me," Amber argued. "I'll live."

"Okay."

Amber unzipped her slacks and stepped out of them. Tossed them on top of the blouse and grabbed the jeans from the end of her bed.

"He called today."

"Nathan did?"

"Yeah." Amber sniffled as she eased her jeans over her hips. Buttoned and zipped them and met Ingrid's eyes. "He asked me if I wanted to have dinner Friday night. So we can…talk about Hadley. How's that for irony? Never married, not divorcing, and we're still gonna have dinner and talk about Hadley, about how best to handle her…relationship with Nathan."

"He asked you to dinner."

Amber nodded.

"Where?"

"Lloyd & Jones."

Ingrid blinked and shook her head.

"What?"

"You think he asked you to dinner at Lloyd & Jones to talk about visitation rights with your daughter?"

"What does that mean?" Amber fished in her drawer for a pair of socks. Perched on the edge of her bed to put them on.

"Do you love him?"

Amber dropped her gaze to the floor between her feet. Nodded. Covered her face with her hands.

"I do."

"Okay. Then let's do this."

"What are we doing?"

"Show me your closet."

Amber looked up with a frown.

"What?"

"What's in your closet? Any sexy little black dresses?"

"Why?"

"Well, what are you planning to wear to dinner with Nathan at Lloyd & Jones? You're not wearing jeans."

"I don't know. Slacks, I guess."

"No. Show some leg. Show a lot of leg. Show me your sexiest dress."

"Sex isn't our problem, Ingrid-"

"Amber." Ingrid dropped her hands on her shoulders when she stood up. "You gotta make him see what he's gonna miss. You gotta make him miss it before it's even gone."

"And if I don't let him put that ring on my finger, none of it matters anyway."

"How bad do you wanna save this relationship?"

"So I have to bend?"

"Bend or break, Amber." Ingrid shrugged.

Amber swallowed hard and turned to her closet. She reached deep into the right hand side and pulled out a short black cocktail dress.

"That it?"

"What's wrong with it?"

"Is it?" Ingrid pushed.

Amber sighed and gestured for Ingrid to have a look for herself.

"Text Liv," Ingrid told her as she perused Amber's clothes.

"Why?"

"Ask her about dinner. Tell her to meet us here."

"Why?" Amber asked again.

"Because this is a fashion thing. This is a sister thing."

"A sister thing?" Amber repeated. "Really?"

"Yes. Text her."

Amber turned her back to Ingrid and moved closer to the nightstand. Pulled her phone from her purse.

"Is that what I tell Liv? We're having a sister thing?"

"If you don't do it, I'm gonna text her and tell her our mission is to get you laid-"

"Again. That's not the problem."

"We'll make you so freaking hot, he'll melt just looking at you. Your job is to blow his mind after dinner."

"Ingrid."

"I'm not talking about sex, Amber," Ingrid said softly. "I'm talking about making him love you. Enough. Making him remember what it feels like to love you."

"Sounds likes sex."

"Don't be a pain," Ingrid mumbled. "Text Liv."

"I did."

"This one." Ingrid pulled a strapless dress from the closet. Black. Thigh length. Slit on the side.

"Are you kidding me?"

"Not even remotely." Ingrid winked. "Show me your sexiest panties."

Amber stared at her silently.

"What if I told you I'm wearing them?"

Ingrid shook her head. "Just saw you change. You're lying."

Amber moved to the dresser again and pulled her drawer open.

"You really think this is gonna work?"

Ingrid cocked her head and studied Amber's face. "If you want it to."

"He's leaving," Amber reminded Ingrid.

"Maybe he's leaving because he thinks there's nothing left for him here."

"Hadley and I are here."

"Exactly, Amber. How badly do you want him to stay?"

Forty-Five

Amber was surprised there were no sirens the way Liv came tearing into the house, like a fireman ready to battle a blaze. In fact, when Liv stopped short in Amber's bedroom and saw Ingrid eyeing the strapless dress and Amber sorting through her underwear drawer, Amber and Ingrid exchanged a glance.

"What?" Liv was actually out of breath.

Amber and Ingrid giggled, but the giggle turned into a good, old-fashioned belly laugh. Liv, still in the dark about the sister thing and the laughter, was a good sport and joined in. Only Hadley coming downstairs and finding the three of them doubled over in laughing fits chased the light-hearted moment away.

She didn't need to say anything. She'd simply leaned into the bedroom and made sure to sweep the whole room with her gaze. And then she'd rolled her eyes and slipped back out to the kitchen. Amber followed half way through the dining room.

"What are you doing?" she called to Hadley.

"Getting a snack."

"Well, don't eat much," Amber answered. "We're going out for dinner."

"Yeah, Mom, it's like three-thirty. Dinner won't be for, like, years."

"Five, Hadley. That's an hour and a half."

"Uncle Wade and Luke can't be there by five. They work."

"We can get there at five," Liv announced. Amber turned to find Liv standing just behind her. "And we can eat chips and salsa."

"I'm eating a cookie." Hadley walked into the dining room with an Oreo in her hand. "That okay?"

"Hey," Ingrid called. Amber saw her standing in the bedroom doorway. "We're going to the mall before we eat. Wanna go with us?"

"The mall?" Liv frowned.

"We are?" Amber looked at Liv and shook her head.

"With you guys?" Hadley almost snorted.

"We are," Ingrid answered Amber. "Sister thing."

Amber laughed out loud. "She doesn't wanna go."

"Since when do young girls not wanna go to the mall?" Liv's gaze followed Hadley to the steps.

"I have homework," Hadley said dismissively.

"Since it would involve being with me."

"I thought things were okay now." Liv reached for Amber, put her arm around her waist.

"Temporary truce," Amber explained. "She's back to hating me."

"Okay." Ingrid appeared in the dining room. She handed Amber her purse.

"Wait." Amber shook her head. "What are we doing?"

"Going to the mall." Ingrid fake punched Amber in the arm. "Keep up, Amber."

"Why? Why are we going to the mall?"

"We're going to Victoria's Secret."

"What?" Amber shook her head. "No. We're not."

"Well. I am. If you want a say in what I buy, then you'll come, too."

"Could you just catch me up first?" Liv asked Ingrid. "Remember me? I just got here-"

"Amber has a dinner date Friday night-"

Liv turned to Amber with a look of uneasy surprise.

"With who?"

"Nathan," Amber mumbled.

"Nathan," Ingrid said louder. "They're getting together to discuss Hadley."

Liv frowned and looked from Ingrid to Amber. "But you're not even…"

"I know," Amber agreed. "Ironic, huh?"

"That's good." Liv pointed at Amber. "So why? Are we-? Why are we going to the mall?"

"To get Amber a thong. God, Amber, one basic wardrobe piece every woman should own, and you're young and sexy, and you don't have-"

"I have dental floss," Amber suggested.

Ingrid snorted. "It's a good thought. But let's go. I'm already hungry."

"Wait." Amber stopped walking. Ingrid was trying to herd her to the door. "Wait."

"What?"

"Wait." Liv held up her hands. "What's she wearing? What-? Are you gonna try to seduce him? Is that the game plan? Send him off with a bang…" Liv glanced at Amber and grinned. "So to speak."

"Lloyd & Jones, Liv," Ingrid huffed impatiently. "Go look at the dress."

"Lloyd & Jones?" Liv whispered, eyes wide with wonder.

"Do you guys both have thongs?"

"Of course." Ingrid shrugged.

"Really?"

"Yep."

"And you wear it? Them?"

"Sometimes." Ingrid grinned. "Luke likes it."

"Wow." Amber shook her head. "Do you, Liv?"

"No," Liv admitted.

"Seriously?" Ingrid sounded surprised. "God, that might be part of your problem. Fruit of the Loom isn't gonna do it-"

"I'd rather go commando than wear a thong," Liv announced as she hurried back through the dining and living rooms. Amber blinked, looking after her, and then turned to Ingrid.

"Did she just say-?"

Ingrid closed her mouth. "Yeah. She did."

"Mm-kay." Amber nodded. "I need a drink."

"Shopping first." Ingrid raised her eyebrows. "You can have a drink once you're ready for Friday."

Amber felt a tingle of nerves in her belly. Felt the same in her fingertips.

"I'm never gonna be ready for Friday."

"Think of it as an audition."

"Not an actress."

"You're gonna be beautiful," Ingrid ignored her. She looked up, over Amber's shoulder as Liv joined them again.

"Okay. Let's go."

"Forgot to ask." Ingrid opened the door and looked back over her shoulder at Amber. "Do you have a strapless bra?"

"Um."

"How does that dress fit?" Liv asked.

"Pretty tight."

"Don't wear one."

"What?" Amber stared at Liv in shock. She pulled the door closed behind Liv. "God, Olivia, are you a nudist or something?"

"Something you aren't telling us?" Ingrid dug around in her purse and finally pulled her keys out.

"Tell me you wear…all layers of clothing…when you're at work." Amber's gaze roamed down over Liv and back up again.

"Eww." Liv shivered. "Of course I do."

Amber sighed with relief.

"Let's go. Clock's ticking." Ingrid tapped her wrist, though she wasn't wearing a watch.

"What if he shows up to pick me up and he's wearing jeans? And I'm decked out for nightlife? I'm gonna feel stupid."

"You're gonna be in command," Ingrid corrected her.

"I'm not, though." Amber climbed into the backseat, letting Liv sit up front with Ingrid. "He is. If I don't say I'll marry him, he'll leave. I mean, he might not even want that now. He might be ready to move on-"

"It's only been a few weeks. No one falls out of love that quickly."

"But-"

"Stop it!" Ingrid looked at Amber in the rearview mirror. "We are confident women!"

"We are?" Liv turned to Ingrid with one eyebrow arched in question.

"What've you got to lose, Amber?"

"Everything." Amber swallowed hard. "Nothing."

"So?" Ingrid shrugged and shook her head, eyes still on Amber in the mirror.

Amber nodded. She had everything to lose if she didn't fight for him. And she had nothing to lose, whether she fought or not.

"Ingrid?"

"Hmm?"

"You're totally freaking me out." Amber leaned forward and pointed around Liv. "Watch what...yeah...there's a curve in the alley..."

Forty-Six

    According to Ingrid, the shopping trip was a success. Amber wasn't so sure. She still had two nights before her dinner with Nathan, and already she was physically uncomfortable thinking about the dress and the tiny black thong, that was really nothing more than a few black strings held together with rhinestones. Looking at her receipt, Amber would have thought she'd bought more than the thong. Then again, if it worked as well as Ingrid predicted it would, it would be worth it.

    When they swung back by the house to pick up Hadley, Amber and Liv climbed out of Ingrid's SUV. Liv and Ingrid went ahead to get a table. Amber went inside to get Hadley and put her purchase in her bedroom. Hadley was no more talkative than she'd been earlier. She'd only grunted when Amber asked her if she'd finished her homework. Since her grades had improved since January, and because Amber simply had no energy to argue, she assumed the grunt was meant to be a yes.

    El Churro wasn't packet yet, but Amber knew it would be before six. The parking lot was never completely empty, and sometimes, the lot was full, and you'd have to park far enough away that you wanted to call a taxi to drop you off at the door. Ingrid and Liv sat together at a table for eight. Hadley grabbed the seat next to Liv, so Amber sat beside Ingrid.

    Amber was glad to see that they'd ordered a pitcher of margaritas, and they'd asked for a glass for her. Chips and salsa dotted the table. Liv and Ingrid were talking about Shay and Ezra. Apparently, Liv had called Ez to invite them to come along, and Ezra had begged off because Shay hadn't had much sleep the night before. As much as Amber liked Shay, she was actually surprised she and Ezra were still together. They'd been a great couple when they were dating. Amber wasn't sure what had happened, other than Samuel, but they weren't really a great couple anymore, and it was rare to see them out anywhere together, enjoying themselves.

Ingrid confessed to being a little wired about speaking to Hadley's class on Friday. Amber offered to go with her, just for moral support. She'd assumed Ingrid would blow her off, but she didn't. Ingrid had looked pleasantly surprised at Amber's offer, and so it was decided Ingrid would swing by the studio and pick her up on the way to the school on Friday morning.

Within twenty or thirty minutes, with a margarita in hand Amber wasn't counting, Wade and the kids showed up, Luke close on their heels. Dinner was a lively event. The guys drank beer, leaving the pitcher to the girls. Hadley fell into easy conversation with Gracie and Charlie. Luke and Wade's conversation jumped between work stuff-sounded like a drywall job-and NBA basketball. Liv and Ingrid had moved on from Ezra and Shay to reminiscing about the good old days, and the tree in the backyard that they'd all climbed and the time Liv took off on her bike and the chain came off and Liv crashed to the ground and scraped the hell out of her knees.

Amber found the ebb and flow of conversation around her somewhat soothing. She listened, mostly, threw in a comment now and then, though she didn't share Liv and Ingrid's memories. And they didn't share hers. Still, missing Nathan was an ache somewhere inside that no amount of conversation or fun or music could touch. She wanted this. What she saw between Liv and Wade, between Ingrid and Luke. The silent glances the couples shared. The ones that Amber knew instinctively were anything but silent. They were saying a million things to each other with only their eyes. Amber wanted Nathan to fill her glass for her automatically; she wanted to send her fork down the table to Nathan, so he could have a bite of her rice because he didn't like it enough to have his own order. She wanted to talk to Liv and Ingrid about her children, Hadley yes, but more than that. She envied that whenever Gracie or Charlie spoke or laughed, Wade and Liv's eyes met from opposite ends of the table, and they smiled, and Amber knew they were proud of the kids they'd had together.

Amber noticed the light catch on Liv's wedding ring every time Liv moved her hands. Every time she reached for her glass. Every time she lifted her fork. Amber's fingers had always been bare. She'd never worn a ring in her life. Made her think of Ingrid, the comment she'd made a while ago about never being pregnant in her life. Ingrid had admitted that it bothered her.

Amber took a deep breath.

It bothered her.

That she would turn thirty soon. And her fingers were bare.

The world didn't stop spinning. The power didn't go out. Liv and Ingrid still talked about sleepovers they'd had with mutual friends, and Wade and Luke talked about the Bulls. Hadley and Gracie had their heads together over their phones, giggling about something, and Amber's heart had just done a frigging three sixty, and her chest hurt and she stared in disbelief as life went on around her.

~

Ingrid was funny. Apparently, she didn't know it. She held the class in the palm of her hand, kept a relaxed control of the room though she mostly let the kids lead her with their questions. The questions had been slow to come at first, and Ingrid tossed out a few stories about some bizarre research situations-like getting stuck in an elevator with a guy she'd sworn was a biker slash murderer and ended up being a Catholic priest. Amber had been impressed with the questions, which mustered some strength and speed as the kids grew more comfortable. Ingrid kind of looked like she was watching a tennis match, her head bobbing back and forth, looking from one kid to another as she laughed and talked, all the while looking so at ease, you'd think she did *this* for a living, and not writing.

Carrie Jackson, Hadley's teacher, had invited Ingrid to come back anytime she'd like, and she'd been delighted to hear that Ingrid had moved back to the area. Amber had been just a little surprised at the pride she felt for her sister as they left the school together. She'd always enjoyed telling people I.G. Arenson was her sister. Just meant more now that she and Ingrid had developed a personal relationship.

Didn't get more personal than it had last night, Amber decided as she climbed out of Ingrid's SUV back at the studio. She decided to spend some time in the dark room, developing some of the pictures she'd taken throughout the week. Old buildings. Rusted out refrigerators and dryers tossed out in yards with brown grass, thriving weeds and no hope. She needed something to keep her mind busy, because between thinking about last night and her date with Nathan tonight, not to mention Hadley meeting Kyle for lunch tomorrow, she was wired like she'd consumed five or six pots of coffee and in reality, she hadn't touched a single cup.

Last night, Ingrid and Liv had come over to play like she was their doll. They'd dressed her in the thong and the strapless dress, and they'd done her hair and makeup, and Amber had to admit she hadn't recognized the woman in the mirror. She'd been just a little bit beautiful, and Amber had never seen that in herself, and yet, she still had to avert her eyes because the ugly she still felt inside wanted to jump out and ruin everything.

Liv had leafed through a Cosmopolitan while Ingrid coached Amber into the thong and the black heels she'd found on the floor of Amber's closet.

"You seriously wear thongs? A lot?" Amber had asked with a frown. "I feel like a science experiment," she whined. She stood in a t-shirt and the thong and the heels, waiting for Ingrid to decide if she was acceptable so far. "Standing here with you studying me like this."

"You don't look like any science experiment I've ever seen," Liv had mumbled, barely lifting her eyes from the magazine. "Although, I am curious how you don't have any stretch marks."

"What?" Amber lifted her t-shirt to expose her stomach to them. "How do you not see my stretch marks?"

"You don't have any on your hips or butt."

"Guess mine all went to my stomach and my boobs," Amber said with a shrug.

"At least you have something to show for them," Ingrid said softly. "I like the heels. You're a dream, Amber."

Amber rolled her eyes at Ingrid.

"Okay. Next."

"What, next?" Amber shook her head.

"Take off the t-shirt."

"Seriously?"

"Mm." Ingrid nodded. "I used to change your diapers, kid. It's not a big deal."

"Yeah, you're not the one parading around naked," Amber groaned.

"No, but my own sister watched me having sex with my boyfriend."

Liv had laughed out loud. Amber had simply sighed and whipped the shirt off over her head.

"I still wanna know where you got those boobs." Ingrid eyed her appreciatively. "Are you sure they're real?"

"Oh my God! Yes!" Amber laughed. "Can I please put something on now?"

"Yep. Time for the dress."

"Thank you." Amber reached for the dress that was draped over her bed.

"This was a good idea, Liv," Ingrid announced

Liv looked up. "What? What was a good idea?"

"What are you reading?" Amber asked her.

"Ten secrets Wade apparently wants me to know when we're in bed-"

"Going without a bra. Imagine Nathan when he unzips the dress and finds nothing but skin."

"Zip me." Amber shook her head and turned her back to Ingrid. "And how do you know he's going to unzip anything? What if he doesn't want this?"

Liv frowned at Amber.

"Are you kidding me? You're gonna blow his mind."

"This is better anyway," Ingrid decided.

"What?" Amber had looked at her over her shoulder as Ingrid zipped the dressed.

"Damn, that's gorgeous!" Liv whistled.

"Serial killers tend to go after the girls whose panties and bras match. We might have just saved you from a serial killer."

"Yeah? What about the girls in the horror movies who always seem to end up topless and then get tortured and killed by demons?"

Ingrid shrugged and waved Amber's concern away. "I don't write horror."

Amber laughed and sighed and then looked down at herself.

"I'm scared."

"About demons?" Liv tossed the magazine aside.

"About Nathan."

That's when they'd escorted her to the mirror. Not the one in the bathroom. She'd seen herself when they'd done her hair and makeup. Fully dressed, heels and tastefully small diamond necklace added, they'd walked Amber over to the full-length mirror on the back of her bedroom door. They'd pronounced her beautiful just as Hadley had knocked at her door.

Liv had opened it, and Ingrid had waved her hands at Amber with a big, loud *ta-da*.

Hadley's eyes had flashed with emotion. Amber saw it all in that two second space. Hadley had approved, marveled even, at Amber. And then she'd remembered Amber and Nathan had split up, and she'd wondered if Amber was seeing someone else.

"Your mom is having dinner with Nathan tomorrow night," Liv had told Hadley. "Whatcha think?"

"Doesn't matter what she wears," Hadley had mumbled. "Nathan wants to marry her. Mom doesn't want to get married. Nothing's gonna change that."

Amber hadn't told Hadley, she hadn't told anyone, that sitting at El Churro the other night, surrounded by her family, she'd had that moment, that life-changing moment when she'd realized how desperately she wanted something different. How desperately she wanted the whole goddamned package. The ring, the wedding, marriage.

A family of her own. With Nathan Marquardt.

Liv had moved to follow Hadley, to lay into her probably, for what she'd said. But Amber had taken Liv's hand, told her to let it go. She'd given Hadley a hundred passes lately for behavior. What was one more going to hurt right now? Either everything would slide back into place and click and lock, and they'd be okay after Friday. Or nothing would ever be okay again, and Amber would just pretend and then she'd deal with Hadley and the behavior and the rest of their lives. Without Nathan.

Forty-Seven

As good as Amber felt about herself earlier, before Nathan had come to pick her up, before his jaw had dropped when he'd found her in the little black dress and the sexy black heels, Amber had asked Hadley to take a picture of her hands. Hadley had stared at her for a moment with a look of utter contempt on her face. She'd finally shaken her head and muttered *what?*

Amber didn't explain; she'd simply repeated her request. Hadley had taken a few shots of Amber's hands, flat on the scarred, faded kitchen counter. Ringless fingers. Empty hands. Old, worn countertop. Amber thought it might be the ugliest picture yet.

Now, Nathan couldn't keep his eyes off her. His eyes roamed over her face, her hair, the necklace-the diamond pendant that rested just below the hollow of her throat. They'd had dinner here before. To celebrate a finished construction project for Nathan. To celebrate a completed book deal for Amber. To celebrate their anniversary.

They'd never had dinner here to discuss how they would salvage a relationship between Nathan and Hadley. Amber swallowed the irony with her wine, half wishing the night was over-no matter how it ended-and half wishing it could go on forever, in case it didn't end well.

"Has Hadley seen her father again?" Nathan asked, his eyes riveted to her diamond pendent. She watched him struggle to look up, to meet her eyes. "Since…"

"Since our last fight."

Nathan pursed his lips and cleared his throat.

"We never used to fight," he said quietly. "Do you remember that?"

She nodded. Played with her fork. They'd already had their salads, though Amber hadn't been able to eat much of hers. Kind of a shame, really, to come here tonight of all nights. Dinner here was expensive, and

Amber had zero appetite. No room inside her for anything with a heart full of fear and a belly full of dread.

"I do."

"What happened?" he asked, and Amber knew he didn't want an answer. Both of them knew exactly what had come between them. What had led to their first fight. The last fight. All the fights in between, though he was right. They tabled it. Whenever the subject came up, they tabled it. Amber had been putting him off for so long. Even in the beginning of their relationship, when things were good, they hadn't fought because she'd pushed him away, gently, and he'd let her.

No wonder he'd finally begun to push back.

"I worry about Hadley," she whispered.

"With Kyle? I thought you said he was just-"

Amber took a sip of her wine-a perfectly smooth, dry red with a spicy finish. Her favorite, and Nathan knew it-and continued, eyes on nothing, to the left of Nathan's chair.

"You know...I mean...I grew up...with a brother and two sisters...but I was alone, Nathan. My sisters were so much older, there was never a connection. Not after Ingrid left. My connection to her was gone by the time I was five." She blinked and looked at him. "I just...I'm scared for that...for Hadley. I'm scared for her to see us together and...feel left out."

Nathan shook his head. "We've never left her out of anything-"

"But what would she feel like?" Amber set her glass down. "If we were married. She and I have been a family. You and I would be a family. Where would that leave her?"

"I'd never do that to her," he argued. "And I know you wouldn't."

The waiter approached the table with their entrees. Amber watched him set her beef tips in front of her and Nathan's crab cakes at his place.

"But what if we didn't realize we were doing it?" Amber picked up her fork and poked at her meat. "I'm sure my parents didn't truly feel the rift between their two families. They had four kids. End of story."

Nathan sighed.

"The job...is...I don't know. It's an office complex. Huge. We're in the negotiations to do the parking garage once the office complex is complete."

"So. You're moving."

He shrugged. Stuck his fork in a crab cake and lifted a bite to his mouth.

"Did you tell Hadley? Last weekend?"

"No."

"What about Nicole?"

"Amber, it was one date."

"But you kissed her good night."

"Look. Other women...this isn't about that. This is-"

"Women?" she repeated.

"What?"

"There was more than one?"

"She doesn't matter-" He tried to wave the other woman or women away, but they were stuck in Amber, like they'd latched their claws in her skin.

"You were with-? Another woman? Other than the blind date?"

Nathan sighed.

"It was one time."

Amber closed her eyes. She set her fork down and then carefully dabbed at her eyes.

"When?"

"Amber."

"When we were together?"

"No!" His answer was quick but heartfelt. "No. Just...after..."

Amber raised her eyebrows. "You've been busy."

"I miss you."

"So you hook up with someone who doesn't matter."

"I've asked you…I don't even know how many times, now…to marry me." He blinked furiously, trying to control himself.

"You know what really scares me?" she whispered.

He swallowed hard and shook his head.

"What if we had a baby together? And Hadley left?"

Nathan rested his elbows on the table. "What if she didn't?"

Amber squeezed her eyes closed. Tears slid from her eyes.

"See? You said I was selfish, and I am, Nathan. I'm scared of a future like this, because of my own childhood."

"Your parents loved you."

"I know they did. I know that." Amber nodded. "But when I was little, I thought of Ingrid as my mom. I didn't understand the difference. And when she left-"

"Here's the thing." He scrubbed his face with his hands. "I have a for sale sign in my yard right now. I leave Sunday."

"Please. Don't go."

Amber reached across the table for his hand. She watched him slide his fingers through hers.

"We could get married. At least give me that much, Amber. Let me adopt Hadley-"

"Can we talk to Hadley about this?" Amber's words were small and tight with emotion. "I don't even know how she feels about us-"

"She wants us to be married. She wants-"

"Having more children together."

Nathan stared at Amber. His shoulders caved as he let out a deep breath.

"Are you saying…" He shook his head. "Are you saying you'll marry me?"

Amber nodded. "Yes."

"Are you sure? You were so-"

"The worst that could happen is happening, Nathan." She ducked her head as tears streaked her face. "You left me…and I found out I can't live without you."

"Amber."

"I don't want to be without you. Ever. Again."

"I don't want you to marry me because I'm pressuring you-"

"I want the ring," she started, "and I want marriage. And a house…that you and I and Hadley make a home. And the hell of it is, Nathan, I've always wanted that. I've always wanted everything with you. I just didn't know it. I was too afraid of…life…to know what I wanted."

Nathan stood up without a word. Amber looked up as he rounded the table for two. Reached for her hand. Hesitantly, aware of the other diners in the romantic room, she let him take it. He drew her out of her chair. Slowly, pressed body to body.

"I love you."

"Please don't leave."

He wrapped his arms around her and held her close.

"I love you so much."

"Don't leave us, Nathan. We love you-"

He shook his head and drew back to look at her. "We'll figure it out. I'll put in for a different site. Different job."

"Are you sure?"

"You belong here." His lips grazed her ear as he pulled her close again. "I don't wanna spend another night without you right here."

Amber rested her forehead on his shoulder.

"We need Hadley here. To celebrate."

She shook her head. Looked up at him. "We can celebrate with Hadley tomorrow. I need you tonight. Just you and me."

"What about her lunch date with her father?"

"I think her mom and dad could drive her there."

Nathan kissed her forehead. Skimmed his fingertips over her cheekbone.

"I think we need champagne."

"I don't." She shook her head when he stepped away from her.

"No?"

"I don't need anything. Not when I'm with you."

He leaned in and kissed her again. This time it was a soft kiss on her lips. Before Amber could protest-they were in public-he stepped back again.

"Do you know how lucky I am to be with the most beautiful woman in the room?"

"Beauty's relative, Nathan," she said softly. "I've never felt uglier than I have since you left me."

"Amber-"

"Inside. When you left, I took a long hard look at myself. That part of me let you go."

"Can I tell you something?" His voice was gruff. Still standing toe to toe, she nodded.

"Tonight was it." He stuck his hands in his pockets. "I was prepared to beg."

Amber covered her mouth with her hands when he pulled the ring box from his pocket.

"I don't wanna move…to Indiana for any reason…but I couldn't stay here. If you said no again."

She swallowed hard when he opened the box. Took the ring-a pear shaped diamond set in white gold. Amber had seen the ring once before, the first time she'd told him no. She sobbed out loud when he eased down on his knee in front of her.

"Amber Williams. Will you marry me?"

Her hand shook when she held it out to him.

"Yes." Their eyes met as he slid the ring over her bare nail and pushed it over her knuckle. She eyed the diamond, the first ring she'd ever worn, and decided her hand looked just a little bit beautiful.

The Williams Legacy

Book 2

Other People's Ugly

Playlist

Lakehouse ~ Of Monsters and Men

Heart and Soul ~ Huey Lewis & The News

Bad Self Portraits ~ Lake Street Drive

Marry Song (Live Acoustic) ~ Band of Horses

Homesick ~ Catfish and the Bottlemen

I Don't Care ~ Fall Out Boy

Never Let Me Go ~ Florence + The Machine

What Happened To Us? ~ Hoobastank

Stolen Dance ~ Milky Chance

Miss You ~ Nickelback

(One of Those) Crazy Girls ~ Paramore

Holding On To You ~ Twenty One Pilots

Shining ~ X Ambassadors

All I Ever Wanted ~ Vance Joy

Time For Letting Go ~ Jude Cole

It Comes Back To You ~ Imagine Dragons

Tears and Rain ~ James Blunt

Don't Let Me Be Lonely Tonight ~ James Taylor

Perfectly Lonely ~ John Mayer

Heart To Heart ~ Kenny Loggins

Pictures Of You ~ The Last Goodnight

I Can't Tell You Why ~ Vince Gill

Why'd You Only Call Me When You're High ~ Arctic Monkeys

Ain't Gonna Drown ~ Elle King